Vampire Kisses

BLOOD RELATIVES

VOLUME III

Ellen Schreiber
Art by Elisa Kwon

HAMBURG // LONDON // LOS ANGELES // TOKYO

KATHERINE TEGEN BOOKS
An Imprint of HarperCollins Publishers

Vampire Kisses: Blood Relatives Vol. 3
By Ellen Schreiber
Art by Elisa Kwon
Cover art by rem (Priscilla Hamby)
Adapted by Diana McKeon Charkalis

Editors - Lillian Diaz-Przybyl and Julie Lansky
Development Editors - Alexis Kirsch and Katherine Schilling
Lettering - Zach Matheny
Inking - Elisa Kwon
Tones - Glass House Graphics
Cover Design - Louis Csontos

Print Production Manager - Lucas Rivera
Managing Editor - Vy Nguyen
Senior Designer - Louis Csontos
Director of Sales and Manufacturing - Allyson De Simone
Associate Publisher - Marco F. Pavia
President and C.O.O. - John Parker
C.E.O. and Chief Creative Officer - Stu Levy

A  Manga

TOKYOPOP and  are trademarks or registered trademarks of TOKYOPOP Inc.

TOKYOPOP Inc.
5900 Wilshire Blvd., Suite 2000
Los Angeles, CA 90036

E-mail: info@TOKYOPOP.com
Come visit us online at www.TOKYOPOP.com

For information address HarperCollins Children's Books, a division of HarperCollins Publishers,
10 East 53rd Street, New York, NY 10022.
www.harperteen.com

Library of Congress catalog card number: 2009930186
ISBN 978-0-06-134083-3

09 10 11 12 13   LP/WOR   10 9 8 7 6 5 4 3 2 1
❖
First Edition

CONTENTS

Welcome to DULLSVILLE

MEET RAVEN MADISON: SPORTING BLACK LIPSTICK, BLACK NAIL POLISH, AND A SHARP WIT, RAVEN IS AN OUTSIDER AT CONSERVATIVE DULLSVILLE HIGH. CURIOUS AND FEARLESS, SHE'S NOT AFRAID TO TAKE ON ANYONE, FROM GOSSIPING GIRLS TO EVEN SCARIER, NEFARIOUS CREATURES OF THE NIGHT. AMAZINGLY, RAVEN'S GREATEST WISH HAS COME TRUE—SHE'S DATING A REAL VAMPIRE. THE ONLY PROBLEM IS THAT SHE HAS TO WAIT UNTIL SUNDOWN TO SEE HIM AND MUST KEEP HIS TRUE IDENTITY A SECRET.

MEET ALEXANDER STERLING:
HANDSOME AND ELUSIVE, ALEXANDER IS THE TEEN VAMPIRE OF RAVEN'S DREAMS. HE LIVES IN A MANSION ON TOP OF BENSON HILL, AND ONLY EMERGES AT NIGHT. A SENSITIVE ARTIST, THIS PALE PRINCE OF DARKNESS HAS SOULFUL EYES AND A HEART TO MATCH. HE IS WITTY WITH A MACABRE SENSE OF HUMOR, BUT KIND AND GENTLE WHEN IT COMES TO RAVEN. WHEN RAVEN FINDS HERSELF IN TROUBLE, HE'S THE FIRST ONE TO SPRING TO HER DEFENSE.

MEET BECKY MILLER:
RAVEN'S ONLY GIRLFRIEND, BECKY IS MORE SHY AND RESERVED THAN HER GOTHIC COUNTERPART. SINCE MEETING IN THE THIRD GRADE, RAVEN HAS BEEN BECKY'S BEST FRIEND AND BODYGUARD, PROTECTING HER FROM NAME CALLING AND PLAYGROUND CLASHES. BECKY OFTEN FINDS HERSELF EMBROILED IN RAVEN'S MISADVENTURES, BUT THESE DAYS SHE HAS SOME EXCITEMENT OF HER OWN. SHE'S HEAD OVER HEELS IN LOVE WITH MATT WELLS, A POPULAR BUT GOOD-HEARTED GUY AT SCHOOL WHOM SHE'S STARTED DATING.

MEET CLAUDE STERLING: CLAUDE IS ALEXANDER'S HOT AND OFTEN HOTHEADED HALF-VAMPIRE COUSIN. COMPETITIVE SINCE BIRTH, CLAUDE HAS ONE THING ON HIS MIND—BECOMING A FULL VAMPIRE. CLAUDE HAS BROUGHT HIS GANG WITH HIM FROM ROMANIA TO DULLSVILLE TO RETRIEVE MUCH NEEDED VIALS OF PURE VAMPIRE BLOOD HIS GRANDMOTHER HAD HIDDEN. DRINKING THESE VIALS IS THE ONLY WAY THEY CAN BE TURNED—AND SINCE ALEXANDER WON'T GIVE THE VIALS UP, CLAUDE THINKS RAVEN IS HIS TICKET TO UNEARTHING THEIR LOCATION.

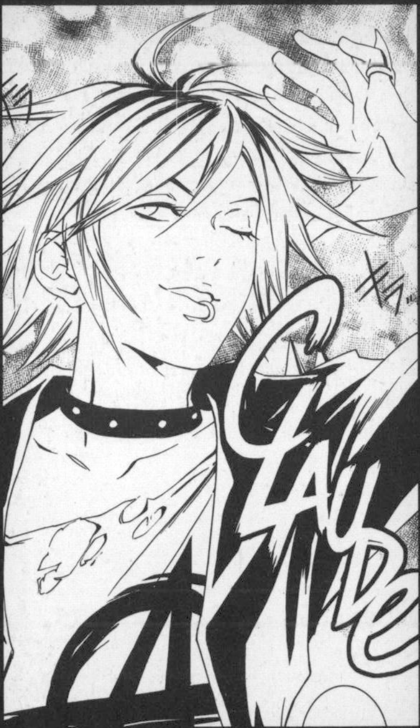
CLAUDE

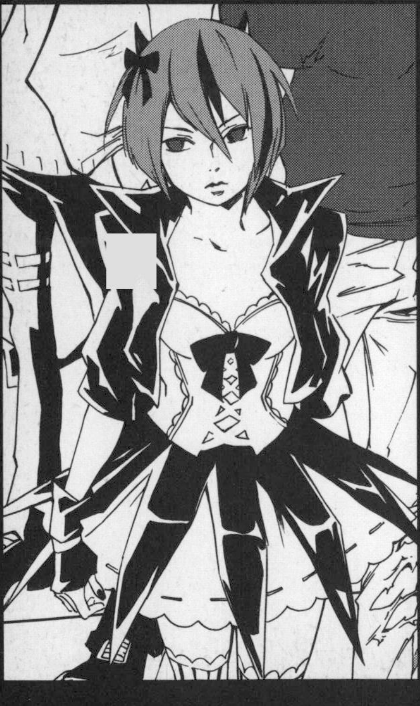

MEET KAT: SULTRY AND DECEPTIVE, KAT IS CLAUDE'S RIGHT-HAND GIRL. SHE USES HER CATLIKE BEGUILES TO CREATE A WEDGE BETWEEN RAVEN AND ALEXANDER. THOUGH SHE'S OFTEN FOUND FILING HER NAILS, SHE'S ONE TOUGH COOKIE AND HATES PLAYING BACKSEAT WHEN PLANS ARE BEING MADE.

MEET ROCCO: THE MUSCLE OF CLAUDE'S GANG, ROCCO WOULD RATHER BE THROWING PUNCHES THAN USING BRAINPOWER TO GET HIS HANDS ON THE VIALS. AND WHILE HE'S JUST AS HUNGRY AS THE OTHERS FOR THE VIALS, ROCCO USUALLY LETS CLAUDE LEAD THE WAY—EVEN IF IT MIGHT BE THE WRONG DIRECTION.

MEET TRIPP: THE BRAINS IN CLAUDE'S GANG, TRIPP CONTRIBUTES HIS TECHNO-SAVVY SKILLS TO HELP THE GANG WHEN NEEDED. NOT ONE WITH MUCH BRAWN, TRIPP IS USUALLY THE FIRST TO HIDE BEHIND ROCCO WHEN DANGER LOOMS NEAR.

MEET TREVOR: RAVEN'S KHAKI-CLAD NEMESIS, TREVOR IS GORGEOUS, RICH, AND A SUPER-JOCK. SO WHAT'S NOT TO LIKE? HIS PERSONALITY. SINCE KINDERGARTEN, TREVOR'S BEEN BENT ON MAKING LIFE MISERABLE FOR RAVEN. HE'D NEVER ADMIT IT, BUT HE'S MORE ATTRACTED TO HER THAN REPULSED AND HAS HAD A CRUSH ON HER SINCE THEY WERE KIDS. WHEN TREVOR'S NOT DOMINATING THE SOCCER FIELD, HE'S USUALLY STARTING RUMORS OR PESTERING RAVEN, HIS "MONSTER GIRL."

Chapter 11: Vampire Vengeance

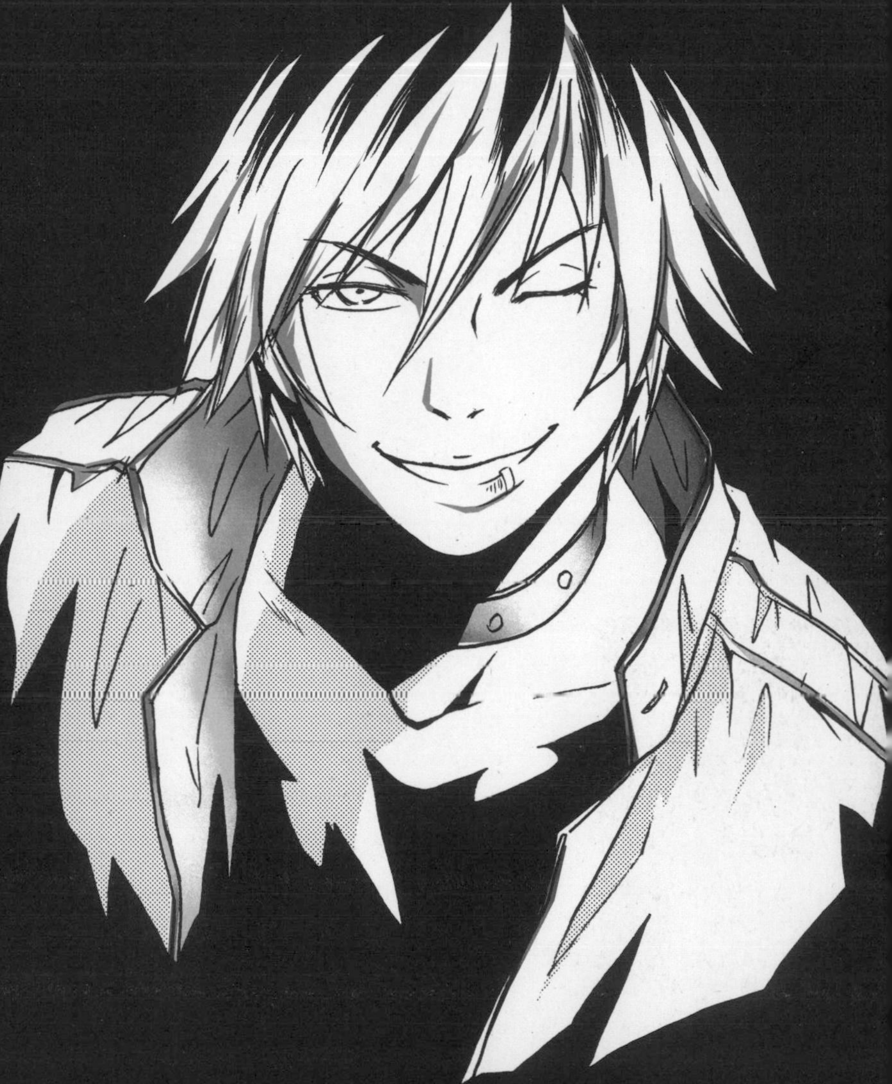

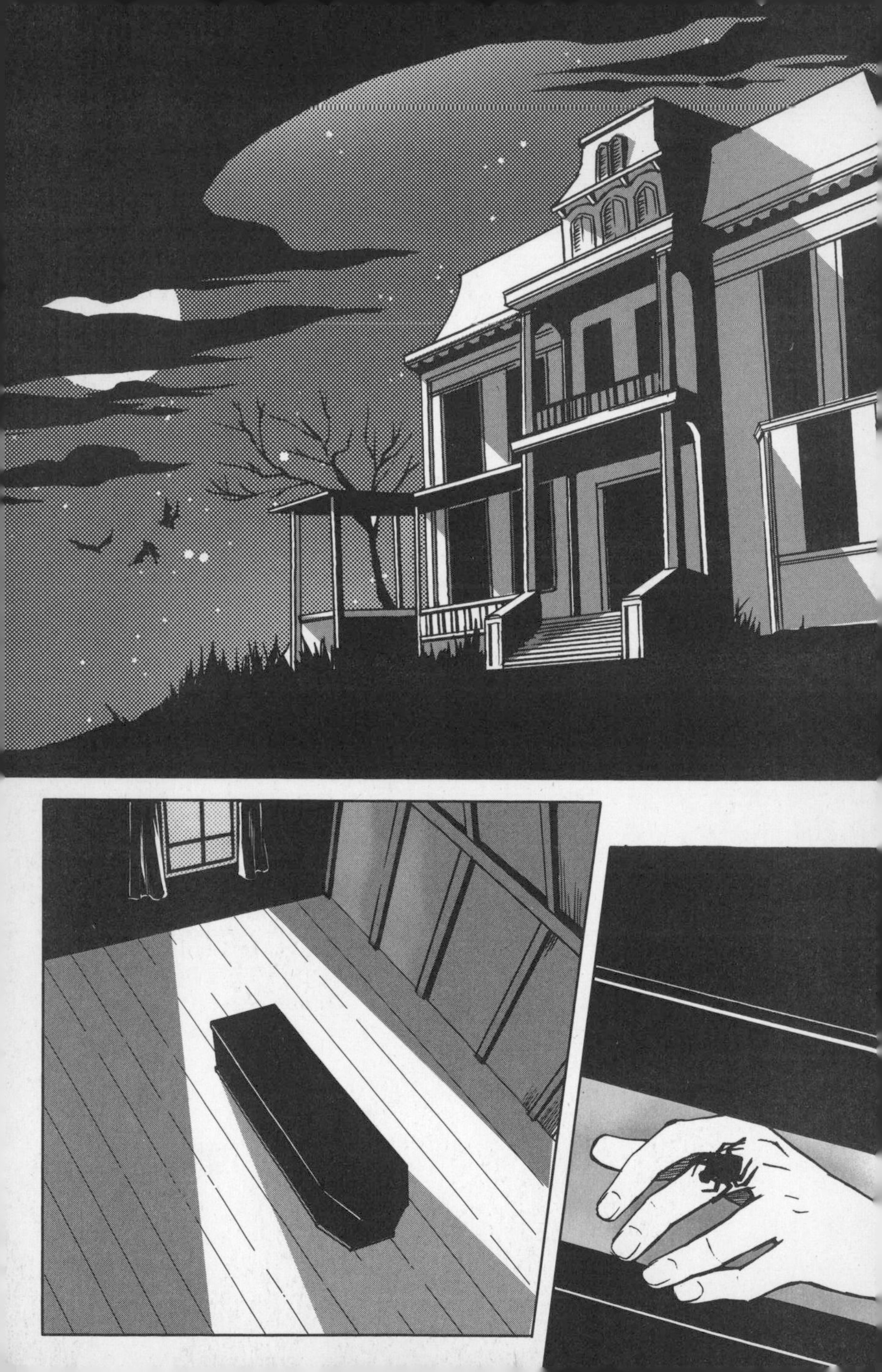

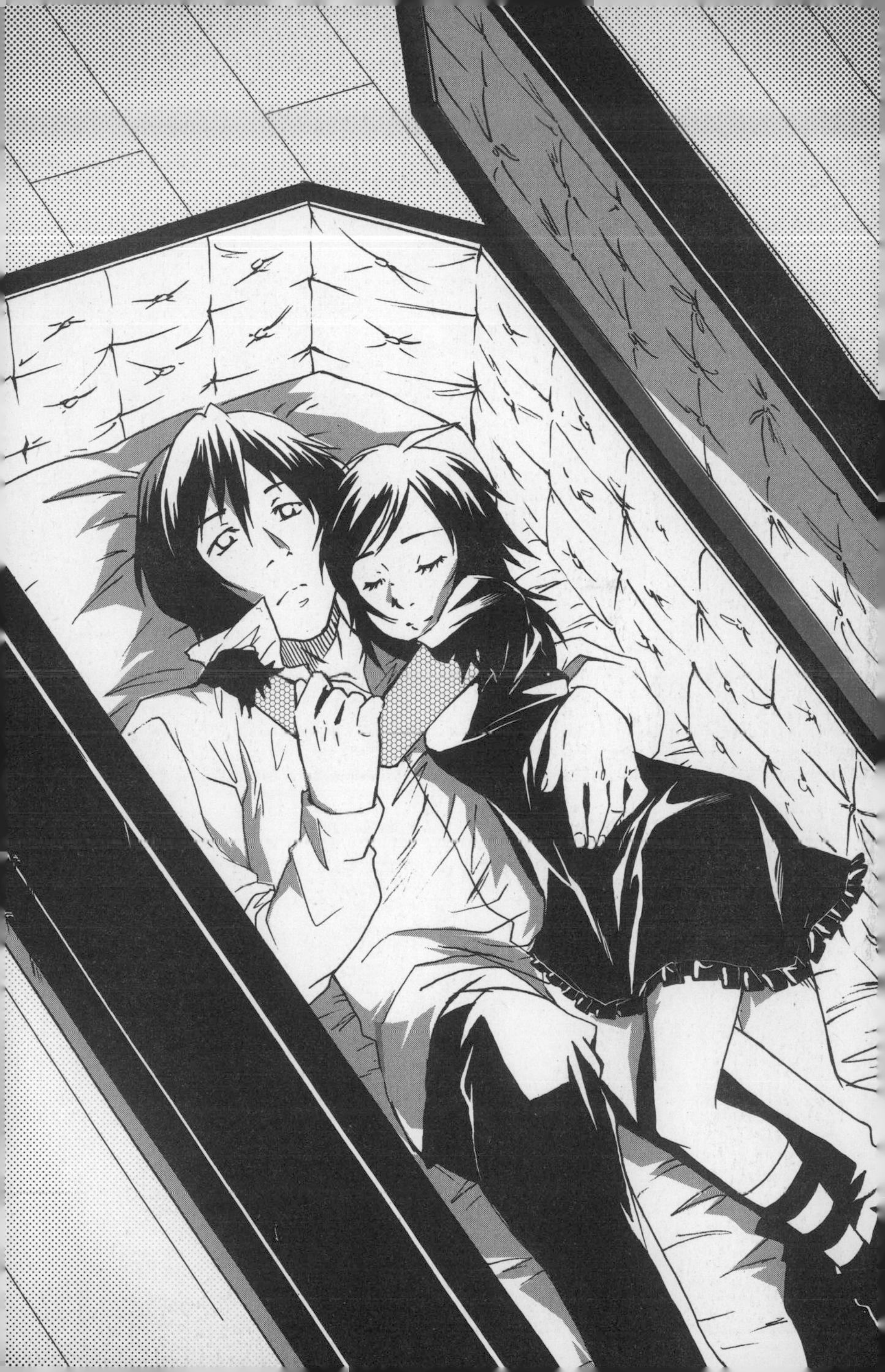

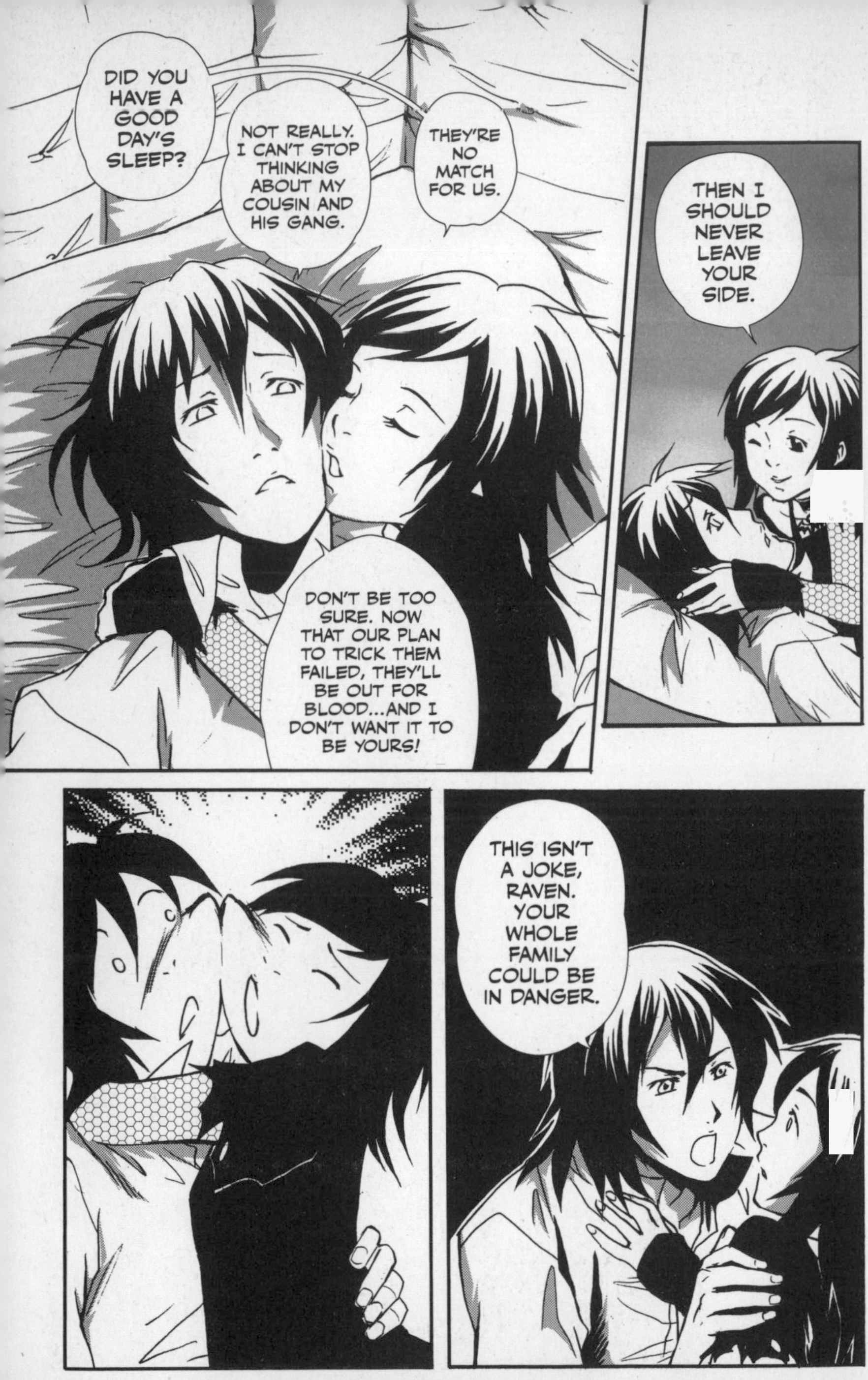
DID YOU HAVE A GOOD DAY'S SLEEP?
NOT REALLY. I CAN'T STOP THINKING ABOUT MY COUSIN AND HIS GANG.
THEY'RE NO MATCH FOR US.
DON'T BE TOO SURE. NOW THAT OUR PLAN TO TRICK THEM FAILED, THEY'LL BE OUT FOR BLOOD...AND I DON'T WANT IT TO BE YOURS!
THEN I SHOULD NEVER LEAVE YOUR SIDE.
THIS ISN'T A JOKE, RAVEN. YOUR WHOLE FAMILY COULD BE IN DANGER.

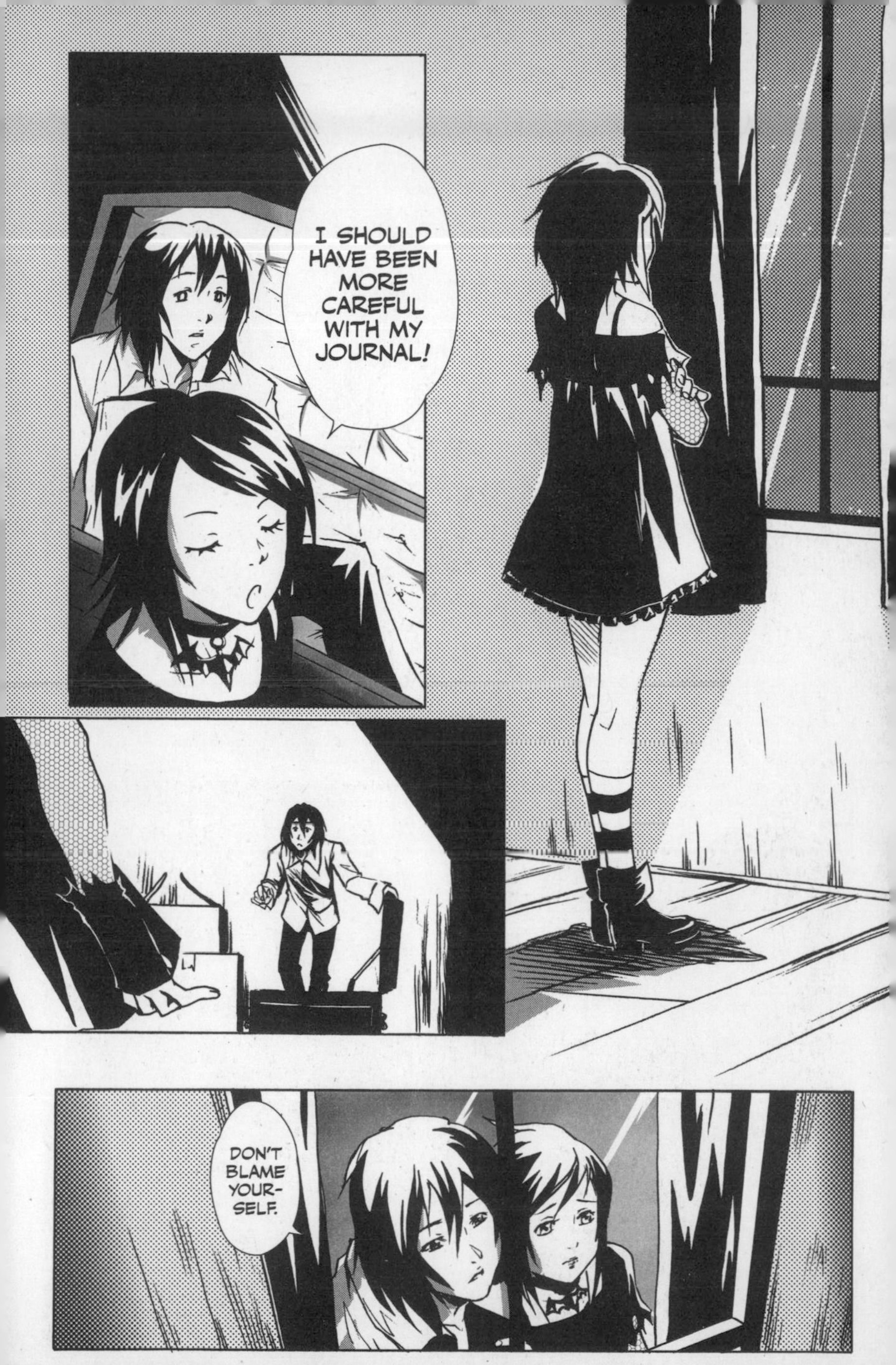
I SHOULD HAVE BEEN MORE CAREFUL WITH MY JOURNAL!
DON'T BLAME YOUR-SELF.

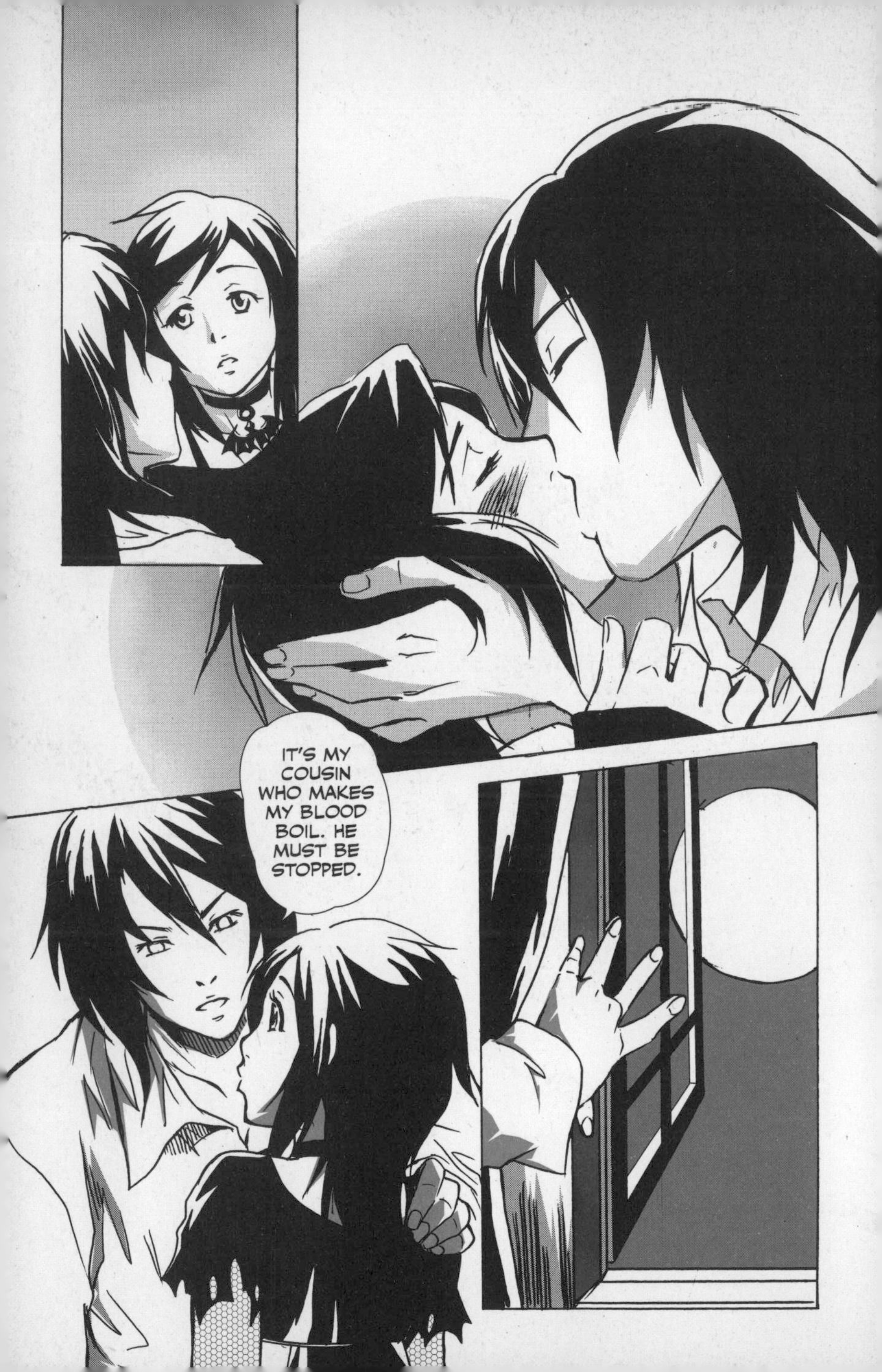
IT'S MY COUSIN WHO MAKES MY BLOOD BOIL. HE MUST BE STOPPED.

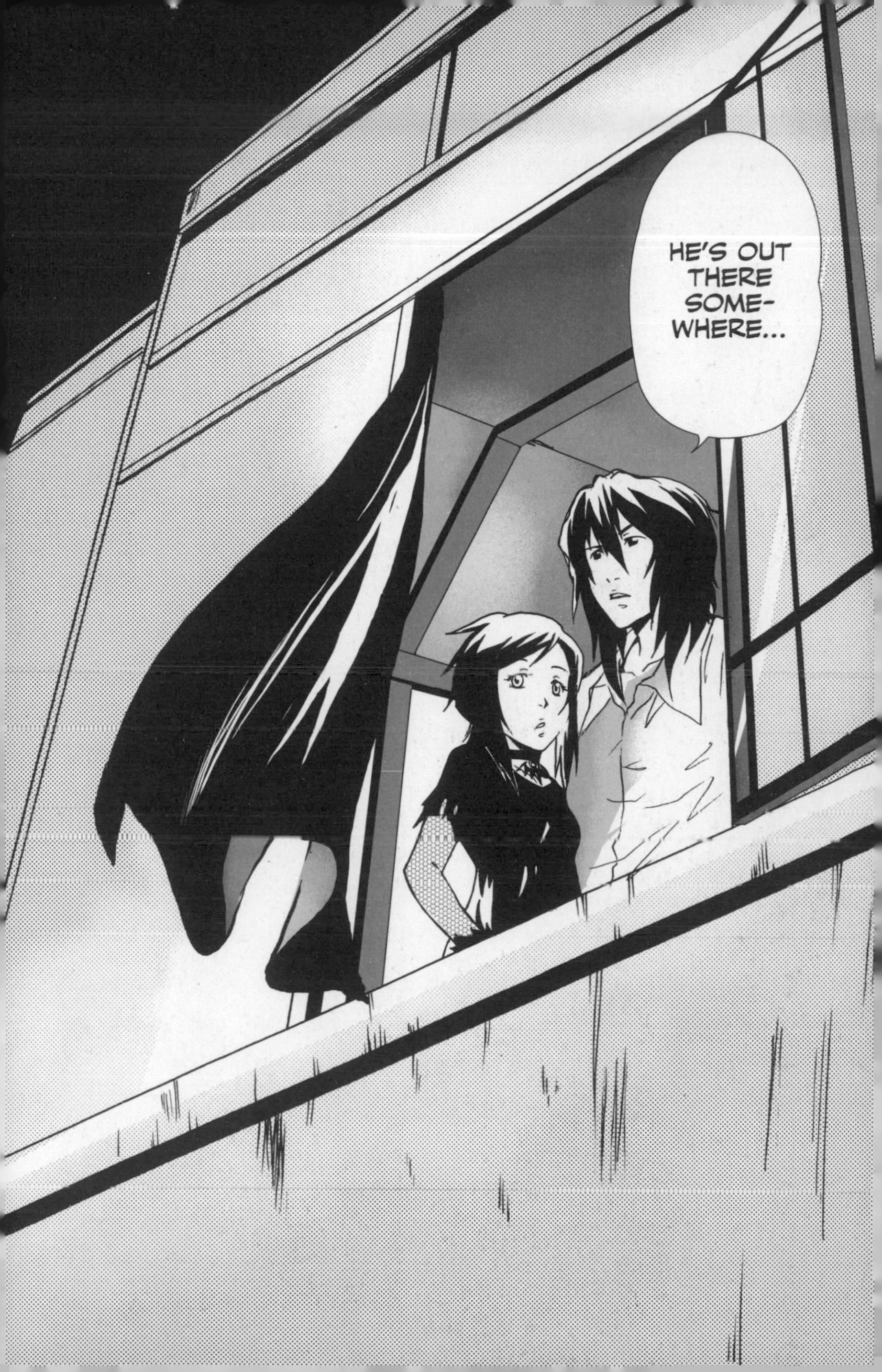
HE'S OUT THERE SOME-WHERE...

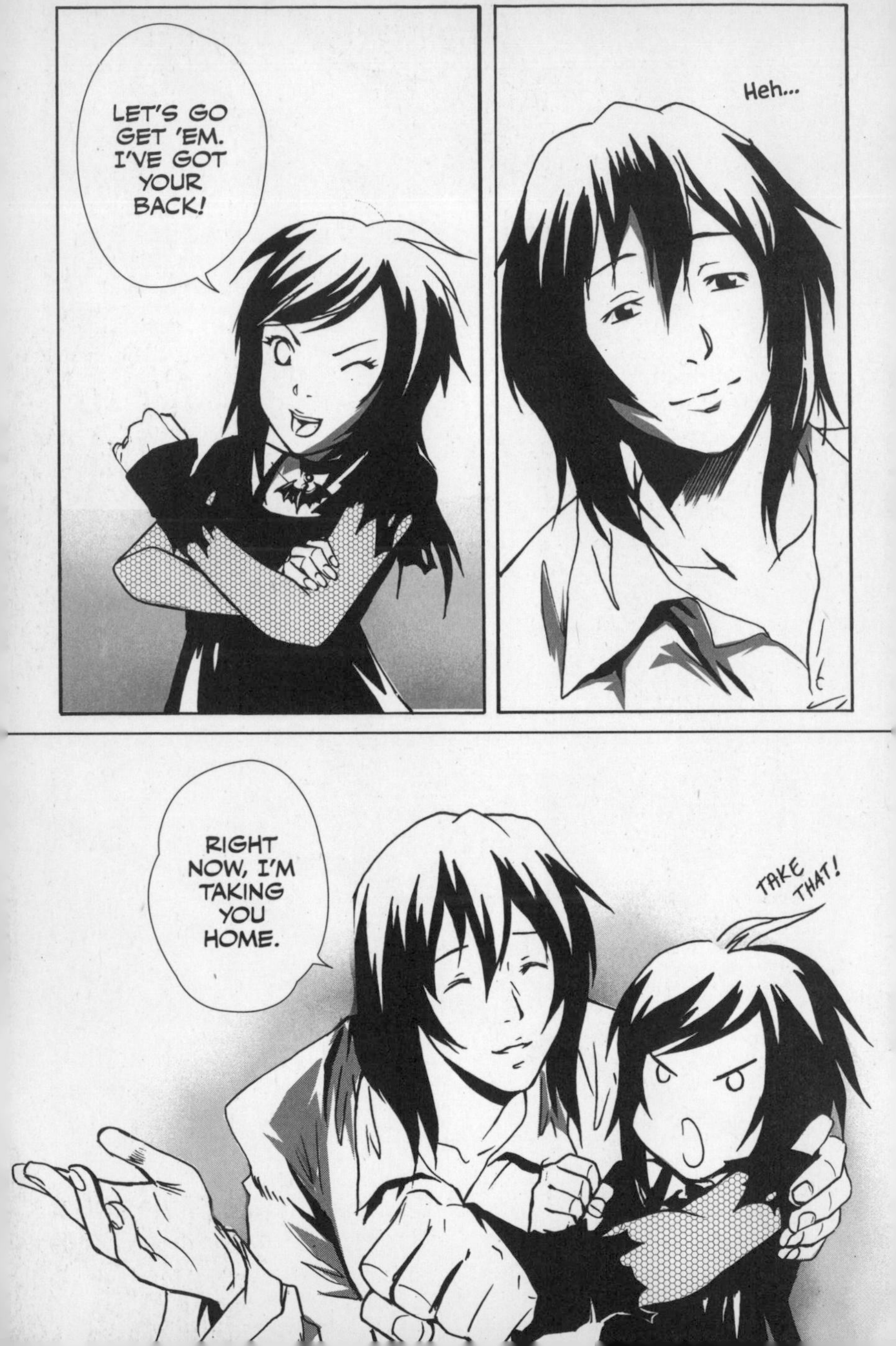

LET'S GO GET 'EM. I'VE GOT YOUR BACK!
Heh...
RIGHT NOW, I'M TAKING YOU HOME.
TAKE THAT!

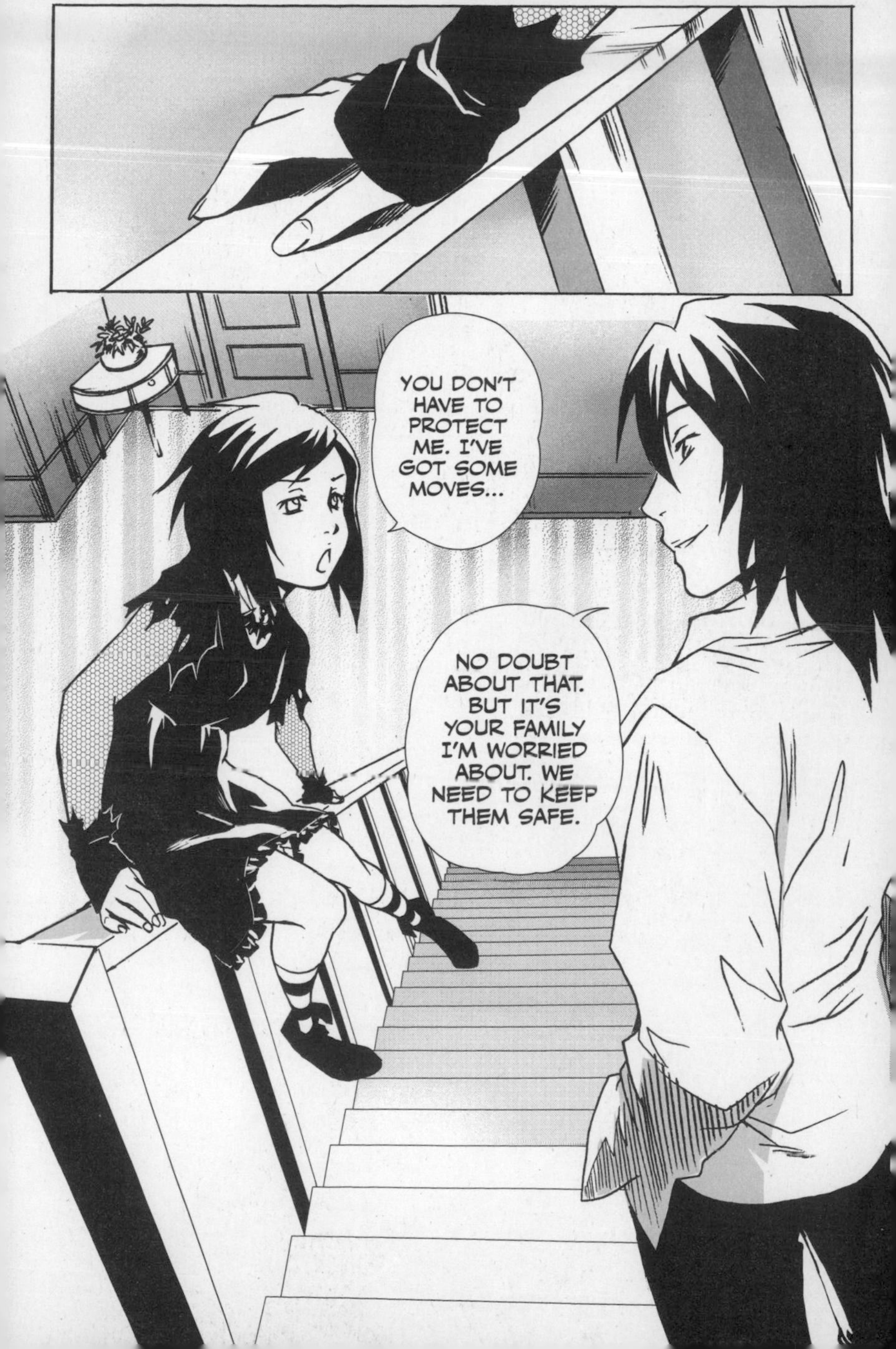
YOU DON'T HAVE TO PROTECT ME. I'VE GOT SOME MOVES...
NO DOUBT ABOUT THAT. BUT IT'S YOUR FAMILY I'M WORRIED ABOUT. WE NEED TO KEEP THEM SAFE.

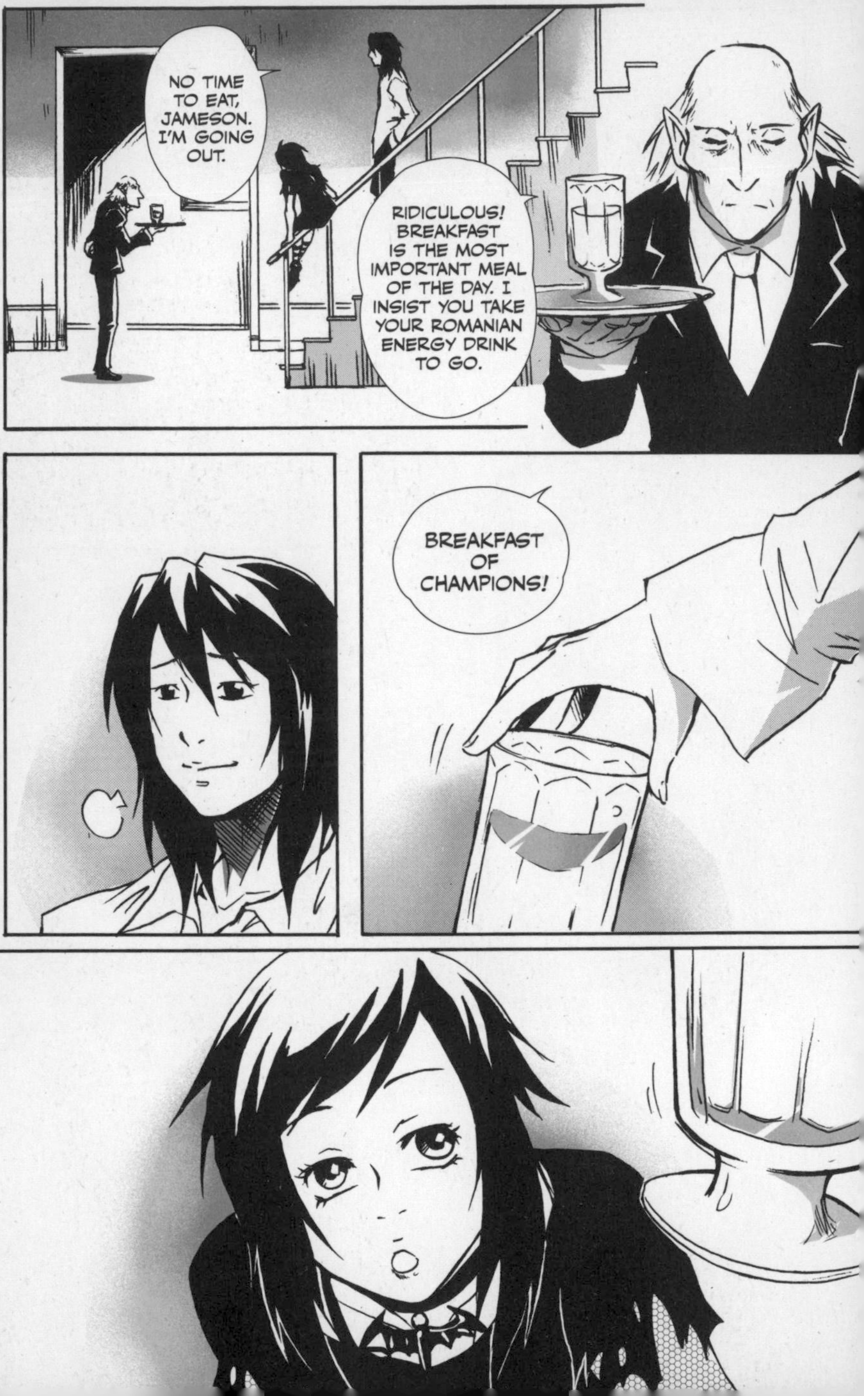
NO TIME TO EAT, JAMESON. I'M GOING OUT.
RIDICULOUS! BREAKFAST IS THE MOST IMPORTANT MEAL OF THE DAY. I INSIST YOU TAKE YOUR ROMANIAN ENERGY DRINK TO GO.
BREAKFAST OF CHAMPIONS!

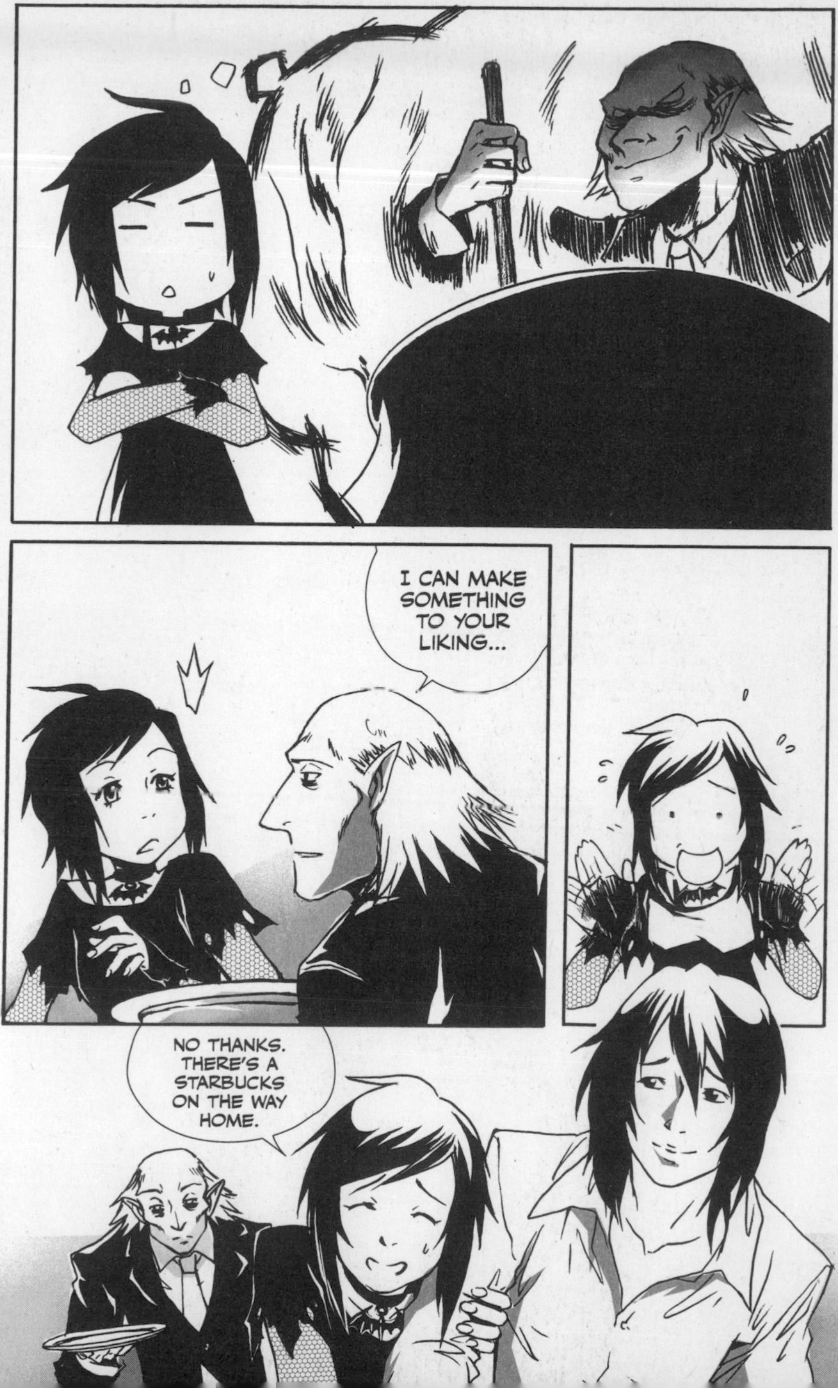
I CAN MAKE SOMETHING TO YOUR LIKING...
NO THANKS. THERE'S A STARBUCKS ON THE WAY HOME.

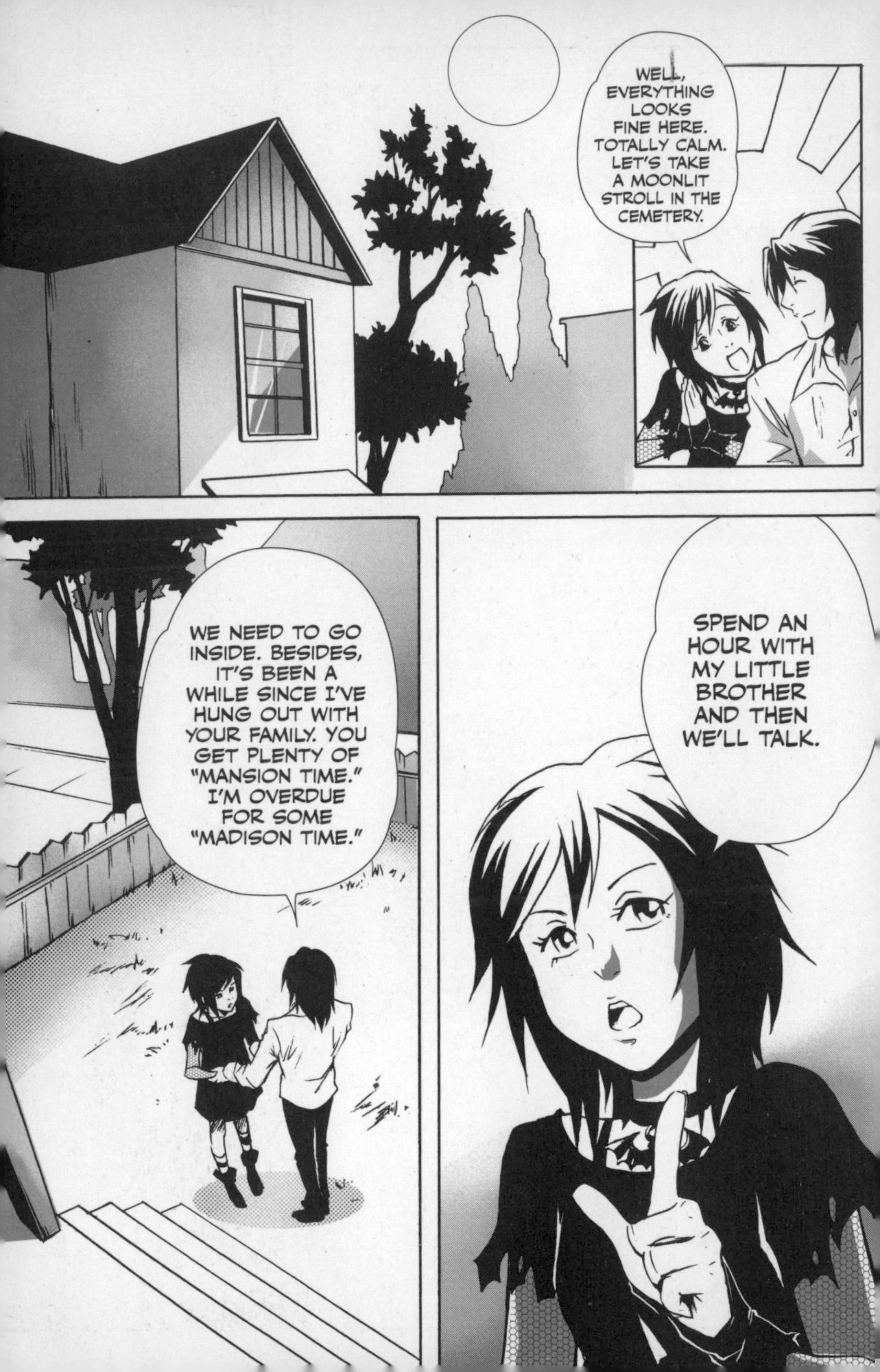
WELL, EVERYTHING LOOKS FINE HERE. TOTALLY CALM. LET'S TAKE A MOONLIT STROLL IN THE CEMETERY.
WE NEED TO GO INSIDE. BESIDES, IT'S BEEN A WHILE SINCE I'VE HUNG OUT WITH YOUR FAMILY. YOU GET PLENTY OF "MANSION TIME." I'M OVERDUE FOR SOME "MADISON TIME."
SPEND AN HOUR WITH MY LITTLE BROTHER AND THEN WE'LL TALK.

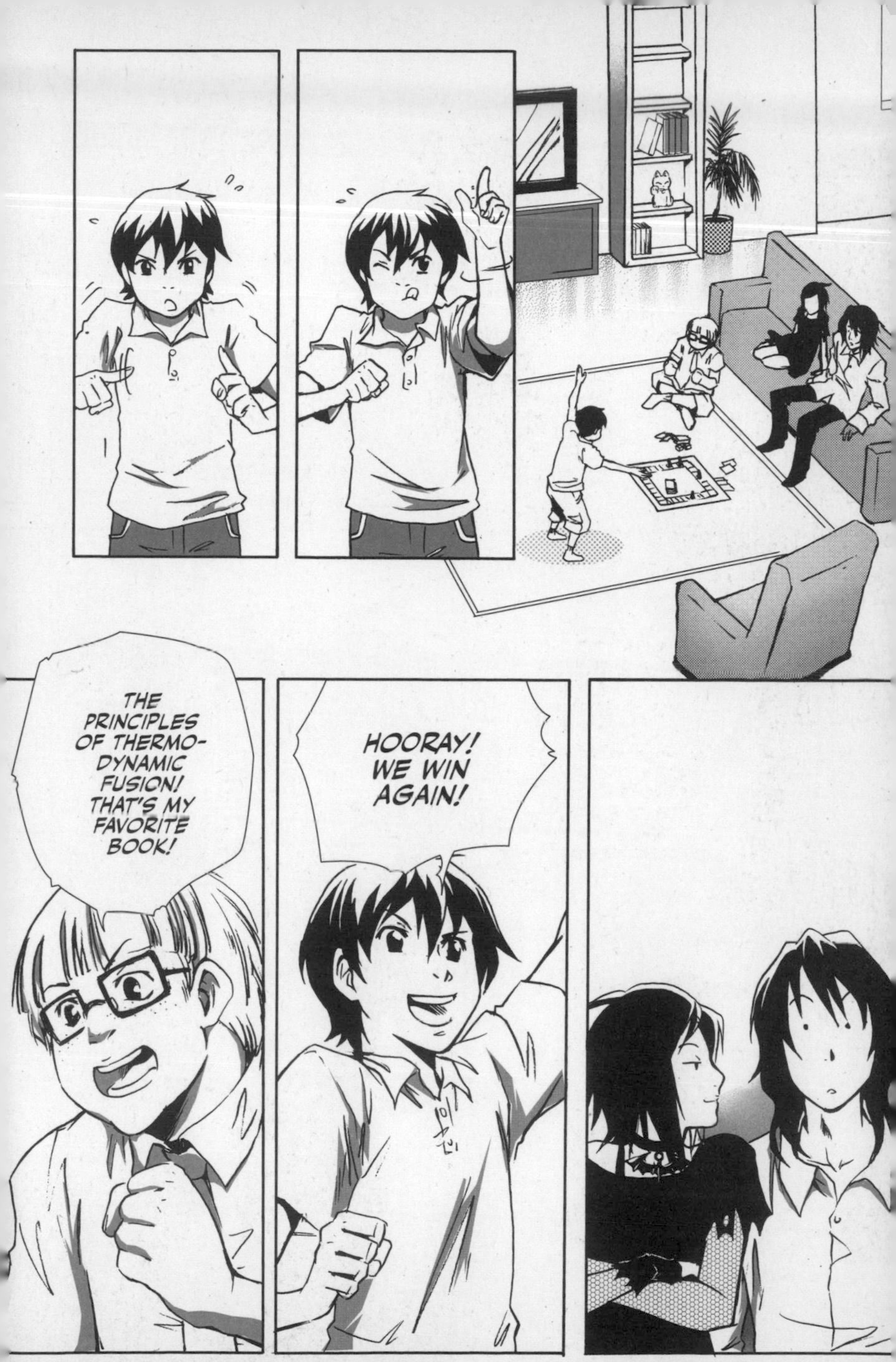
THE PRINCIPLES OF THERMO-DYNAMIC FUSION! THAT'S MY FAVORITE BOOK!
HOORAY! WE WIN AGAIN!

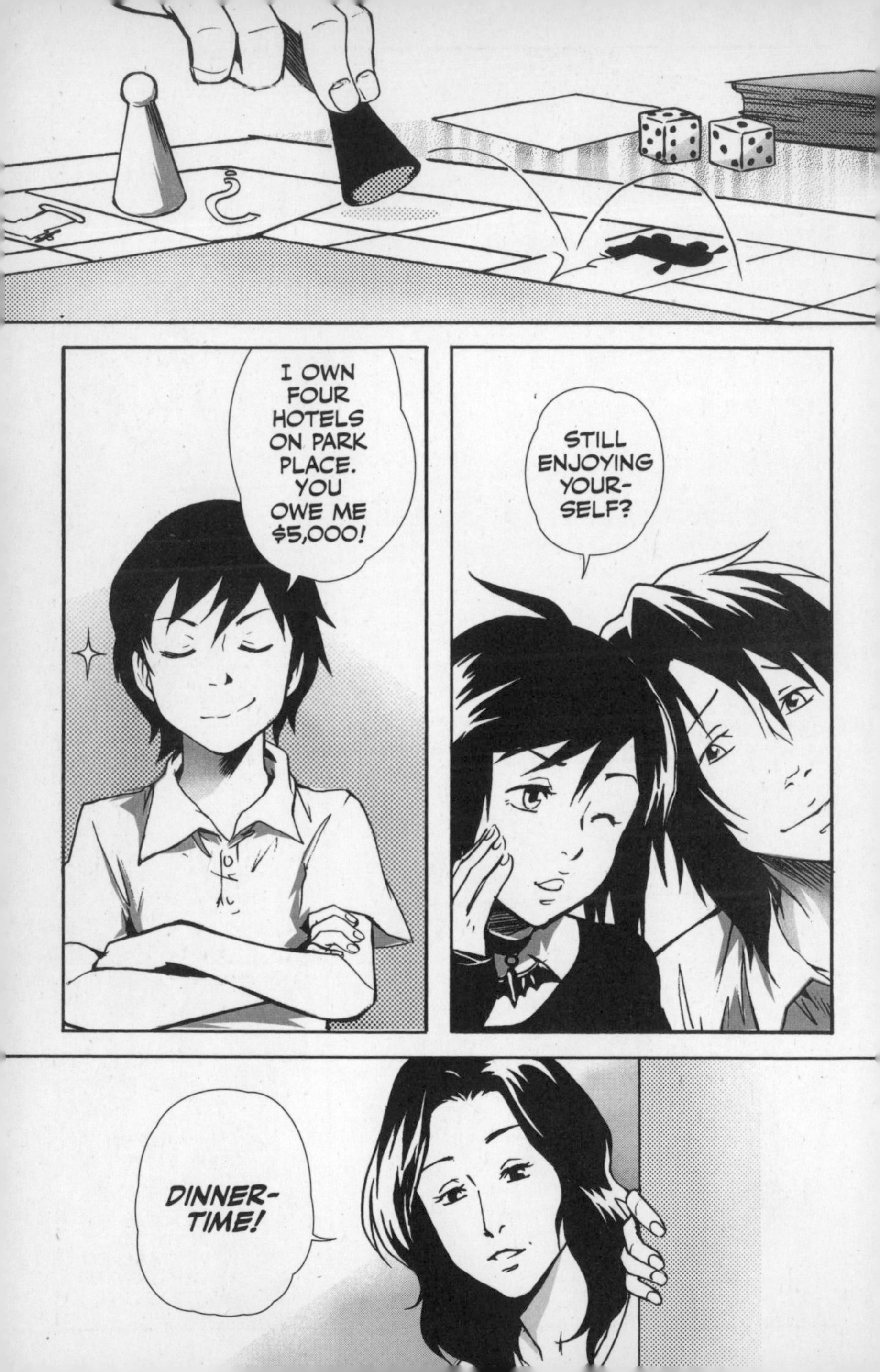
I OWN FOUR HOTELS ON PARK PLACE. YOU OWE ME $5,000!
STILL ENJOYING YOUR-SELF?
DINNER-TIME!

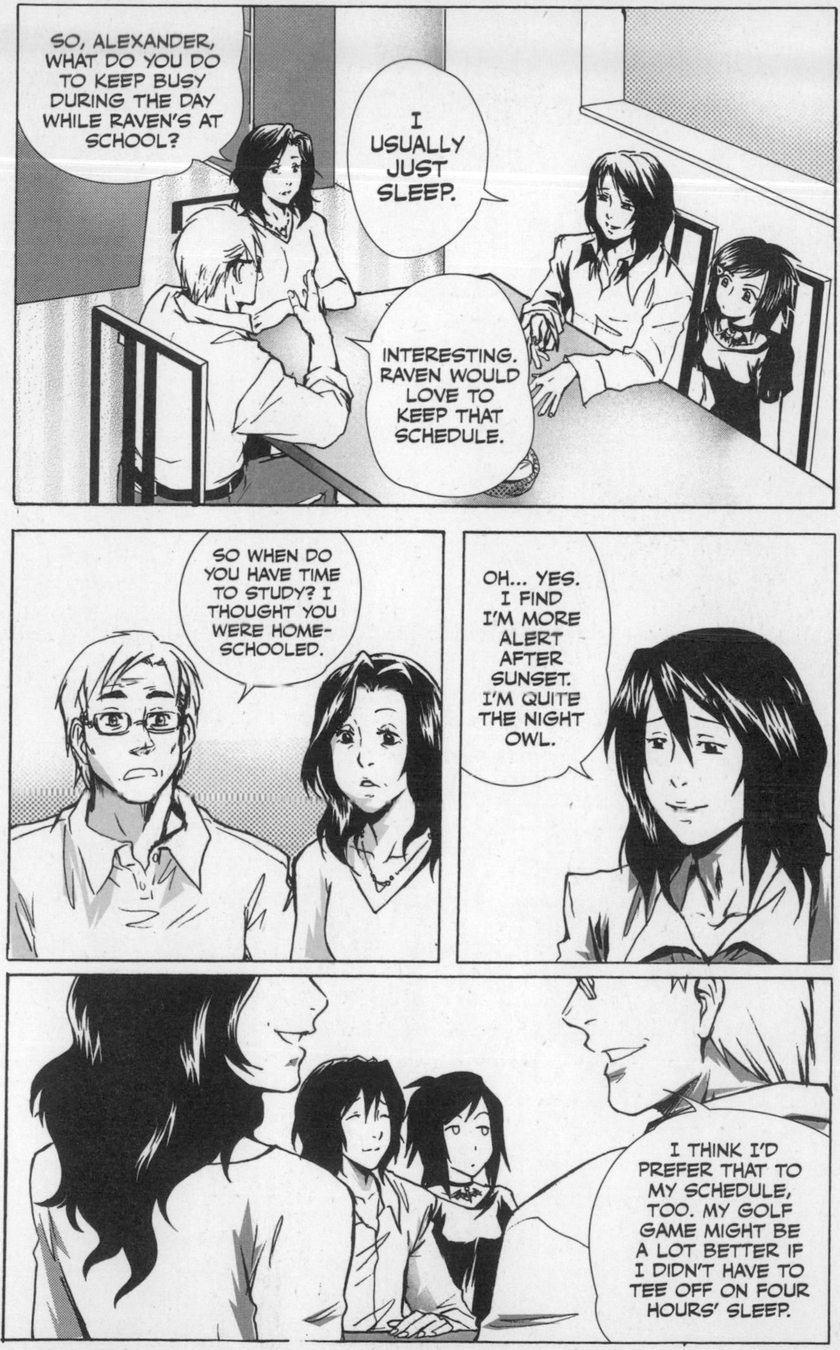
SO, ALEXANDER, WHAT DO YOU DO TO KEEP BUSY DURING THE DAY WHILE RAVEN'S AT SCHOOL?
I USUALLY JUST SLEEP.
INTERESTING. RAVEN WOULD LOVE TO KEEP THAT SCHEDULE.
SO WHEN DO YOU HAVE TIME TO STUDY? I THOUGHT YOU WERE HOME-SCHOOLED.
OH... YES. I FIND I'M MORE ALERT AFTER SUNSET. I'M QUITE THE NIGHT OWL.
I THINK I'D PREFER THAT TO MY SCHEDULE, TOO. MY GOLF GAME MIGHT BE A LOT BETTER IF I DIDN'T HAVE TO TEE OFF ON FOUR HOURS' SLEEP.

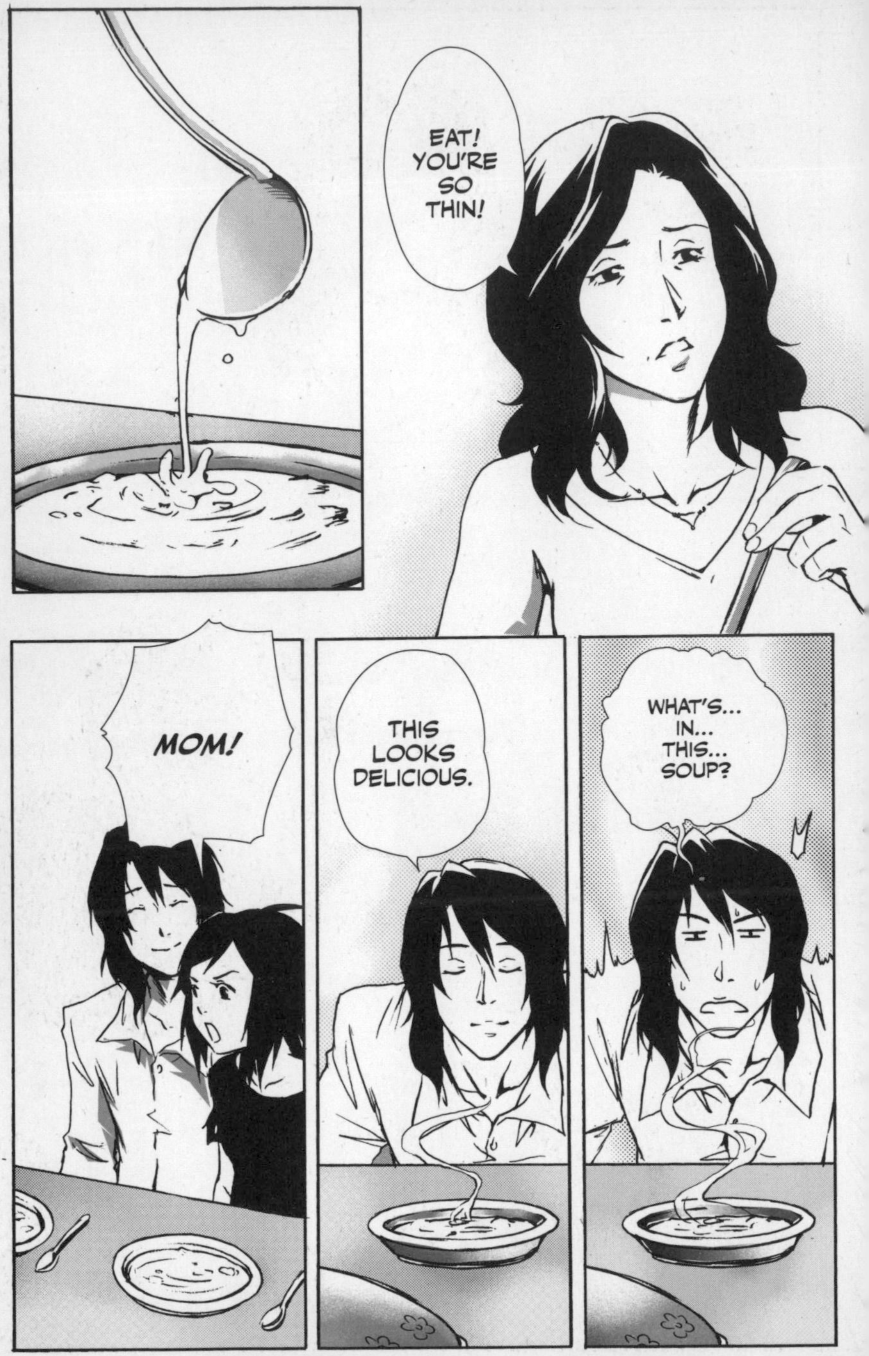
EAT! YOU'RE SO THIN!
MOM!
THIS LOOKS DELICIOUS.
WHAT'S... IN... THIS... SOUP?

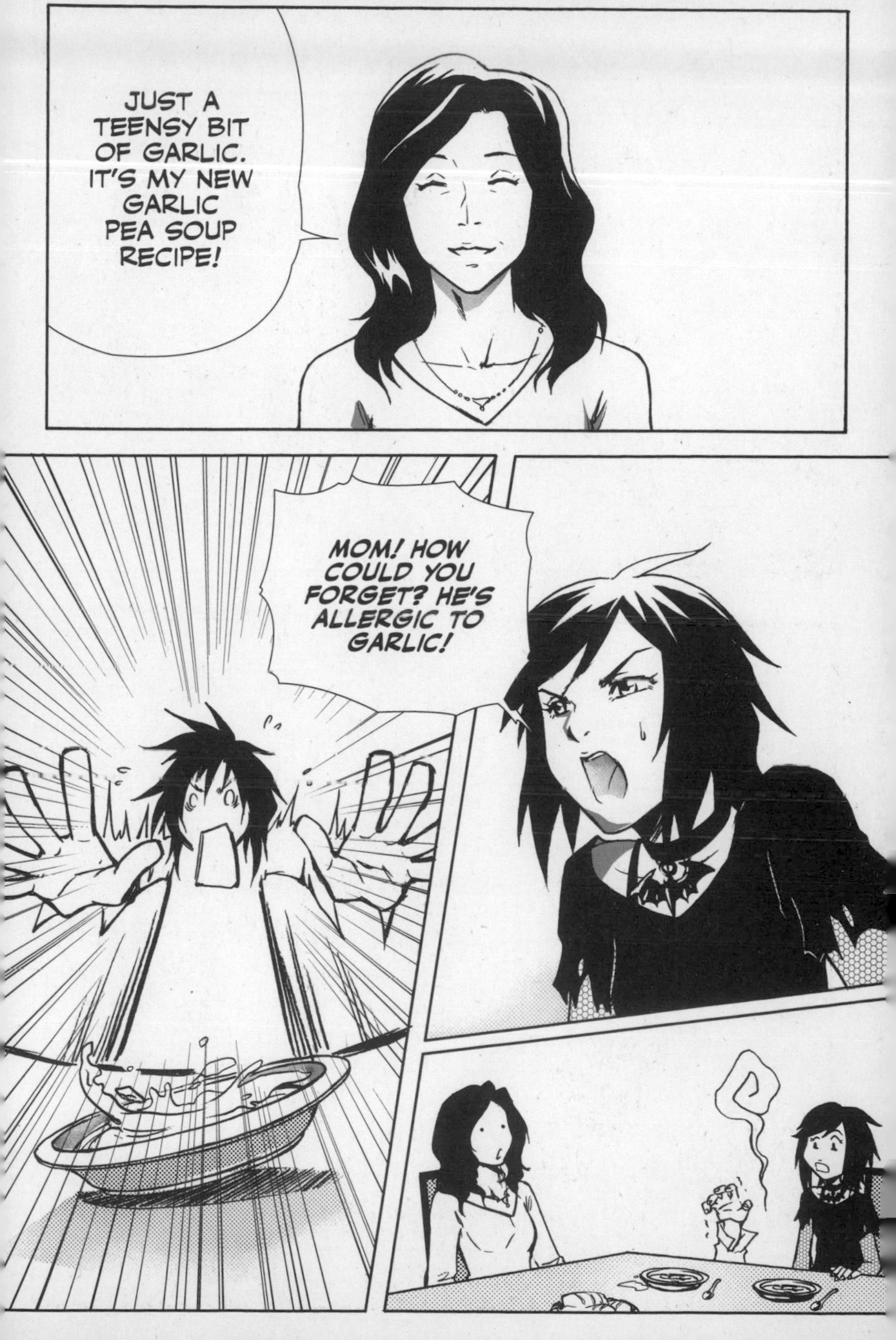
JUST A TEENSY BIT OF GARLIC. IT'S MY NEW GARLIC PEA SOUP RECIPE!
MOM! HOW COULD YOU FORGET? HE'S ALLERGIC TO GARLIC!

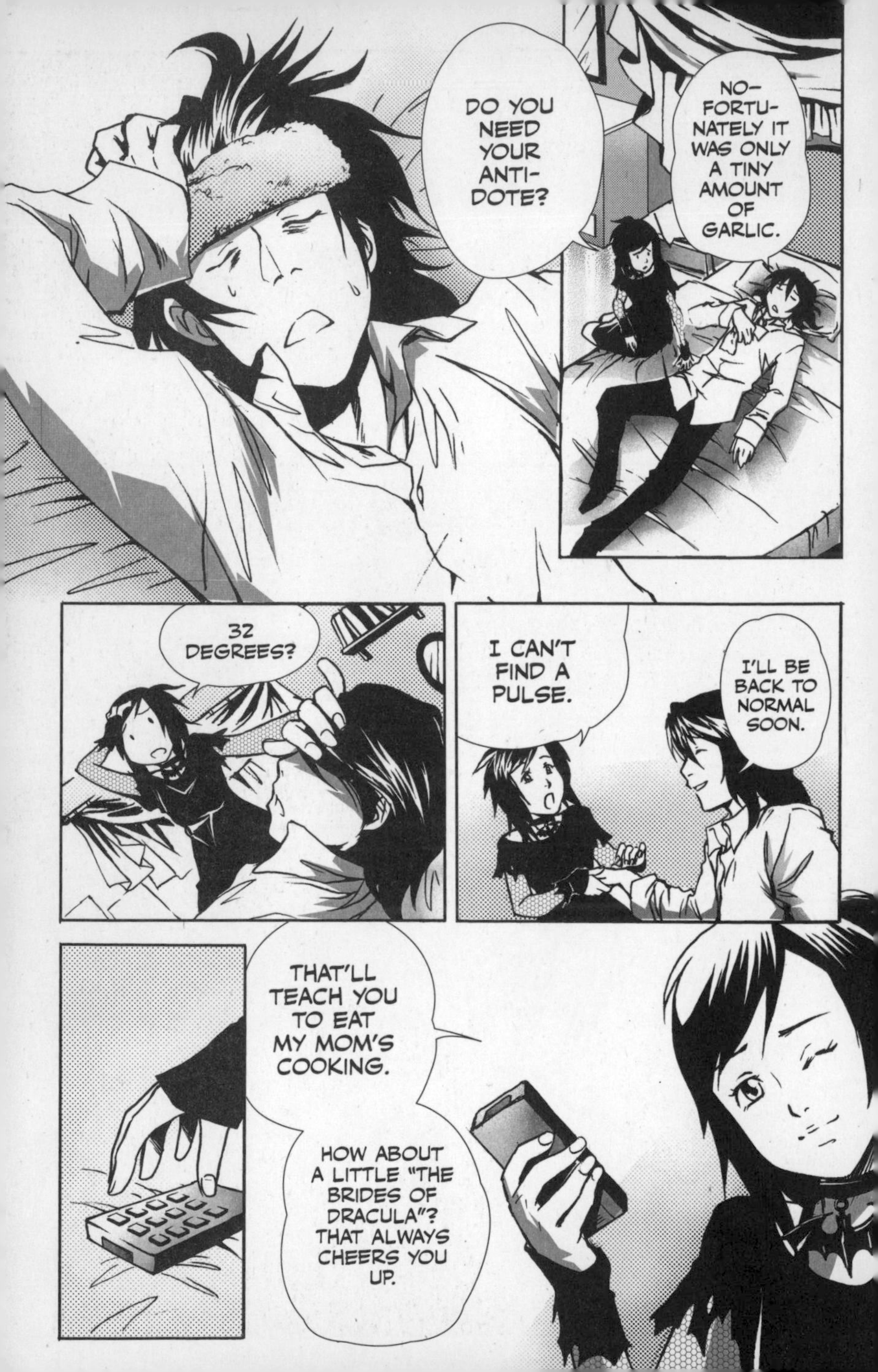
DO YOU NEED YOUR ANTI-DOTE?
NO—FORTU-NATELY IT WAS ONLY A TINY AMOUNT OF GARLIC.
32 DEGREES?
I CAN'T FIND A PULSE.
I'LL BE BACK TO NORMAL SOON.
THAT'LL TEACH YOU TO EAT MY MOM'S COOKING.
HOW ABOUT A LITTLE "THE BRIDES OF DRACULA"? THAT ALWAYS CHEERS YOU UP.

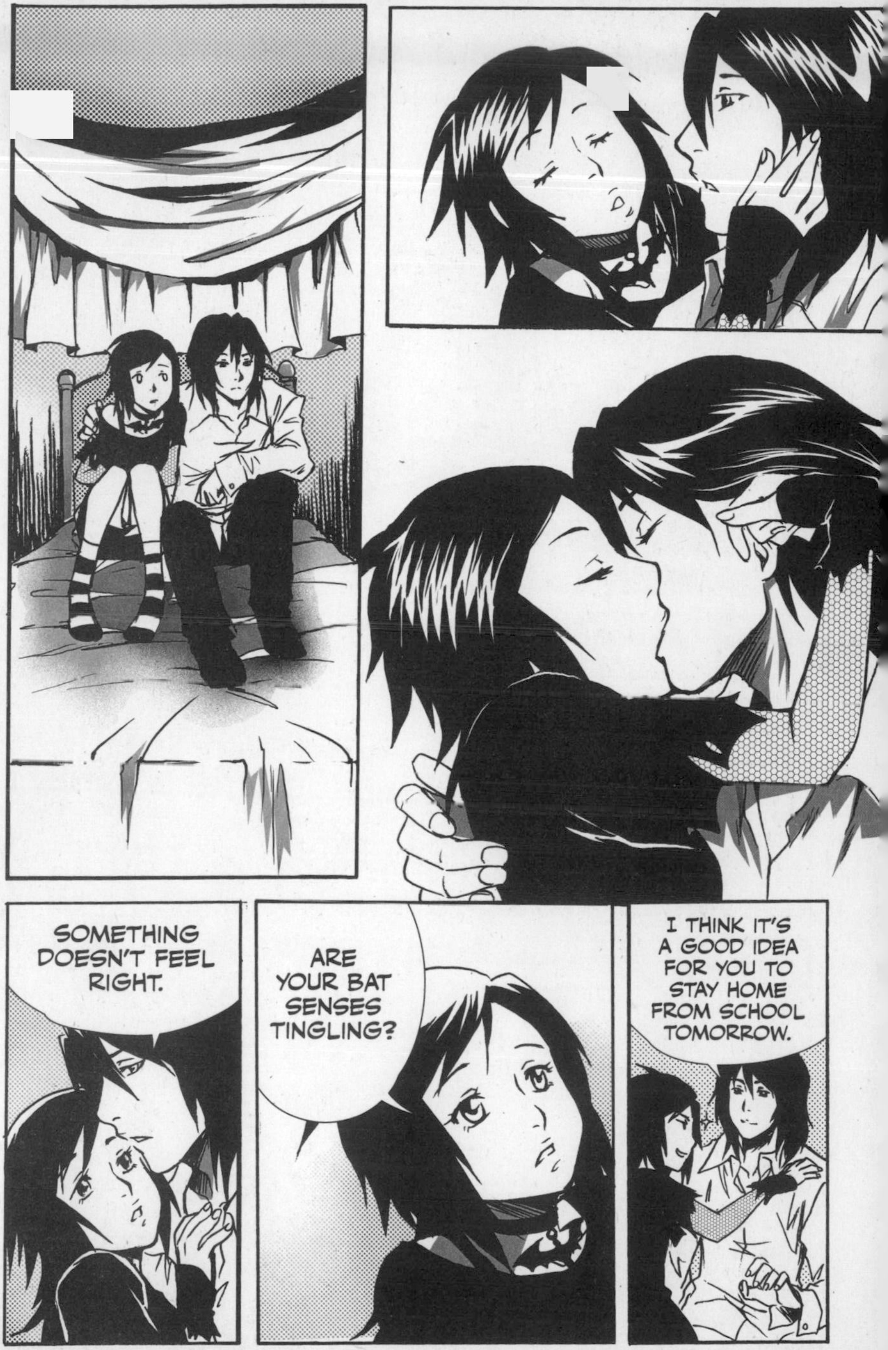
SOMETHING DOESN'T FEEL RIGHT.
ARE YOUR BAT SENSES TINGLING?
I THINK IT'S A GOOD IDEA FOR YOU TO STAY HOME FROM SCHOOL TOMORROW.

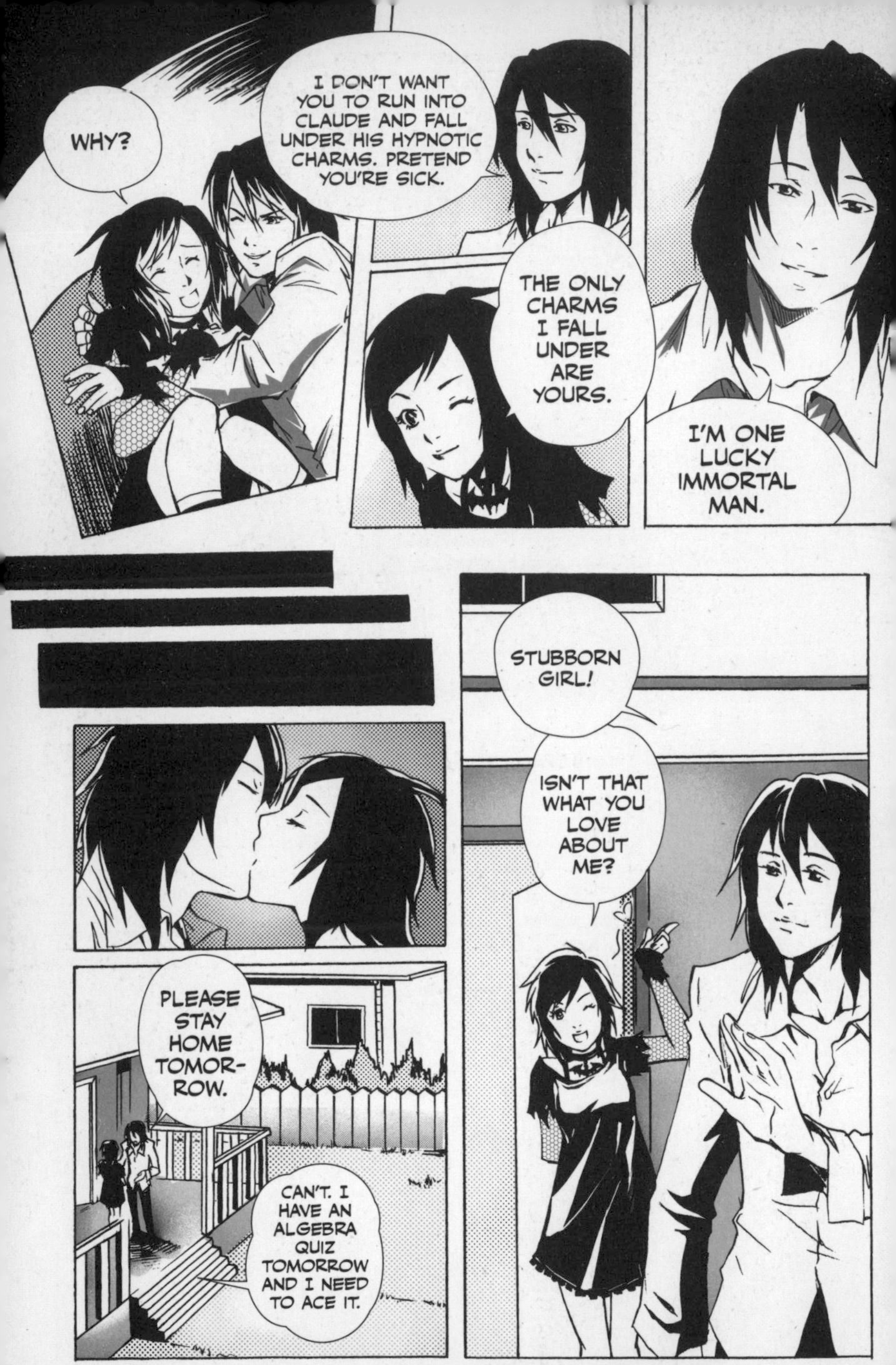
WHY?
I DON'T WANT YOU TO RUN INTO CLAUDE AND FALL UNDER HIS HYPNOTIC CHARMS. PRETEND YOU'RE SICK.
THE ONLY CHARMS I FALL UNDER ARE YOURS.
I'M ONE LUCKY IMMORTAL MAN.
PLEASE STAY HOME TOMOR-ROW.
CAN'T. I HAVE AN ALGEBRA QUIZ TOMORROW AND I NEED TO ACE IT.
STUBBORN GIRL!
ISN'T THAT WHAT YOU LOVE ABOUT ME?

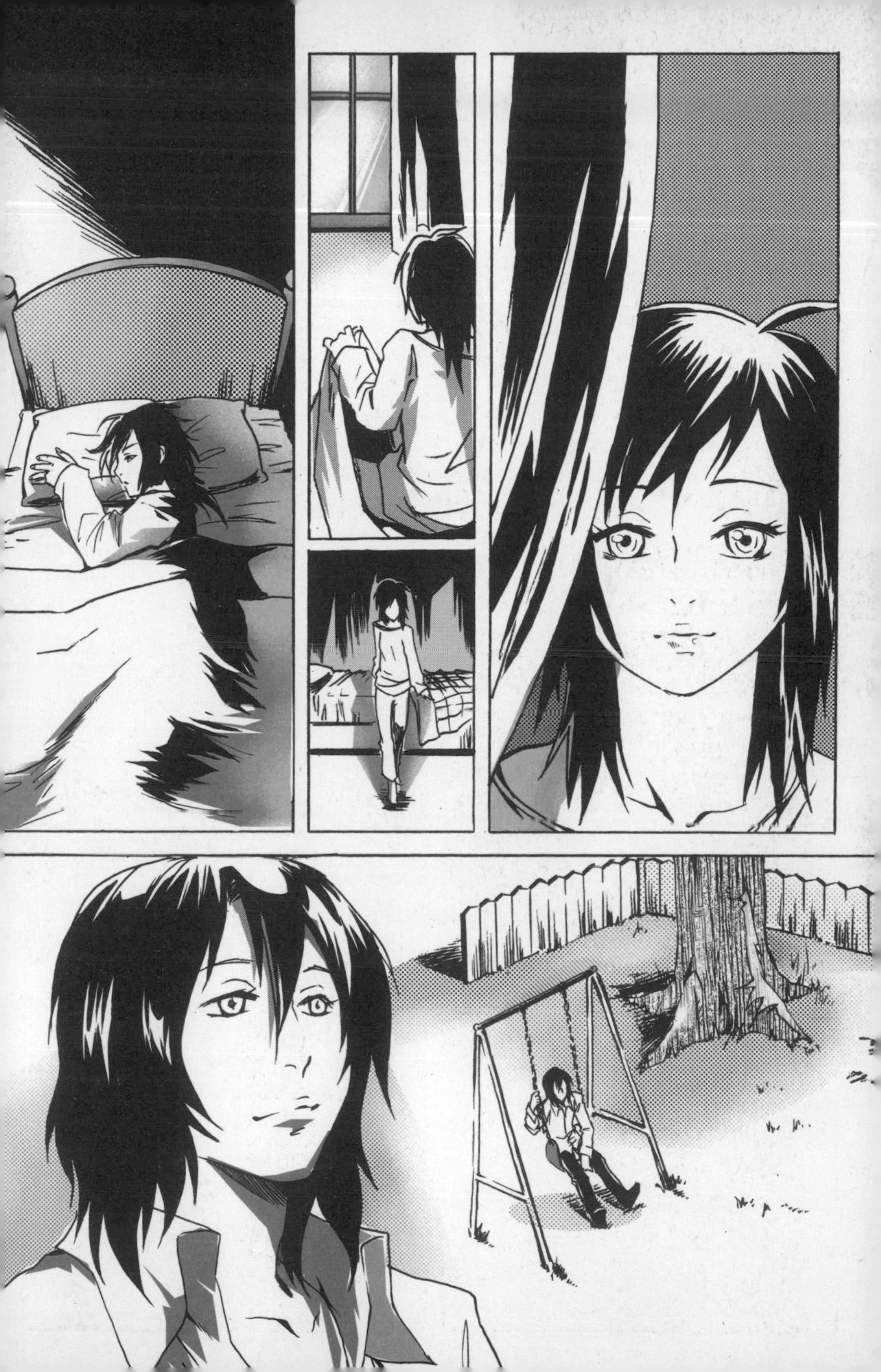

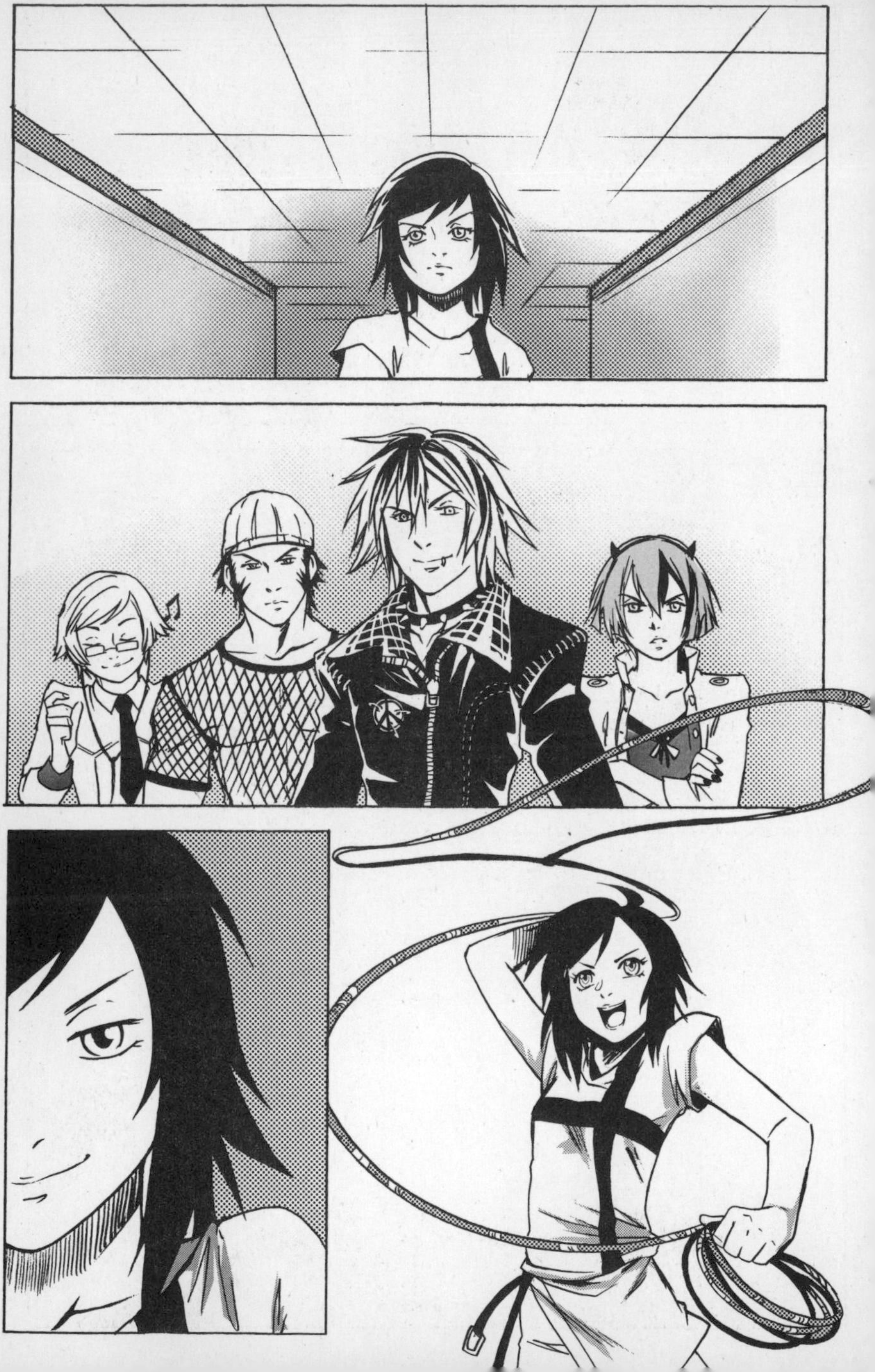

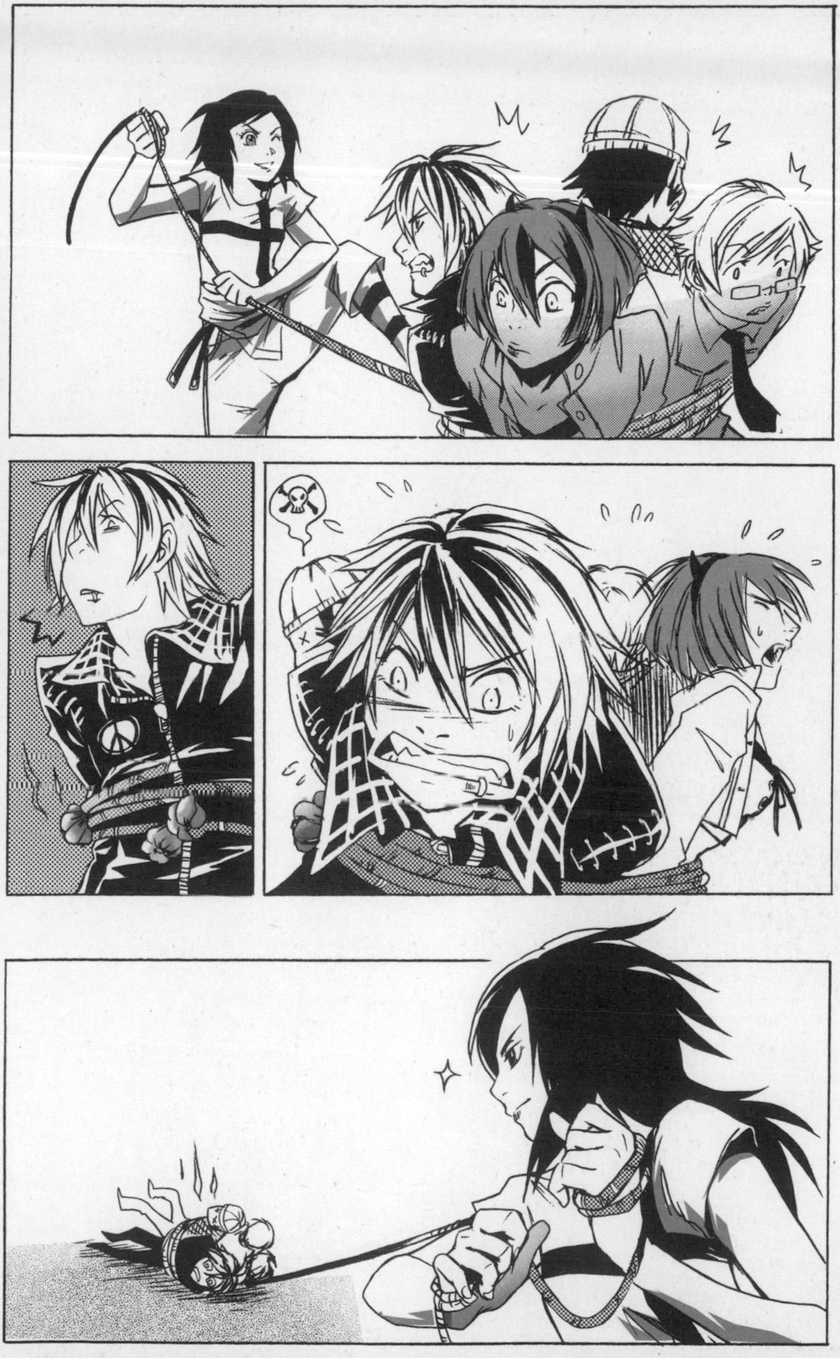

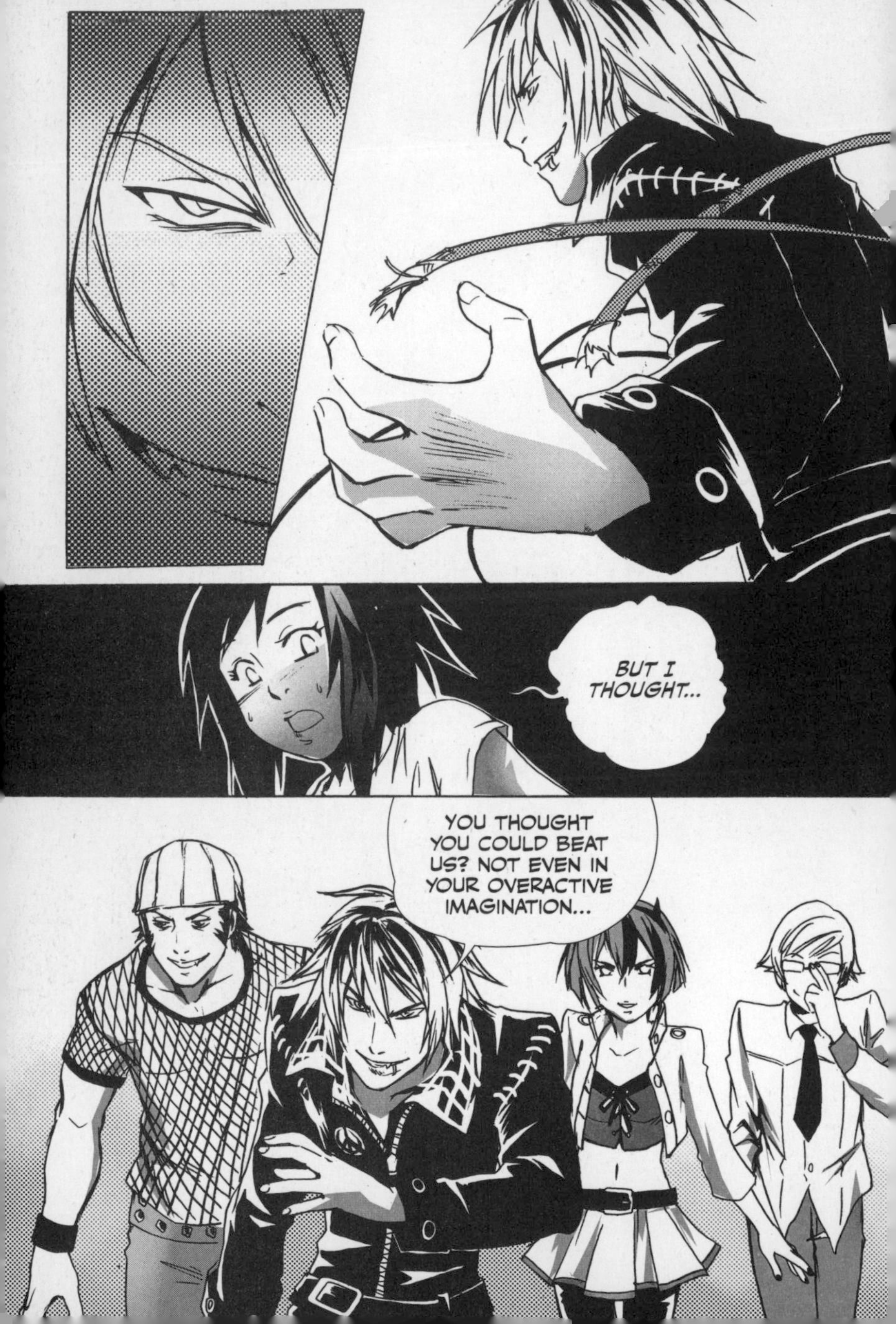
BUT I THOUGHT...
YOU THOUGHT YOU COULD BEAT US? NOT EVEN IN YOUR OVERACTIVE IMAGINATION...

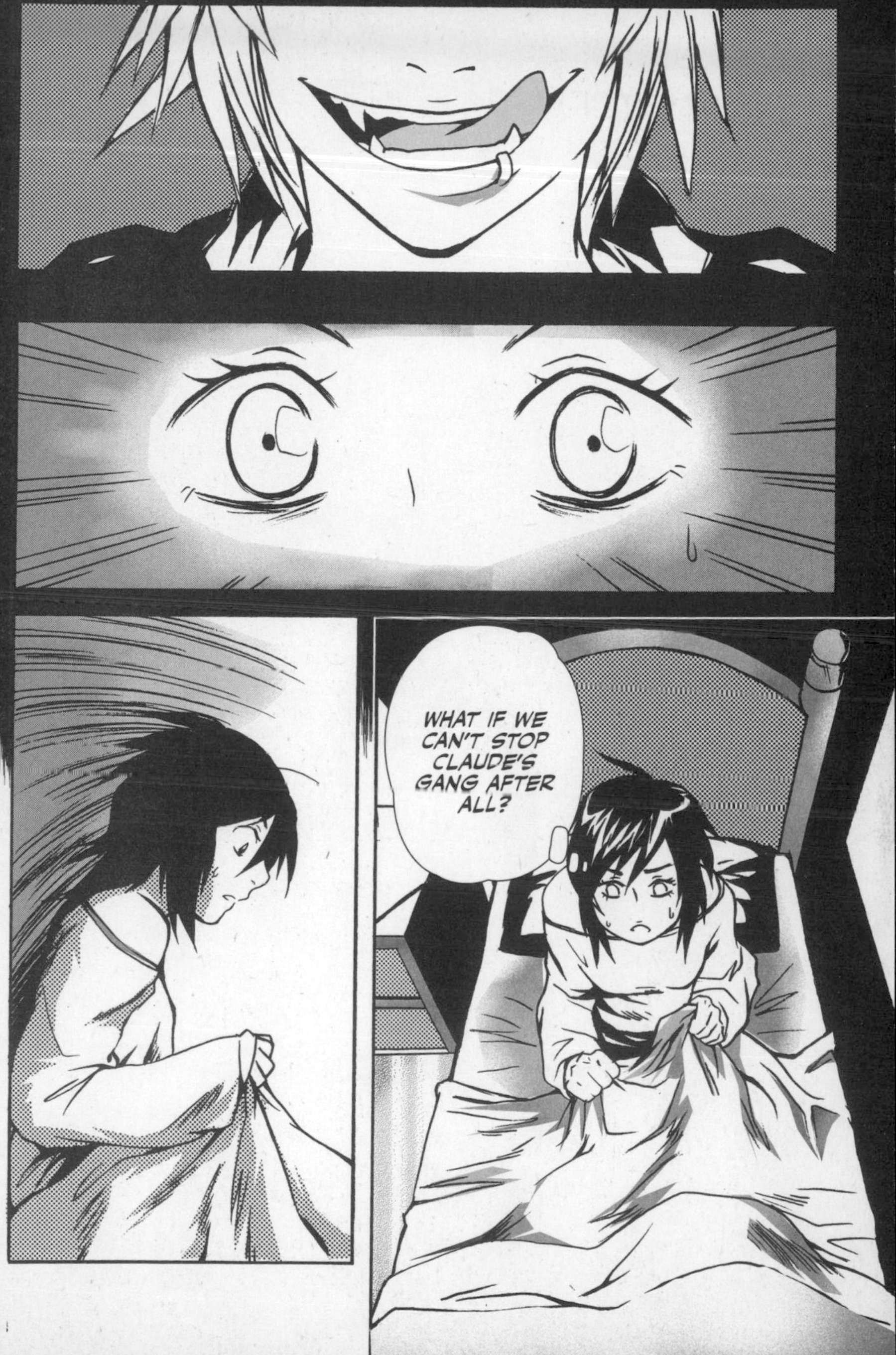
WHAT IF WE CAN'T STOP CLAUDE'S GANG AFTER ALL?

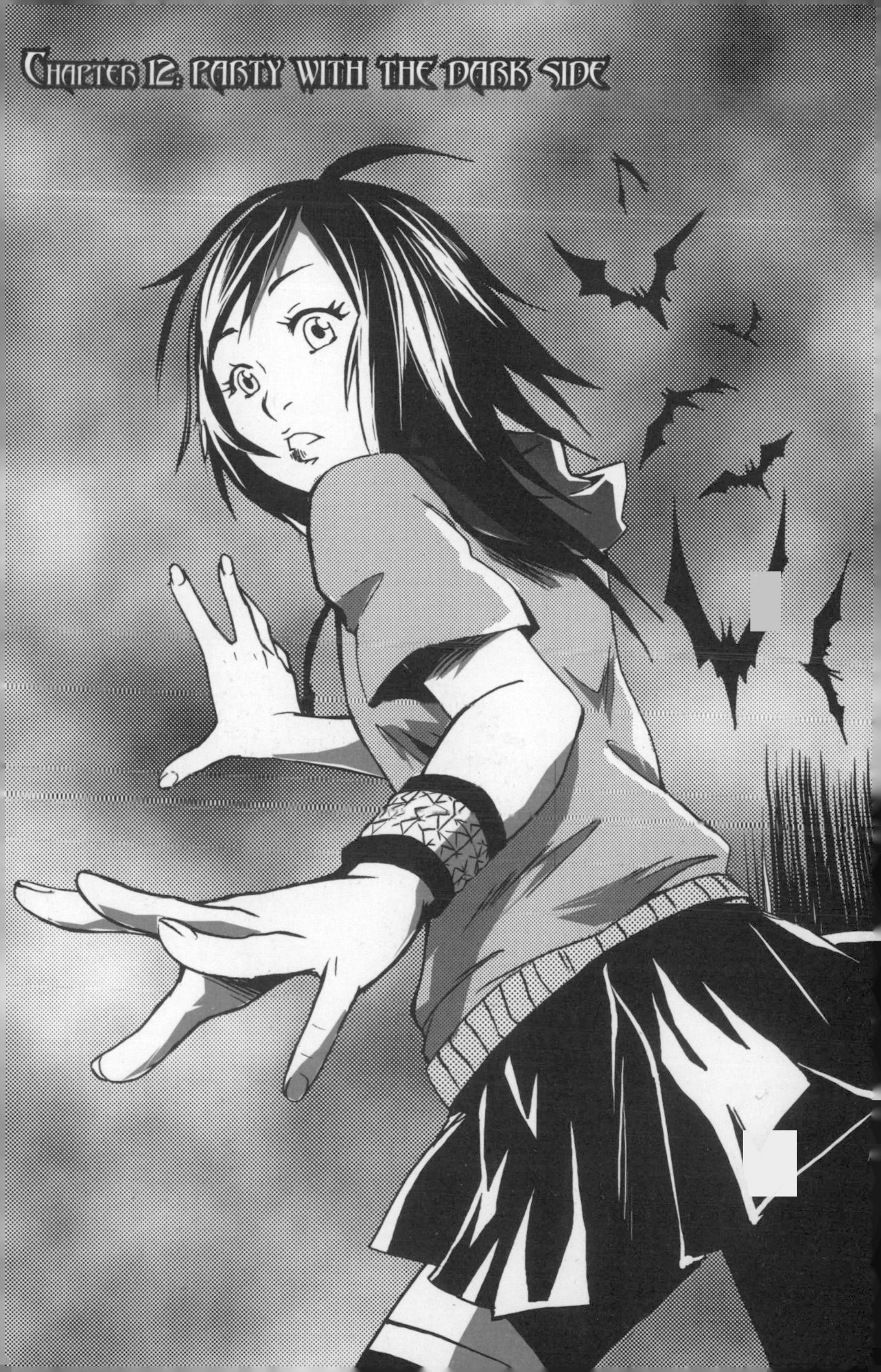
Chapter 12: Party with the Dark Side

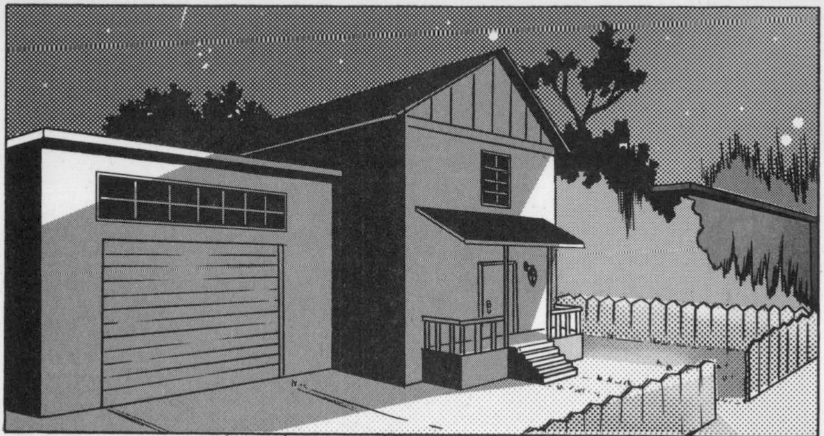
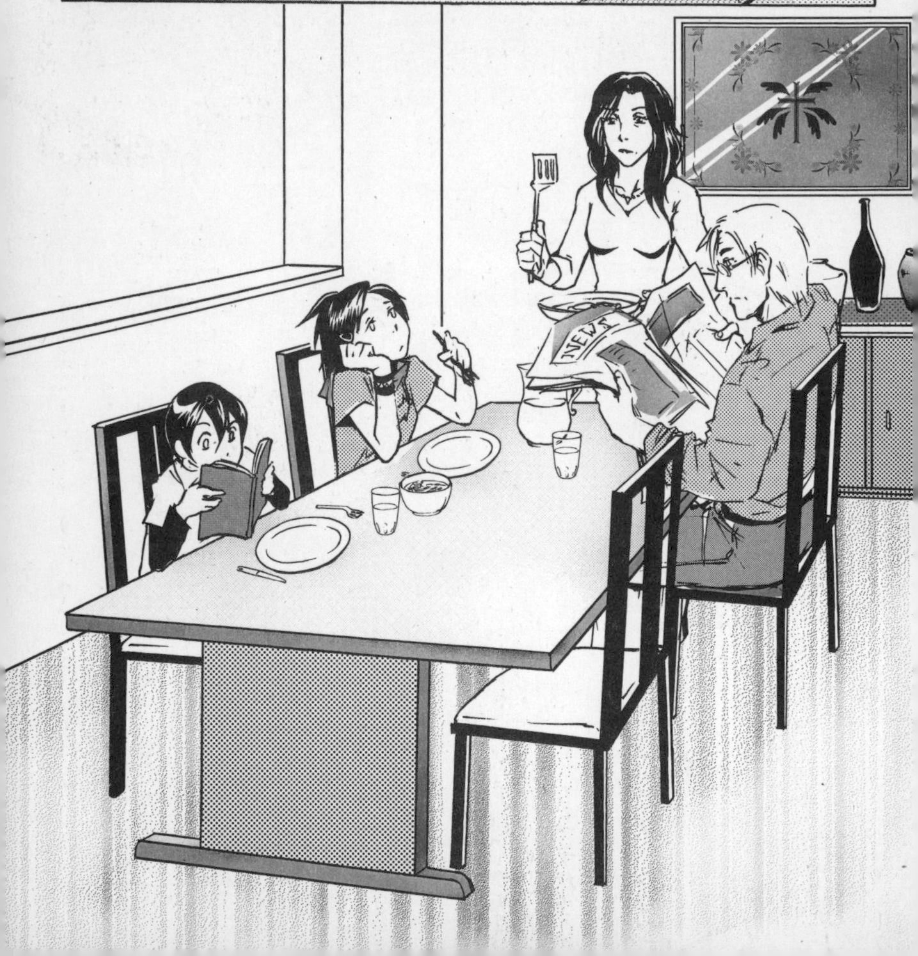
NEWS

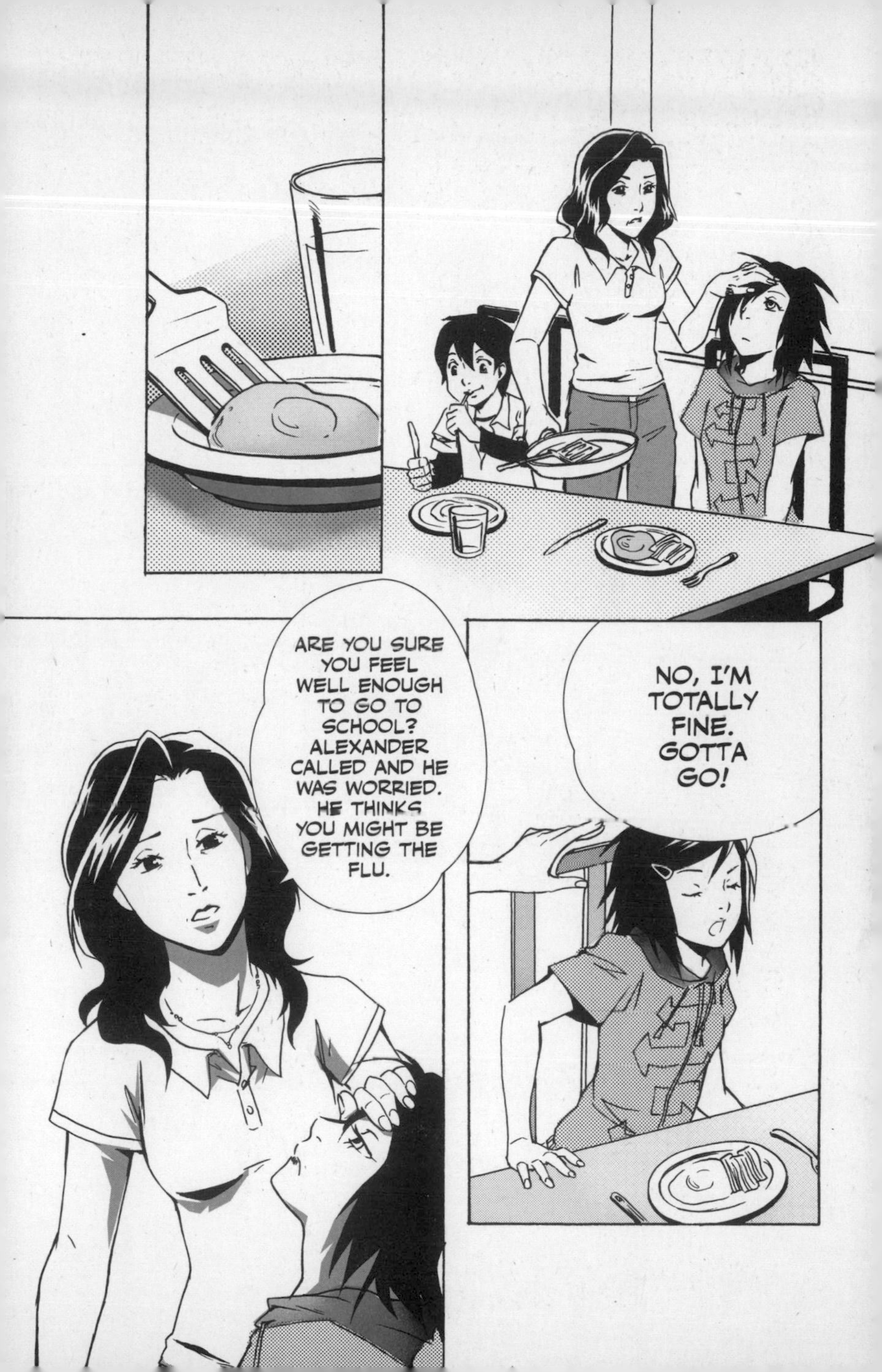
ARE YOU SURE YOU FEEL WELL ENOUGH TO GO TO SCHOOL? ALEXANDER CALLED AND HE WAS WORRIED. HE THINKS YOU MIGHT BE GETTING THE FLU.
NO, I'M TOTALLY FINE. GOTTA GO!

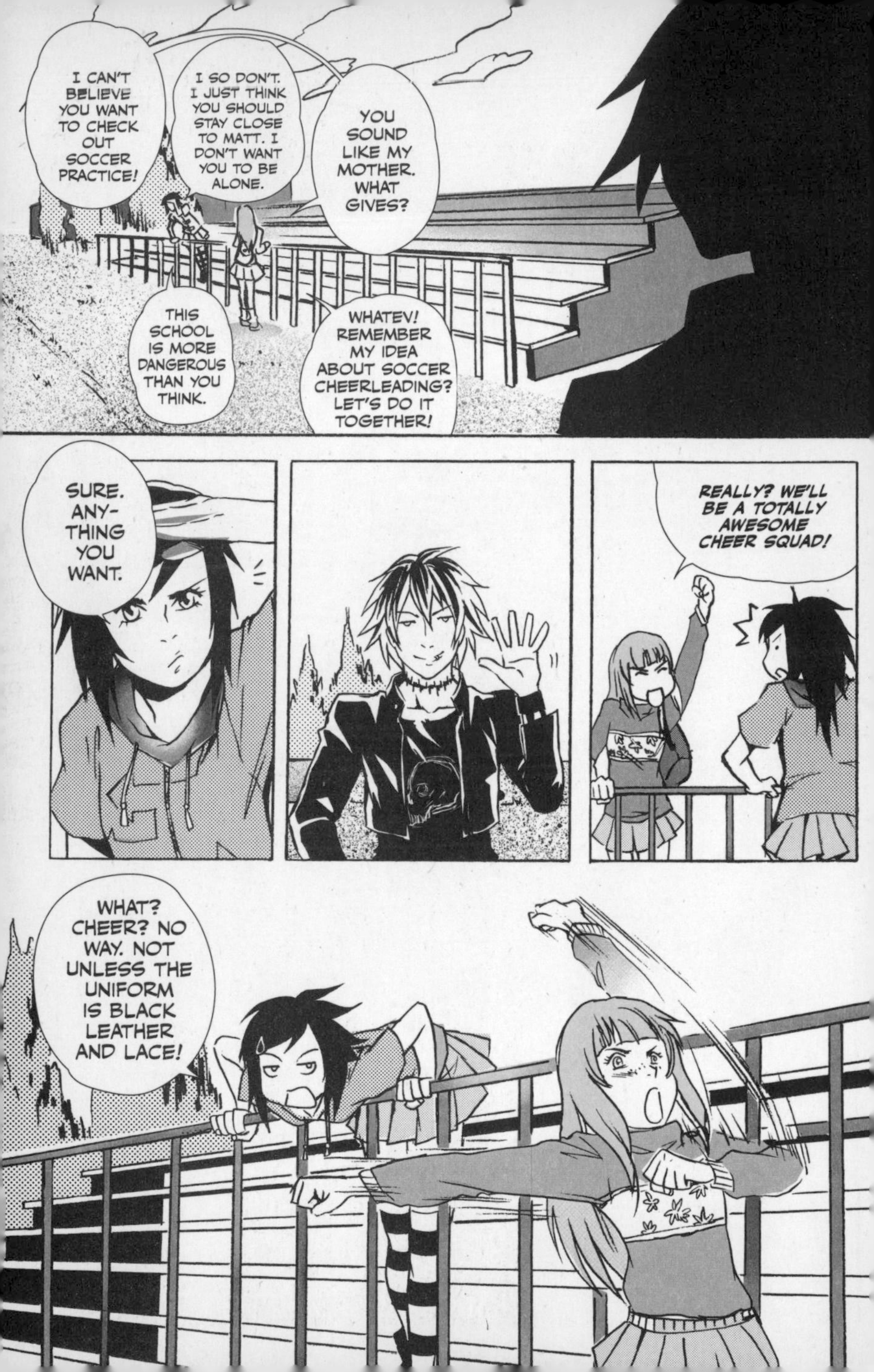
I CAN'T BELIEVE YOU WANT TO CHECK OUT SOCCER PRACTICE!
I SO DON'T. I JUST THINK YOU SHOULD STAY CLOSE TO MATT. I DON'T WANT YOU TO BE ALONE.
YOU SOUND LIKE MY MOTHER. WHAT GIVES?
THIS SCHOOL IS MORE DANGEROUS THAN YOU THINK.
WHATEV! REMEMBER MY IDEA ABOUT SOCCER CHEERLEADING? LET'S DO IT TOGETHER!
SURE. ANY-THING YOU WANT.
REALLY? WE'LL BE A TOTALLY AWESOME CHEER SQUAD!
WHAT? CHEER? NO WAY. NOT UNLESS THE UNIFORM IS BLACK LEATHER AND LACE!

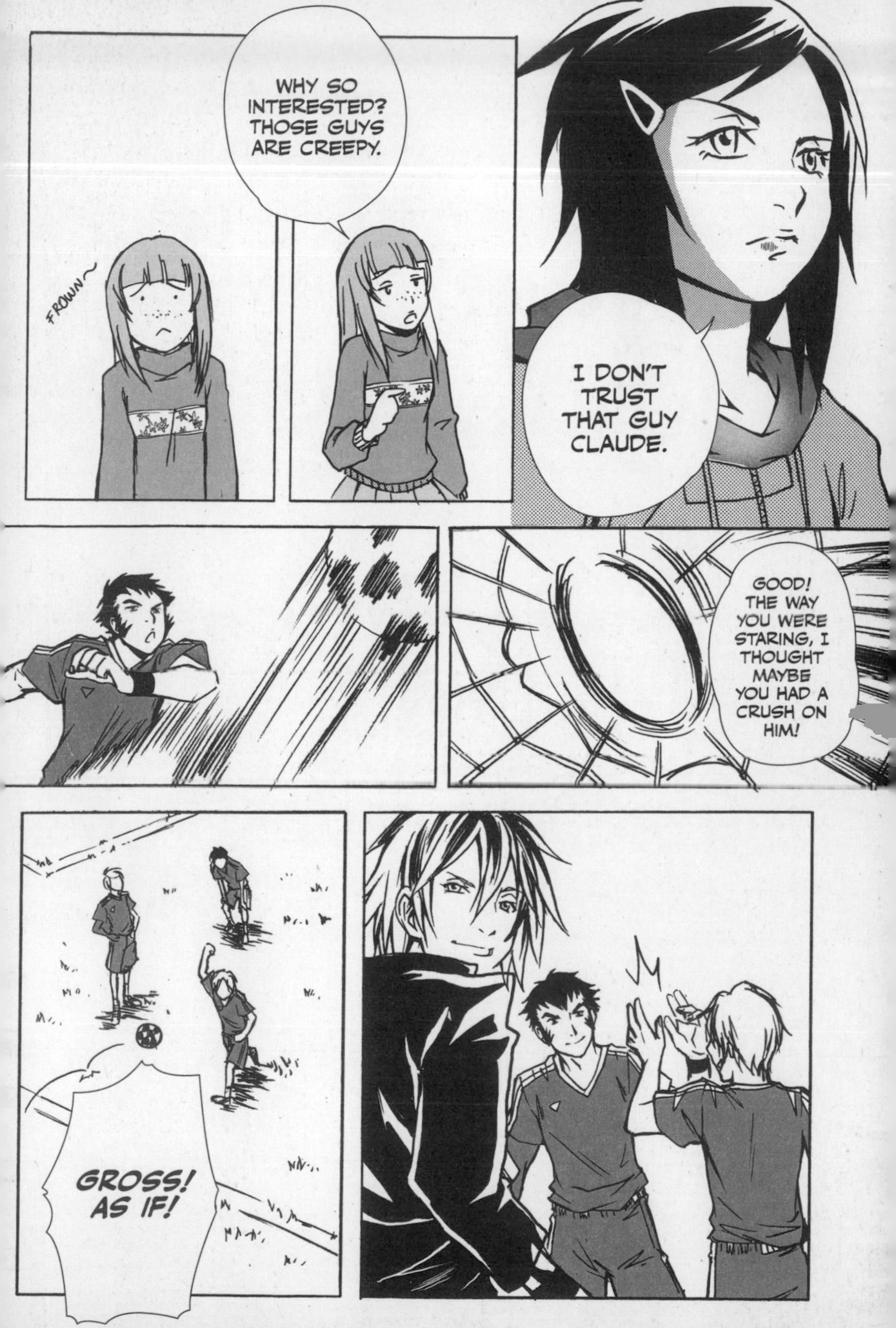
FROWN~
WHY SO INTERESTED? THOSE GUYS ARE CREEPY.
I DON'T TRUST THAT GUY CLAUDE.
GOOD! THE WAY YOU WERE STARING, I THOUGHT MAYBE YOU HAD A CRUSH ON HIM!
GROSS! AS IF!

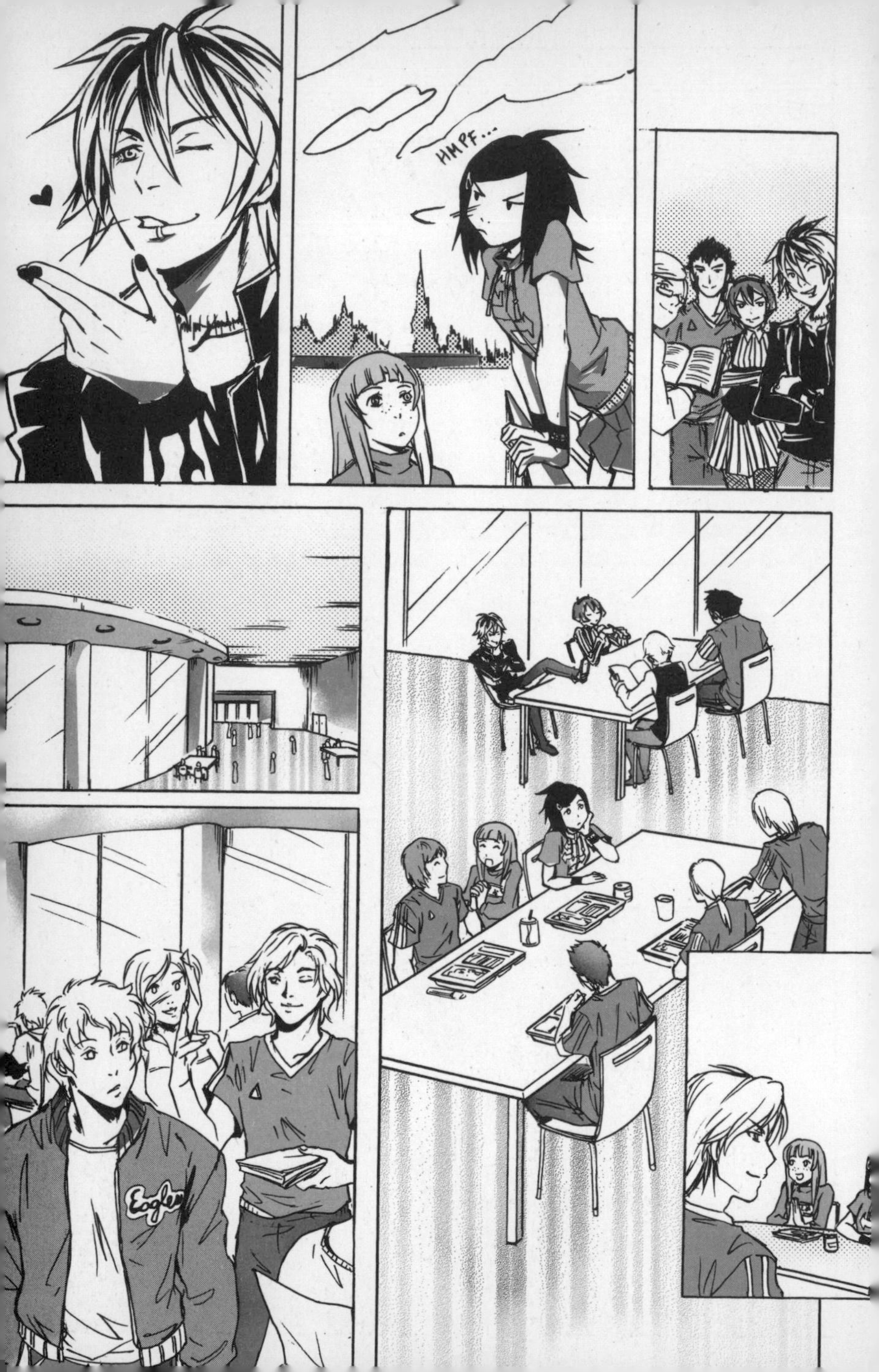
HMPF...

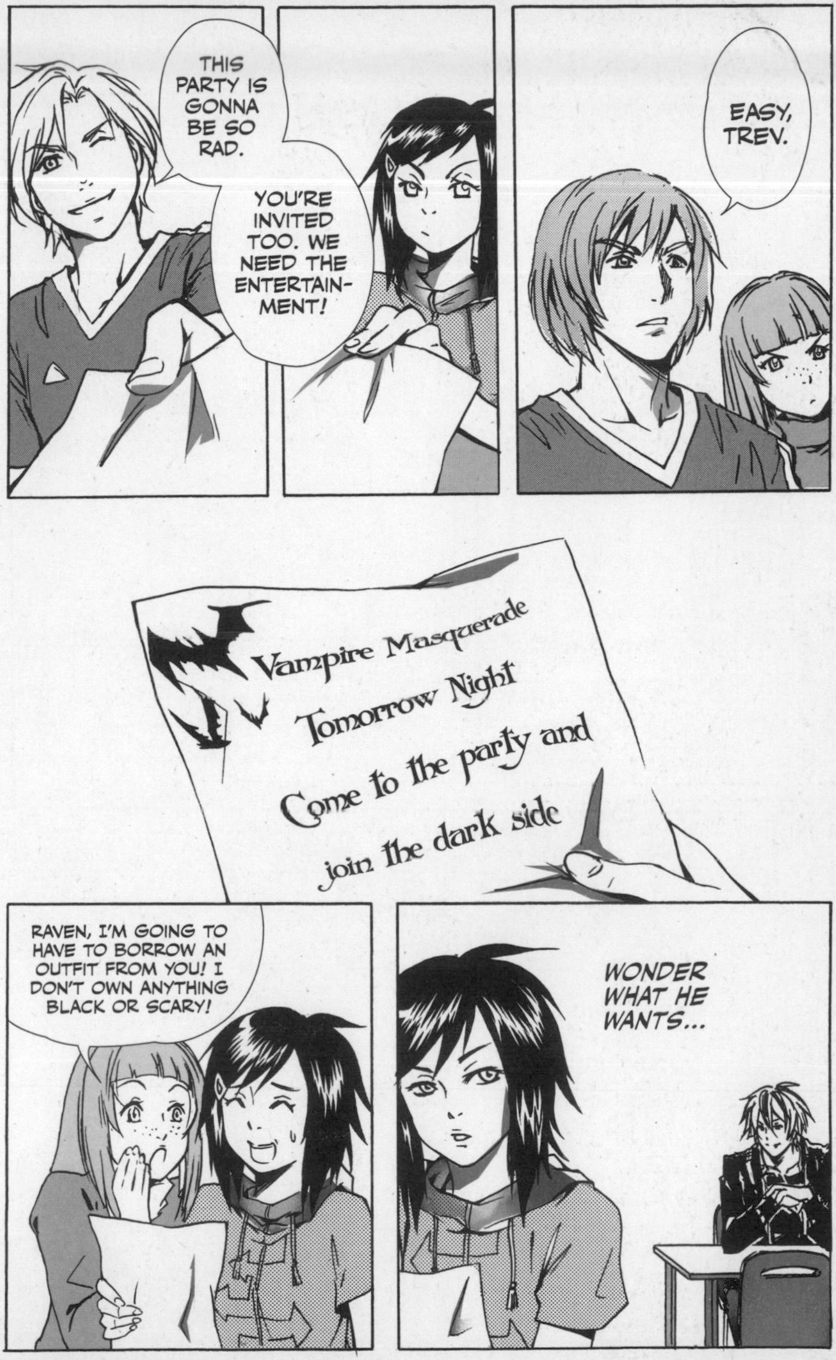
THIS PARTY IS GONNA BE SO RAD.
YOU'RE INVITED TOO. WE NEED THE ENTERTAIN-MENT!
EASY, TREV.
Vampire Masquerade
Tomorrow Night
Come to the party and
join the dark side
RAVEN, I'M GOING TO HAVE TO BORROW AN OUTFIT FROM YOU! I DON'T OWN ANYTHING BLACK OR SCARY!
WONDER WHAT HE WANTS...

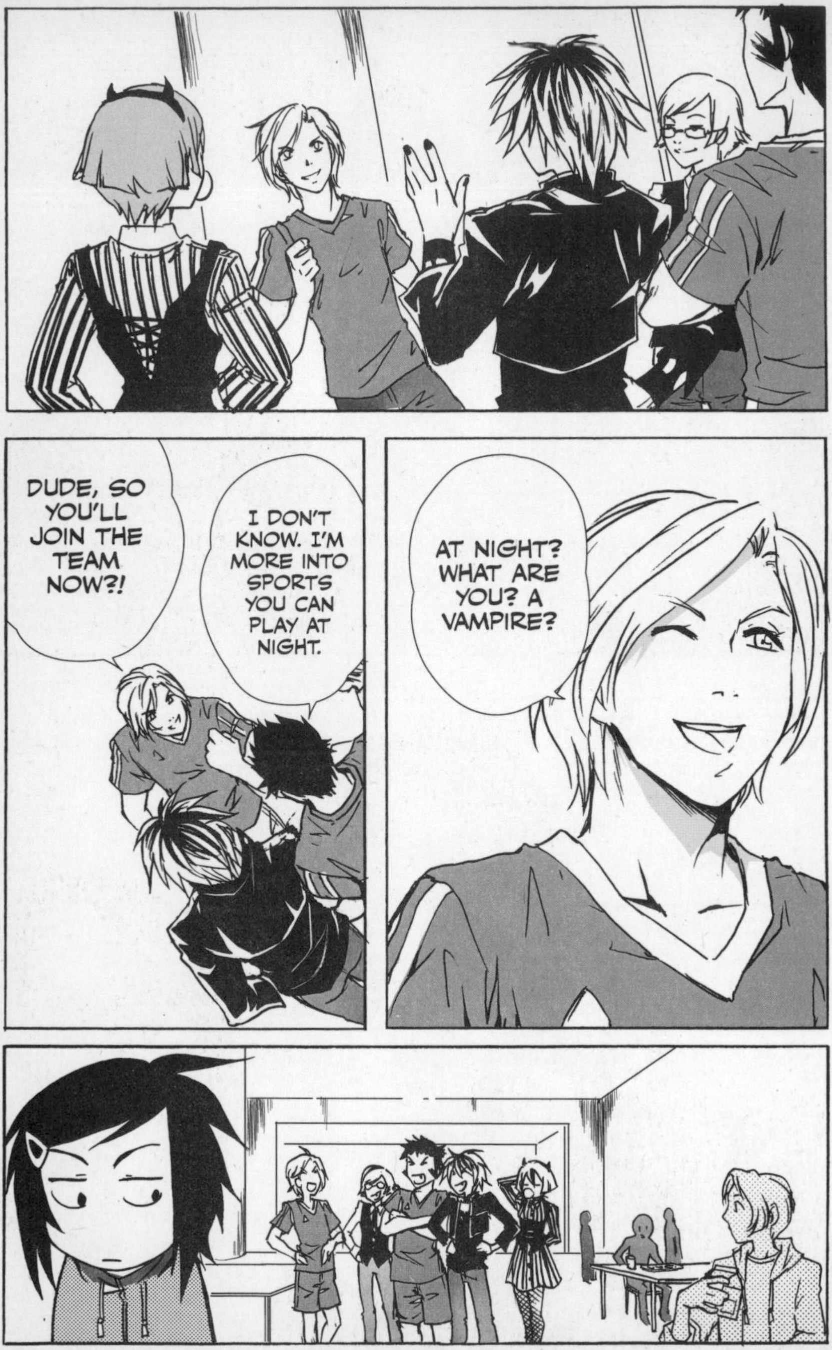
DUDE, SO YOU'LL JOIN THE TEAM NOW?!
I DON'T KNOW. I'M MORE INTO SPORTS YOU CAN PLAY AT NIGHT.
AT NIGHT? WHAT ARE YOU? A VAMPIRE?

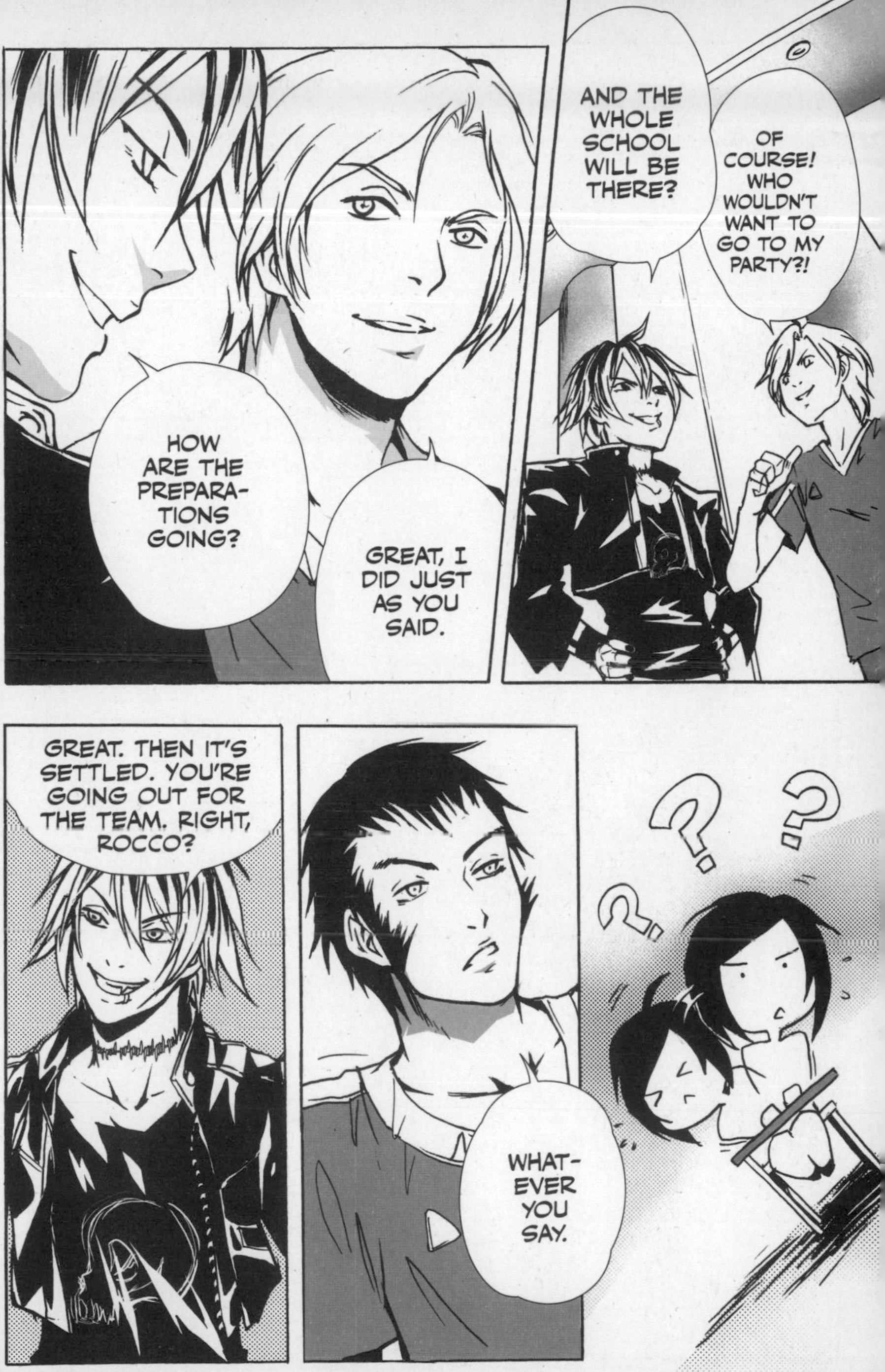
HOW ARE THE PREPARATIONS GOING?
GREAT, I DID JUST AS YOU SAID.
AND THE WHOLE SCHOOL WILL BE THERE?
OF COURSE! WHO WOULDN'T WANT TO GO TO MY PARTY?!
GREAT. THEN IT'S SETTLED. YOU'RE GOING OUT FOR THE TEAM. RIGHT, ROCCO?
WHAT-EVER YOU SAY.

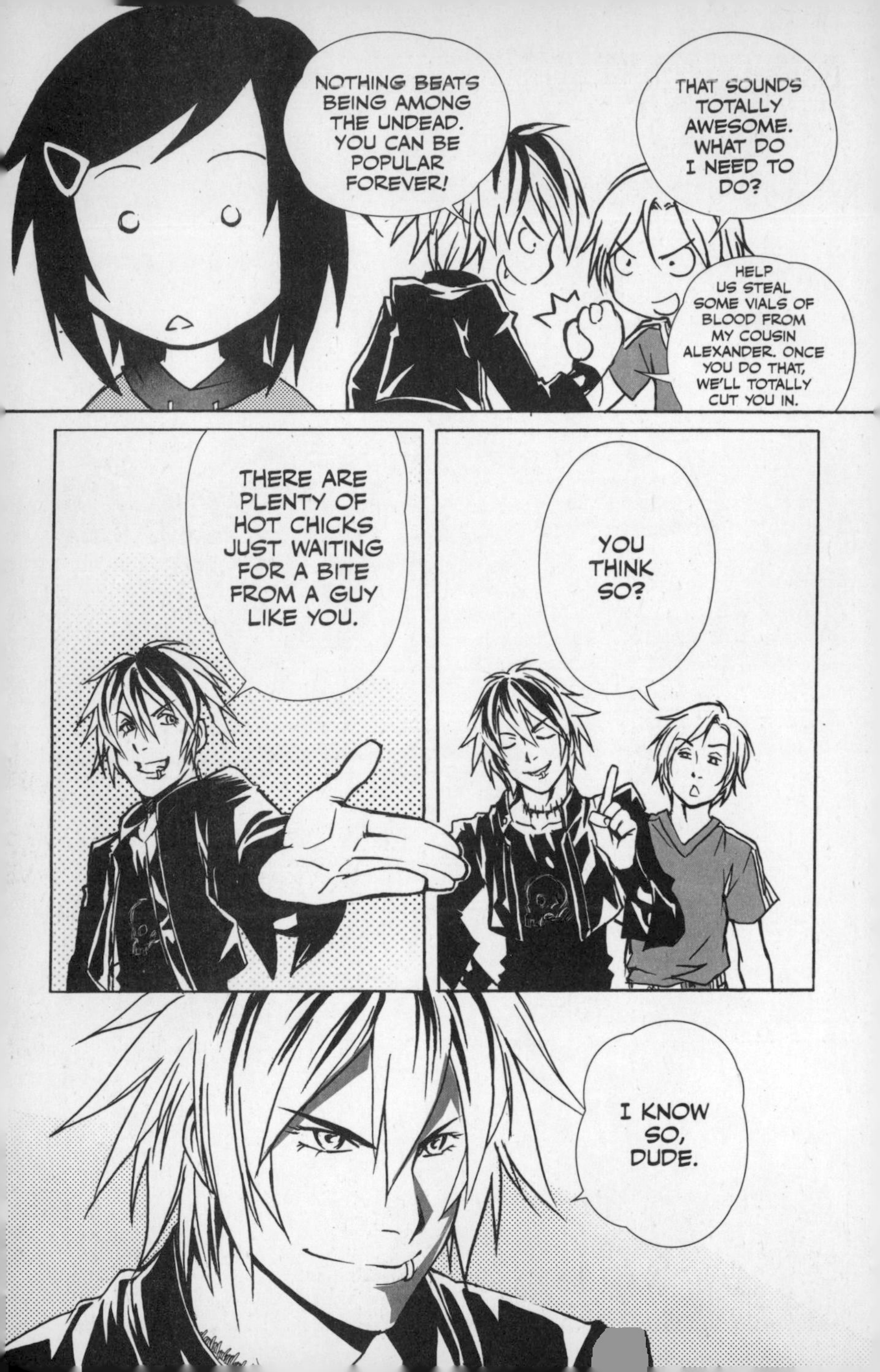
NOTHING BEATS BEING AMONG THE UNDEAD. YOU CAN BE POPULAR FOREVER!
THAT SOUNDS TOTALLY AWESOME. WHAT DO I NEED TO DO?
HELP US STEAL SOME VIALS OF BLOOD FROM MY COUSIN ALEXANDER. ONCE YOU DO THAT, WE'LL TOTALLY CUT YOU IN.
THERE ARE PLENTY OF HOT CHICKS JUST WAITING FOR A BITE FROM A GUY LIKE YOU.
YOU THINK SO?
I KNOW SO, DUDE.

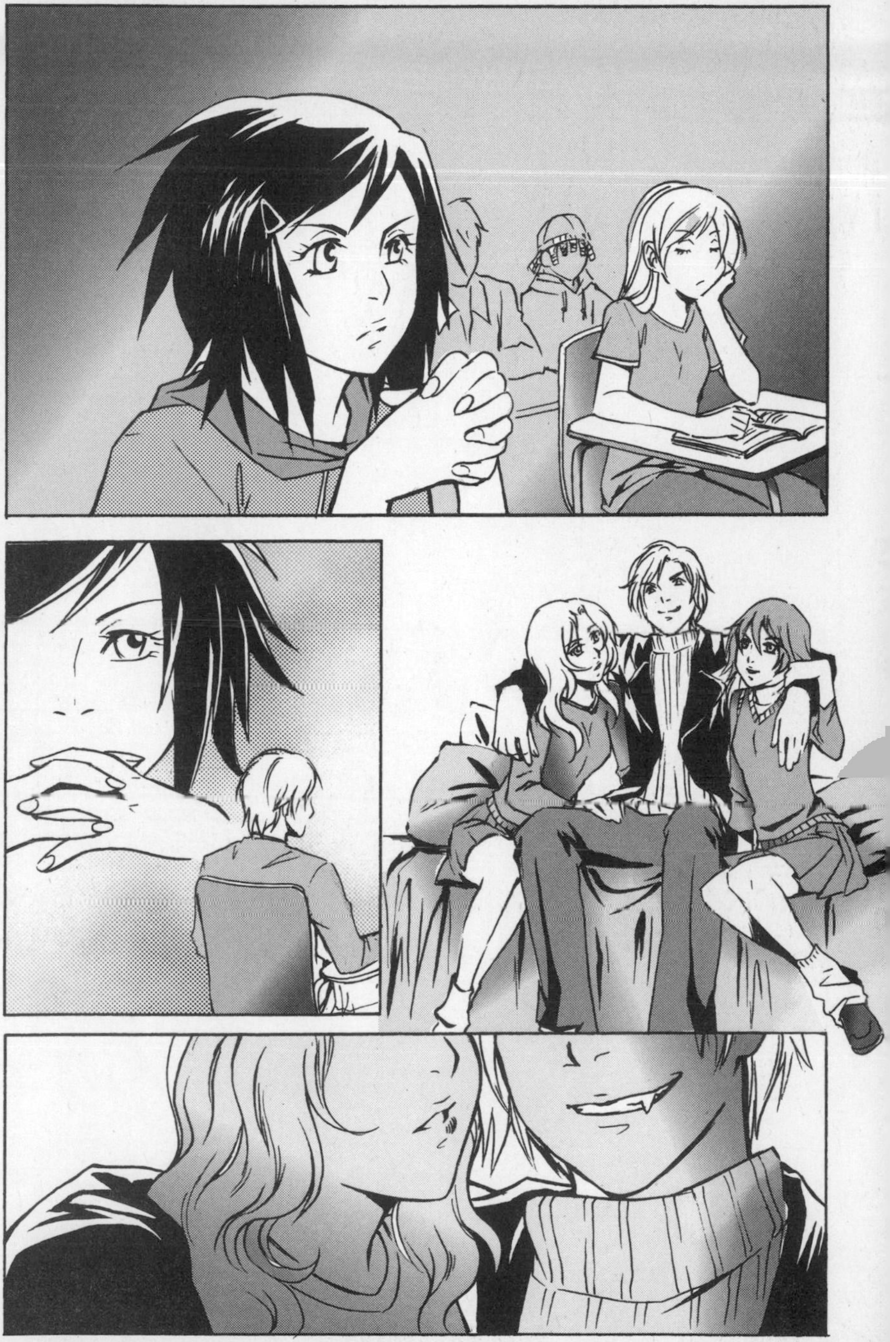

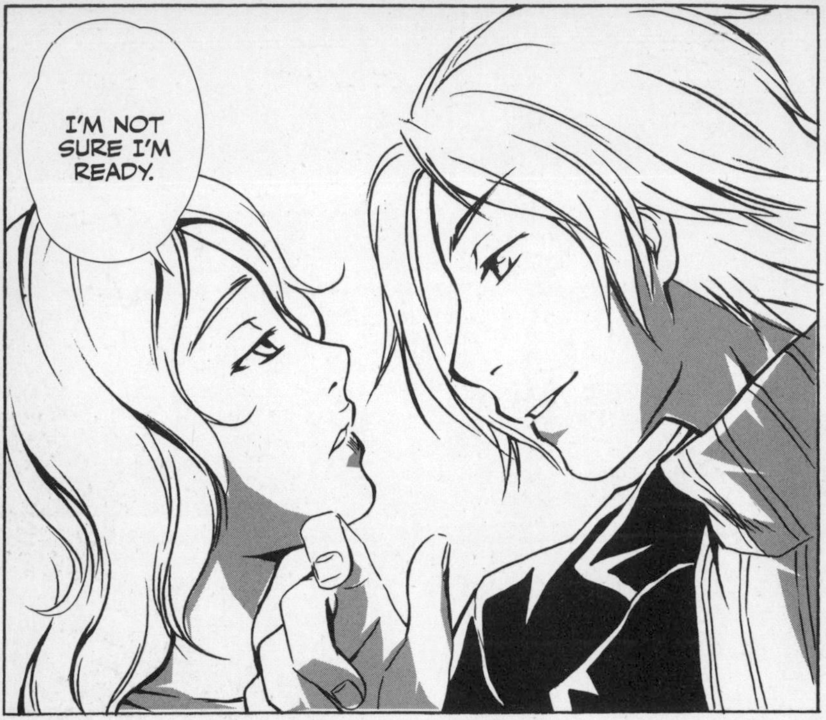
I'M NOT SURE I'M READY.

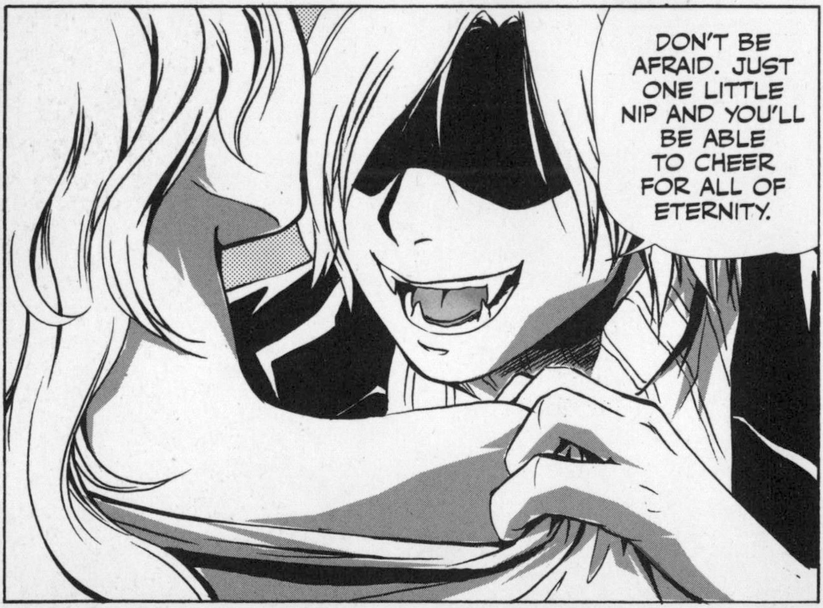
DON'T BE AFRAID. JUST ONE LITTLE NIP AND YOU'LL BE ABLE TO CHEER FOR ALL OF ETERNITY.

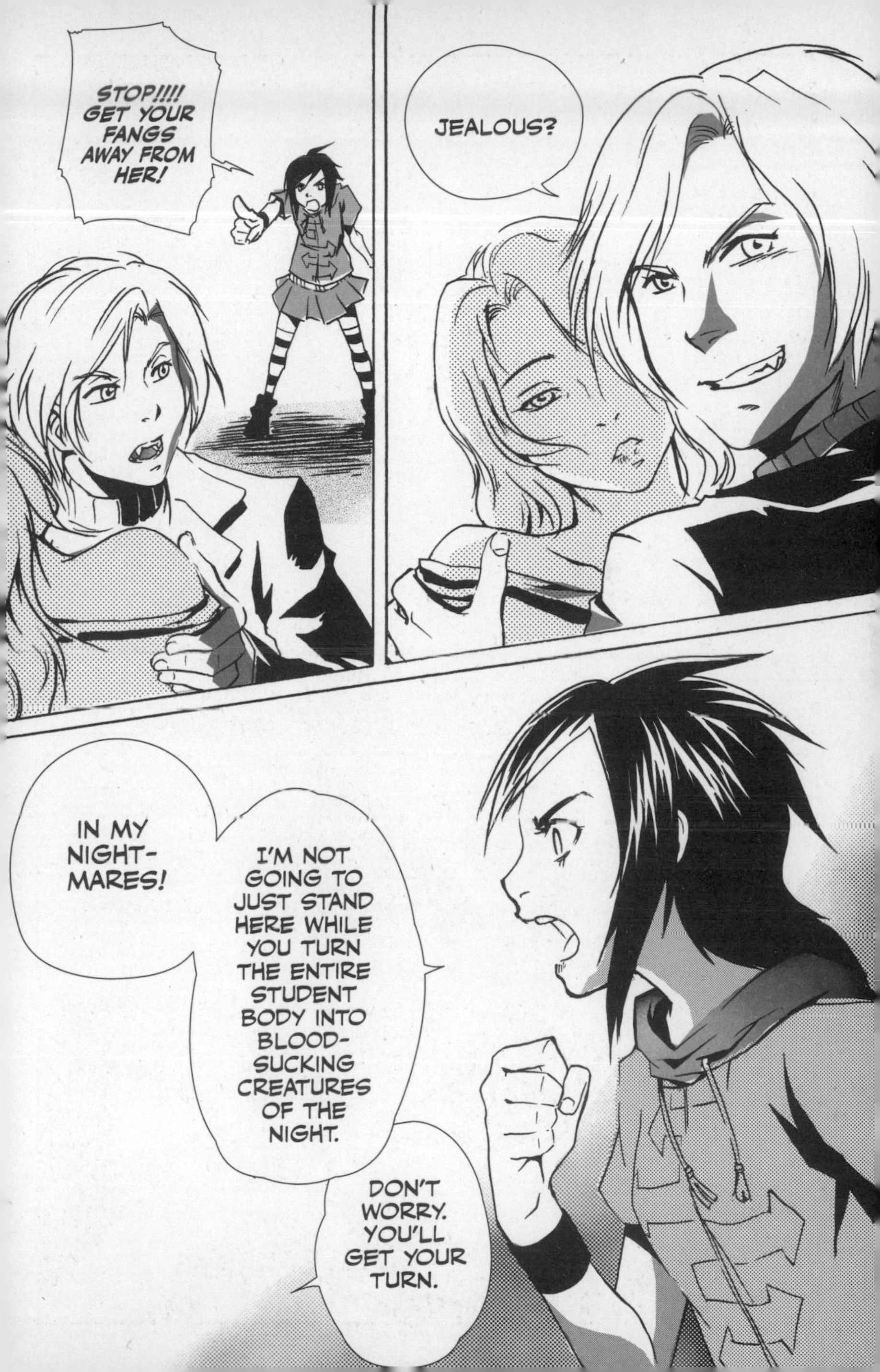
STOP!!!! GET YOUR FANGS AWAY FROM HER!
JEALOUS?
IN MY NIGHT-MARES!
I'M NOT GOING TO JUST STAND HERE WHILE YOU TURN THE ENTIRE STUDENT BODY INTO BLOOD-SUCKING CREATURES OF THE NIGHT.
DON'T WORRY. YOU'LL GET YOUR TURN.

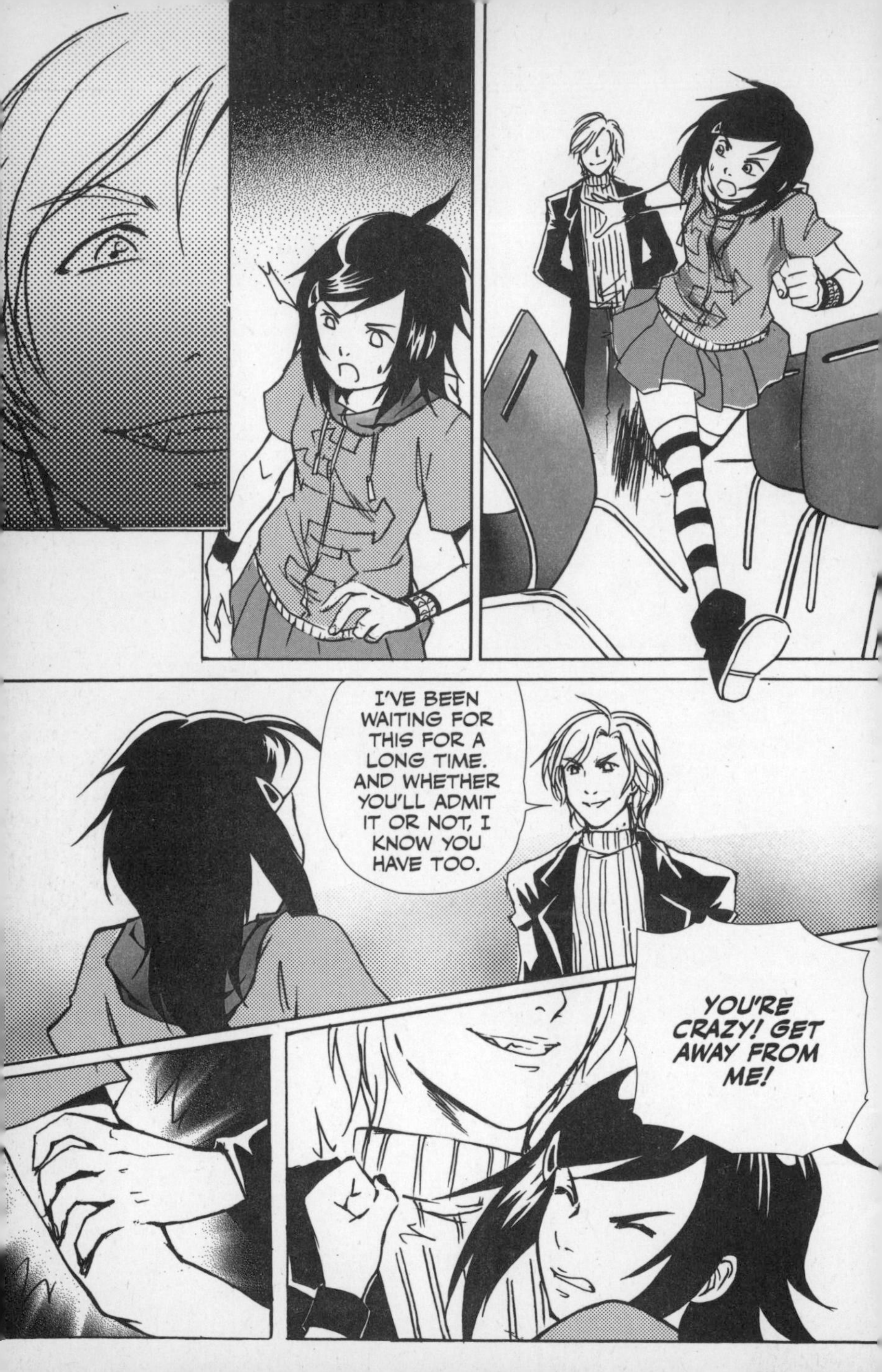
I'VE BEEN WAITING FOR THIS FOR A LONG TIME. AND WHETHER YOU'LL ADMIT IT OR NOT, I KNOW YOU HAVE TOO.
YOU'RE CRAZY! GET AWAY FROM ME!

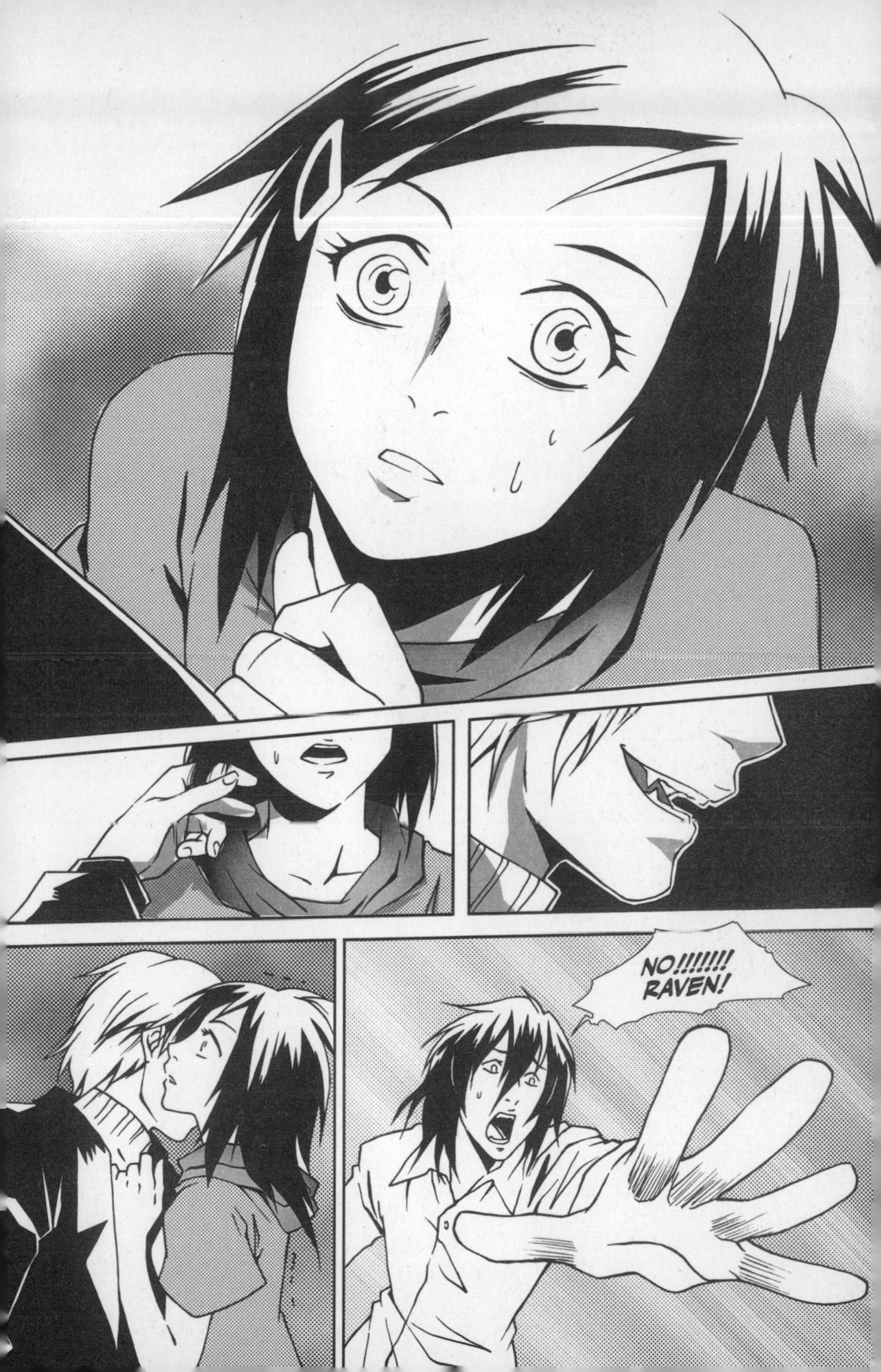
NO!!!!!!!! RAVEN!

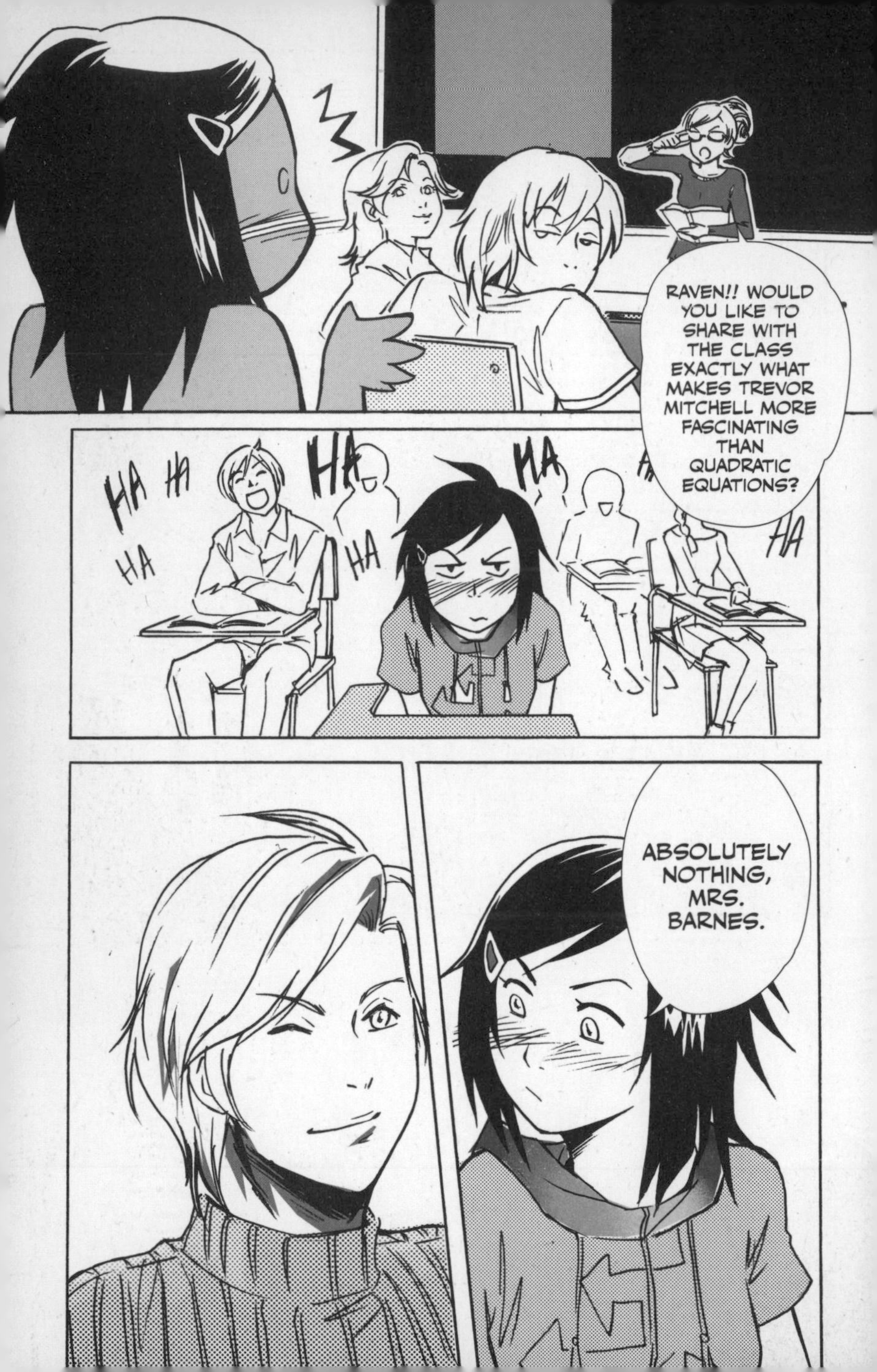
RAVEN!! WOULD YOU LIKE TO SHARE WITH THE CLASS EXACTLY WHAT MAKES TREVOR MITCHELL MORE FASCINATING THAN QUADRATIC EQUATIONS?
HA HA
HA
HA
HA
HA
HA
ABSOLUTELY NOTHING, MRS. BARNES.

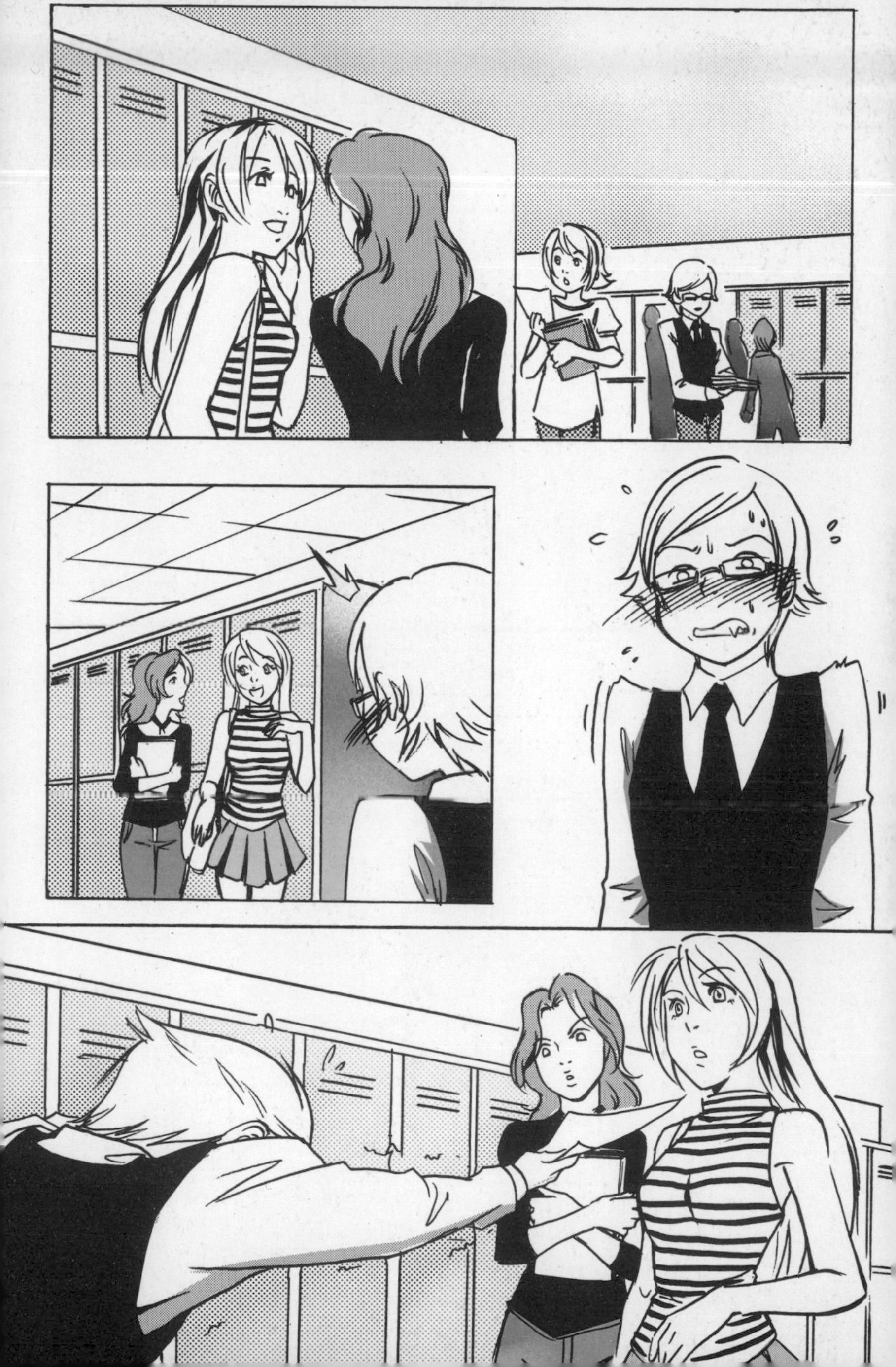

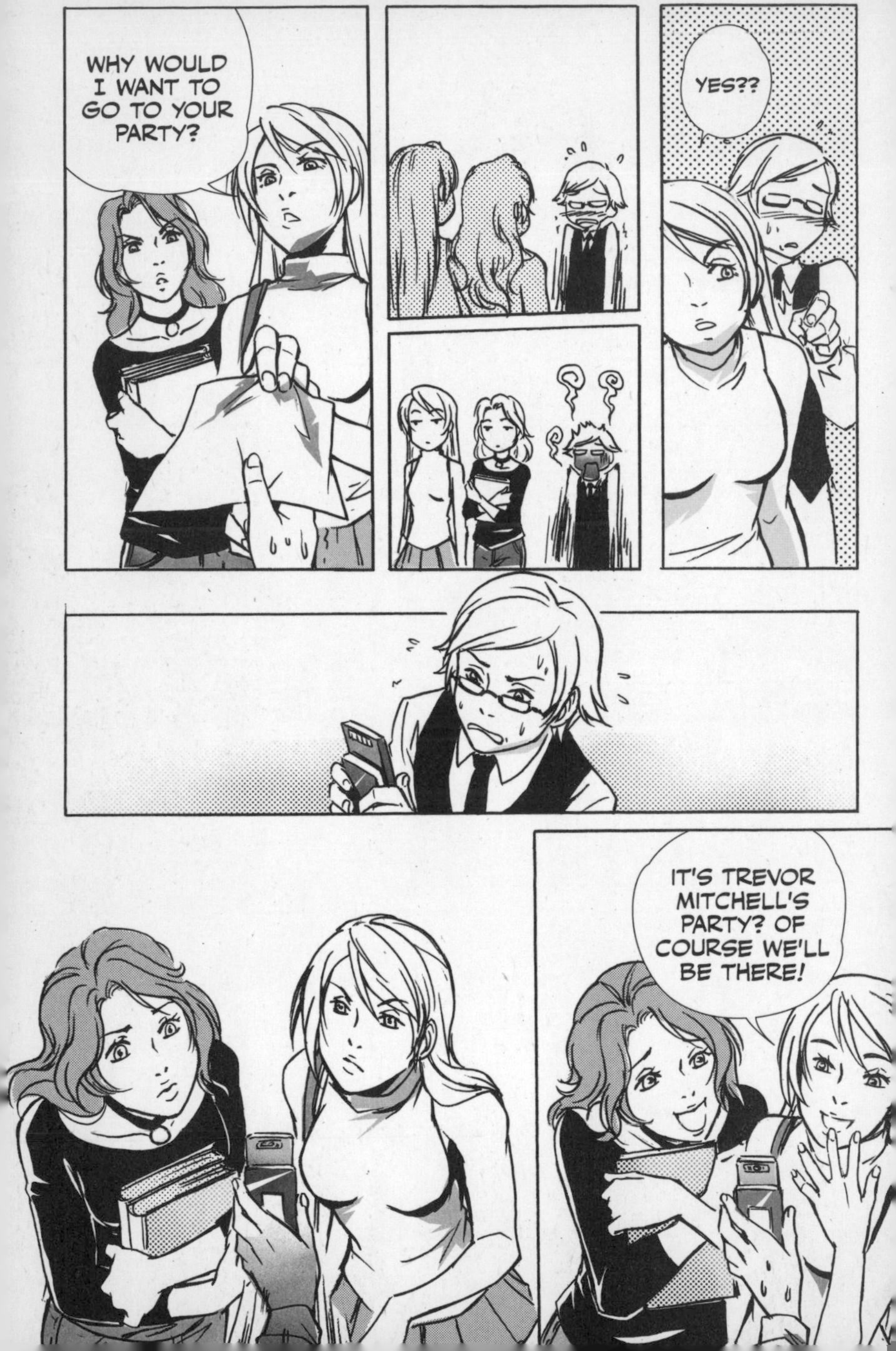
WHY WOULD I WANT TO GO TO YOUR PARTY?
YES??
IT'S TREVOR MITCHELL'S PARTY? OF COURSE WE'LL BE THERE!

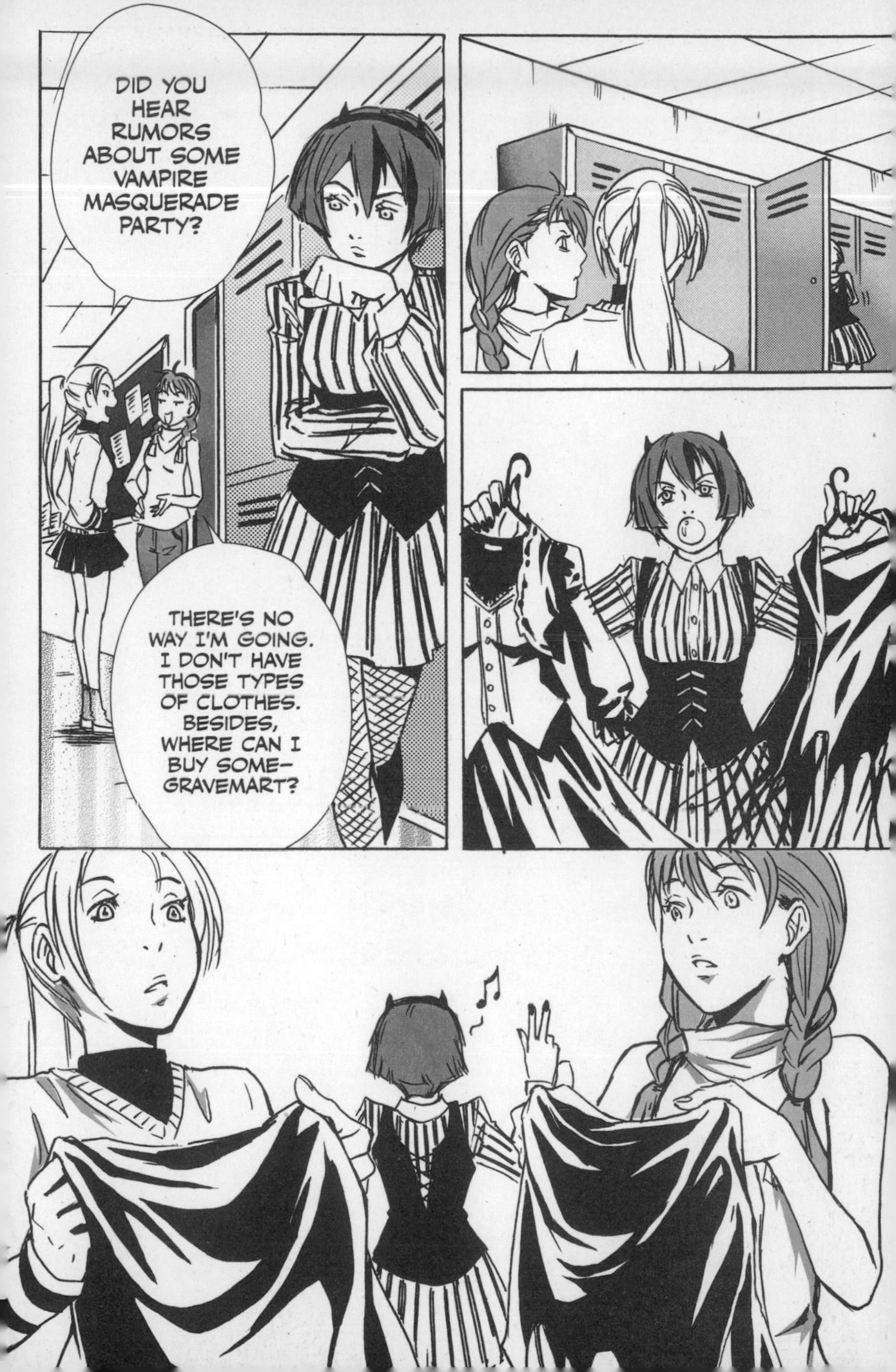
DID YOU HEAR RUMORS ABOUT SOME VAMPIRE MASQUERADE PARTY?
THERE'S NO WAY I'M GOING. I DON'T HAVE THOSE TYPES OF CLOTHES. BESIDES, WHERE CAN I BUY SOME-GRAVEMART?

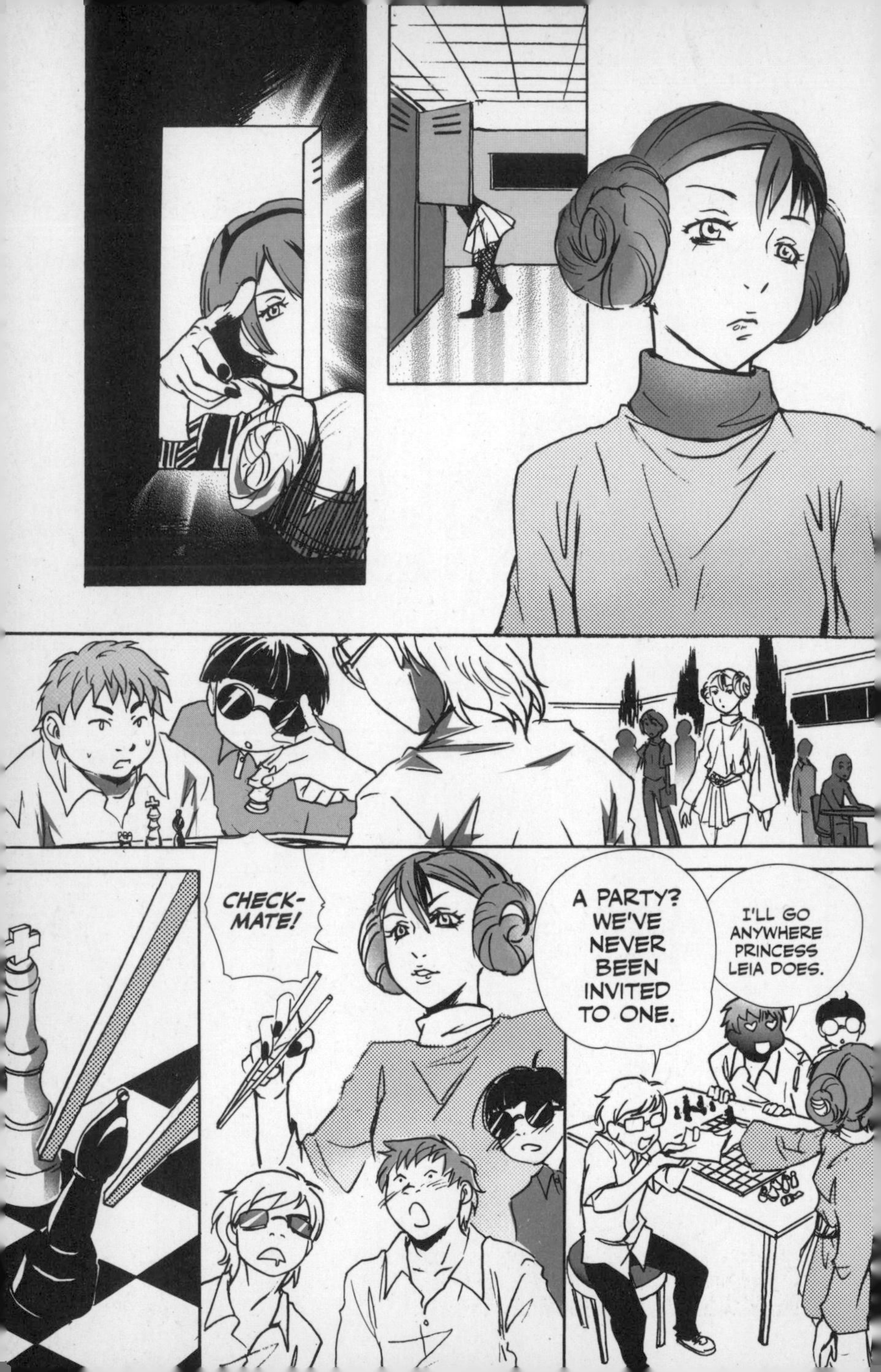
CHECK-MATE!
A PARTY? WE'VE NEVER BEEN INVITED TO ONE.
I'LL GO ANYWHERE PRINCESS LEIA DOES.

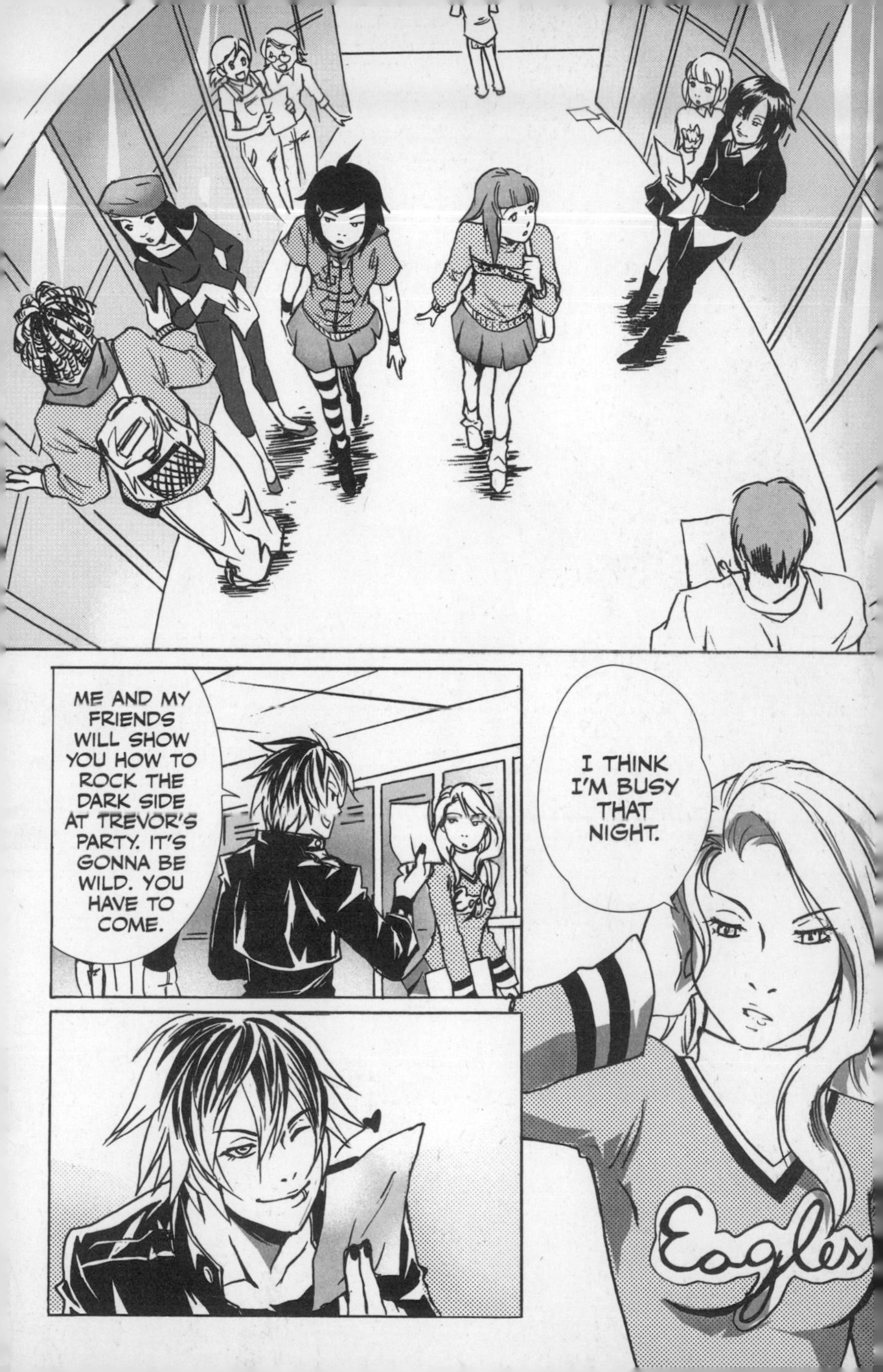
ME AND MY FRIENDS WILL SHOW YOU HOW TO ROCK THE DARK SIDE AT TREVOR'S PARTY. IT'S GONNA BE WILD. YOU HAVE TO COME.
I THINK I'M BUSY THAT NIGHT.
Eagles

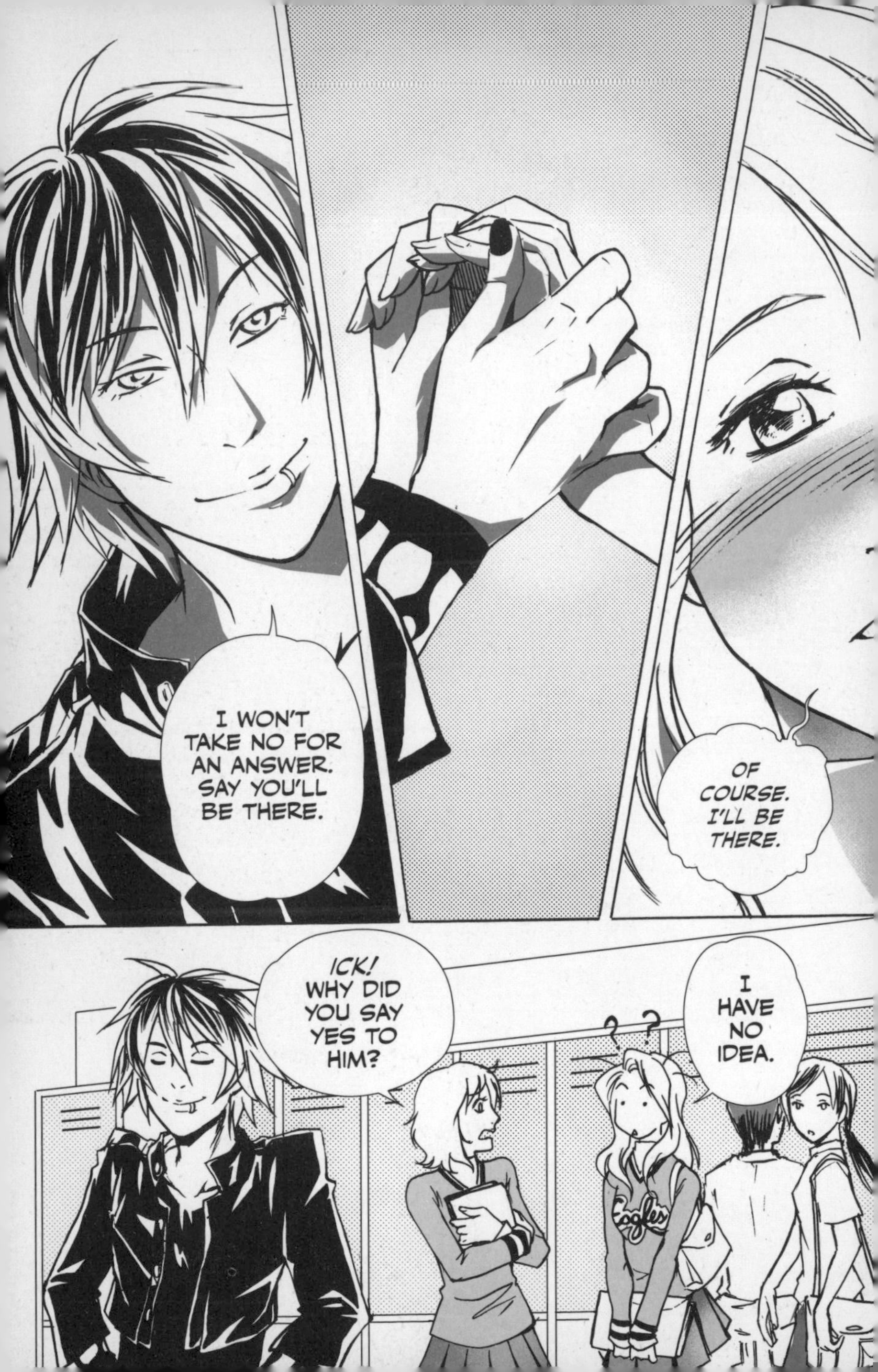
I WON'T TAKE NO FOR AN ANSWER. SAY YOU'LL BE THERE.
OF COURSE. I'LL BE THERE.
ICK! WHY DID YOU SAY YES TO HIM?
I HAVE NO IDEA.
Eagles

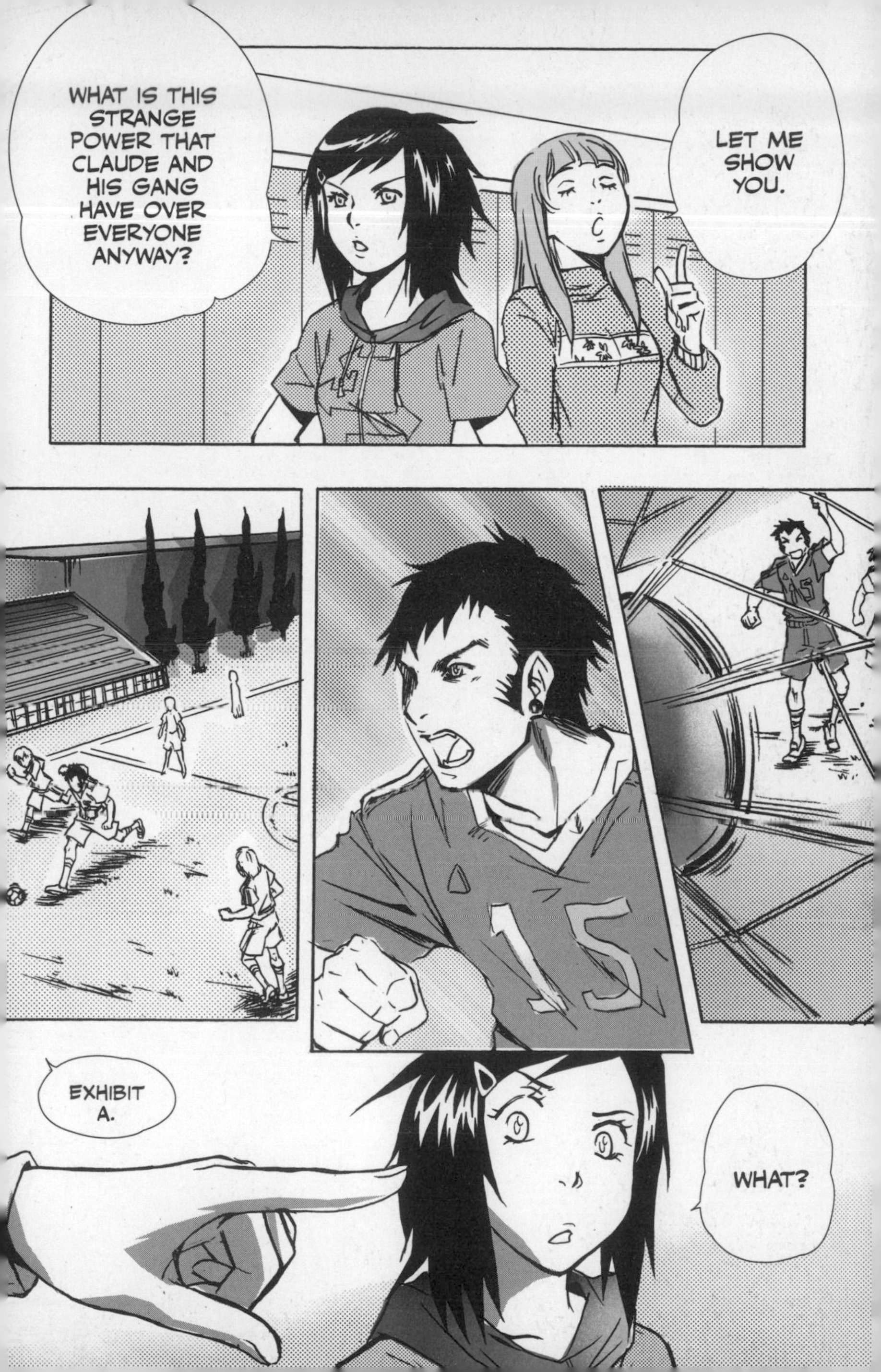
WHAT IS THIS STRANGE POWER THAT CLAUDE AND HIS GANG HAVE OVER EVERYONE ANYWAY?
LET ME SHOW YOU.
15
EXHIBIT A.
WHAT?

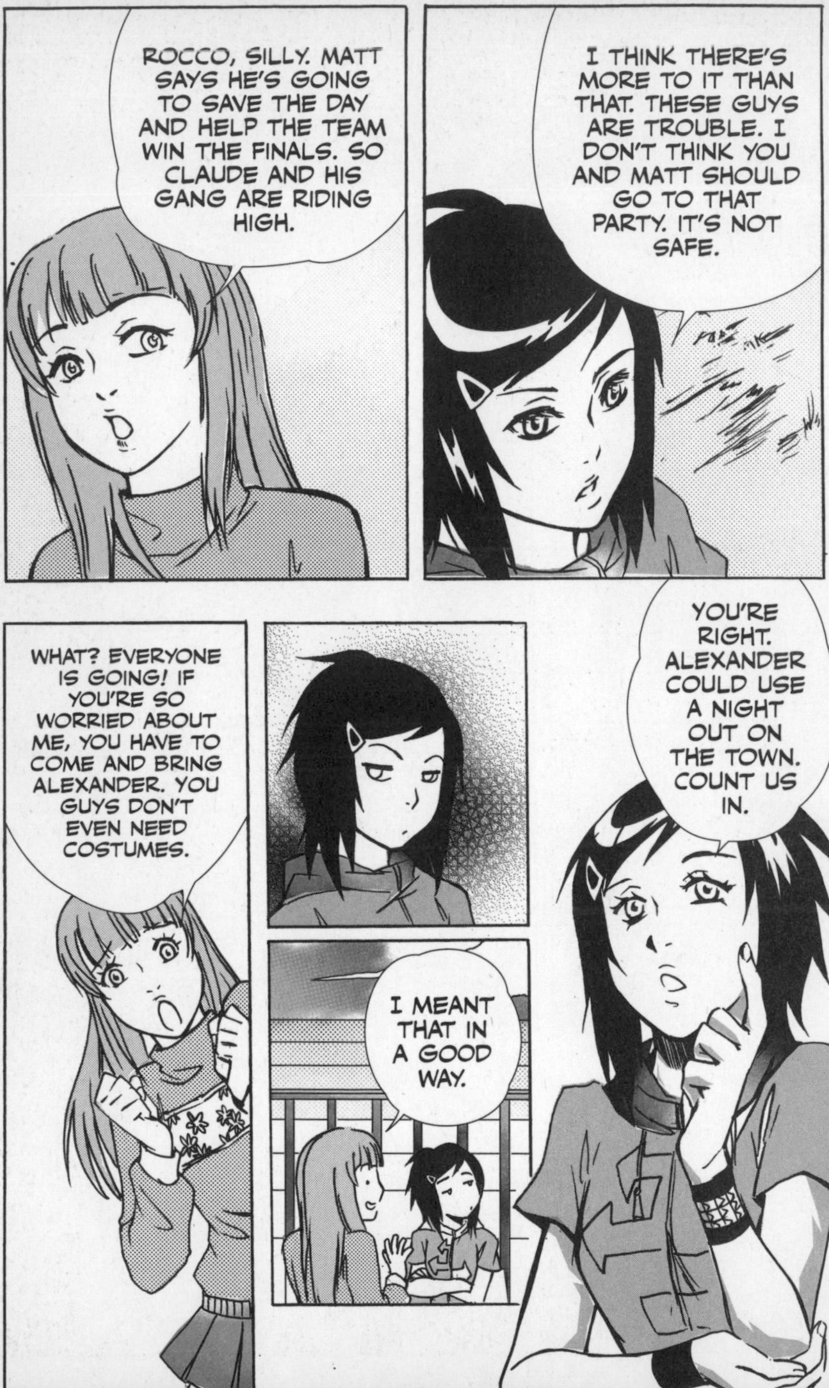
ROCCO, SILLY. MATT SAYS HE'S GOING TO SAVE THE DAY AND HELP THE TEAM WIN THE FINALS. SO CLAUDE AND HIS GANG ARE RIDING HIGH.
I THINK THERE'S MORE TO IT THAN THAT. THESE GUYS ARE TROUBLE. I DON'T THINK YOU AND MATT SHOULD GO TO THAT PARTY. IT'S NOT SAFE.
WHAT? EVERYONE IS GOING! IF YOU'RE SO WORRIED ABOUT ME, YOU HAVE TO COME AND BRING ALEXANDER. YOU GUYS DON'T EVEN NEED COSTUMES.
I MEANT THAT IN A GOOD WAY.
YOU'RE RIGHT. ALEXANDER COULD USE A NIGHT OUT ON THE TOWN. COUNT US IN.

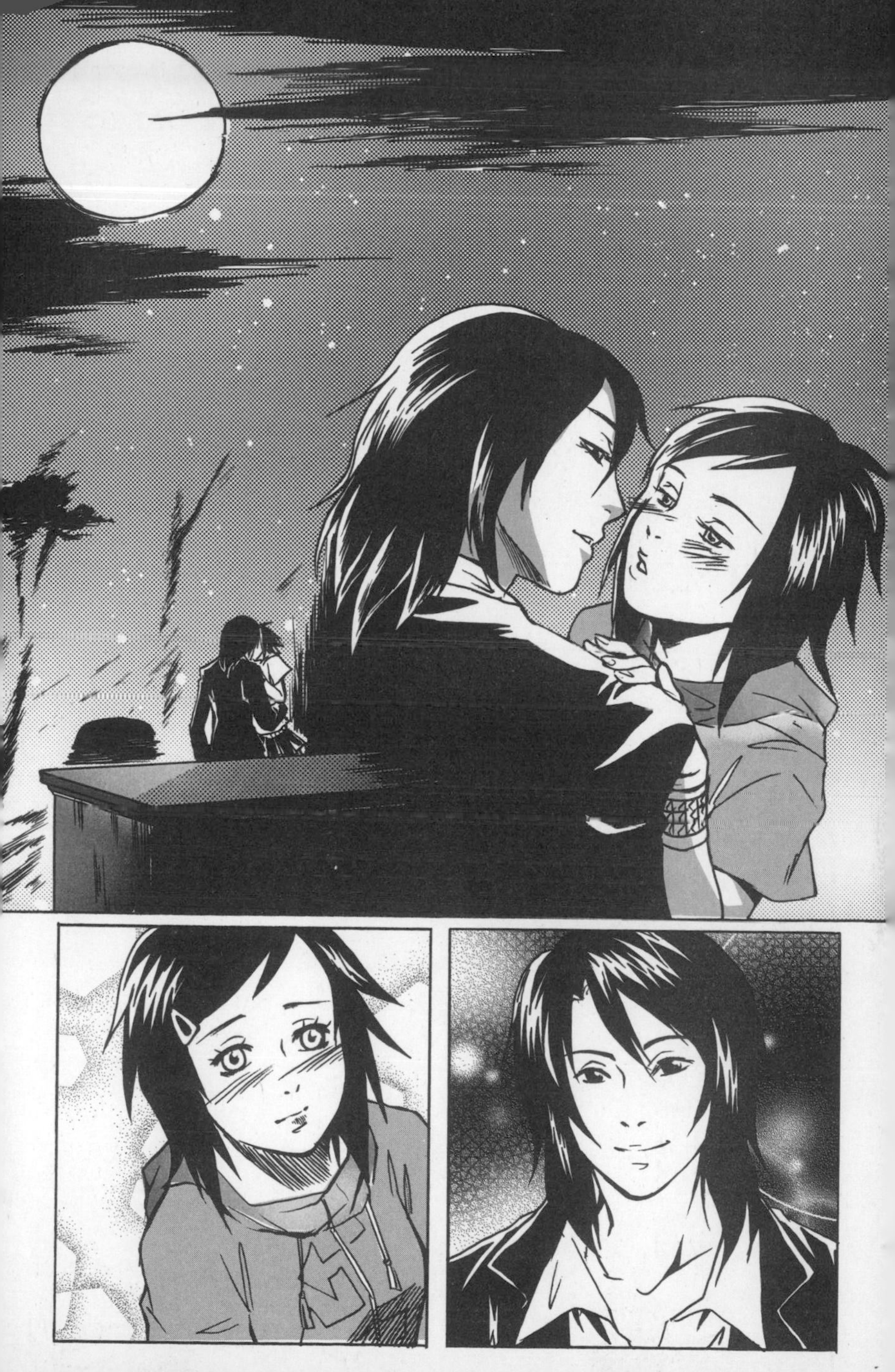

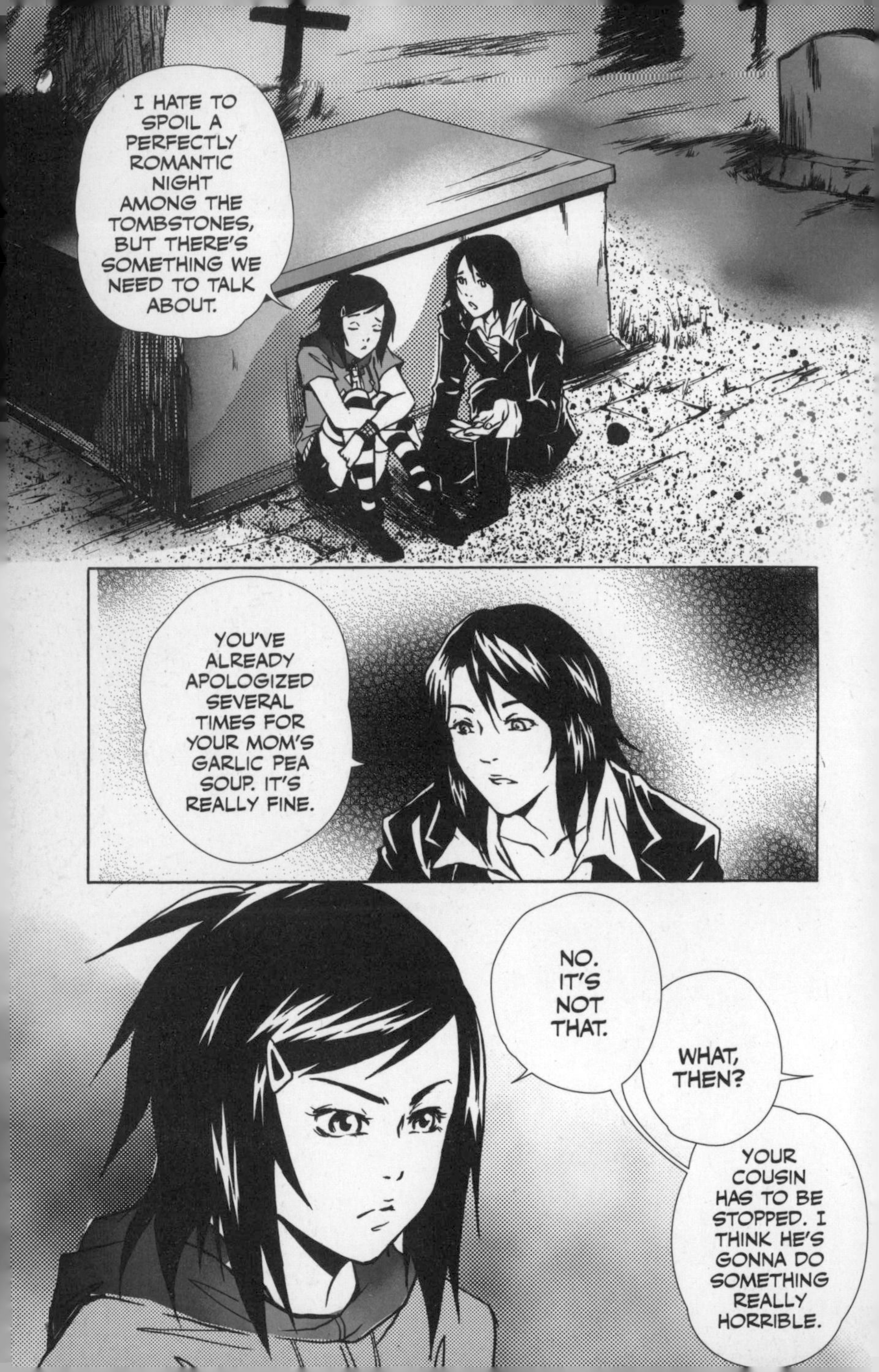
I HATE TO SPOIL A PERFECTLY ROMANTIC NIGHT AMONG THE TOMBSTONES, BUT THERE'S SOMETHING WE NEED TO TALK ABOUT.
YOU'VE ALREADY APOLOGIZED SEVERAL TIMES FOR YOUR MOM'S GARLIC PEA SOUP. IT'S REALLY FINE.
NO. IT'S NOT THAT.
WHAT, THEN?
YOUR COUSIN HAS TO BE STOPPED. I THINK HE'S GONNA DO SOMETHING REALLY HORRIBLE.

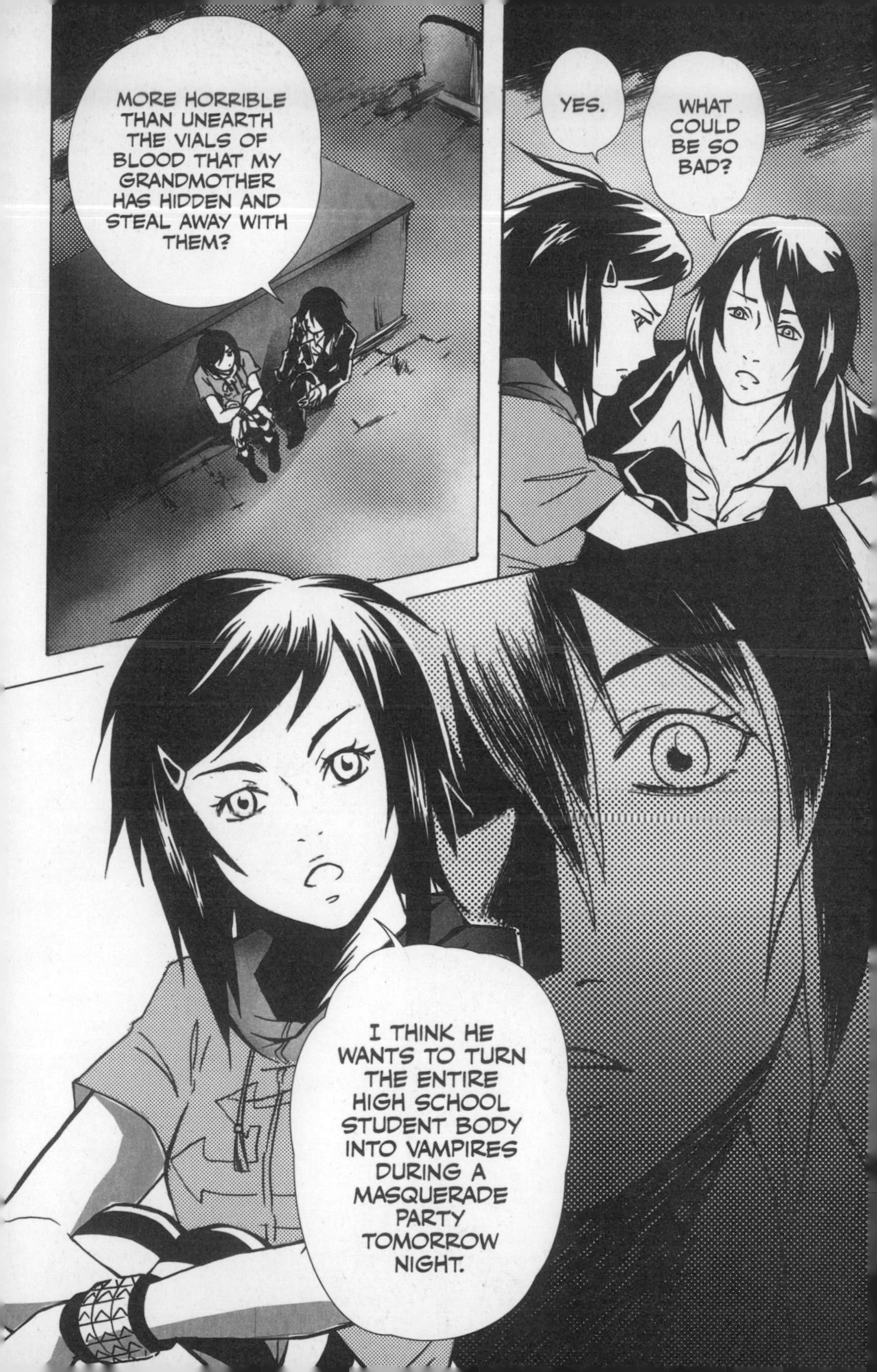
MORE HORRIBLE THAN UNEARTH THE VIALS OF BLOOD THAT MY GRANDMOTHER HAS HIDDEN AND STEAL AWAY WITH THEM?
YES.
WHAT COULD BE SO BAD?
I THINK HE WANTS TO TURN THE ENTIRE HIGH SCHOOL STUDENT BODY INTO VAMPIRES DURING A MASQUERADE PARTY TOMORROW NIGHT.

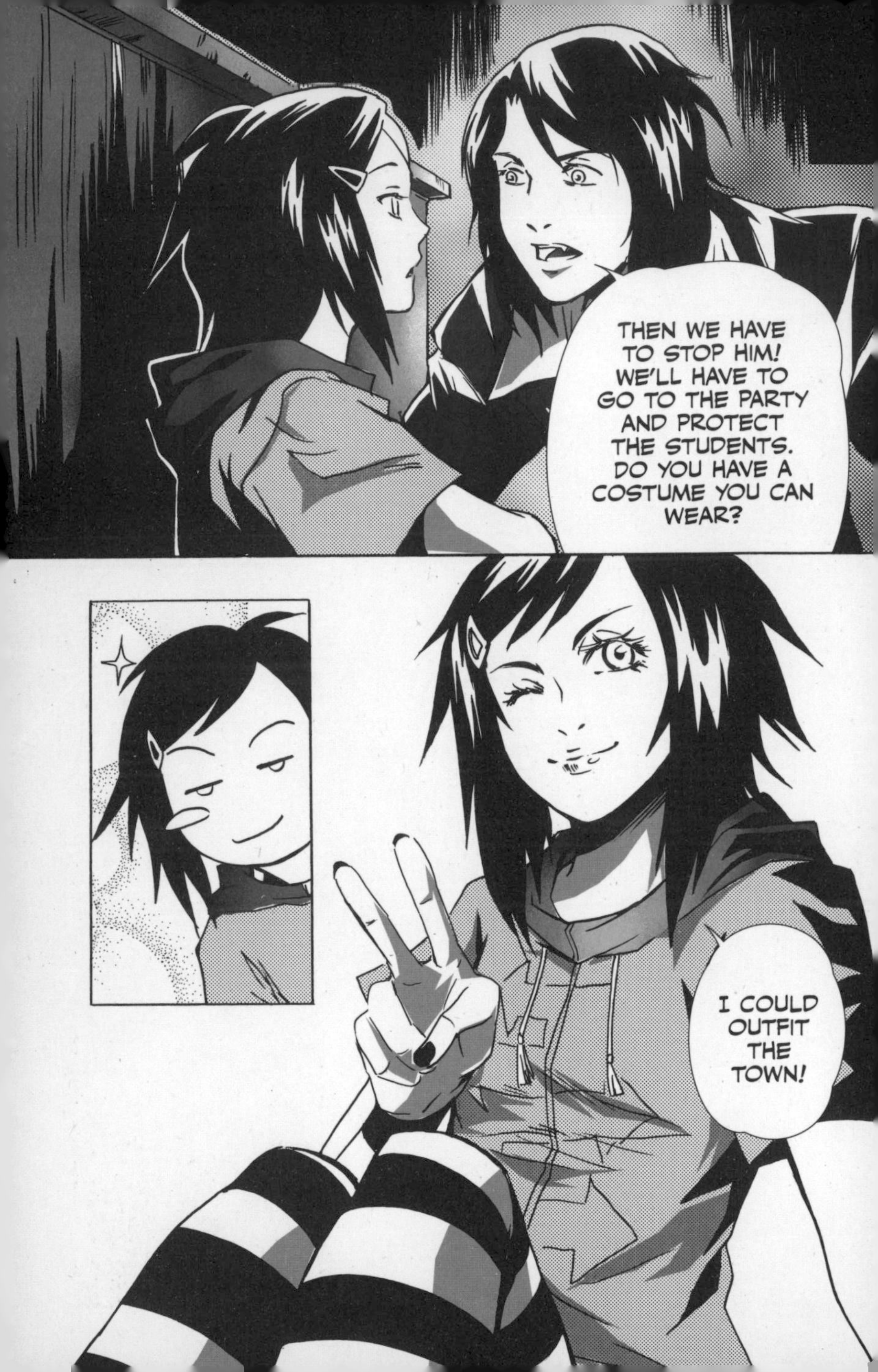
THEN WE HAVE TO STOP HIM! WE'LL HAVE TO GO TO THE PARTY AND PROTECT THE STUDENTS. DO YOU HAVE A COSTUME YOU CAN WEAR?
I COULD OUTFIT THE TOWN!

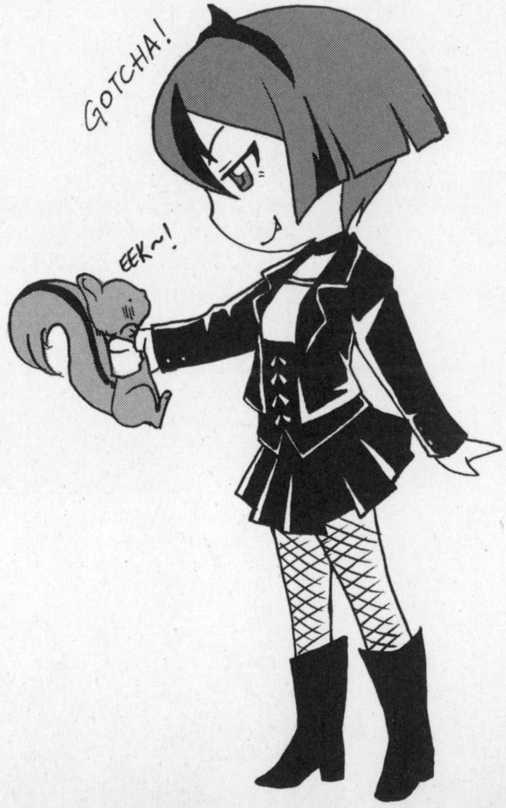
GOTCHA!
EEK~!

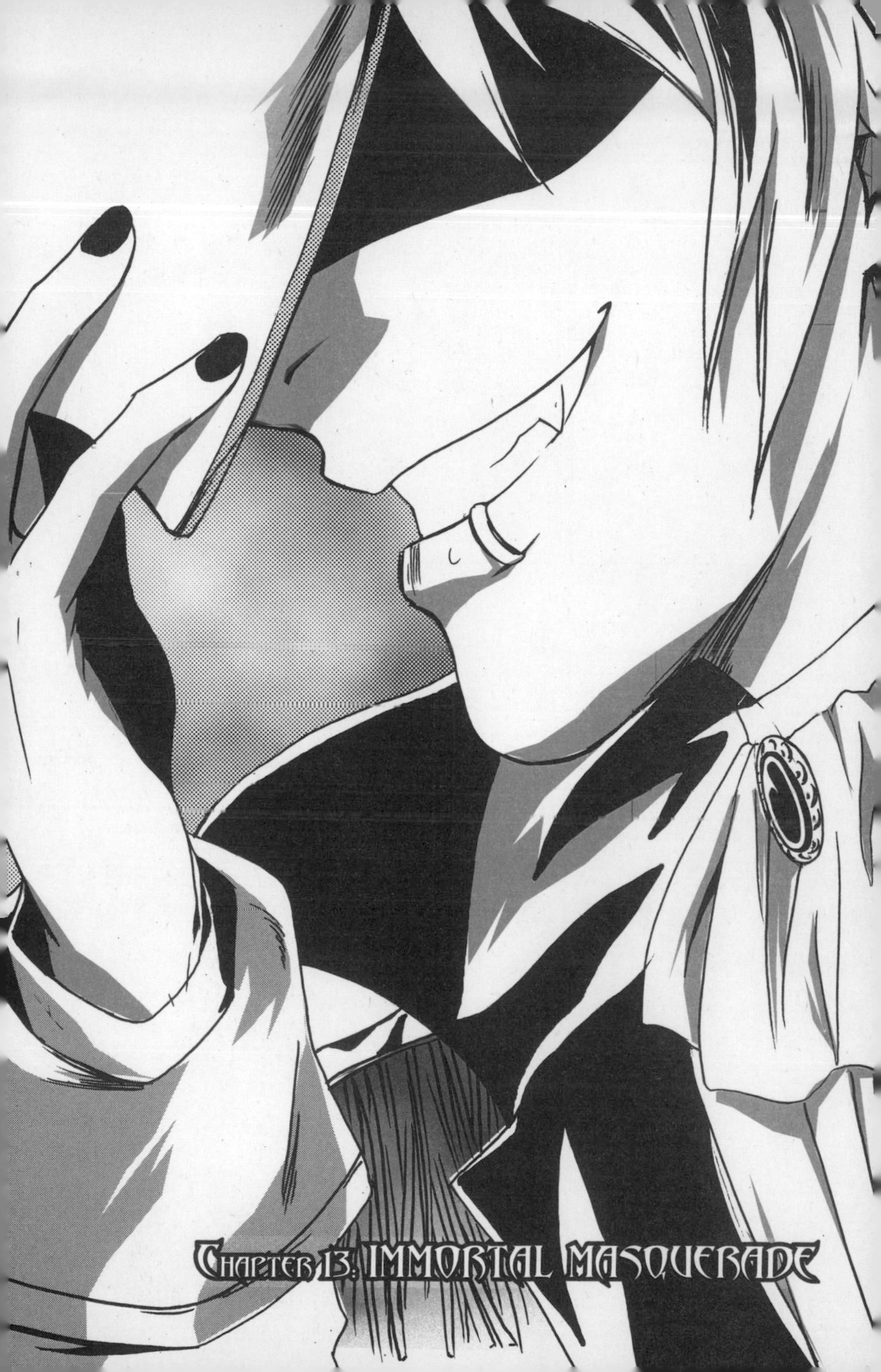
Chapter 13: Immortal Masquerade

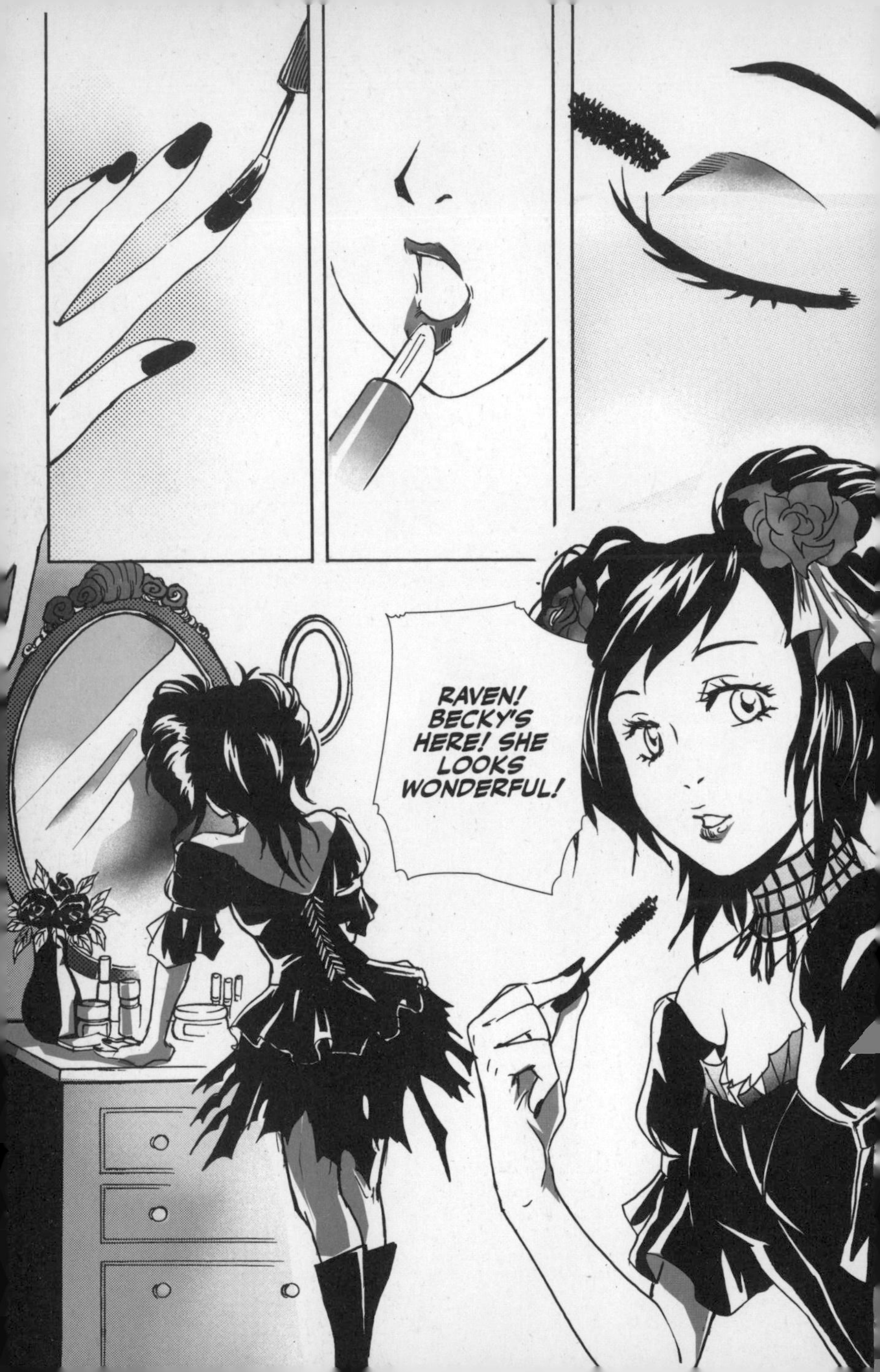
RAVEN! BECKY'S HERE! SHE LOOKS WONDERFUL!

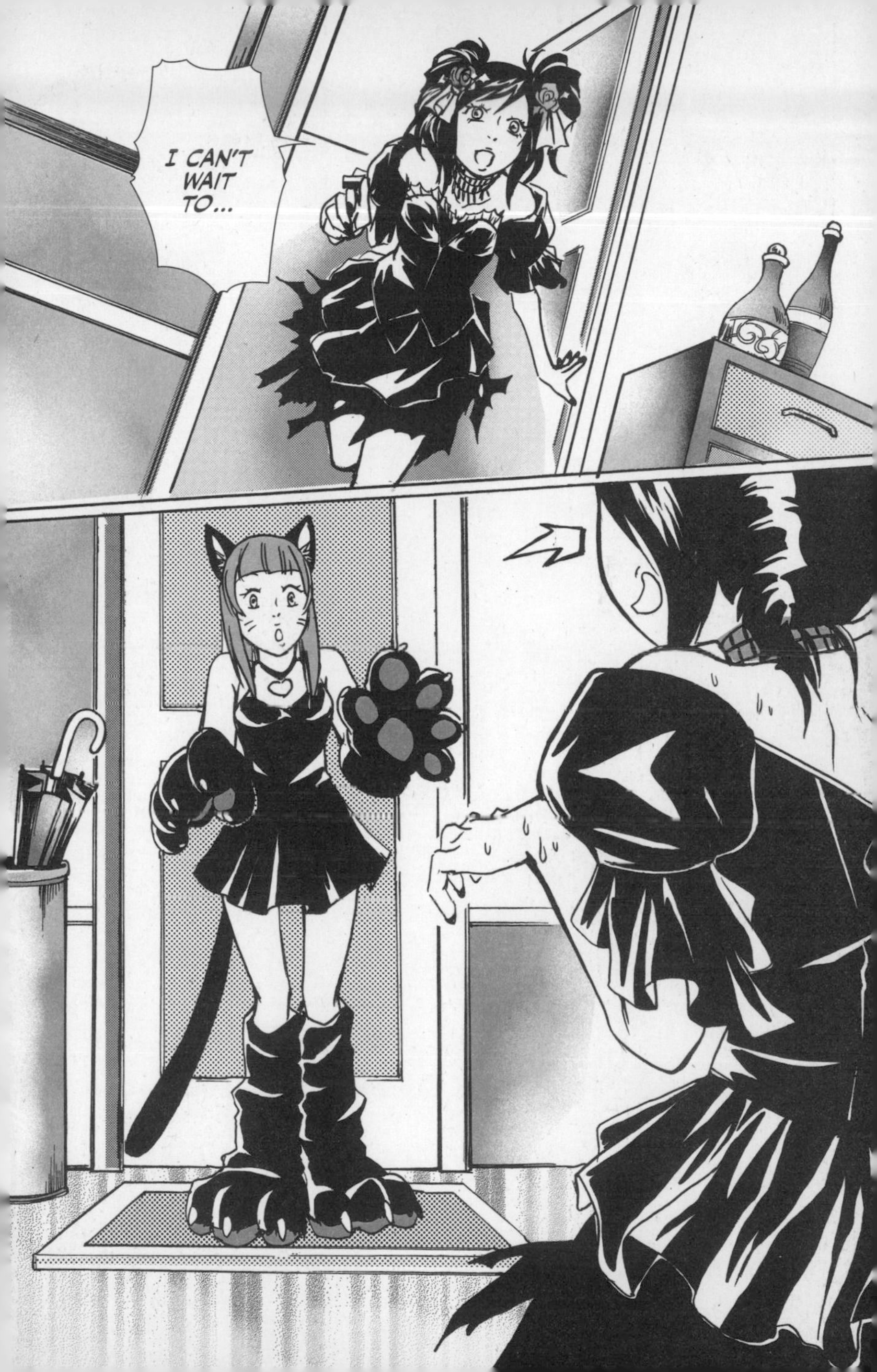
I CAN'T WAIT TO...

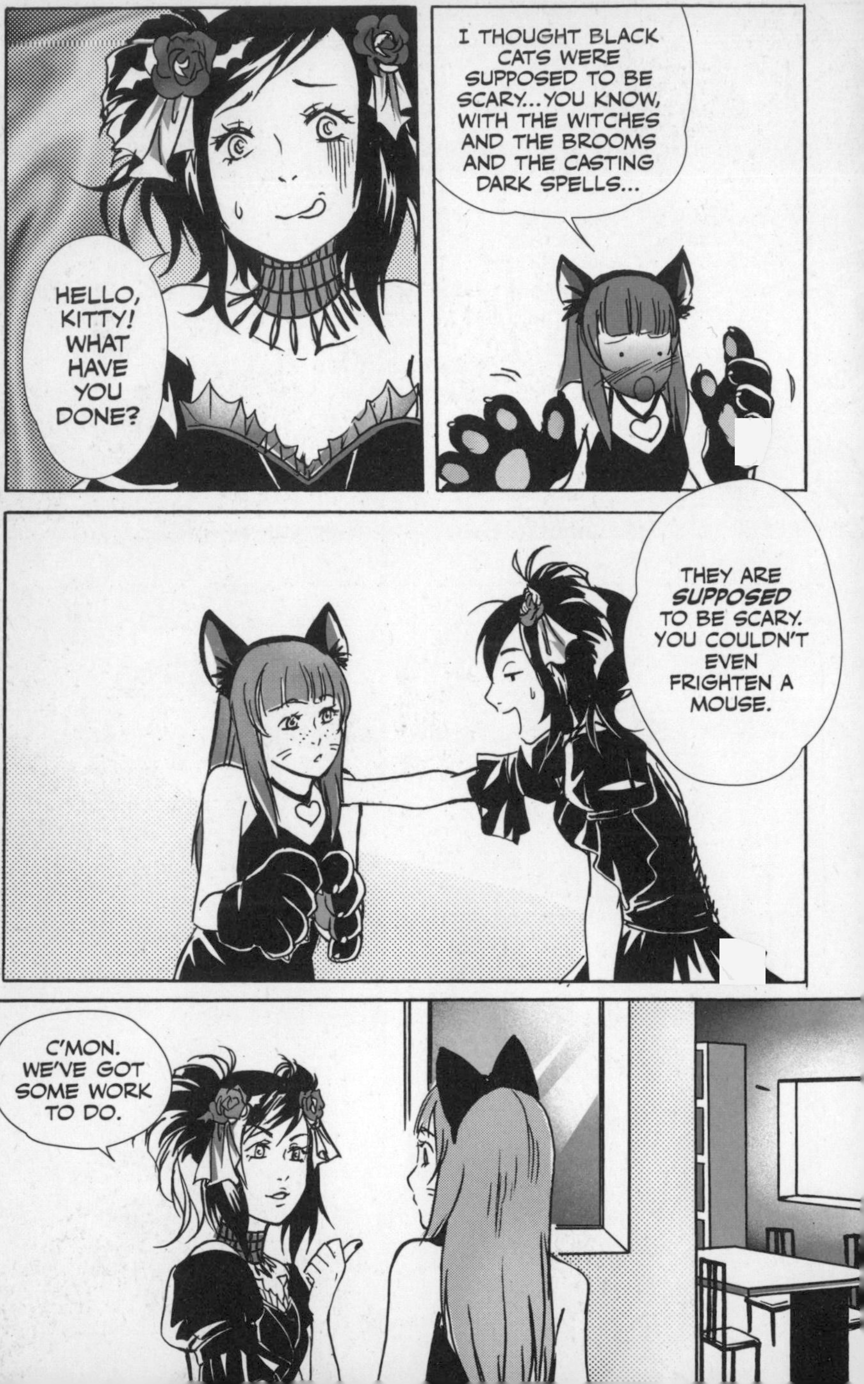
HELLO, KITTY! WHAT HAVE YOU DONE?
I THOUGHT BLACK CATS WERE SUPPOSED TO BE SCARY...YOU KNOW, WITH THE WITCHES AND THE BROOMS AND THE CASTING DARK SPELLS...
THEY ARE *SUPPOSED* TO BE SCARY. YOU COULDN'T EVEN FRIGHTEN A MOUSE.
C'MON. WE'VE GOT SOME WORK TO DO.

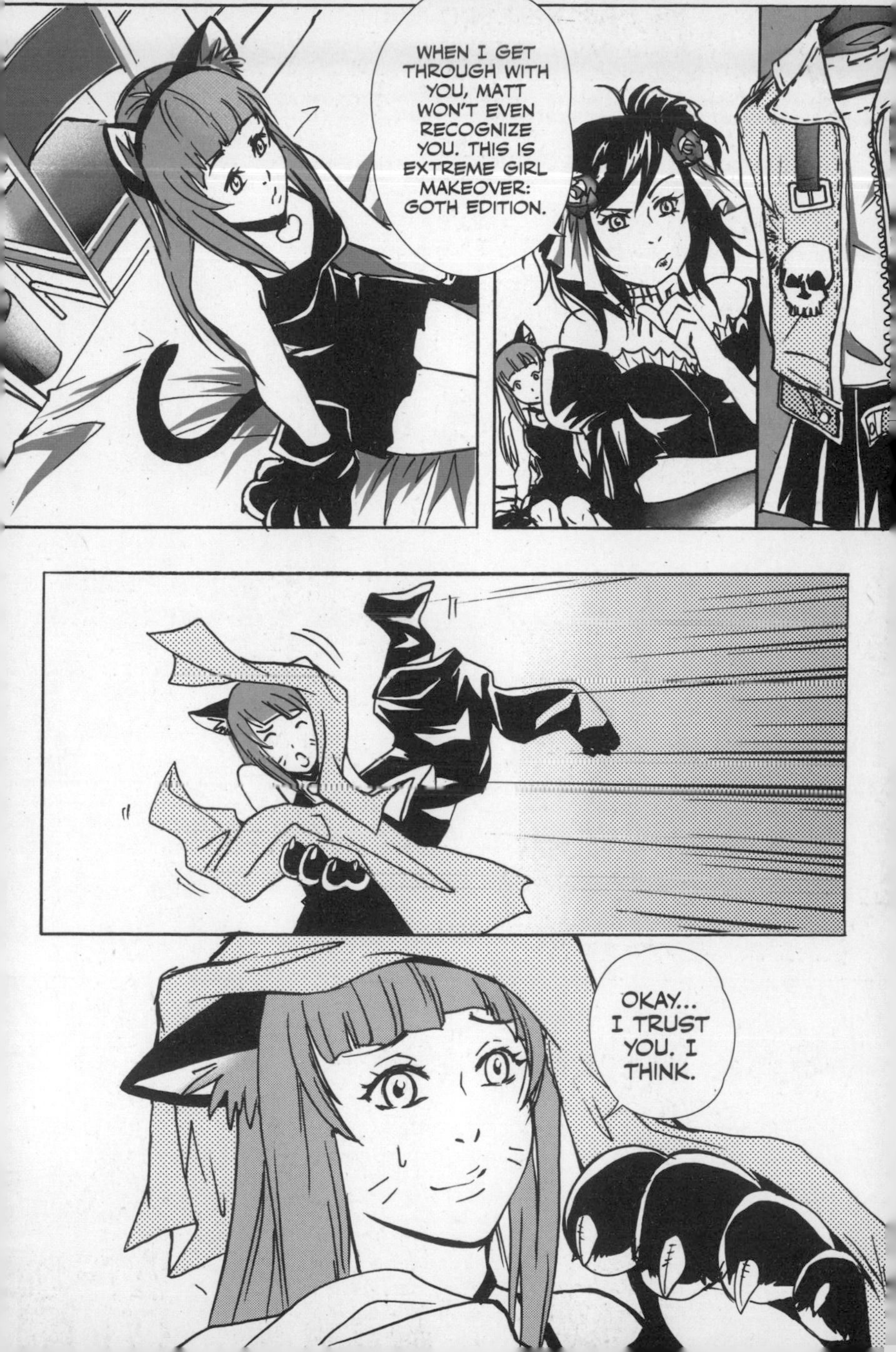
WHEN I GET THROUGH WITH YOU, MATT WON'T EVEN RECOGNIZE YOU. THIS IS EXTREME GIRL MAKEOVER: GOTH EDITION.
OKAY... I TRUST YOU. I THINK.

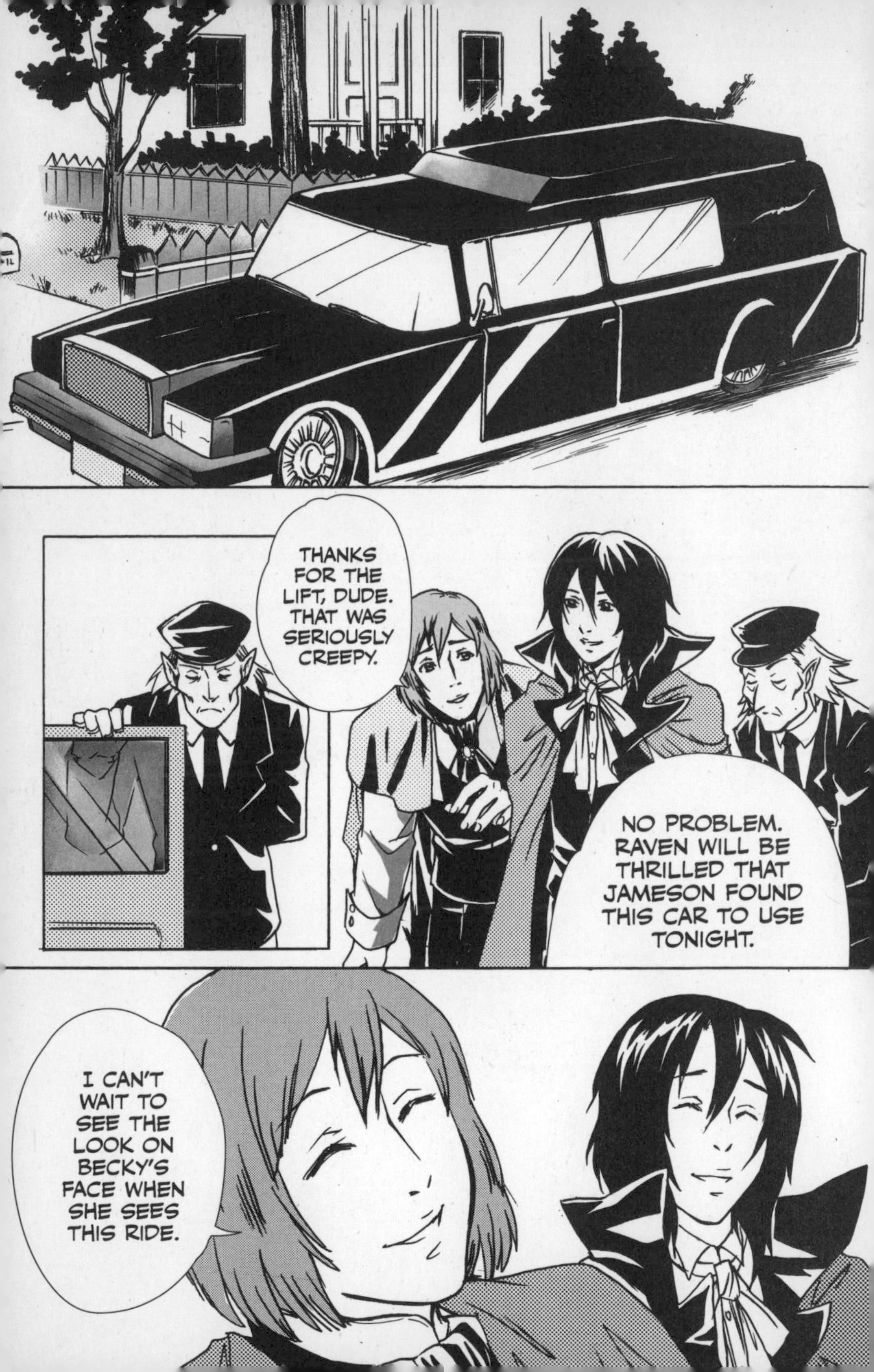
THANKS FOR THE LIFT, DUDE. THAT WAS SERIOUSLY CREEPY.
NO PROBLEM. RAVEN WILL BE THRILLED THAT JAMESON FOUND THIS CAR TO USE TONIGHT.
I CAN'T WAIT TO SEE THE LOOK ON BECKY'S FACE WHEN SHE SEES THIS RIDE.

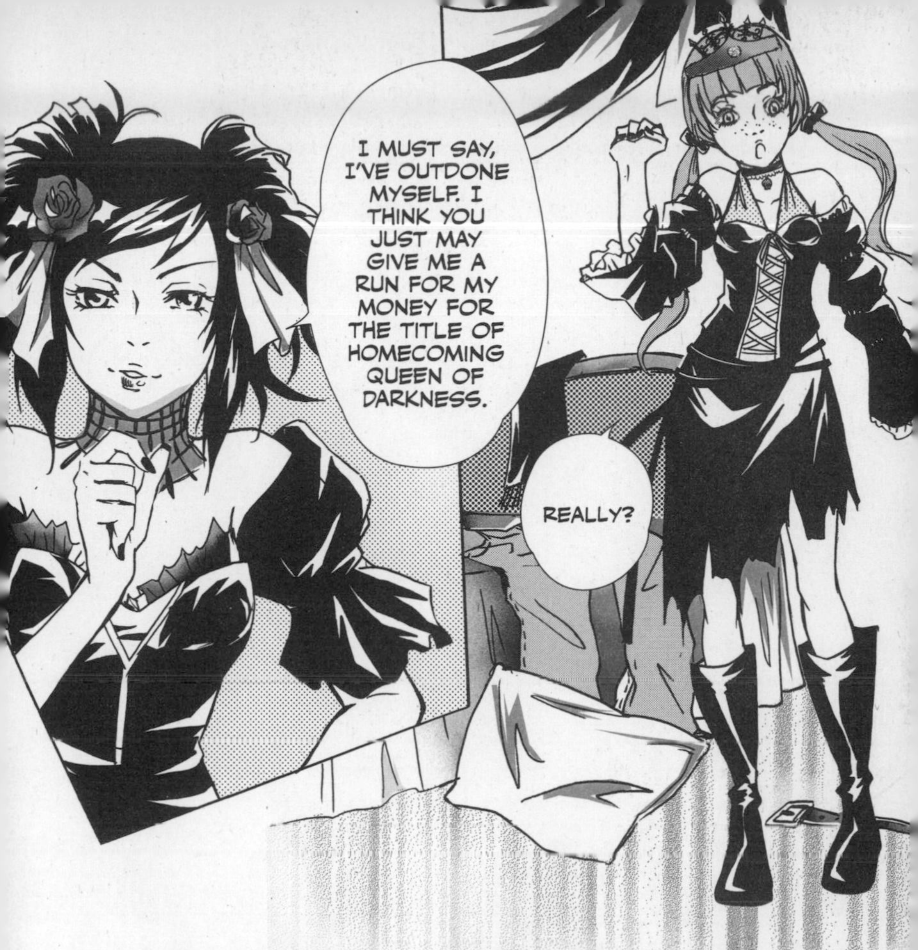
I MUST SAY, I'VE OUTDONE MYSELF. I THINK YOU JUST MAY GIVE ME A RUN FOR MY MONEY FOR THE TITLE OF HOMECOMING QUEEN OF DARKNESS.
REALLY?

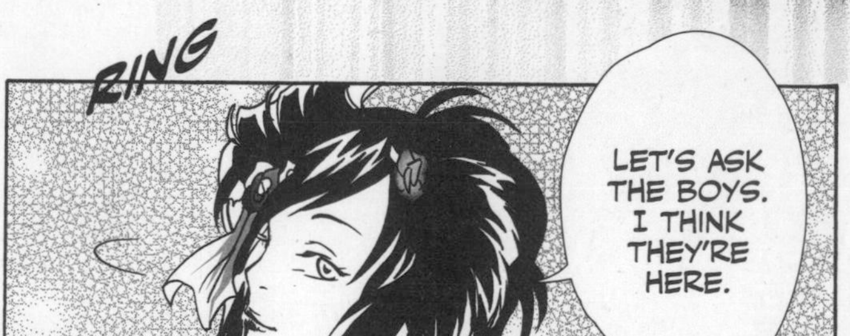
RING
LET'S ASK THE BOYS. I THINK THEY'RE HERE.

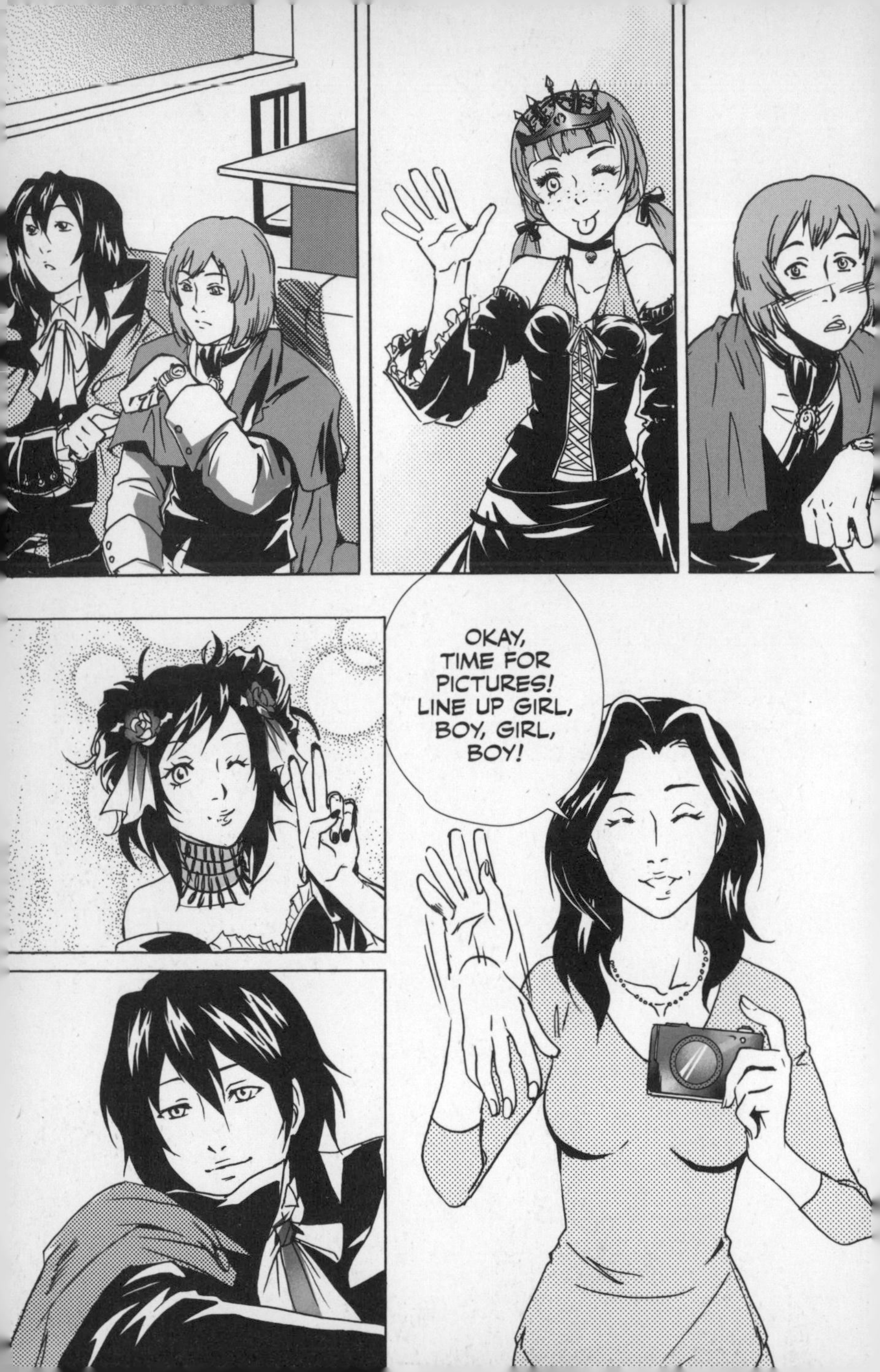
OKAY, TIME FOR PICTURES! LINE UP GIRL, BOY, GIRL, BOY!

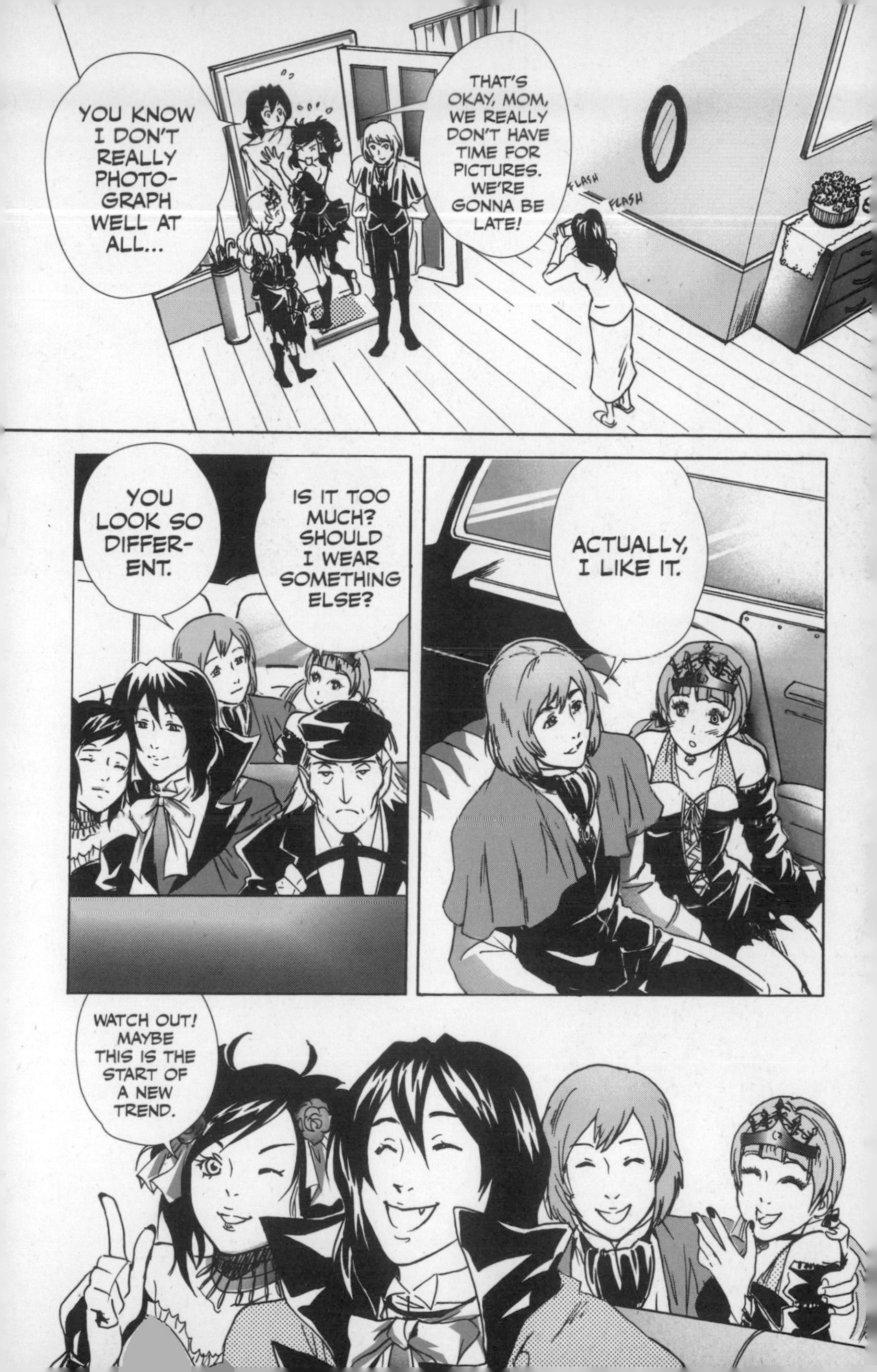
YOU KNOW I DON'T REALLY PHOTO-GRAPH WELL AT ALL...
THAT'S OKAY, MOM, WE REALLY DON'T HAVE TIME FOR PICTURES. WE'RE GONNA BE LATE!
FLASH
FLASH
YOU LOOK SO DIFFER-ENT.
IS IT TOO MUCH? SHOULD I WEAR SOMETHING ELSE?
ACTUALLY, I LIKE IT.
WATCH OUT! MAYBE THIS IS THE START OF A NEW TREND.

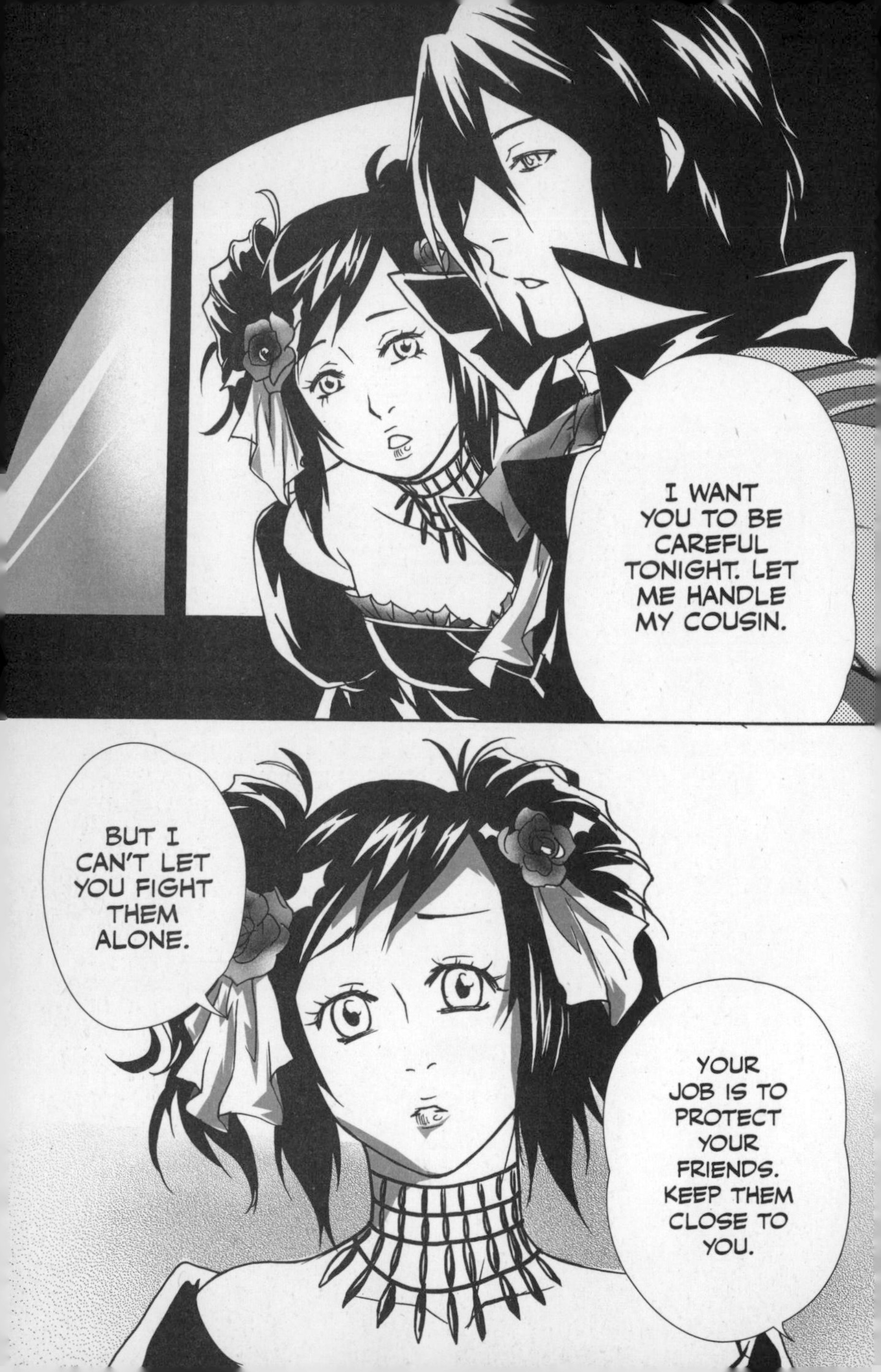
I WANT YOU TO BE CAREFUL TONIGHT. LET ME HANDLE MY COUSIN.
BUT I CAN'T LET YOU FIGHT THEM ALONE.
YOUR JOB IS TO PROTECT YOUR FRIENDS. KEEP THEM CLOSE TO YOU.

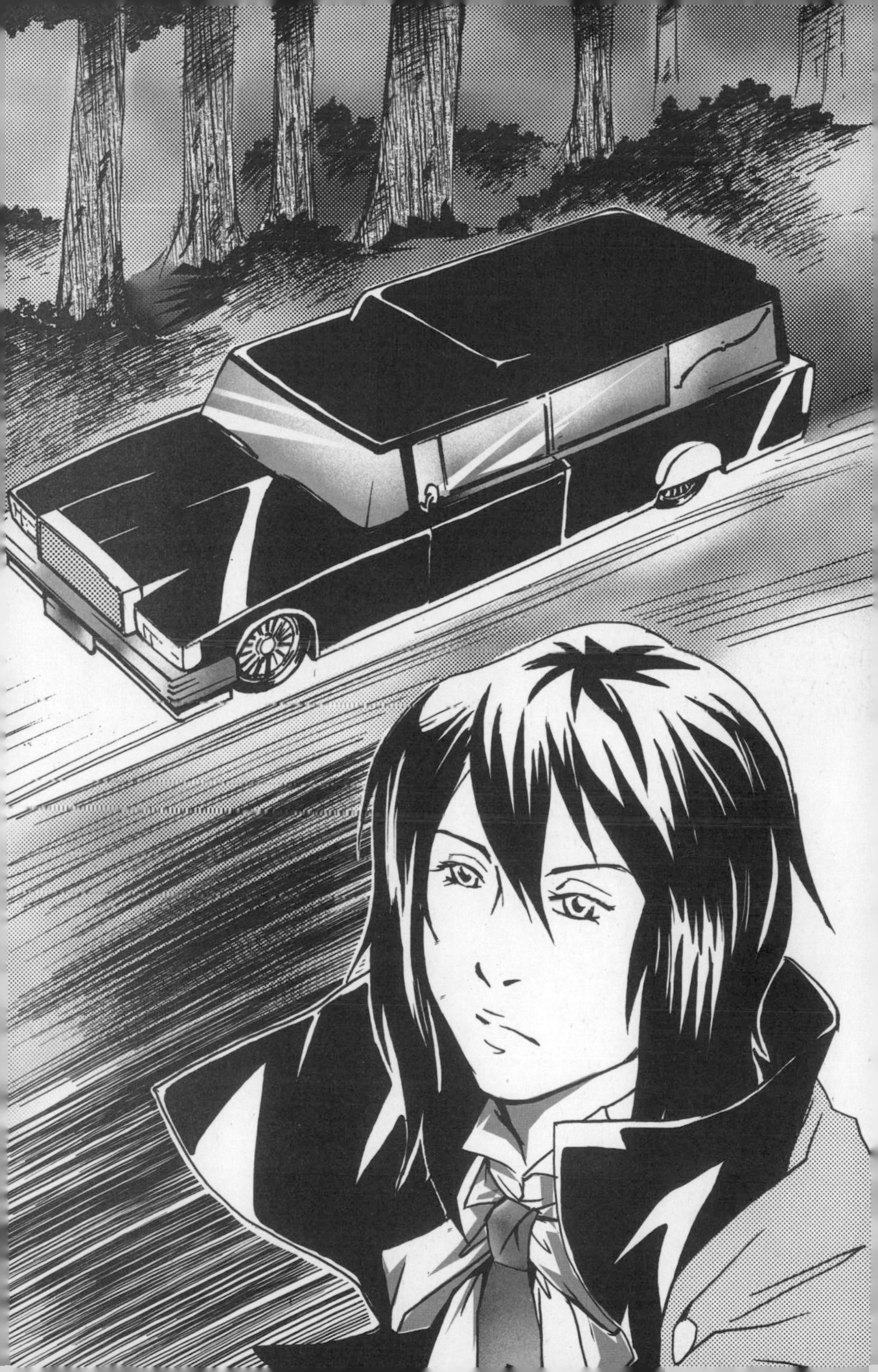

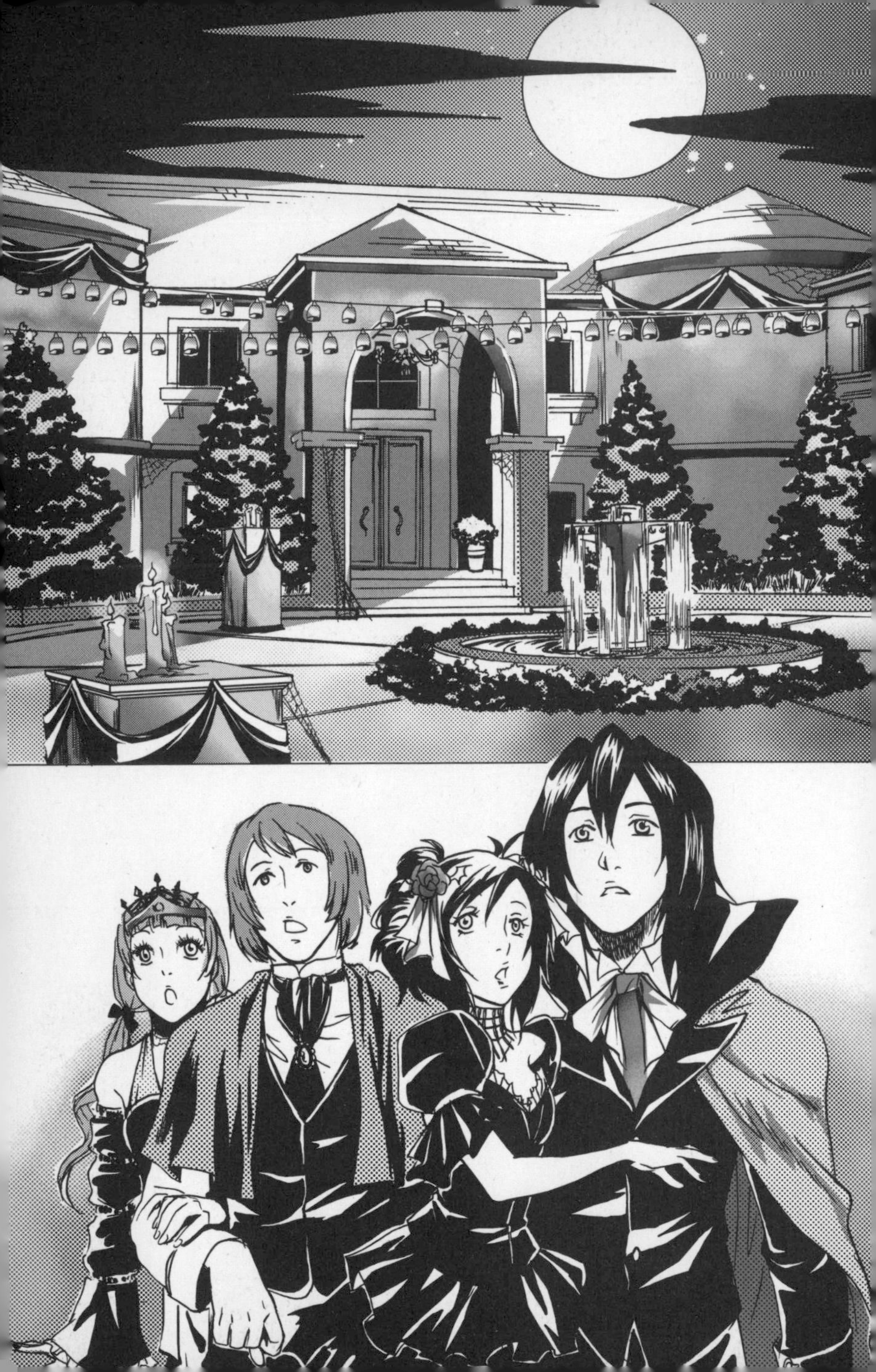

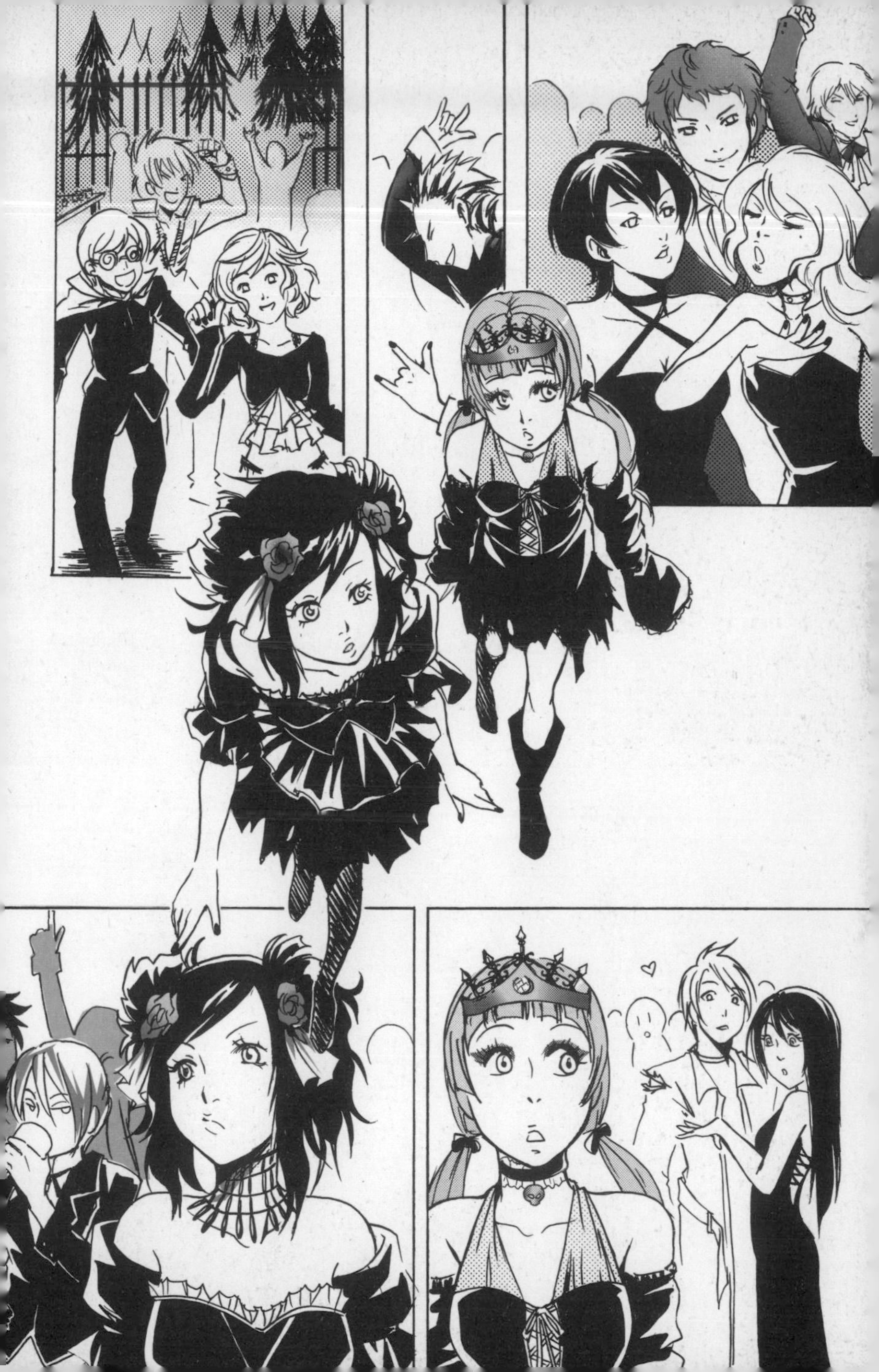

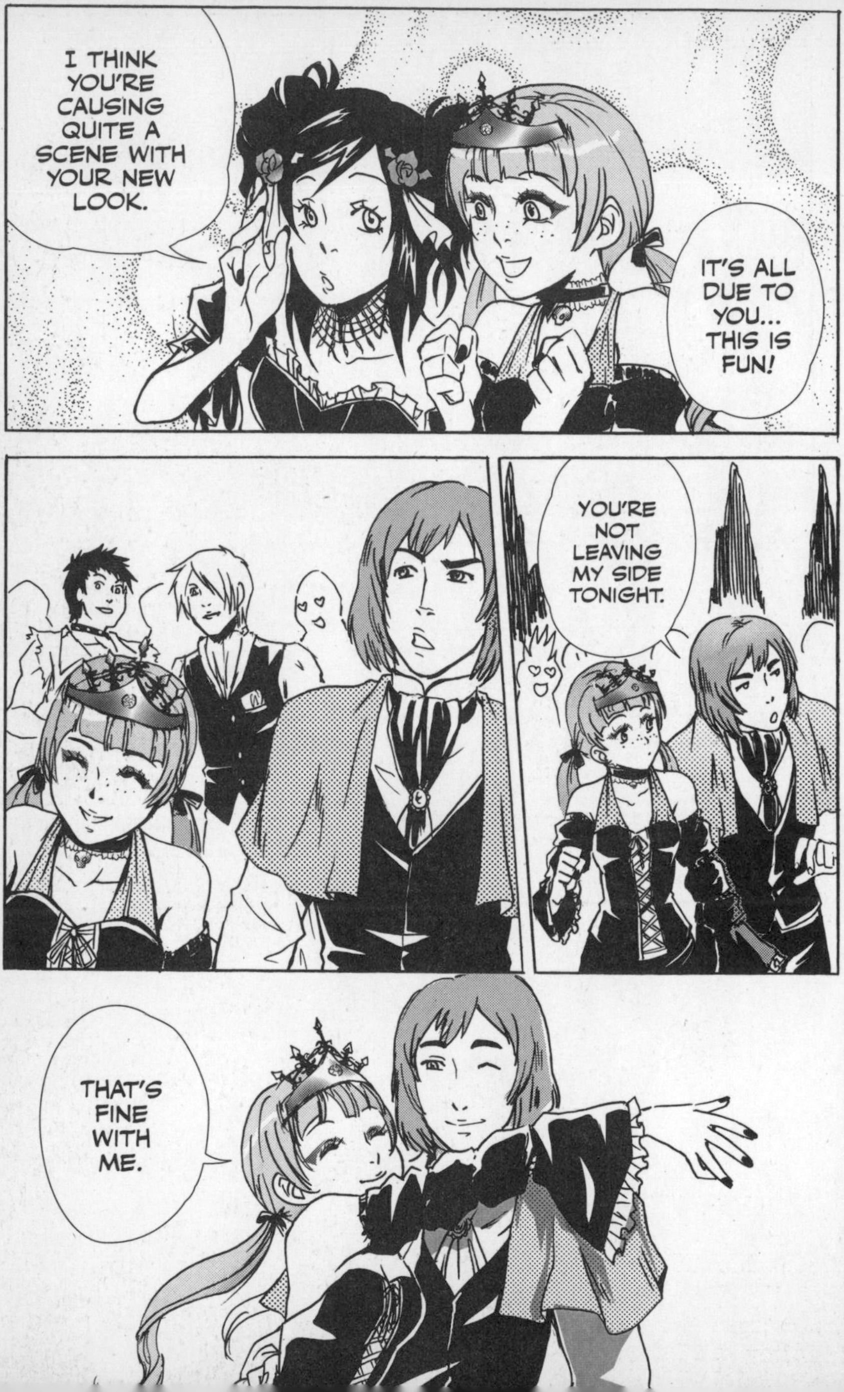
I THINK YOU'RE CAUSING QUITE A SCENE WITH YOUR NEW LOOK.
IT'S ALL DUE TO YOU... THIS IS FUN!
YOU'RE NOT LEAVING MY SIDE TONIGHT.
THAT'S FINE WITH ME.

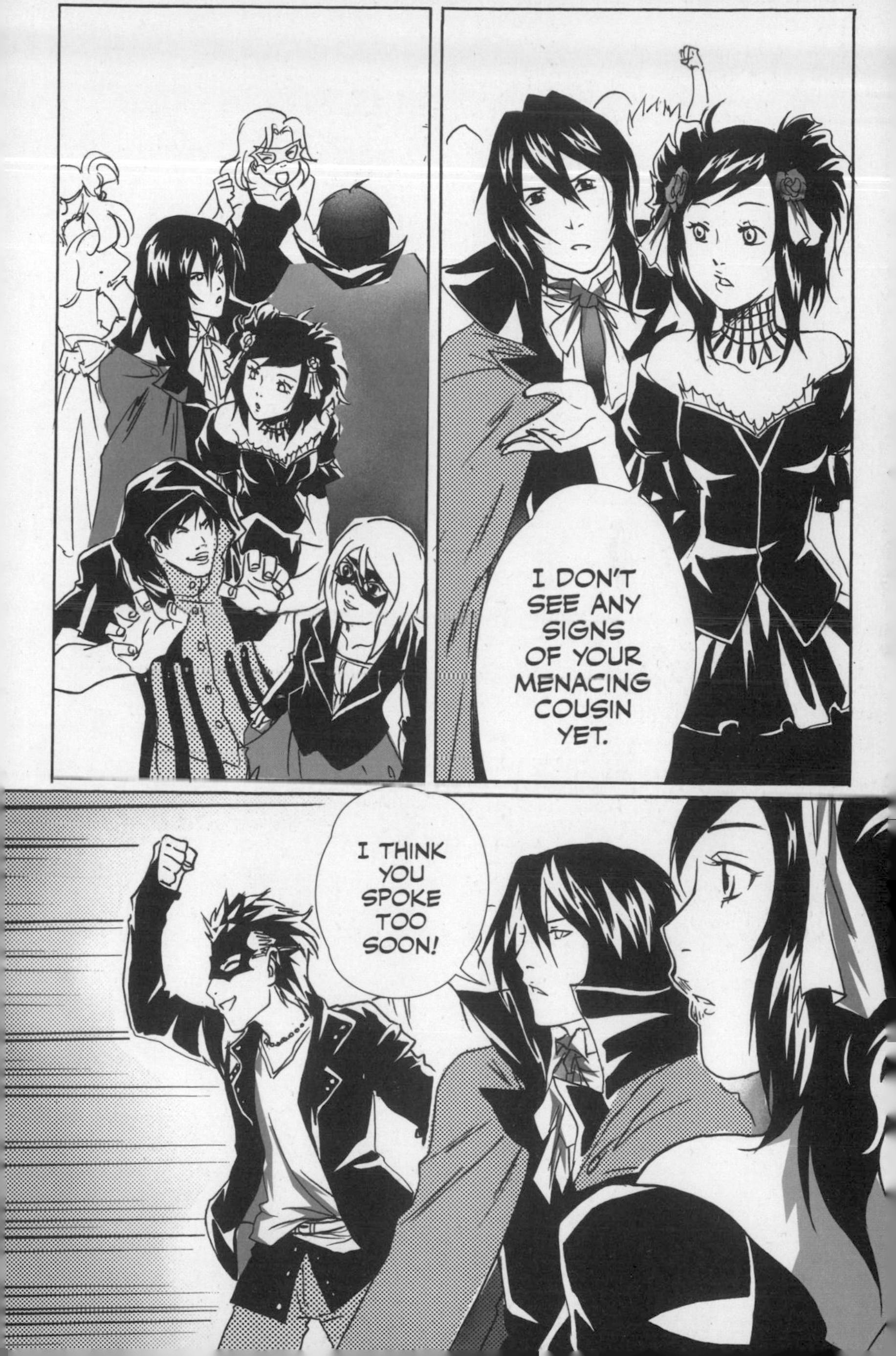
I DON'T SEE ANY SIGNS OF YOUR MENACING COUSIN YET.
I THINK YOU SPOKE TOO SOON!

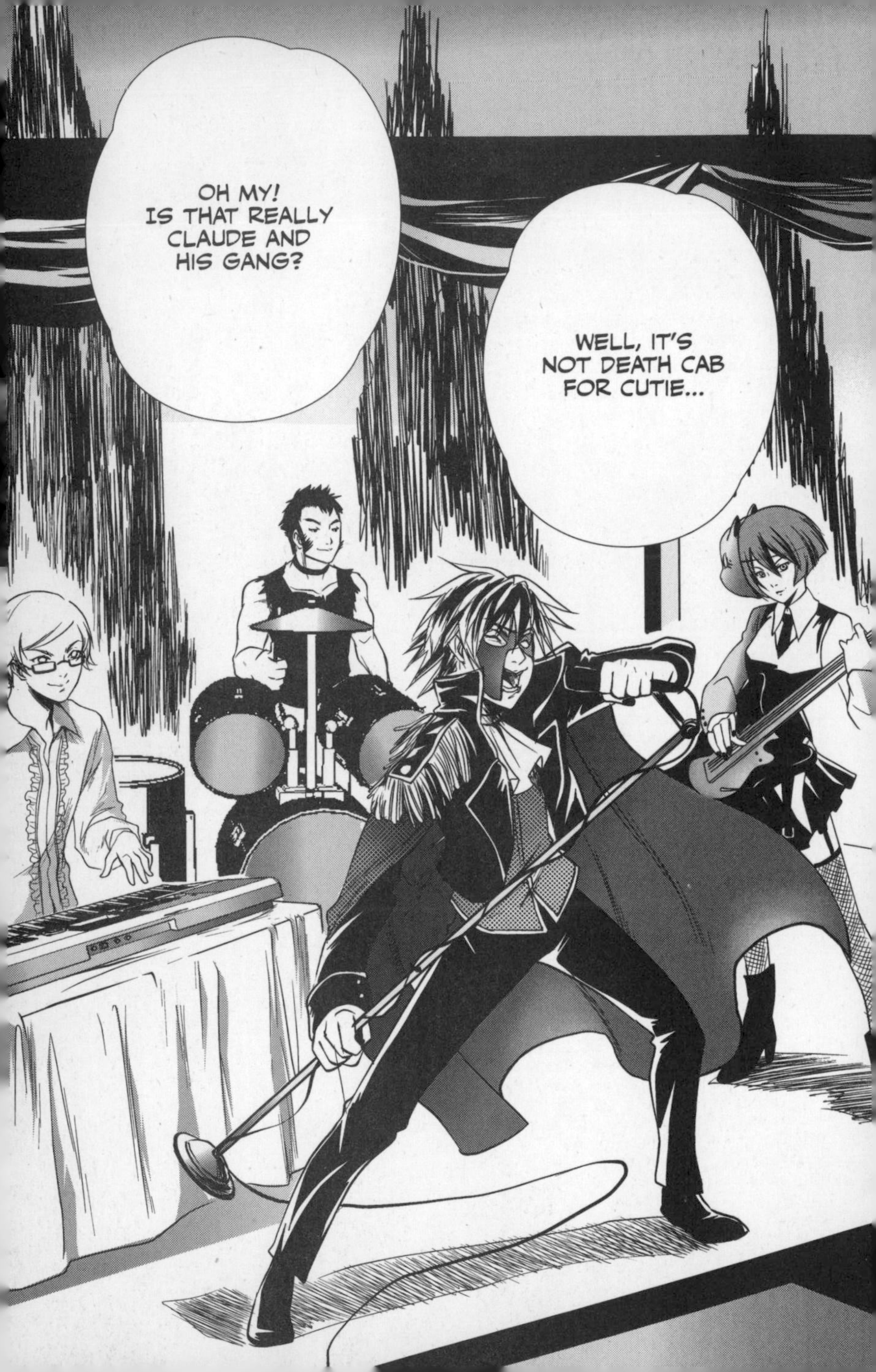
OH MY! IS THAT REALLY CLAUDE AND HIS GANG?
WELL, IT'S NOT DEATH CAB FOR CUTIE...

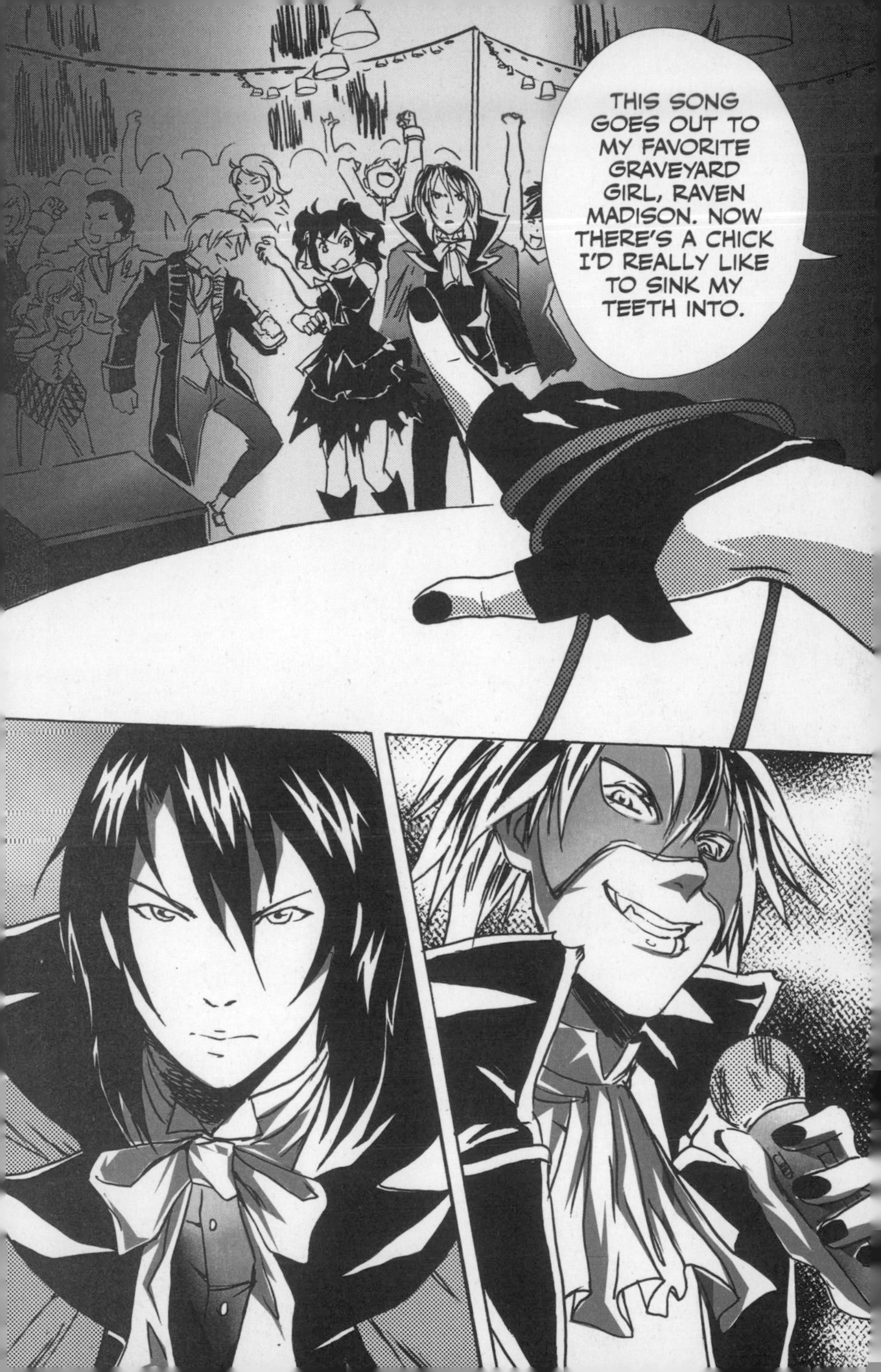
THIS SONG GOES OUT TO MY FAVORITE GRAVEYARD GIRL, RAVEN MADISON. NOW THERE'S A CHICK I'D REALLY LIKE TO SINK MY TEETH INTO.

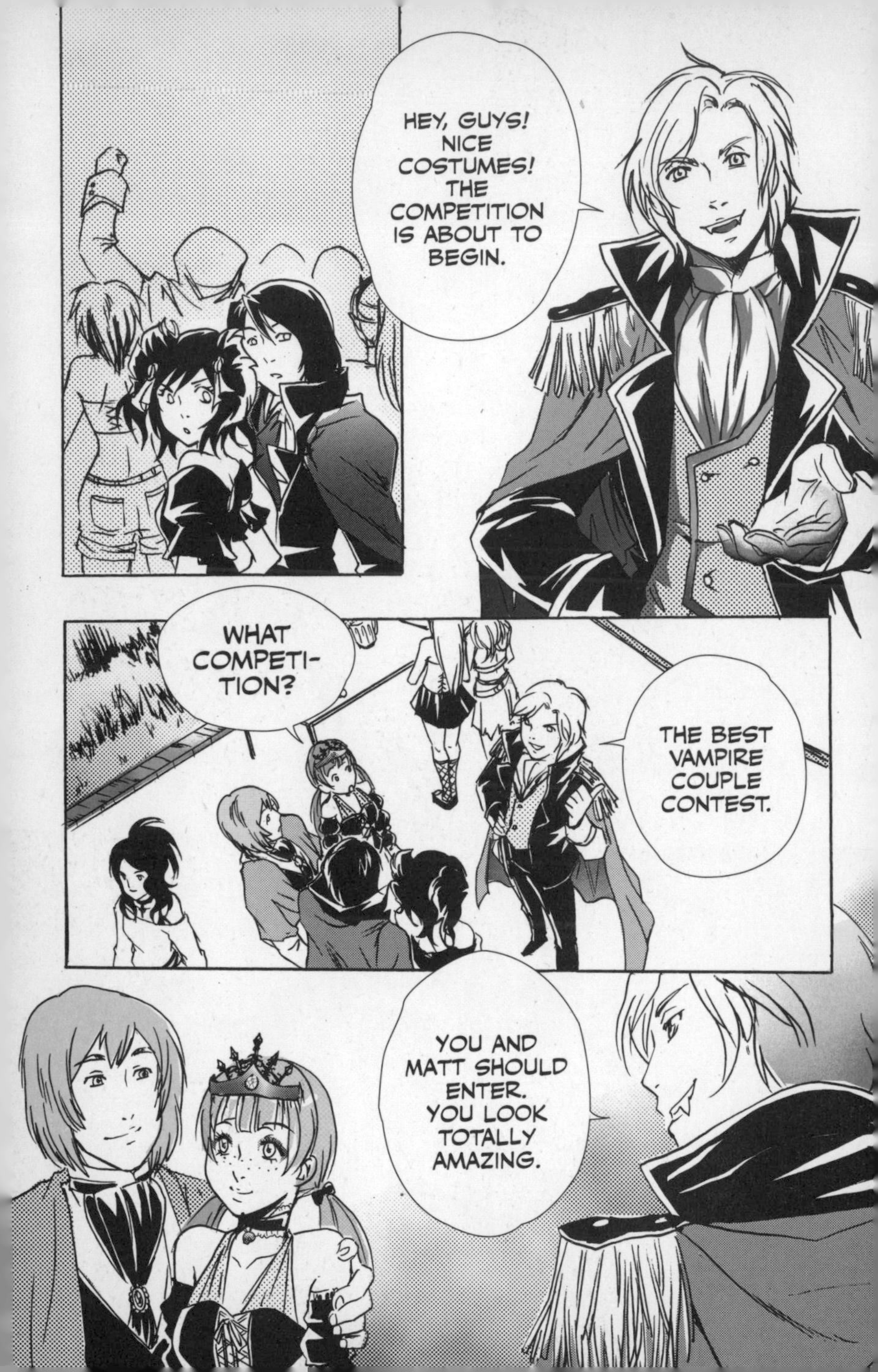
HEY, GUYS! NICE COSTUMES! THE COMPETITION IS ABOUT TO BEGIN.
WHAT COMPETITION?
THE BEST VAMPIRE COUPLE CONTEST.
YOU AND MATT SHOULD ENTER. YOU LOOK TOTALLY AMAZING.

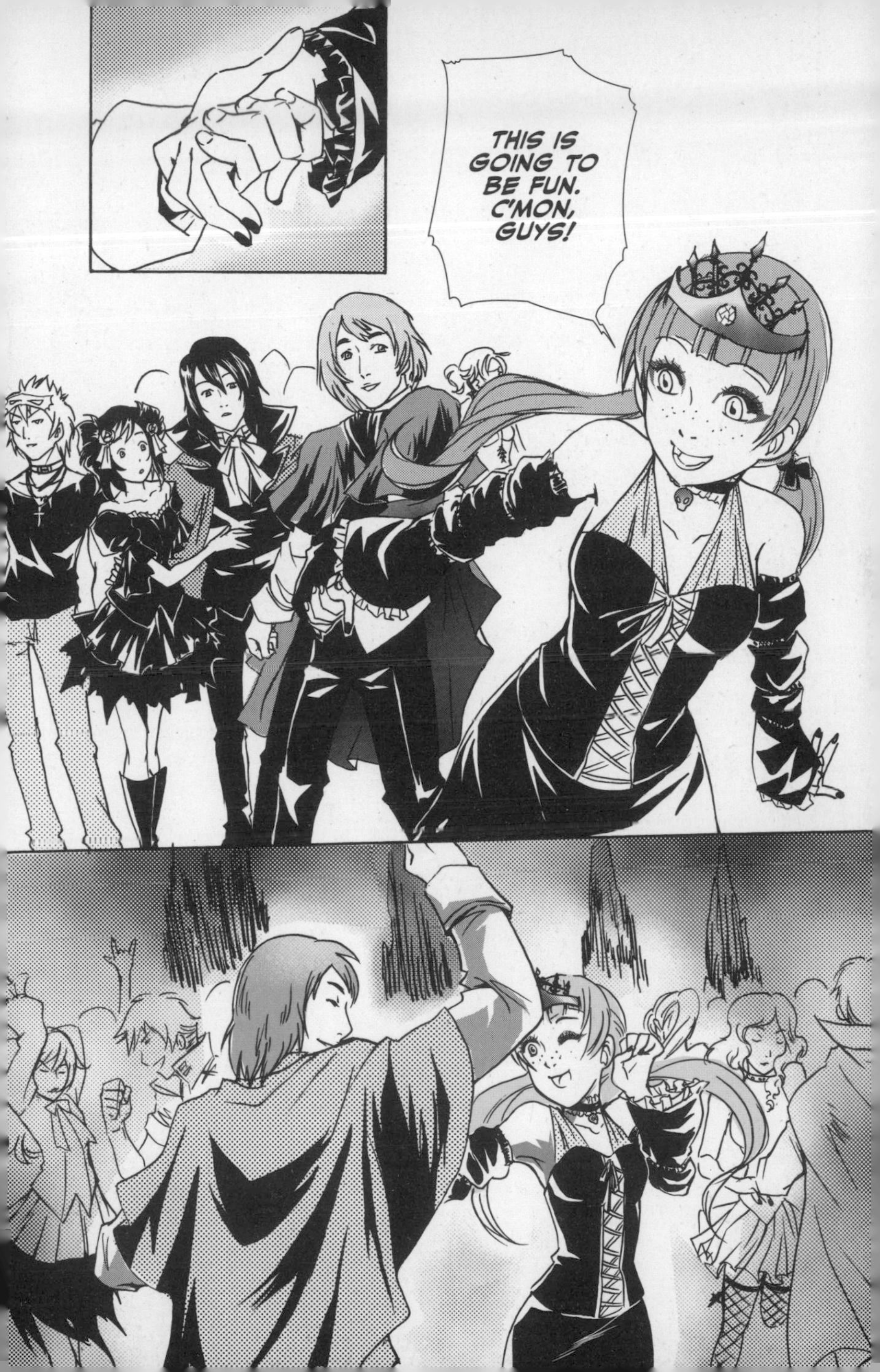
THIS IS GOING TO BE FUN. C'MON, GUYS!

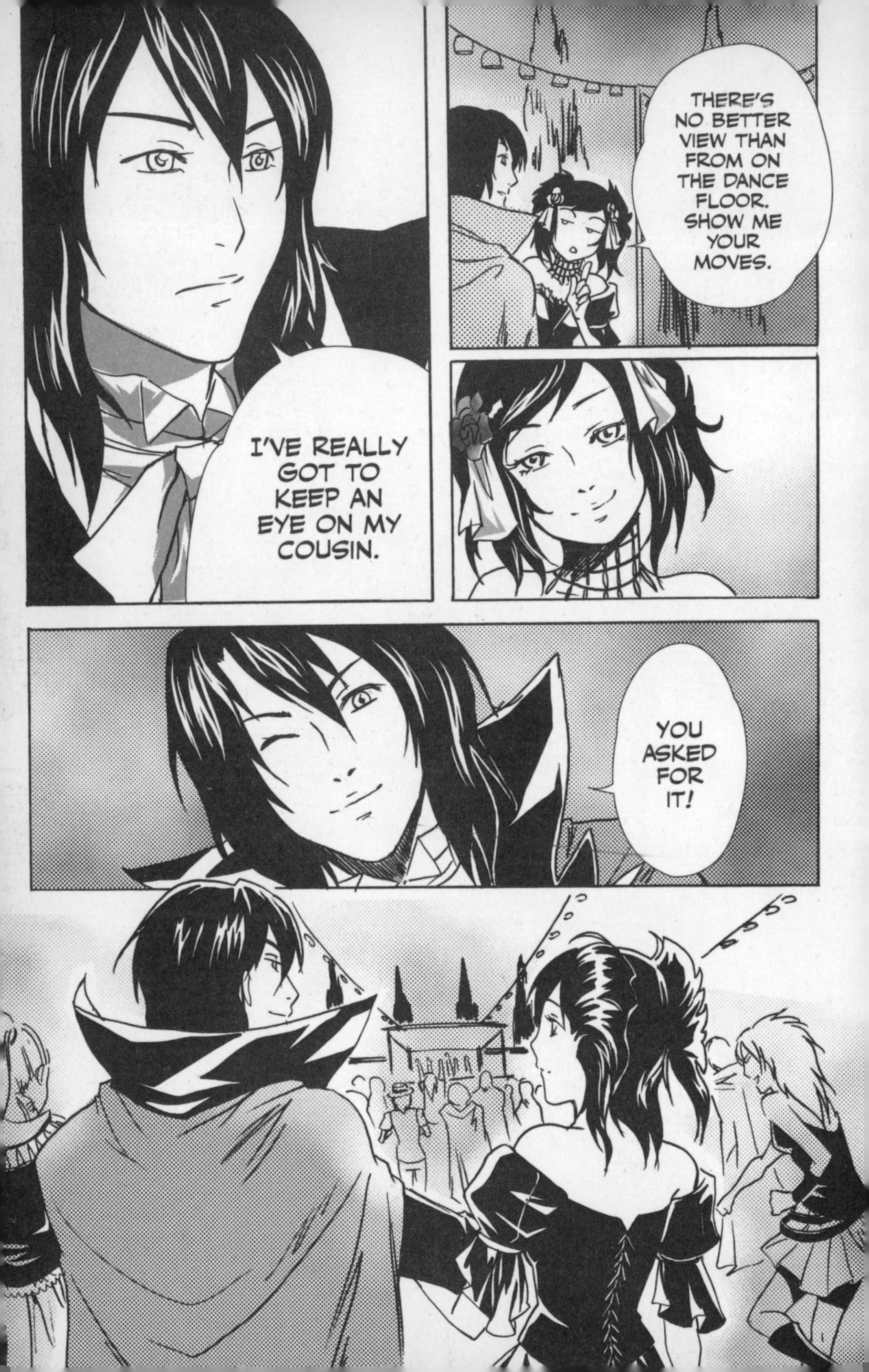
I'VE REALLY GOT TO KEEP AN EYE ON MY COUSIN.
THERE'S NO BETTER VIEW THAN FROM ON THE DANCE FLOOR. SHOW ME YOUR MOVES.
YOU ASKED FOR IT!

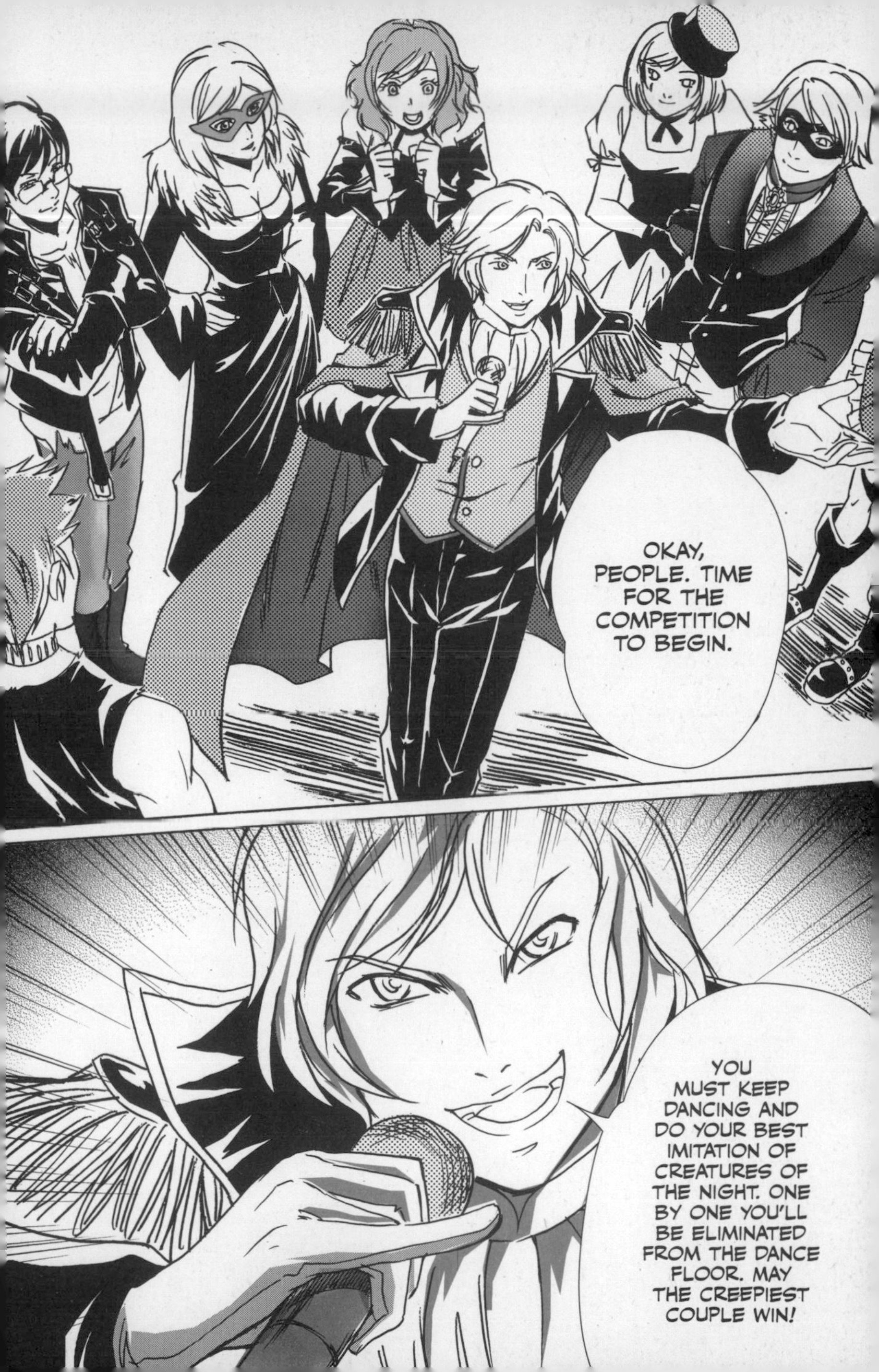
OKAY, PEOPLE. TIME FOR THE COMPETITION TO BEGIN.
YOU MUST KEEP DANCING AND DO YOUR BEST IMITATION OF CREATURES OF THE NIGHT. ONE BY ONE YOU'LL BE ELIMINATED FROM THE DANCE FLOOR. MAY THE CREEPIEST COUPLE WIN!

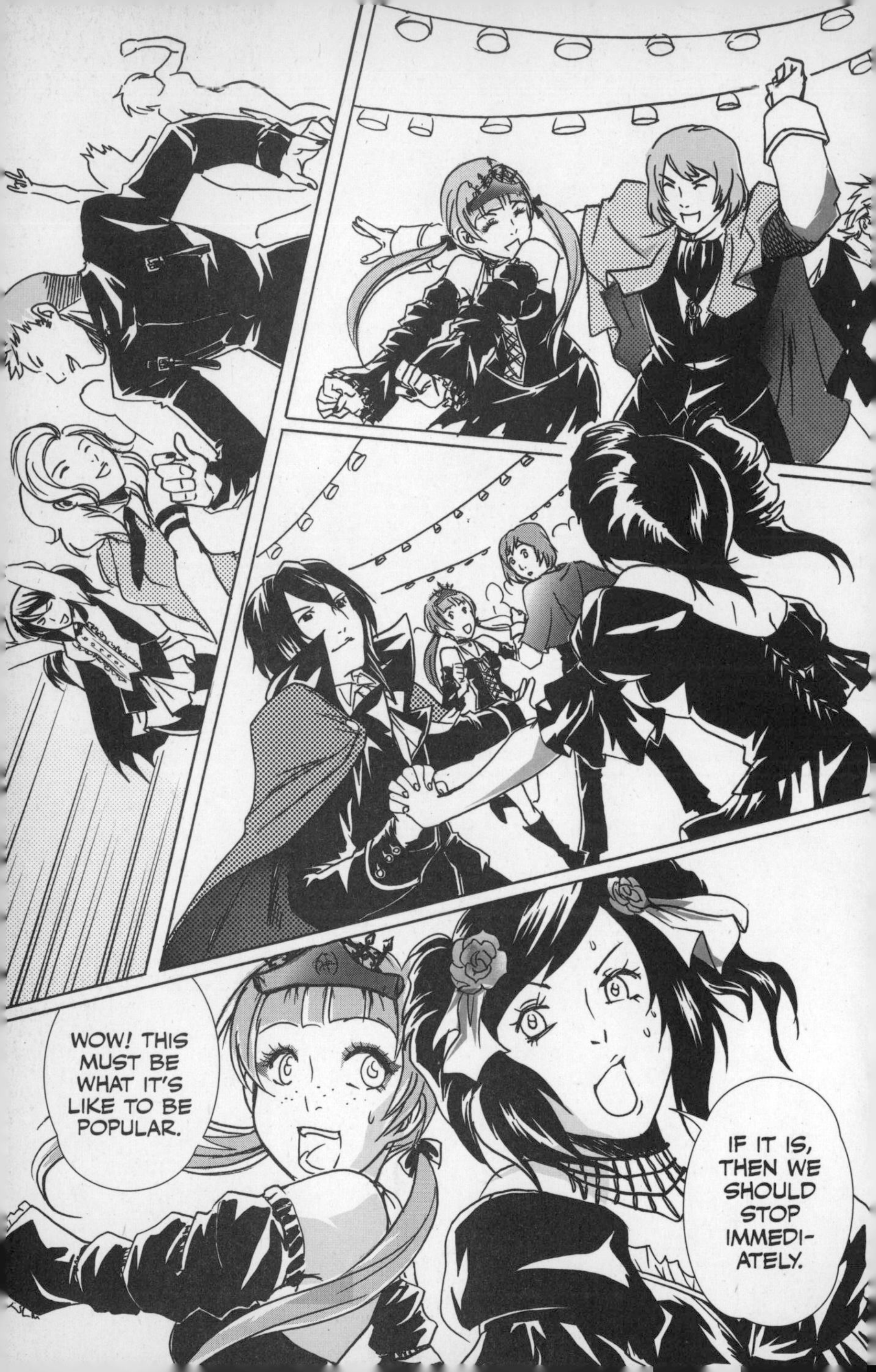
WOW! THIS MUST BE WHAT IT'S LIKE TO BE POPULAR.
IF IT IS, THEN WE SHOULD STOP IMMEDI-ATELY.

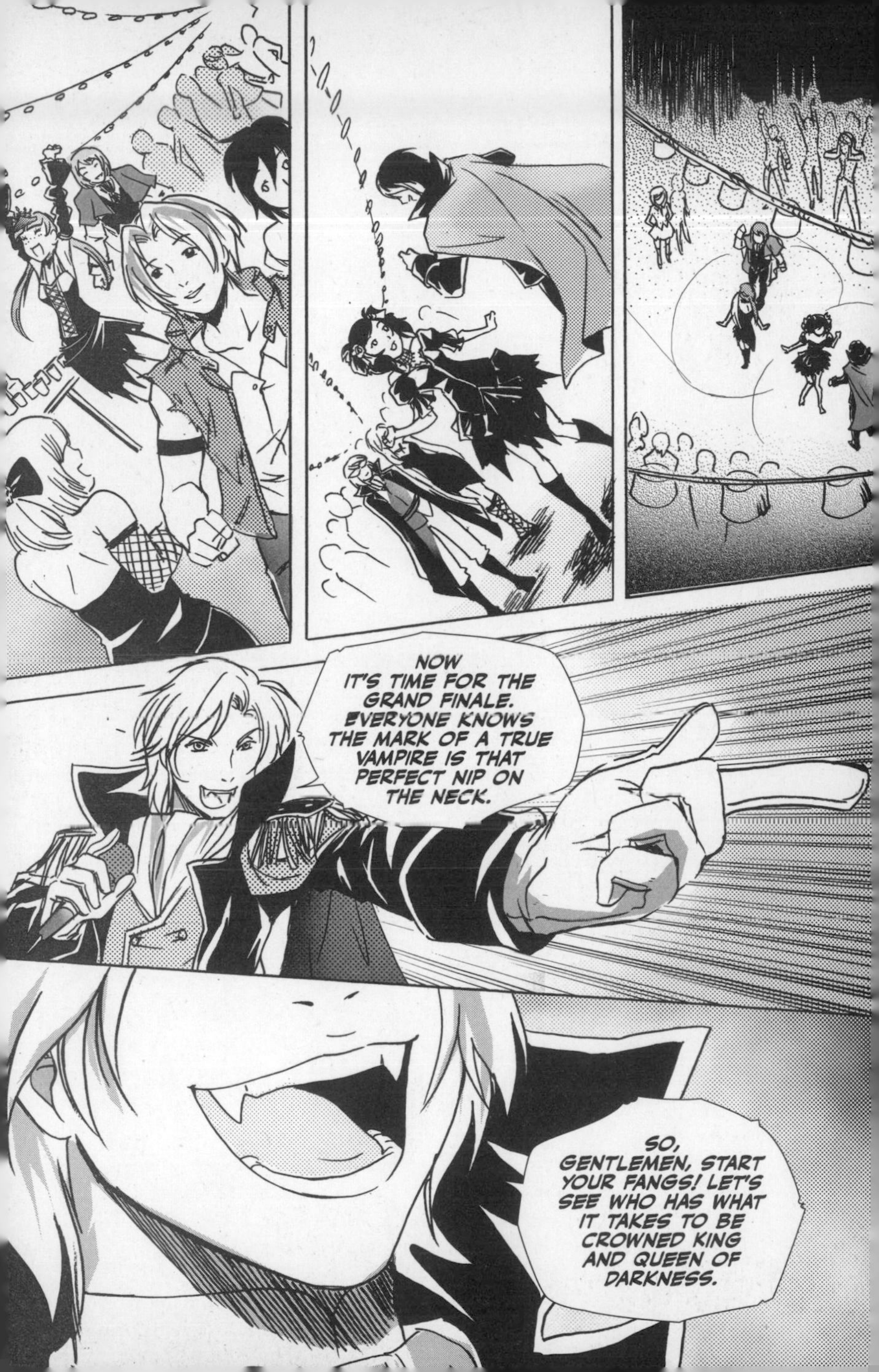
NOW IT'S TIME FOR THE GRAND FINALE. EVERYONE KNOWS THE MARK OF A TRUE VAMPIRE IS THAT PERFECT NIP ON THE NECK.
SO, GENTLEMEN, START YOUR FANGS! LET'S SEE WHO HAS WHAT IT TAKES TO BE CROWNED KING AND QUEEN OF DARKNESS.

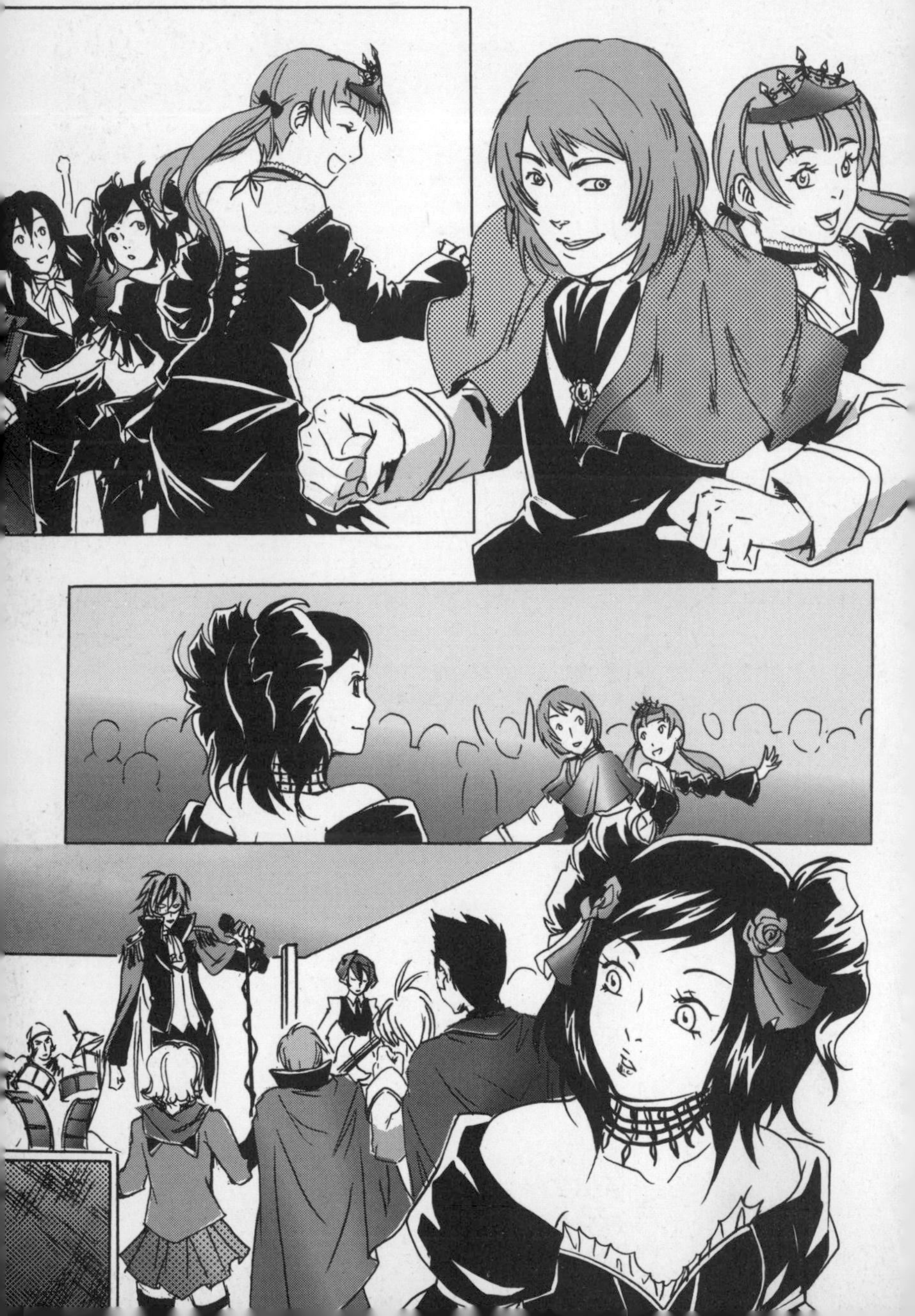

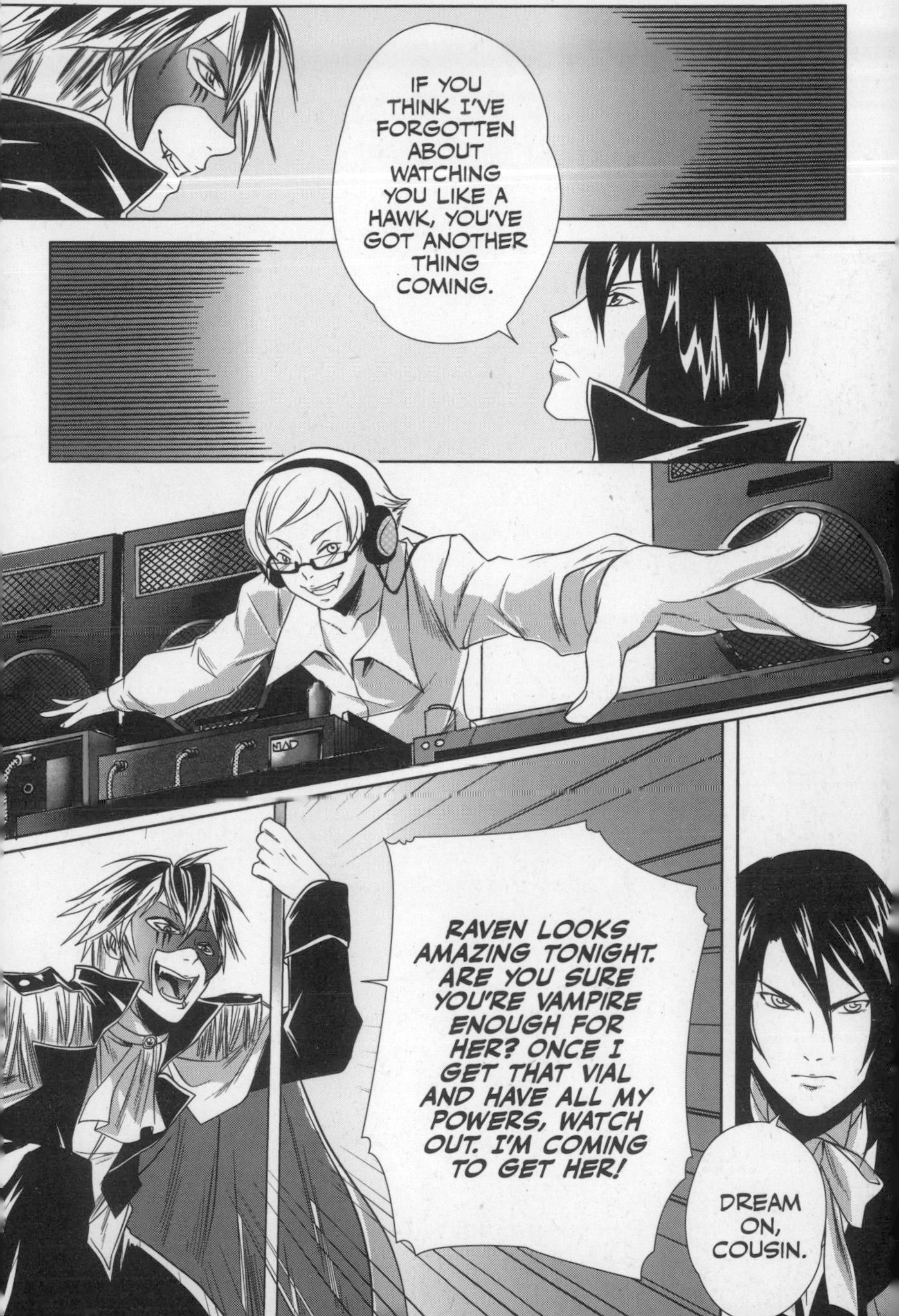
IF YOU THINK I'VE FORGOTTEN ABOUT WATCHING YOU LIKE A HAWK, YOU'VE GOT ANOTHER THING COMING.
RAVEN LOOKS AMAZING TONIGHT. ARE YOU SURE YOU'RE VAMPIRE ENOUGH FOR HER? ONCE I GET THAT VIAL AND HAVE ALL MY POWERS, WATCH OUT. I'M COMING TO GET HER!
DREAM ON, COUSIN.

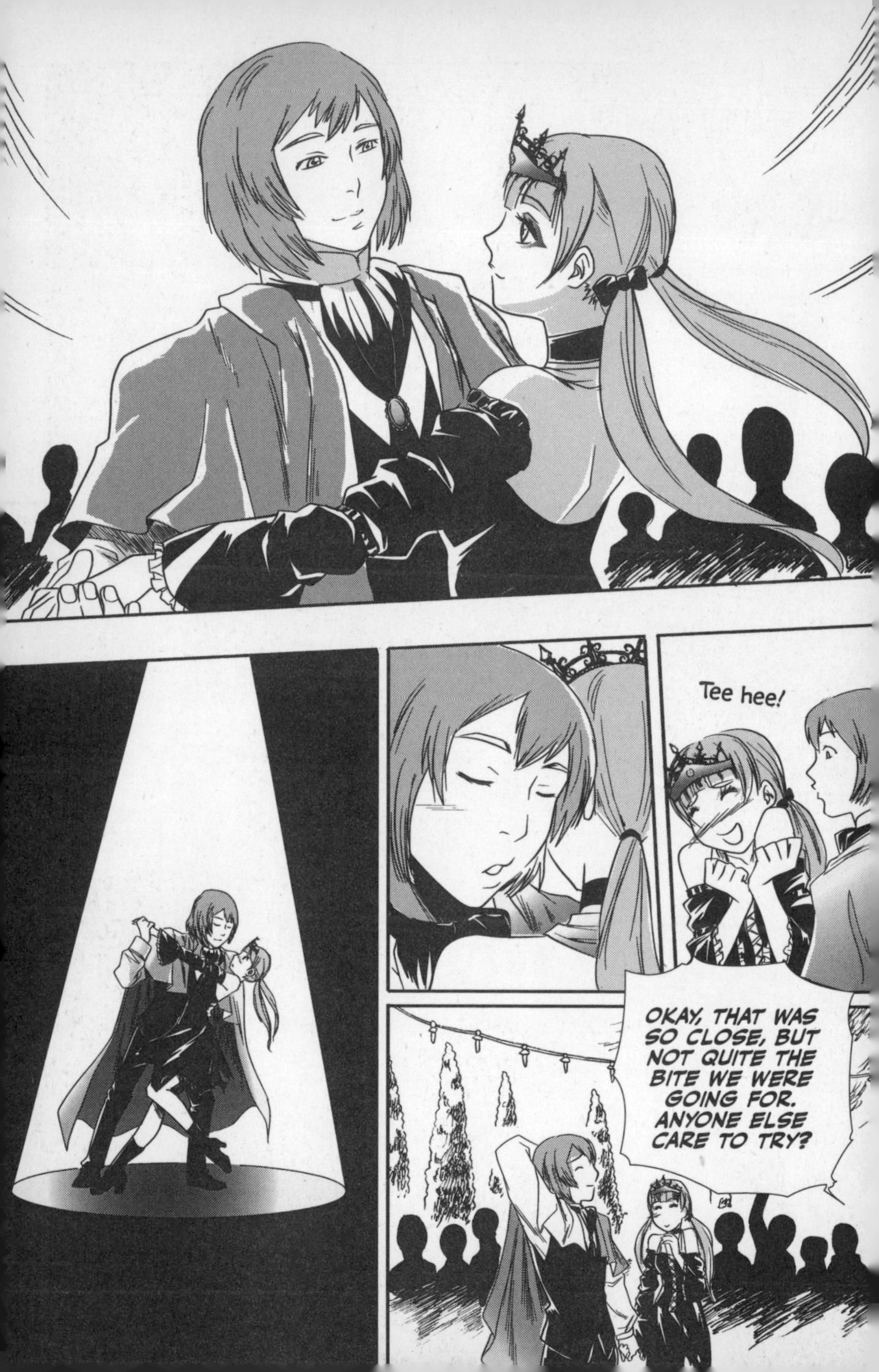
Tee hee!
OKAY, THAT WAS SO CLOSE, BUT NOT QUITE THE BITE WE WERE GOING FOR. ANYONE ELSE CARE TO TRY?

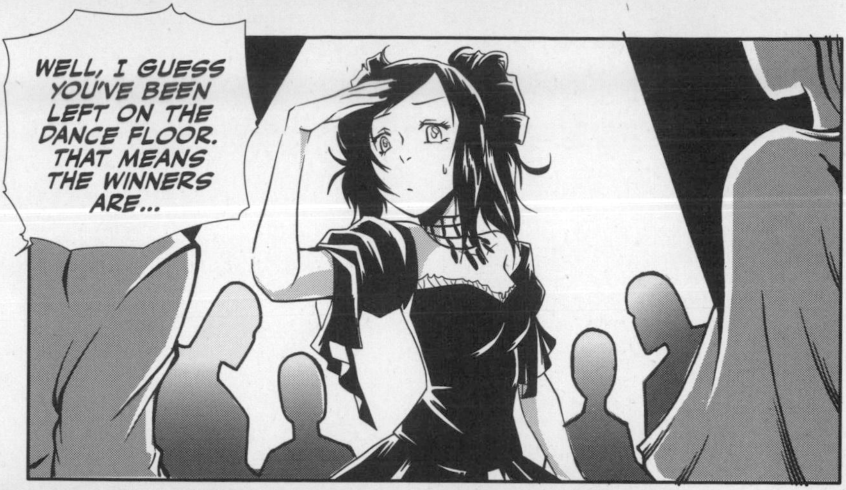
WELL, I GUESS YOU'VE BEEN LEFT ON THE DANCE FLOOR. THAT MEANS THE WINNERS ARE...

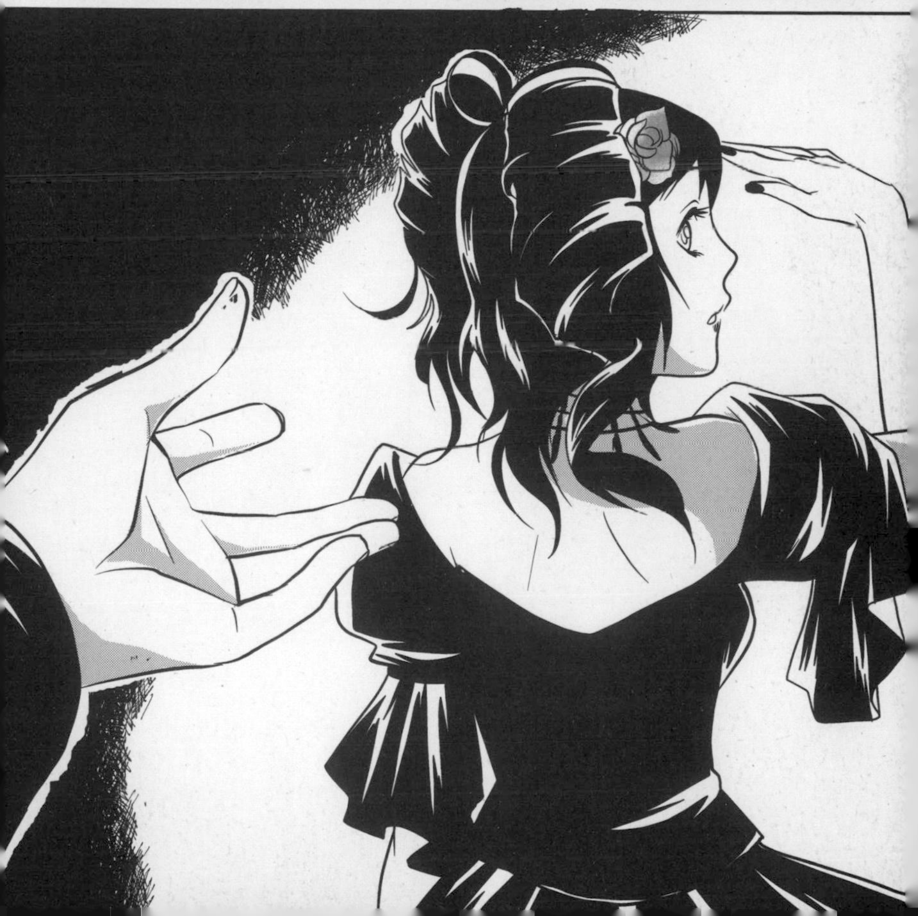

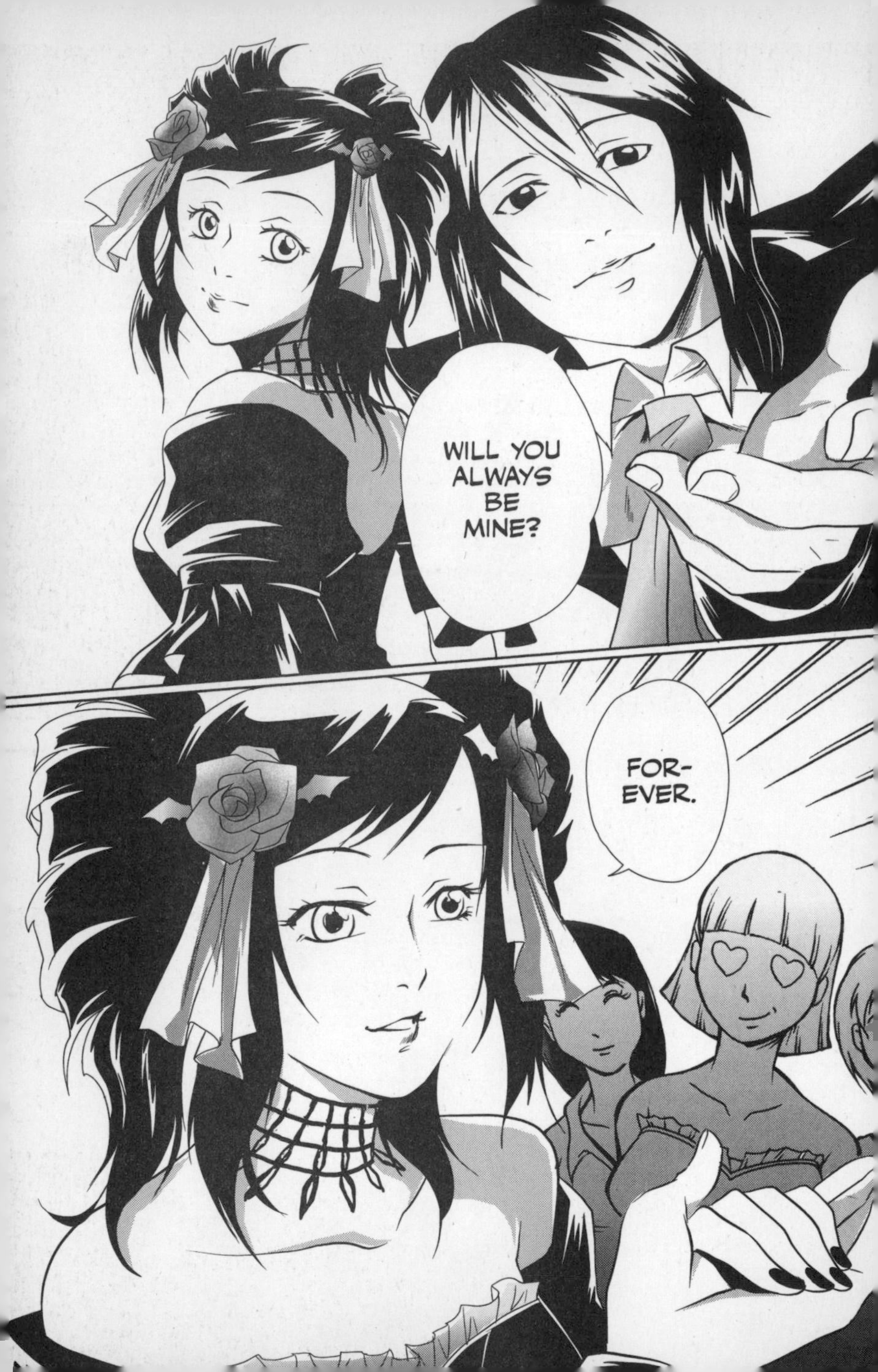
WILL YOU ALWAYS BE MINE?
FOR-EVER.

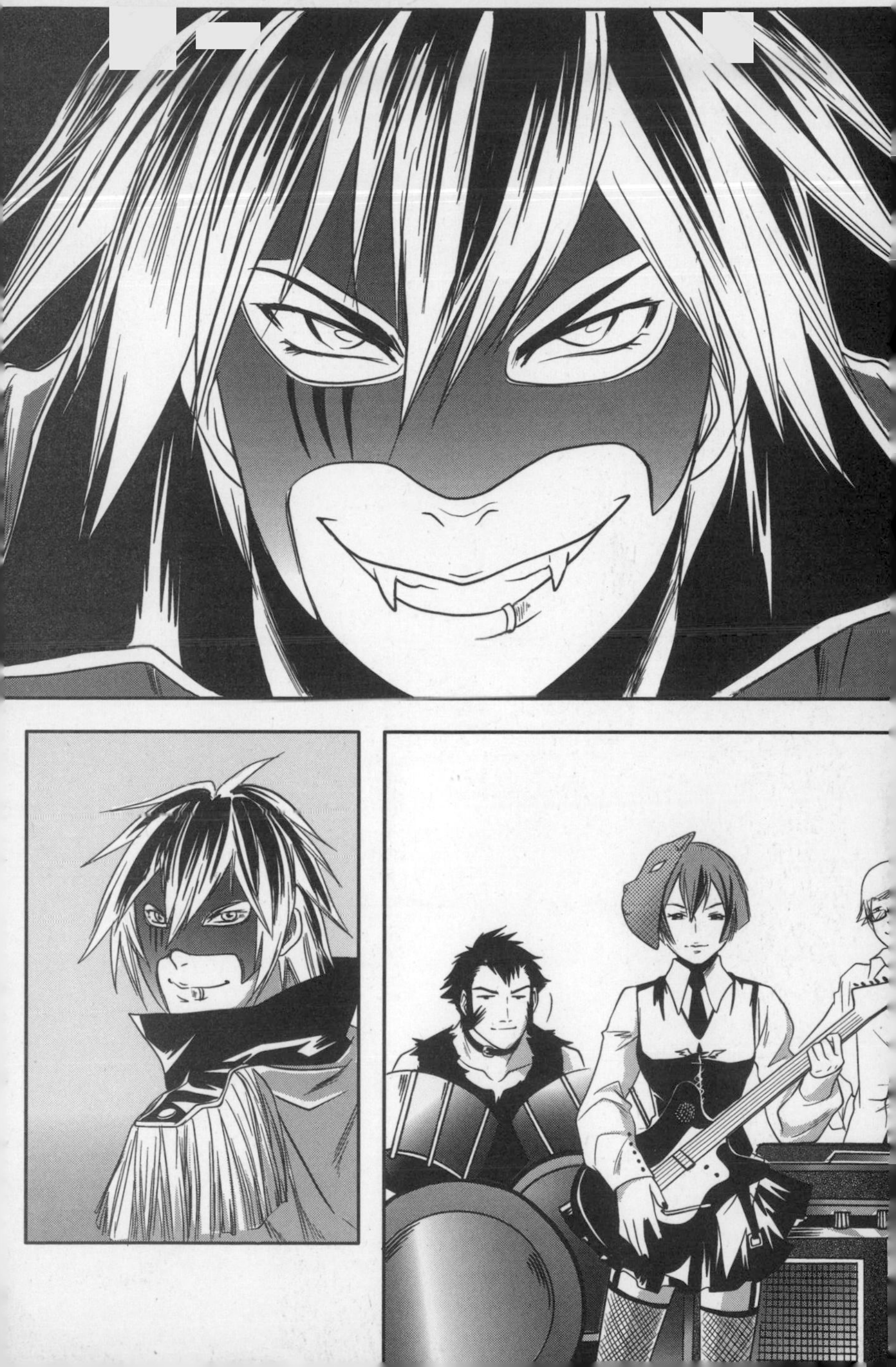

CHAPTER 14: GHOULISH SURPRISE

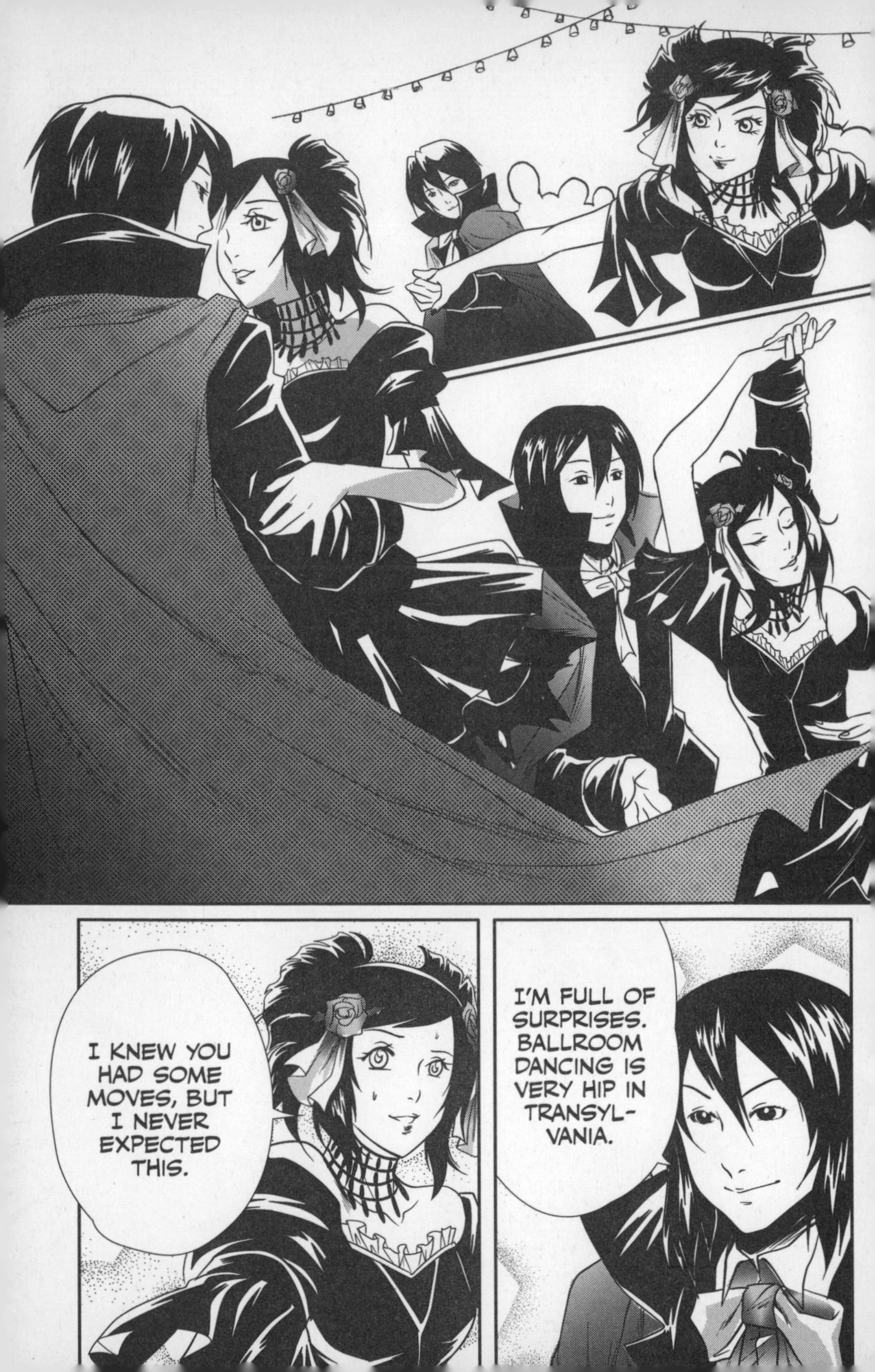
I KNEW YOU HAD SOME MOVES, BUT I NEVER EXPECTED THIS.
I'M FULL OF SURPRISES. BALLROOM DANCING IS VERY HIP IN TRANSYL-VANIA.

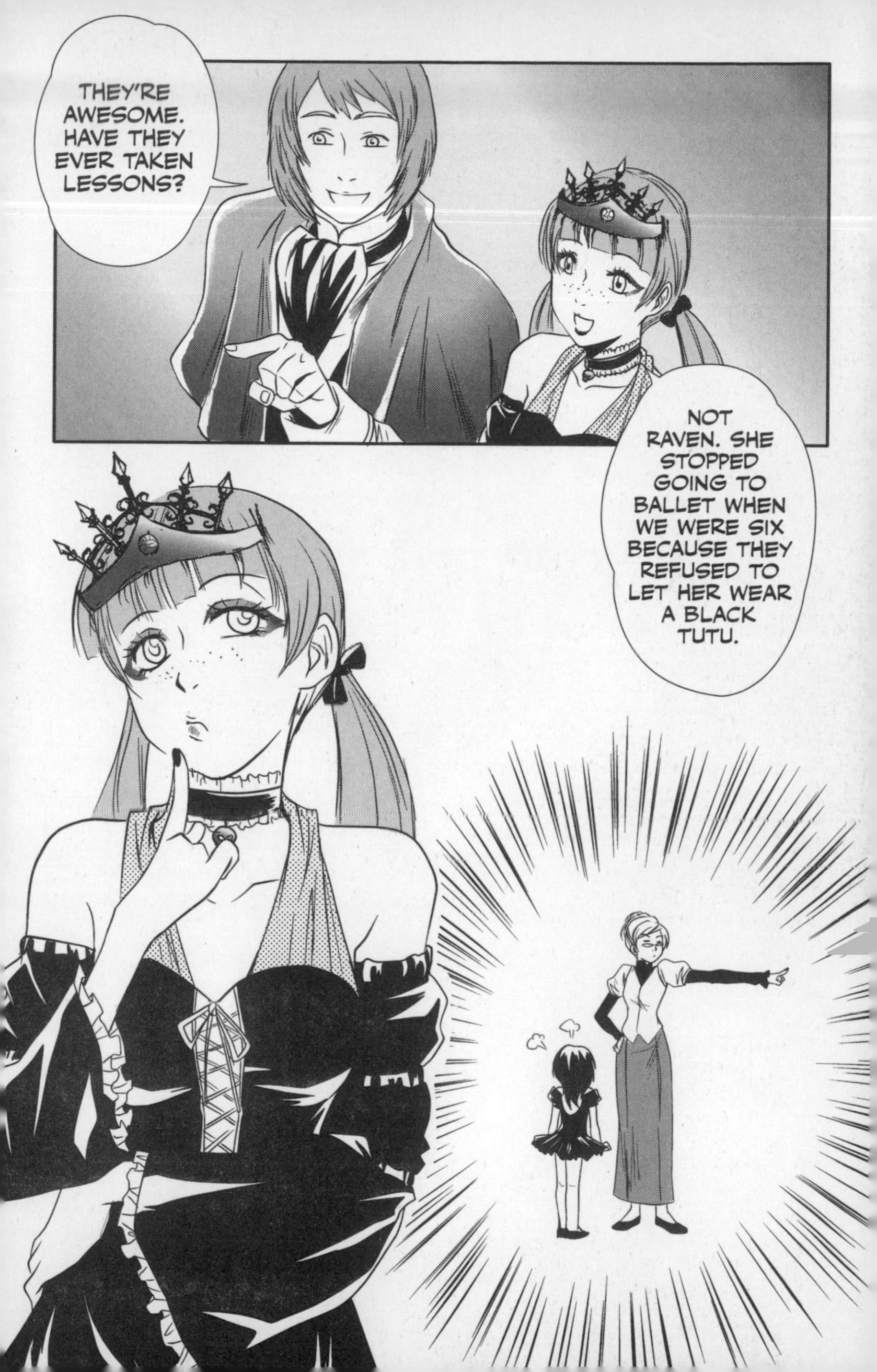
THEY'RE AWESOME. HAVE THEY EVER TAKEN LESSONS?
NOT RAVEN. SHE STOPPED GOING TO BALLET WHEN WE WERE SIX BECAUSE THEY REFUSED TO LET HER WEAR A BLACK TUTU.

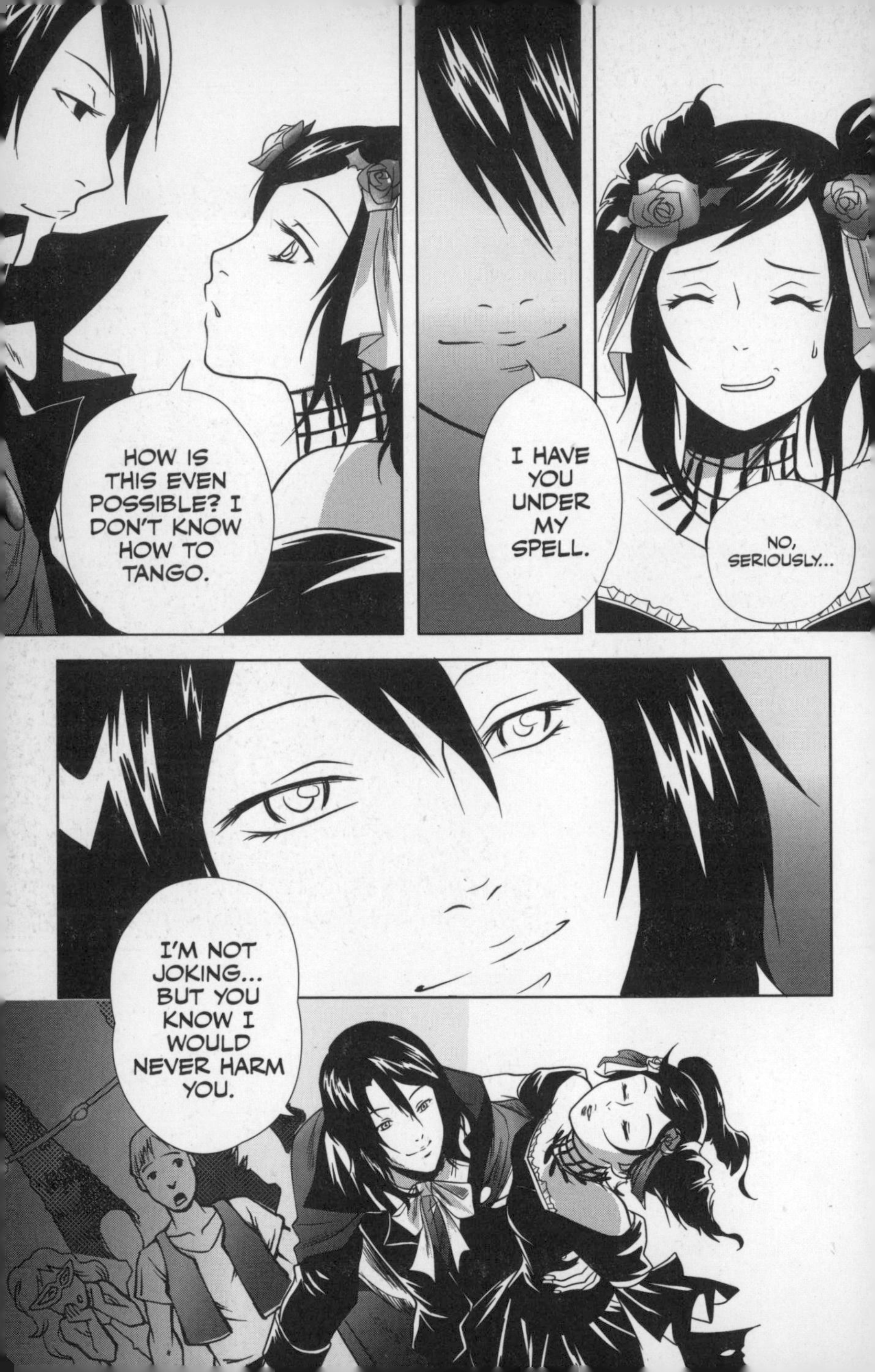
HOW IS THIS EVEN POSSIBLE? I DON'T KNOW HOW TO TANGO.
I HAVE YOU UNDER MY SPELL.
NO, SERIOUSLY...
I'M NOT JOKING... BUT YOU KNOW I WOULD NEVER HARM YOU.

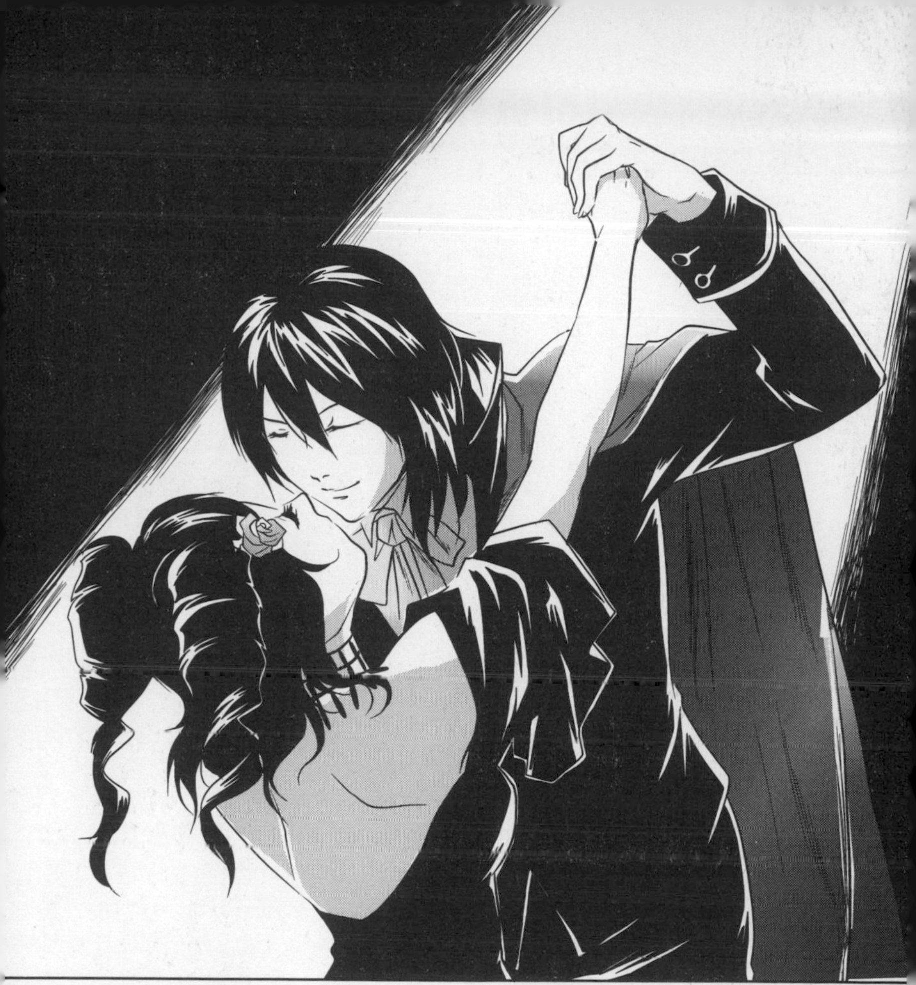

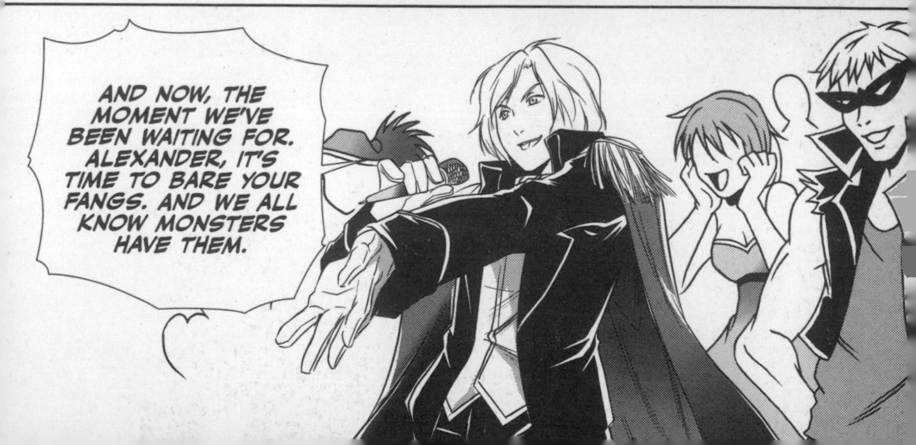
AND NOW, THE MOMENT WE'VE BEEN WAITING FOR. ALEXANDER, IT'S TIME TO BARE YOUR FANGS. AND WE ALL KNOW MONSTERS HAVE THEM.

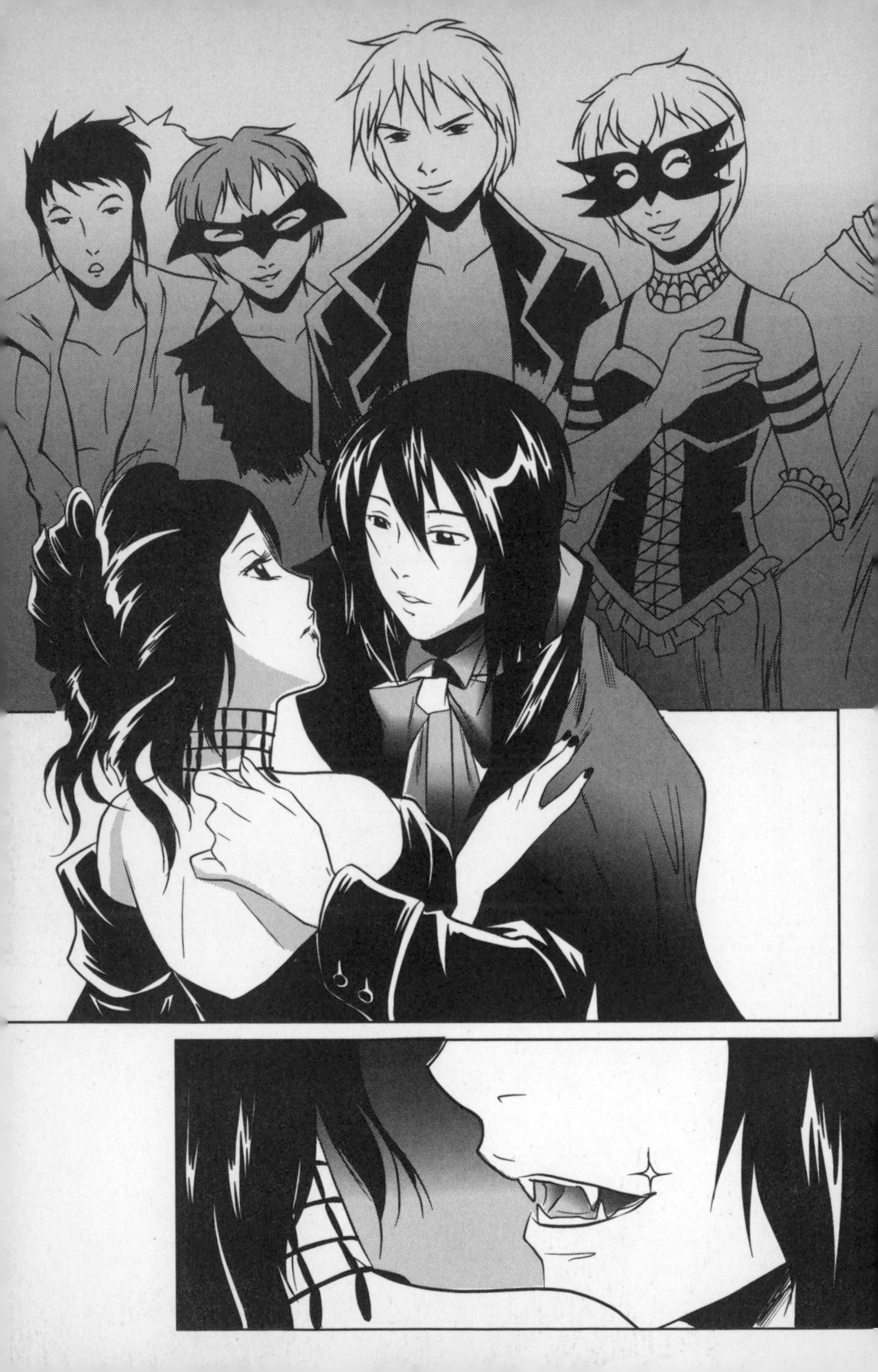

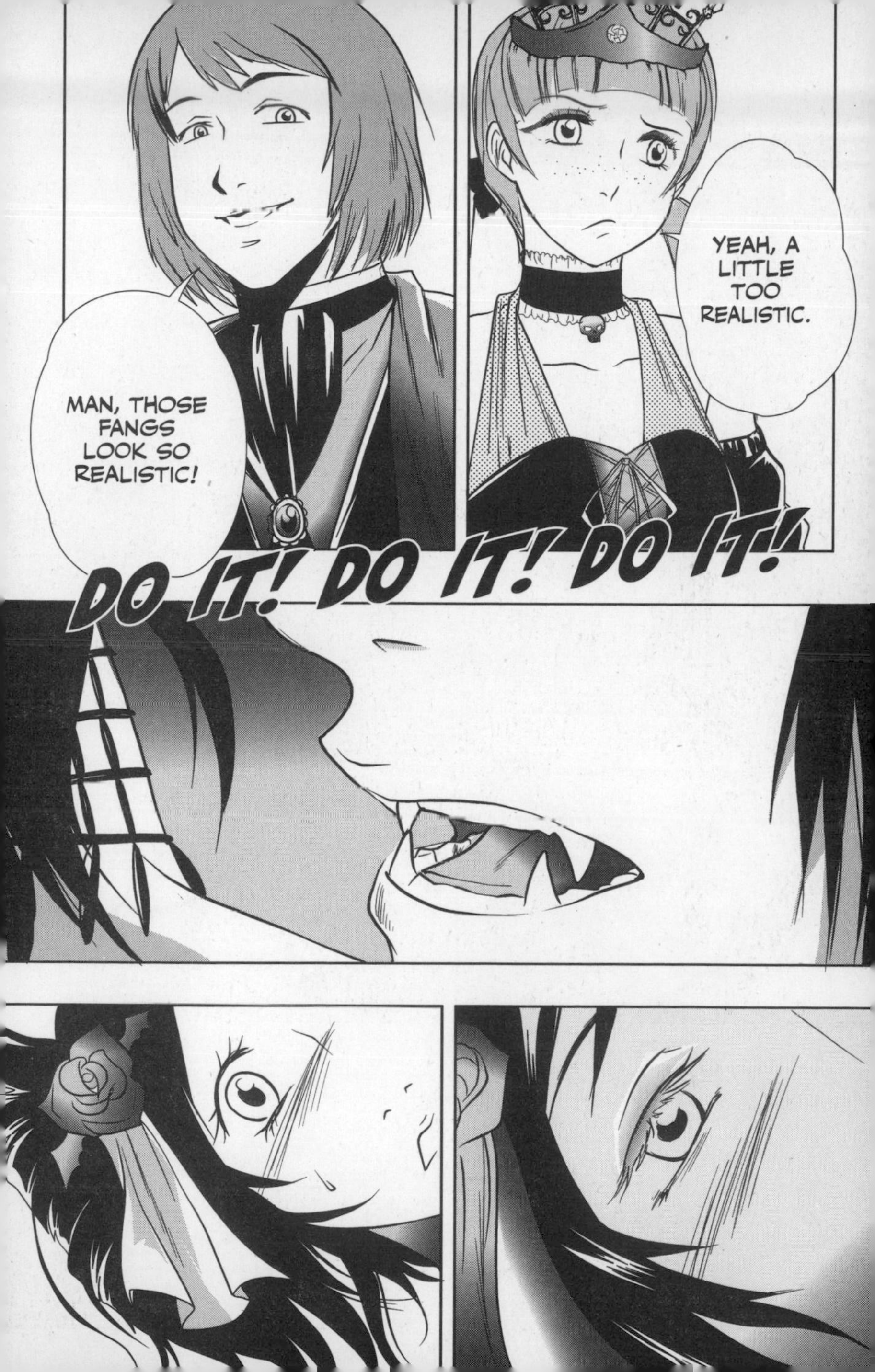
MAN, THOSE FANGS LOOK SO REALISTIC!
YEAH, A LITTLE TOO REALISTIC.
DO IT! DO IT! DO IT!

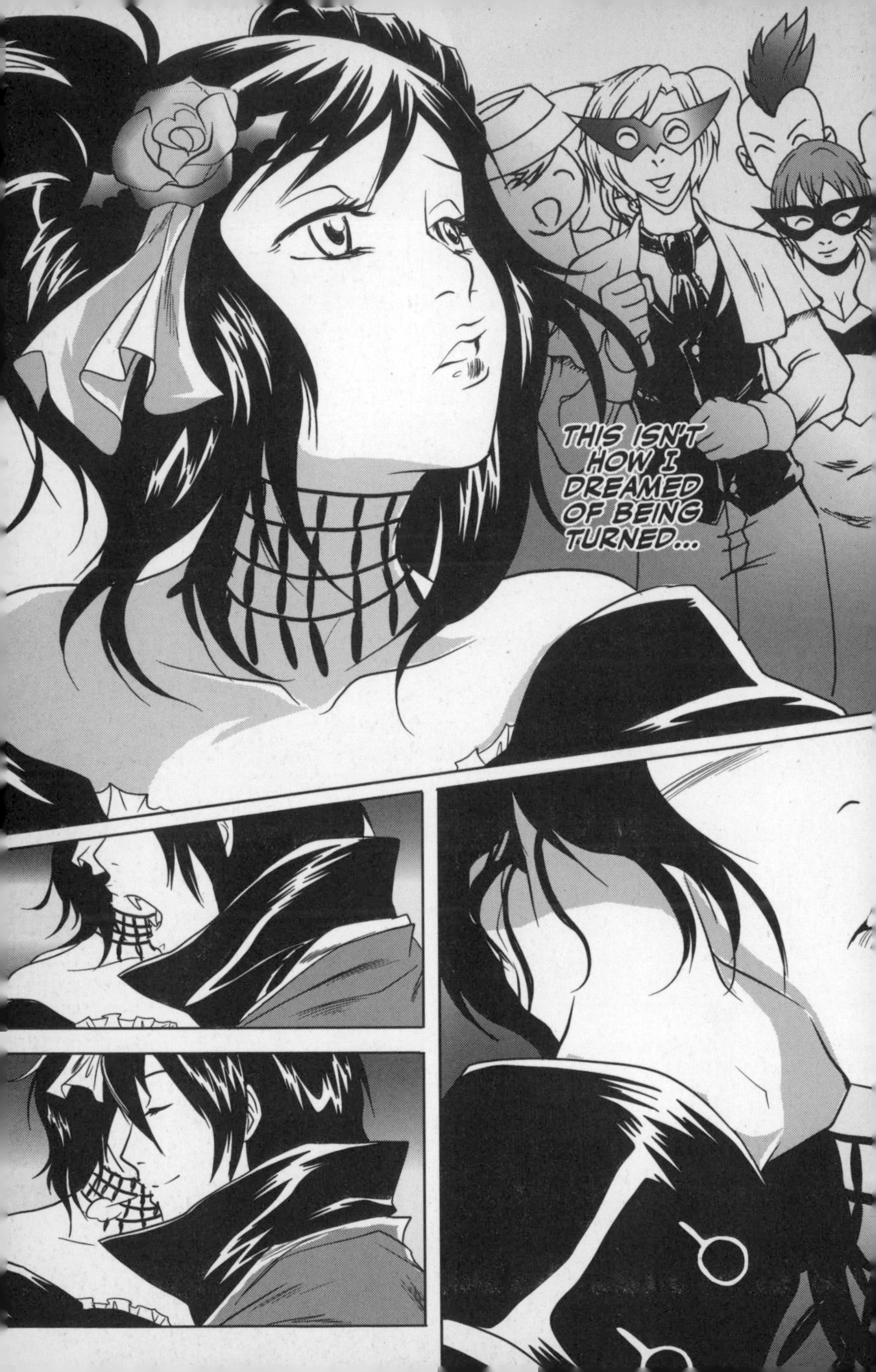
THIS ISN'T HOW I DREAMED OF BEING TURNED...

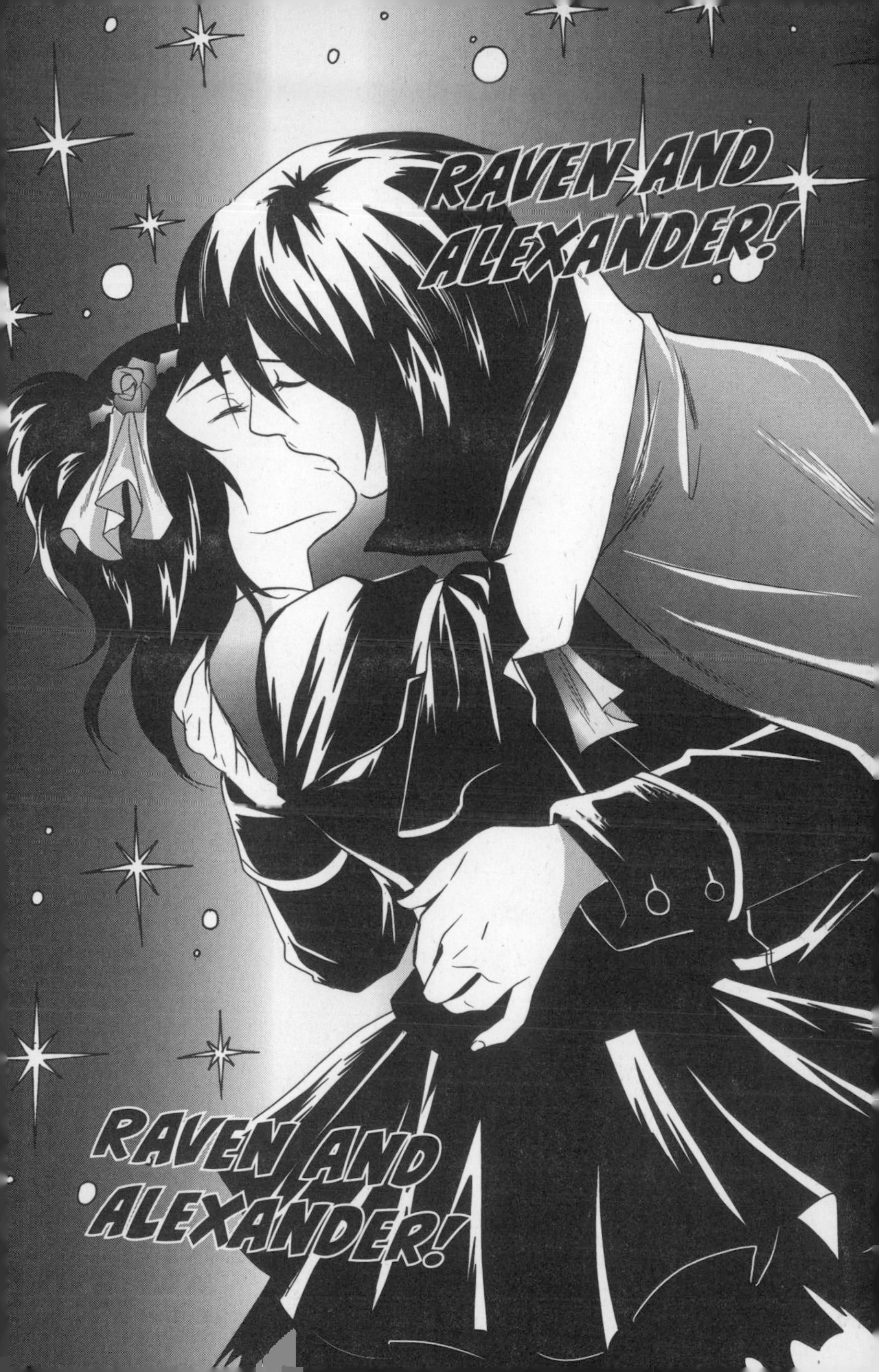
RAVEN AND ALEXANDER!
RAVEN AND ALEXANDER!

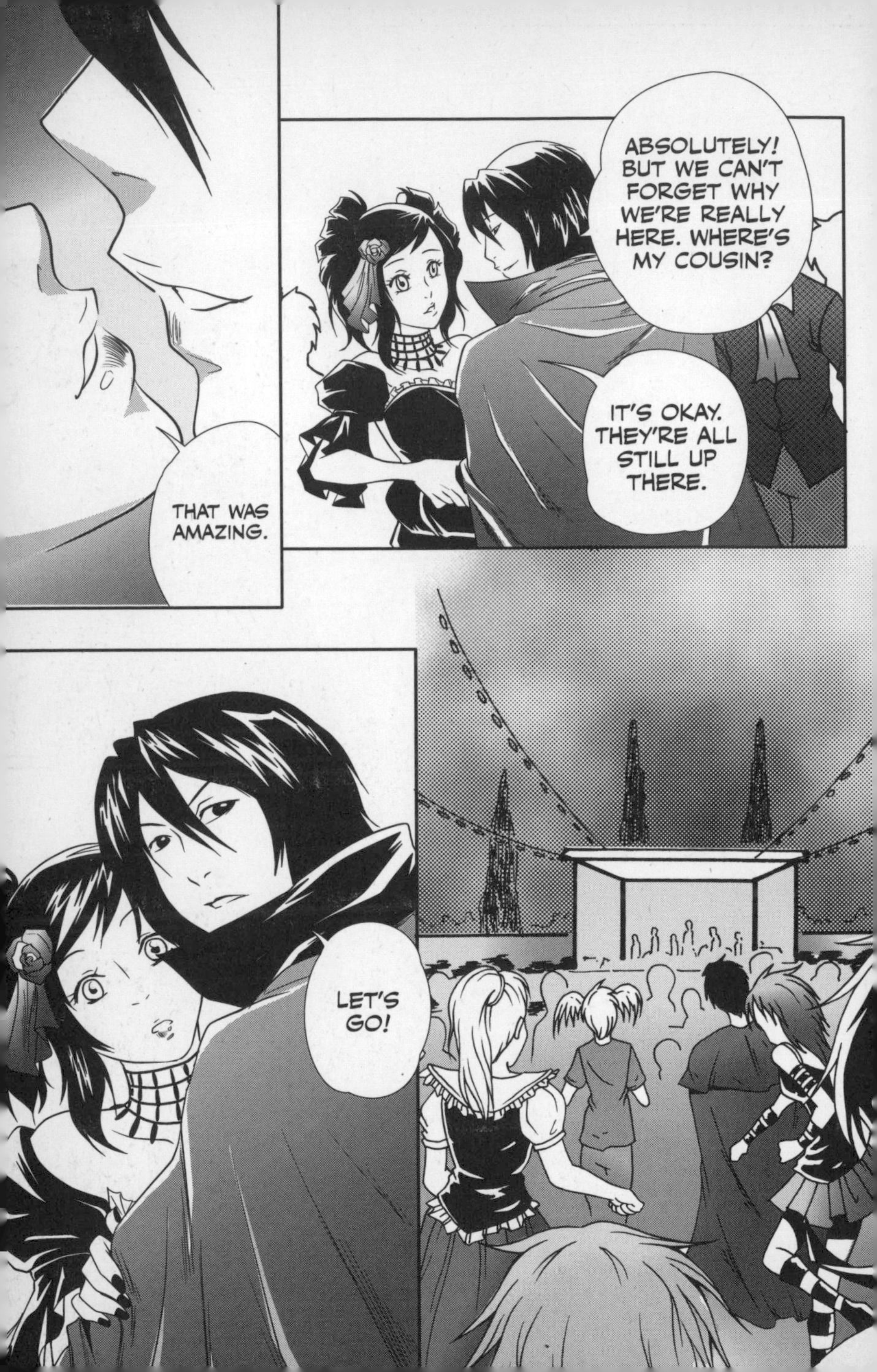
THAT WAS AMAZING.
ABSOLUTELY! BUT WE CAN'T FORGET WHY WE'RE REALLY HERE. WHERE'S MY COUSIN?
IT'S OKAY. THEY'RE ALL STILL UP THERE.
LET'S GO!

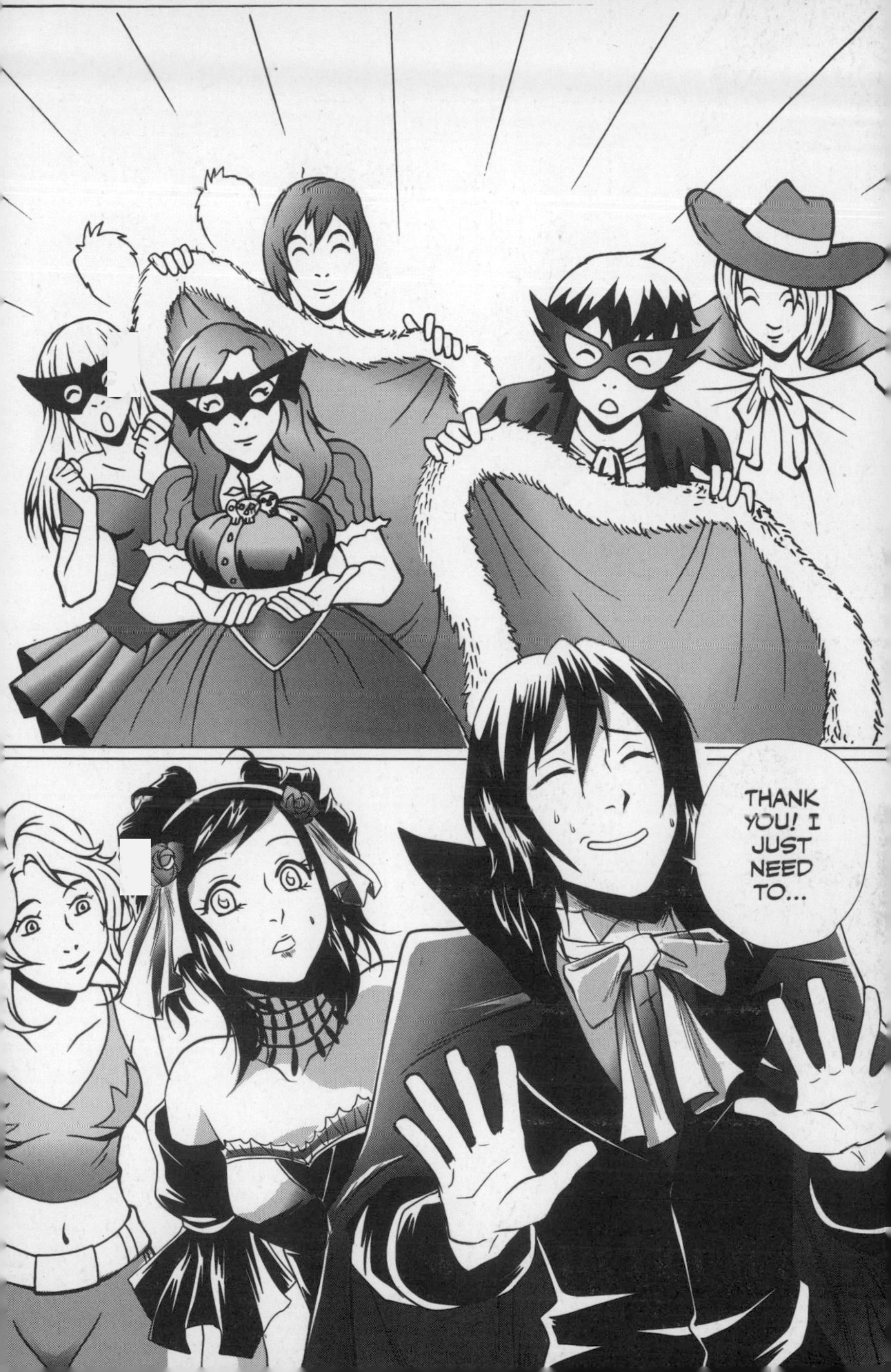
THANK YOU! I JUST NEED TO...

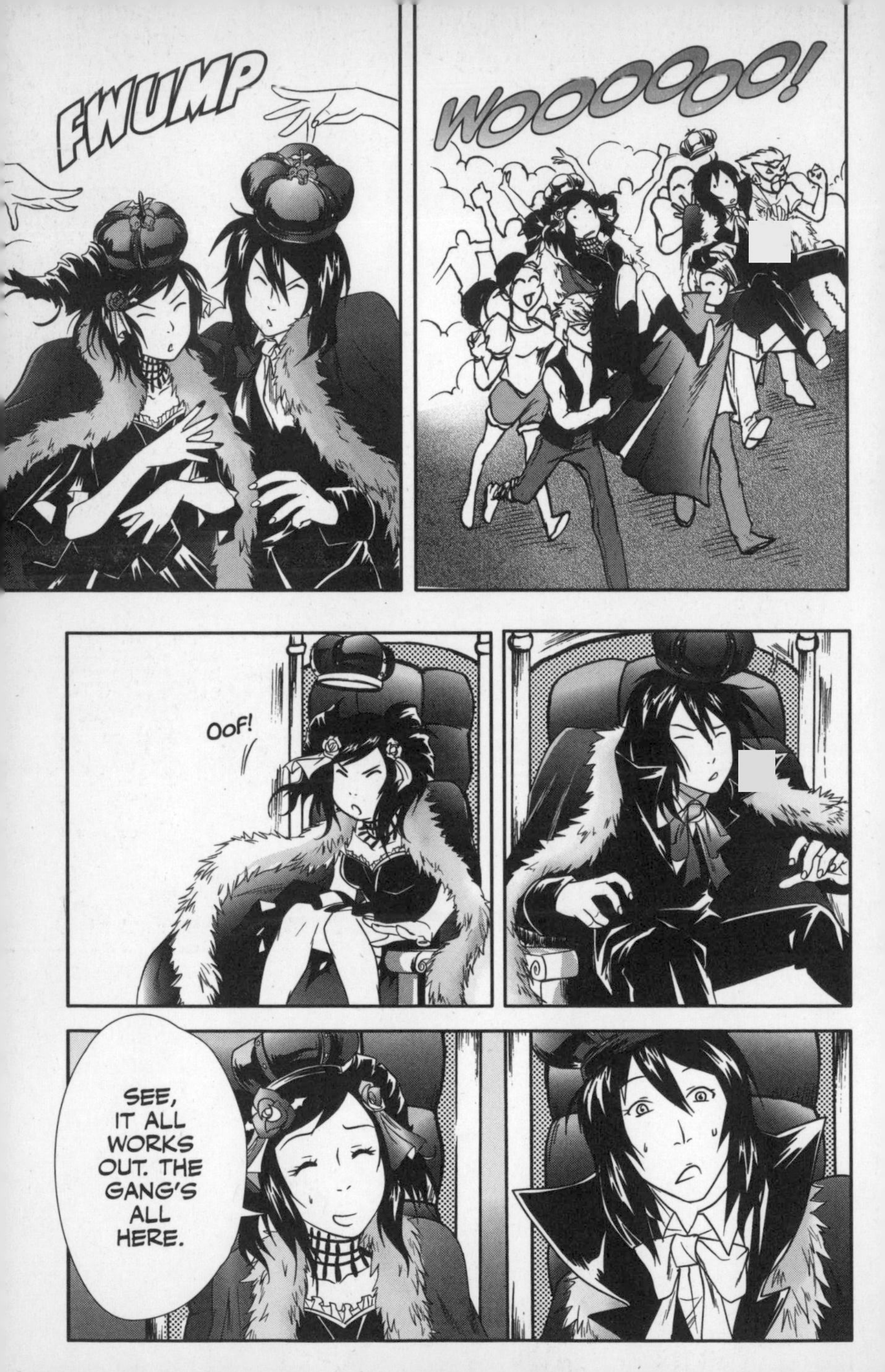
FWUMP
WOOOOOO!
OOF!
SEE, IT ALL WORKS OUT. THE GANG'S ALL HERE.

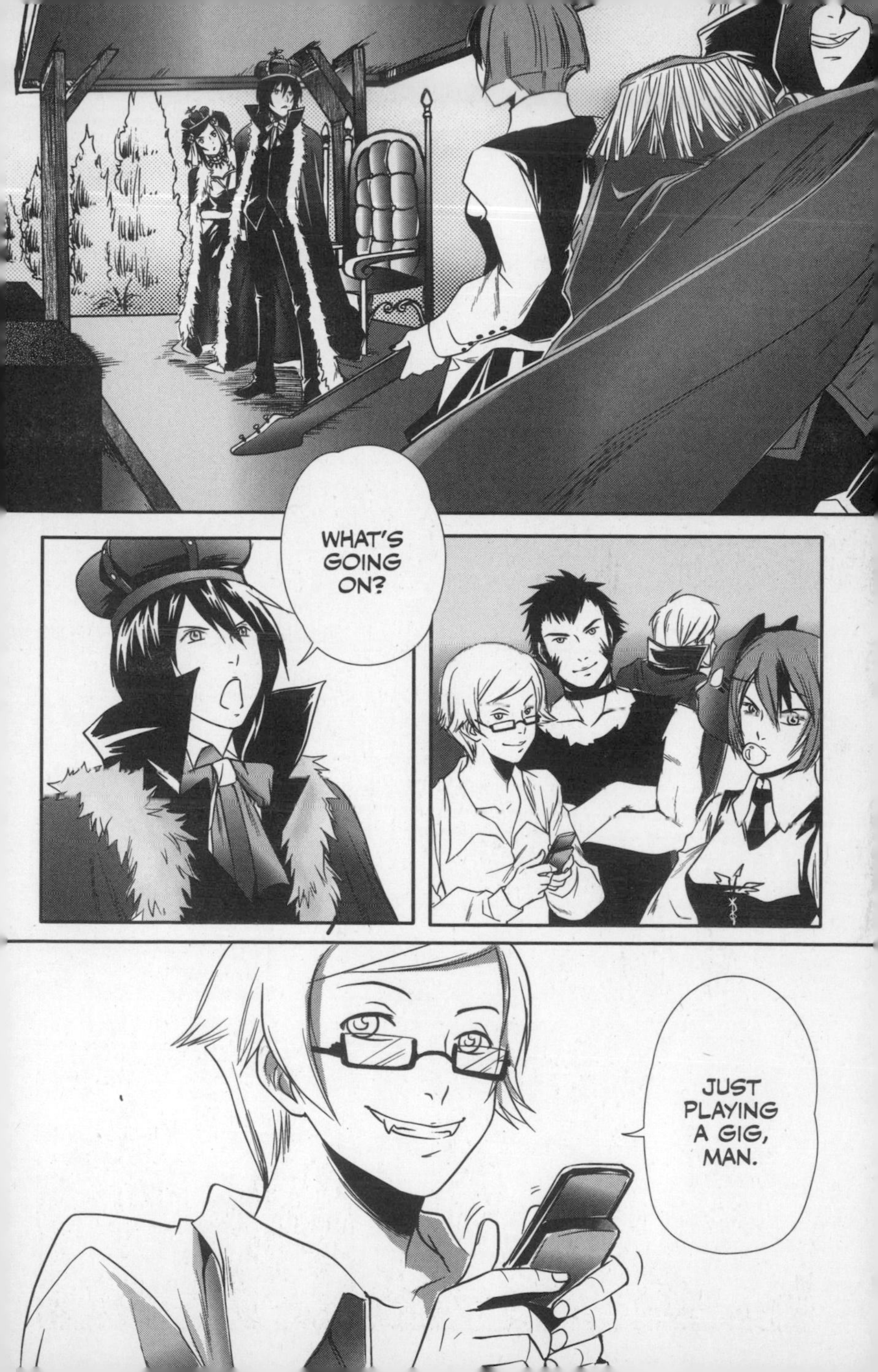
WHAT'S GOING ON?
JUST PLAYING A GIG, MAN.

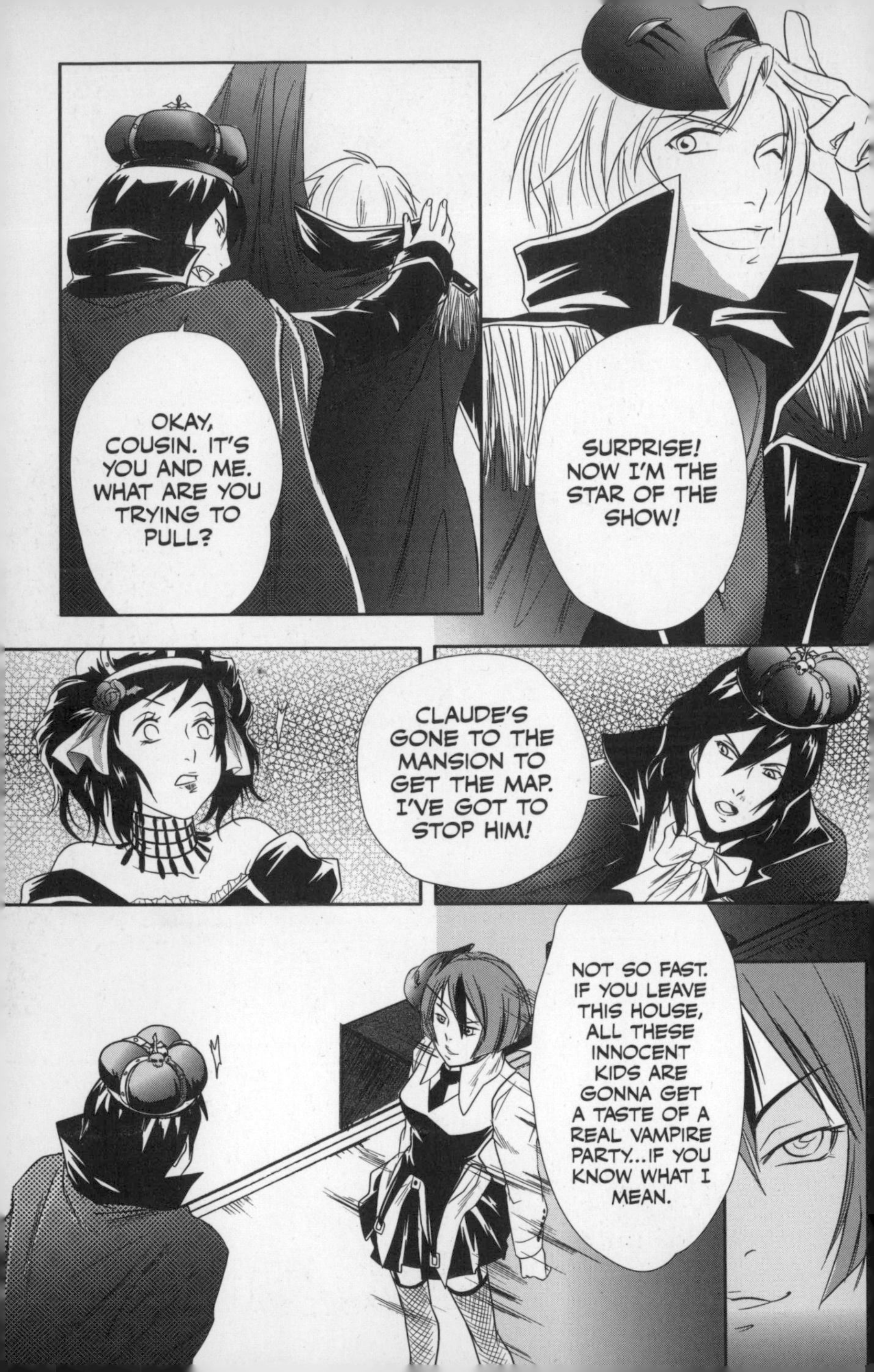
OKAY, COUSIN. IT'S YOU AND ME. WHAT ARE YOU TRYING TO PULL?
SURPRISE! NOW I'M THE STAR OF THE SHOW!
CLAUDE'S GONE TO THE MANSION TO GET THE MAP. I'VE GOT TO STOP HIM!
NOT SO FAST. IF YOU LEAVE THIS HOUSE, ALL THESE INNOCENT KIDS ARE GONNA GET A TASTE OF A REAL VAMPIRE PARTY...IF YOU KNOW WHAT I MEAN.

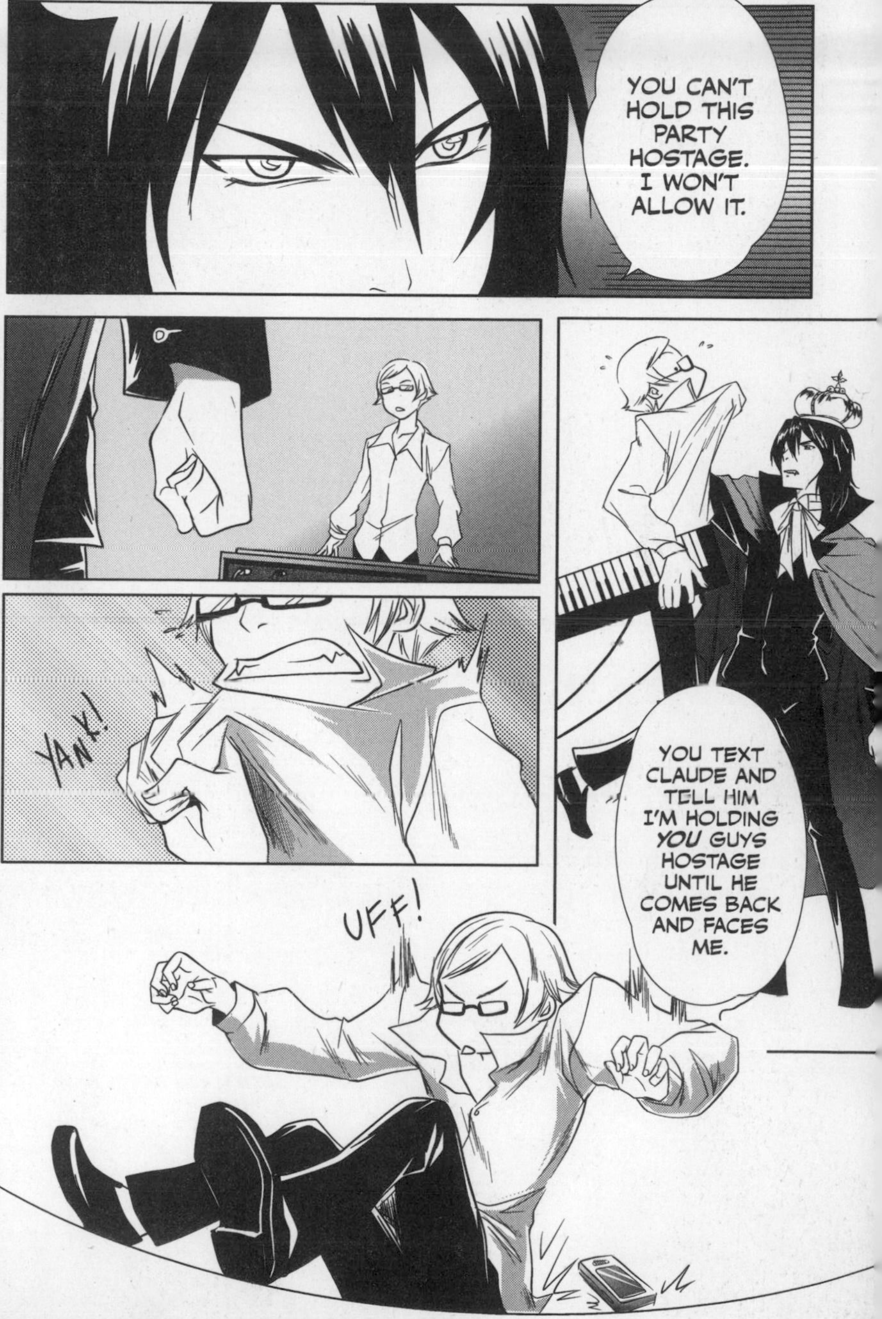
YOU CAN'T HOLD THIS PARTY HOSTAGE. I WON'T ALLOW IT.
YANK!
YOU TEXT CLAUDE AND TELL HIM I'M HOLDING *YOU* GUYS HOSTAGE UNTIL HE COMES BACK AND FACES ME.
UFF!

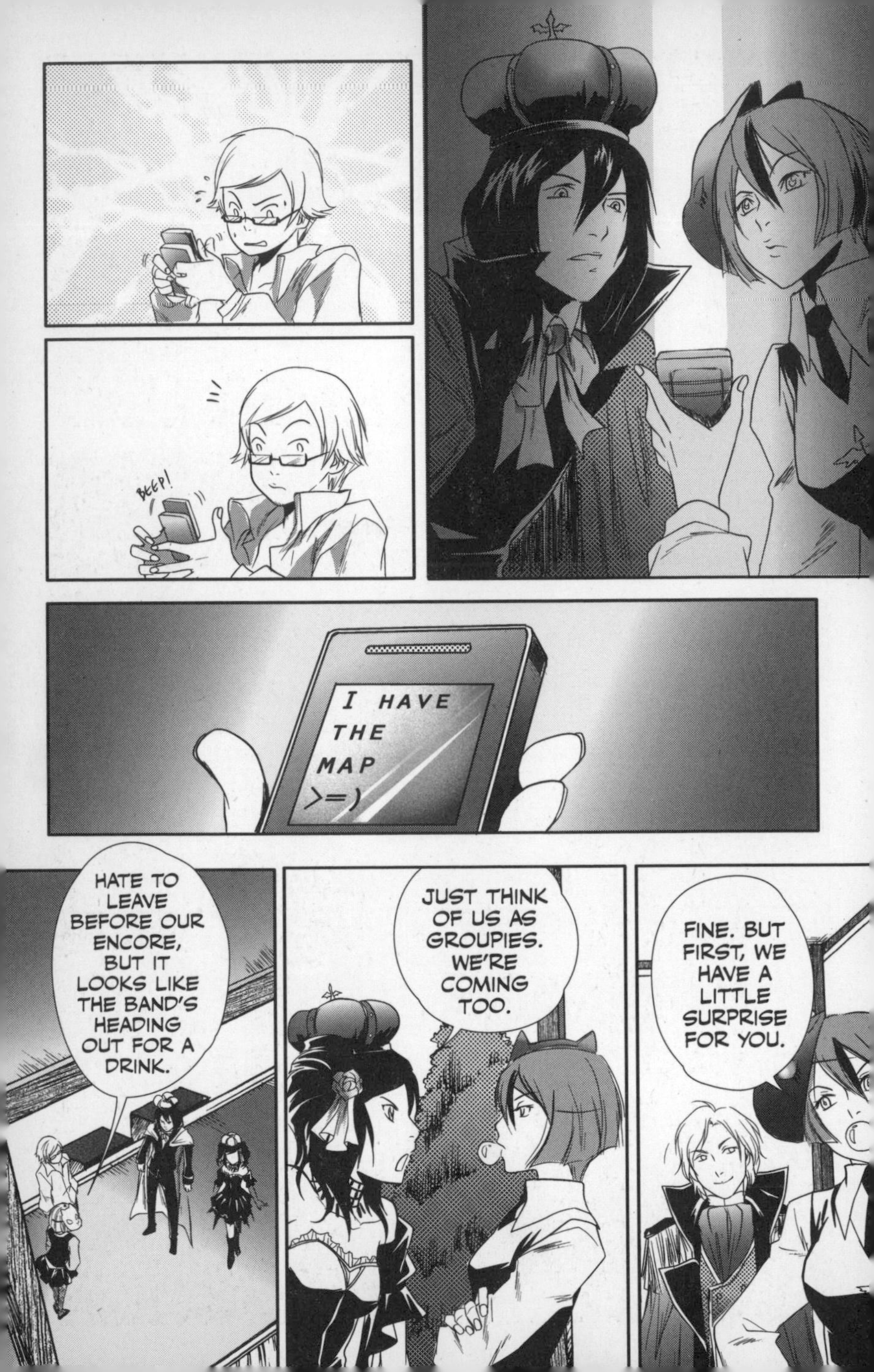
BEEP!
I HAVE THE MAP >=)
HATE TO LEAVE BEFORE OUR ENCORE, BUT IT LOOKS LIKE THE BAND'S HEADING OUT FOR A DRINK.
JUST THINK OF US AS GROUPIES. WE'RE COMING TOO.
FINE. BUT FIRST, WE HAVE A LITTLE SURPRISE FOR YOU.

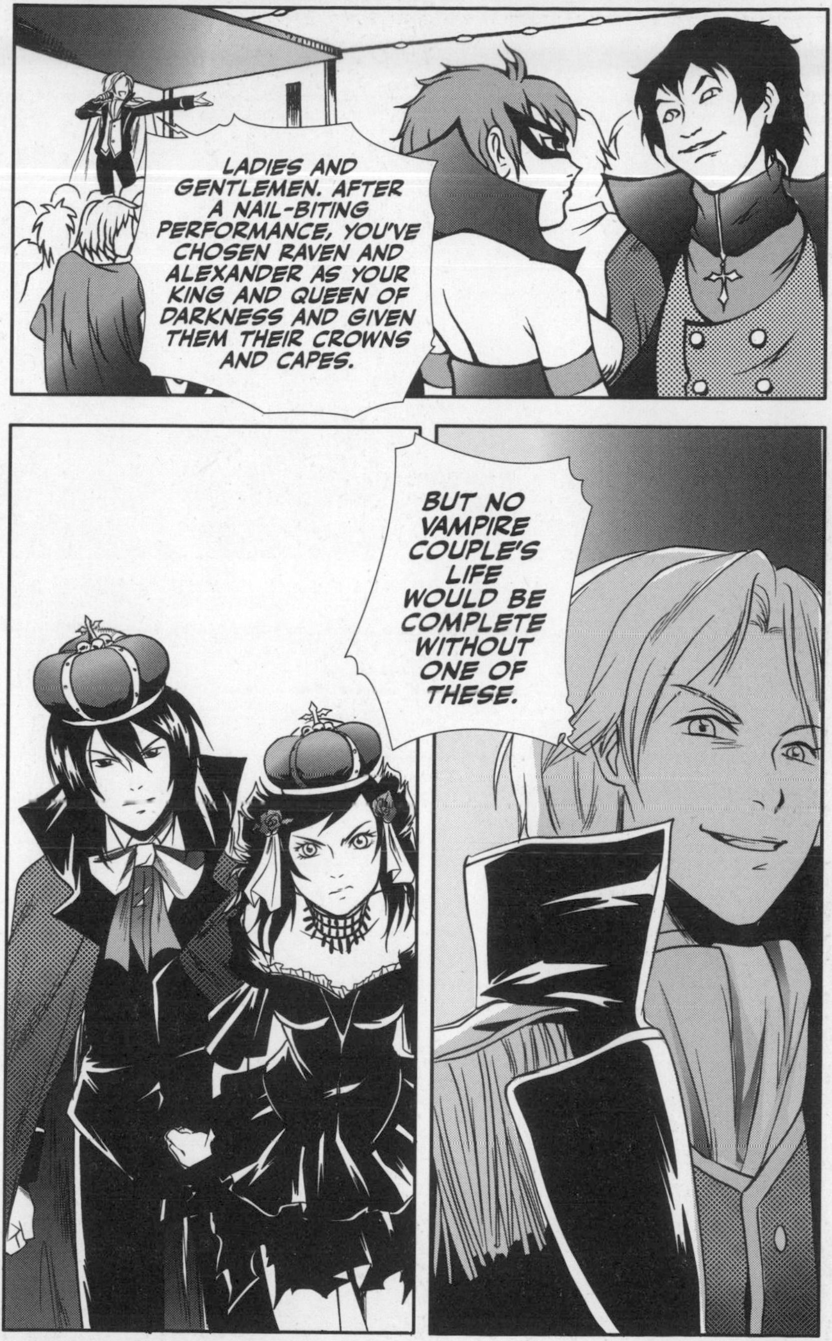
LADIES AND GENTLEMEN. AFTER A NAIL-BITING PERFORMANCE, YOU'VE CHOSEN RAVEN AND ALEXANDER AS YOUR KING AND QUEEN OF DARKNESS AND GIVEN THEM THEIR CROWNS AND CAPES.
BUT NO VAMPIRE COUPLE'S LIFE WOULD BE COMPLETE WITHOUT ONE OF THESE.

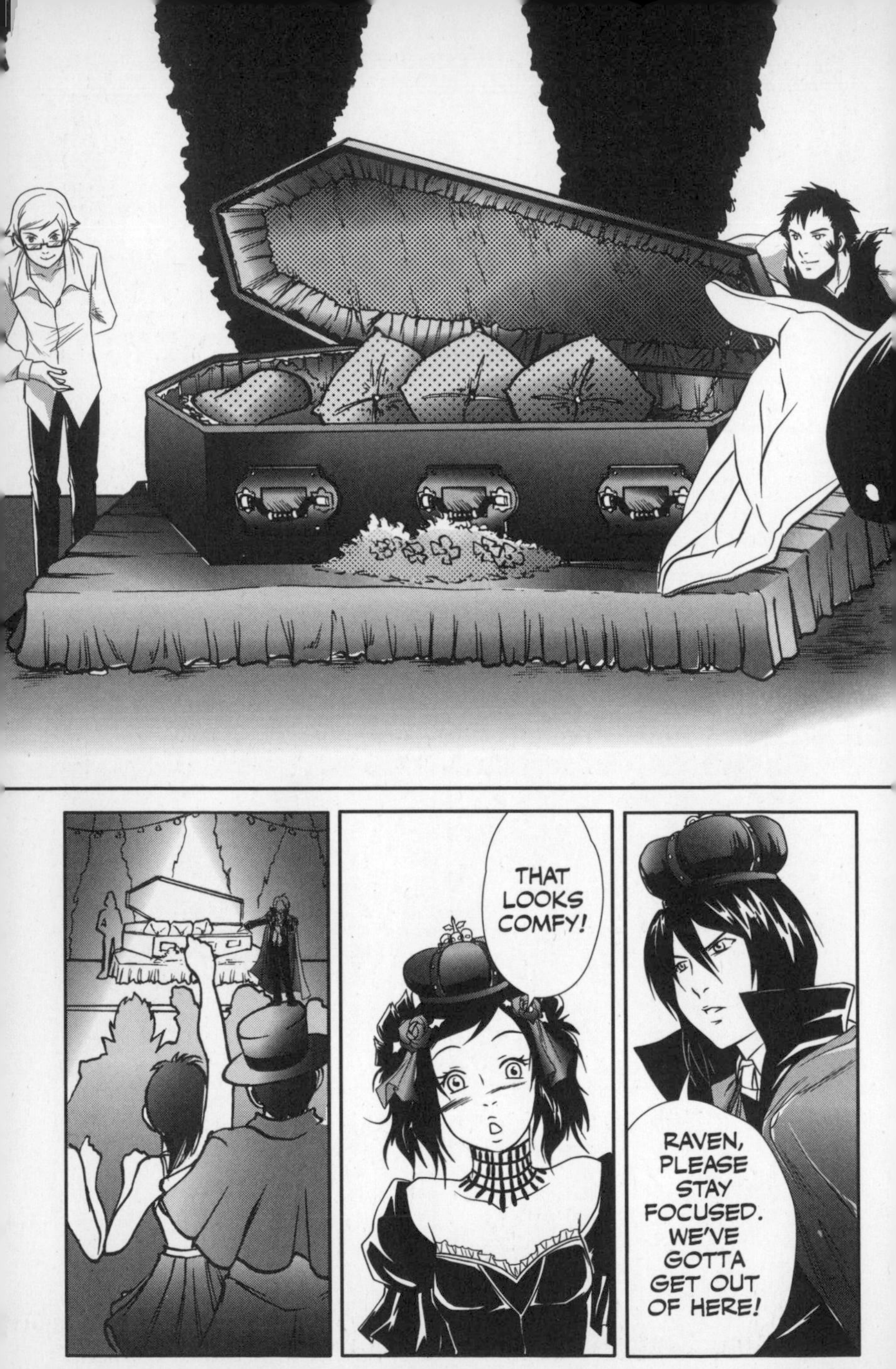
THAT LOOKS COMFY!
RAVEN, PLEASE STAY FOCUSED. WE'VE GOTTA GET OUT OF HERE!

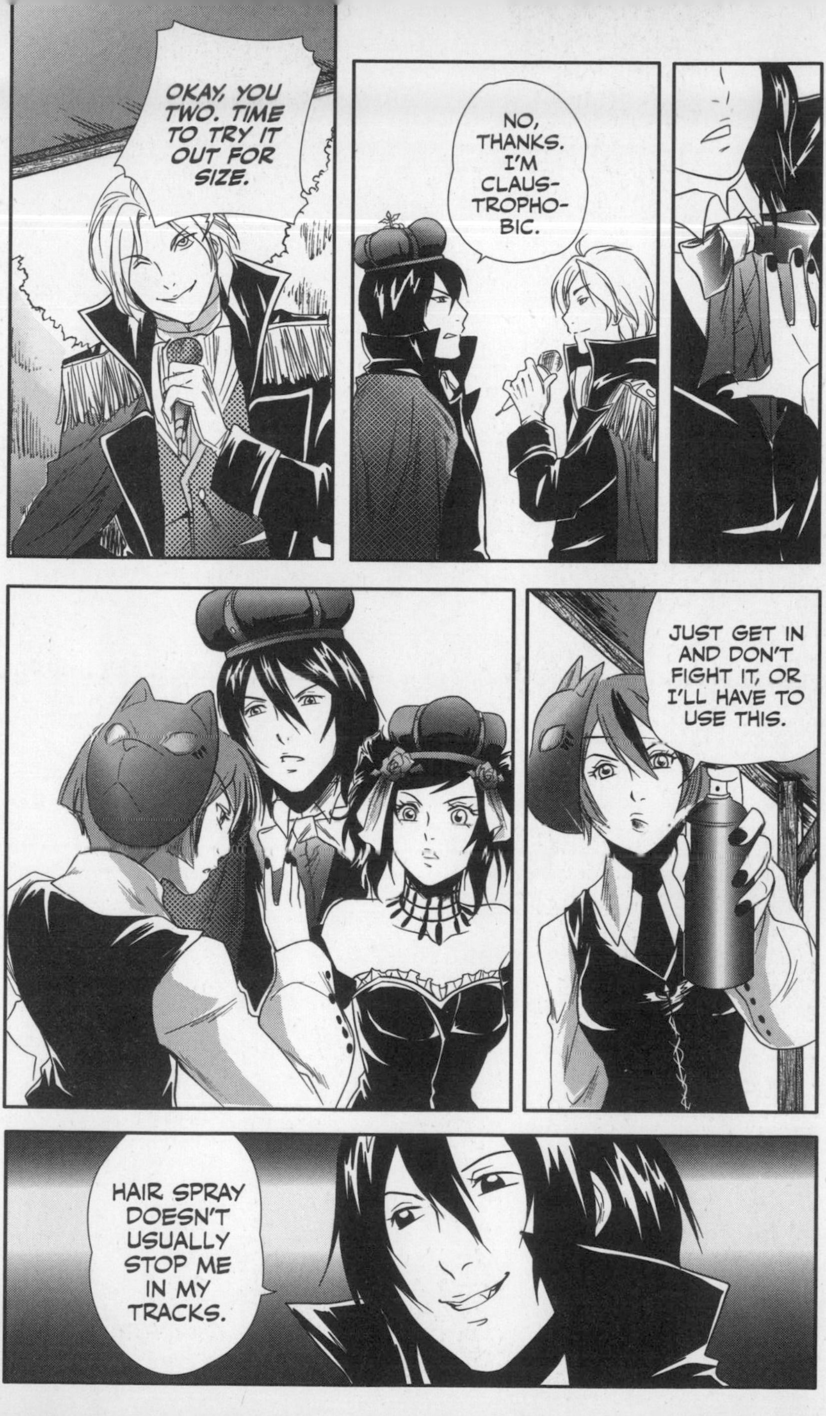
OKAY, YOU TWO. TIME TO TRY IT OUT FOR SIZE.
NO, THANKS. I'M CLAUS-TROPHO-BIC.
JUST GET IN AND DON'T FIGHT IT, OR I'LL HAVE TO USE THIS.
HAIR SPRAY DOESN'T USUALLY STOP ME IN MY TRACKS.

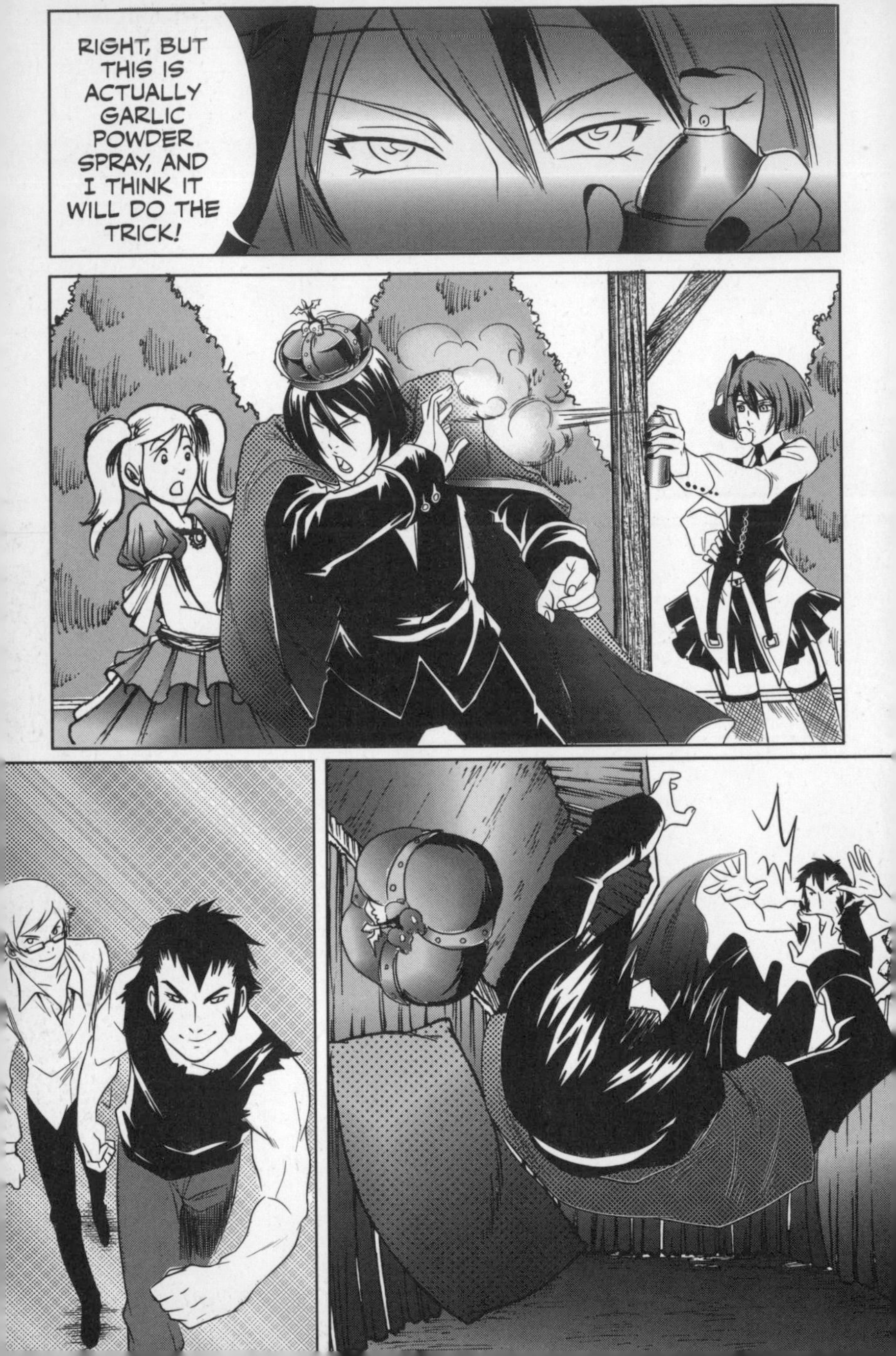
RIGHT, BUT THIS IS ACTUALLY GARLIC POWDER SPRAY, AND I THINK IT WILL DO THE TRICK!

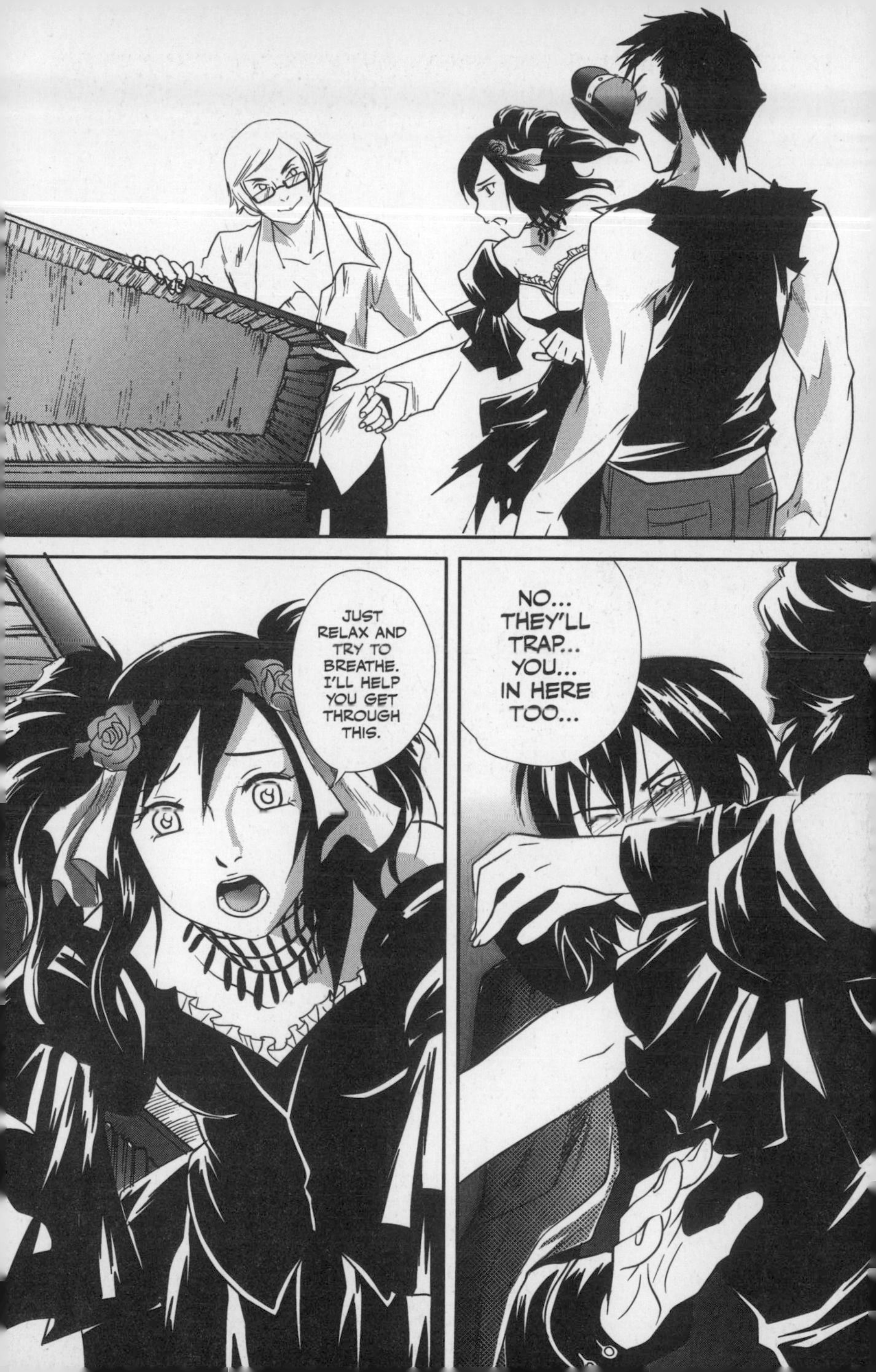
JUST RELAX AND TRY TO BREATHE. I'LL HELP YOU GET THROUGH THIS.
NO... THEY'LL TRAP... YOU... IN HERE TOO...

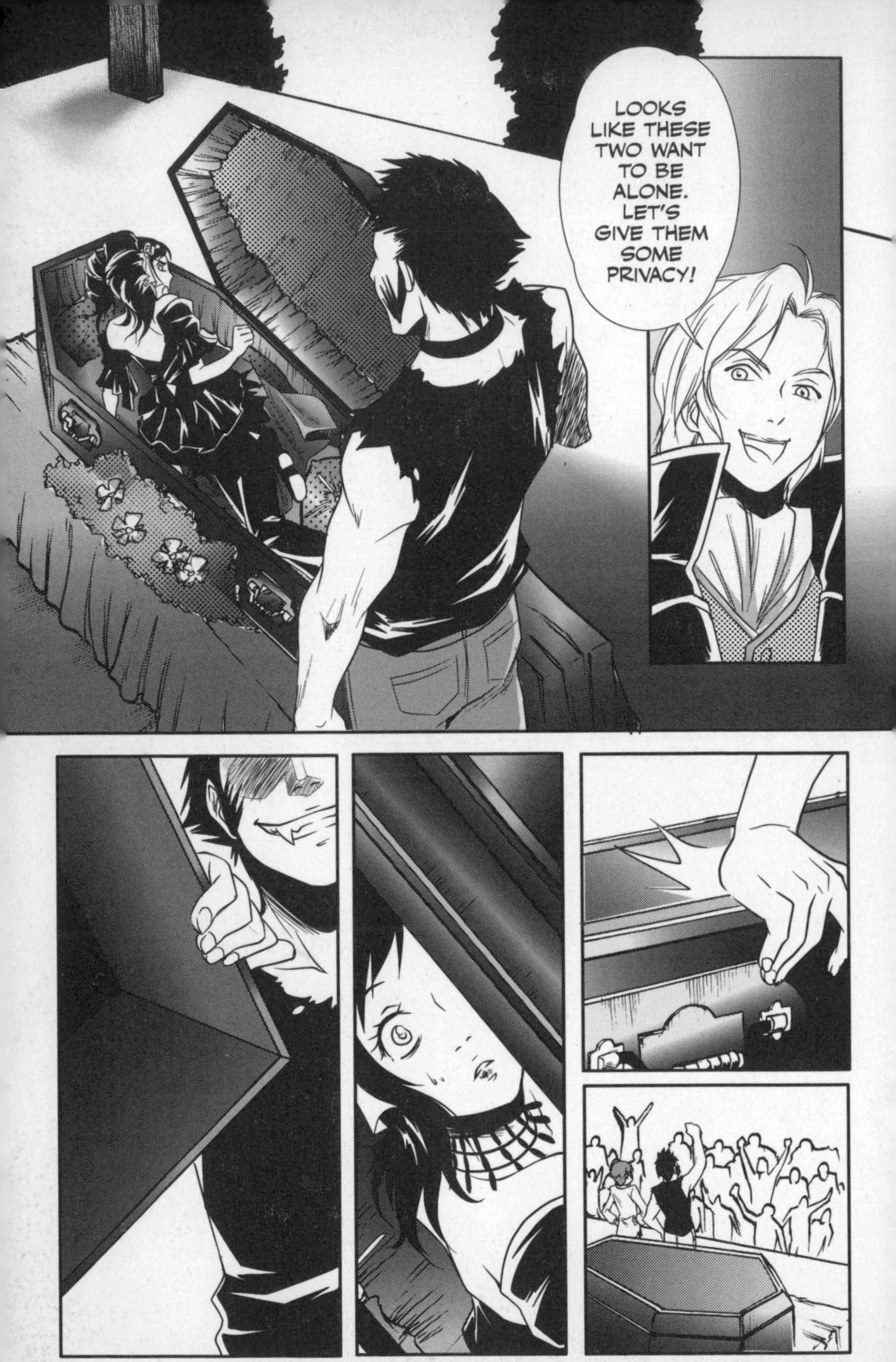
LOOKS LIKE THESE TWO WANT TO BE ALONE. LET'S GIVE THEM SOME PRIVACY!

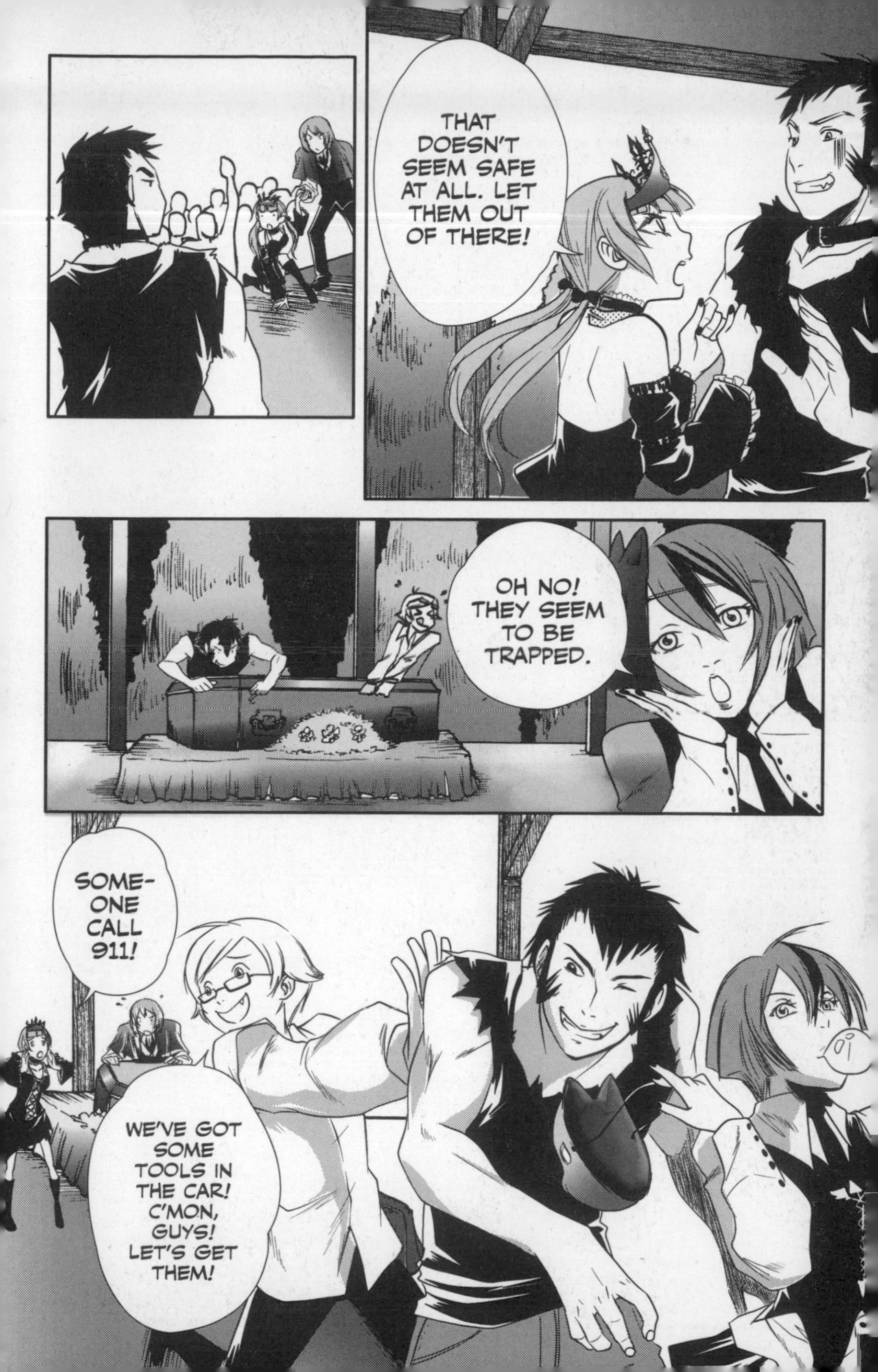
THAT DOESN'T SEEM SAFE AT ALL. LET THEM OUT OF THERE!
OH NO! THEY SEEM TO BE TRAPPED.
SOME-ONE CALL 911!
WE'VE GOT SOME TOOLS IN THE CAR! C'MON, GUYS! LET'S GET THEM!

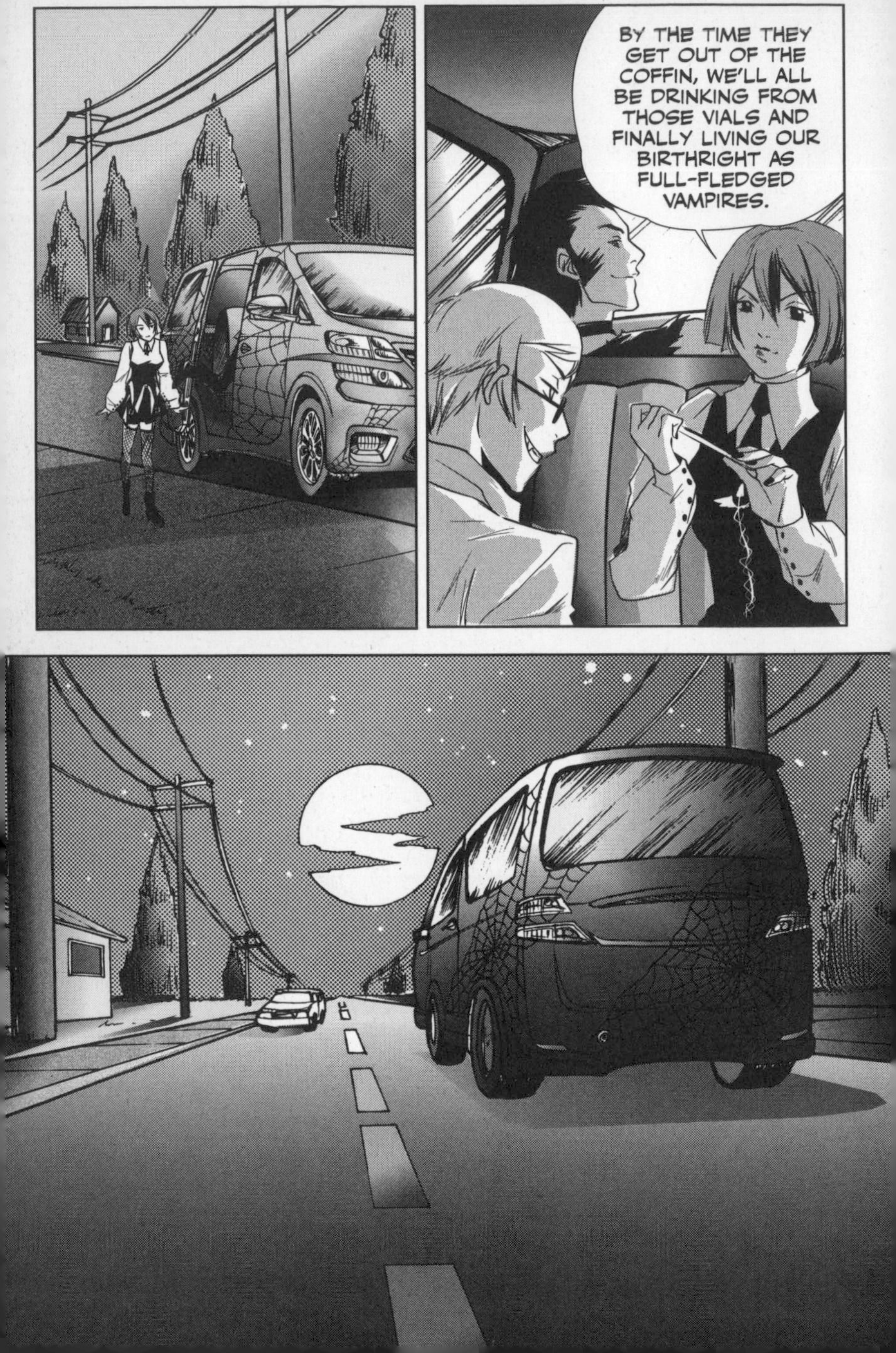
BY THE TIME THEY GET OUT OF THE COFFIN, WE'LL ALL BE DRINKING FROM THOSE VIALS AND FINALLY LIVING OUR BIRTHRIGHT AS FULL-FLEDGED VAMPIRES.

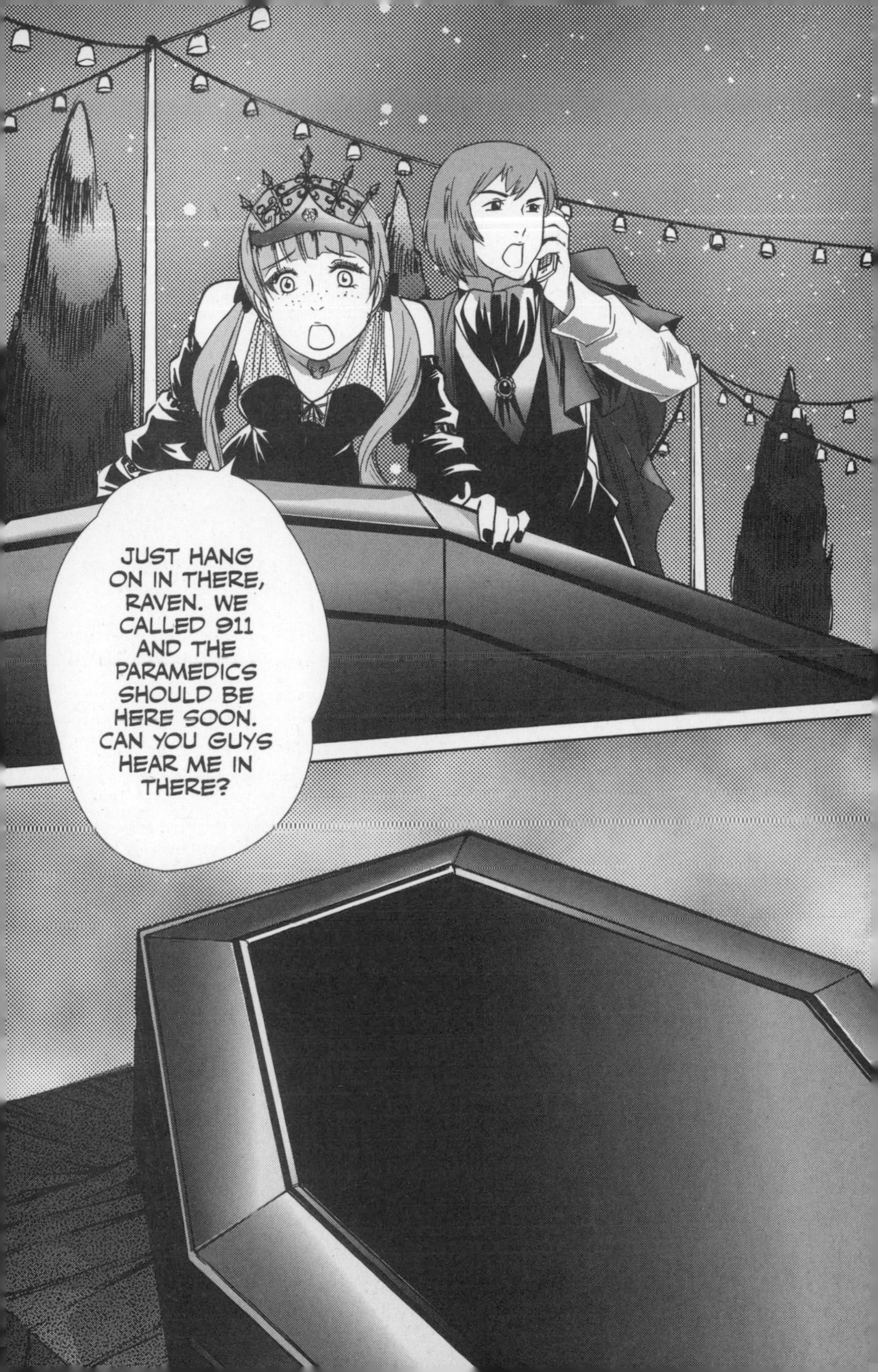
JUST HANG ON IN THERE, RAVEN. WE CALLED 911 AND THE PARAMEDICS SHOULD BE HERE SOON. CAN YOU GUYS HEAR ME IN THERE?

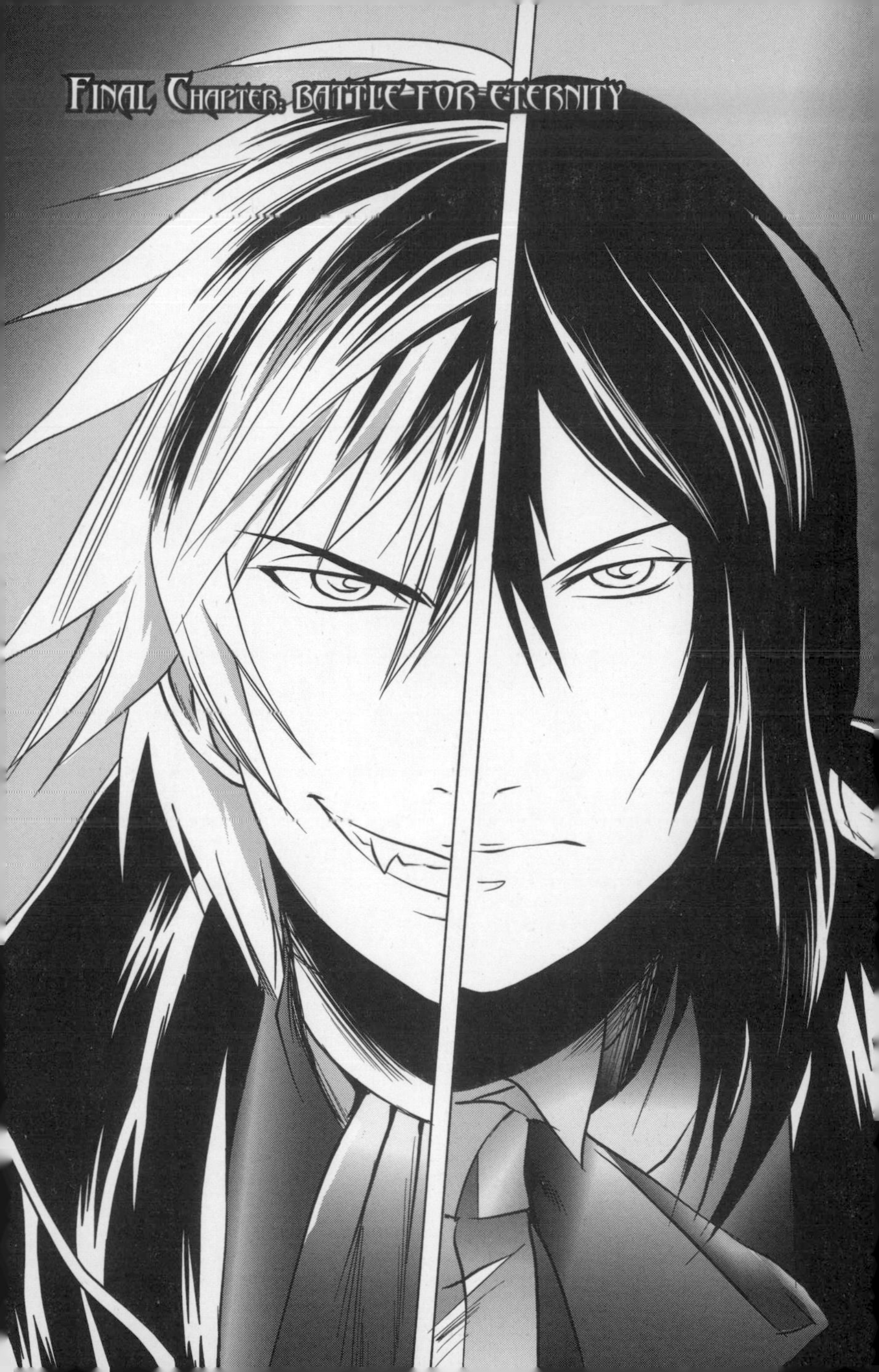
Final Chapter: Battle for Eternity

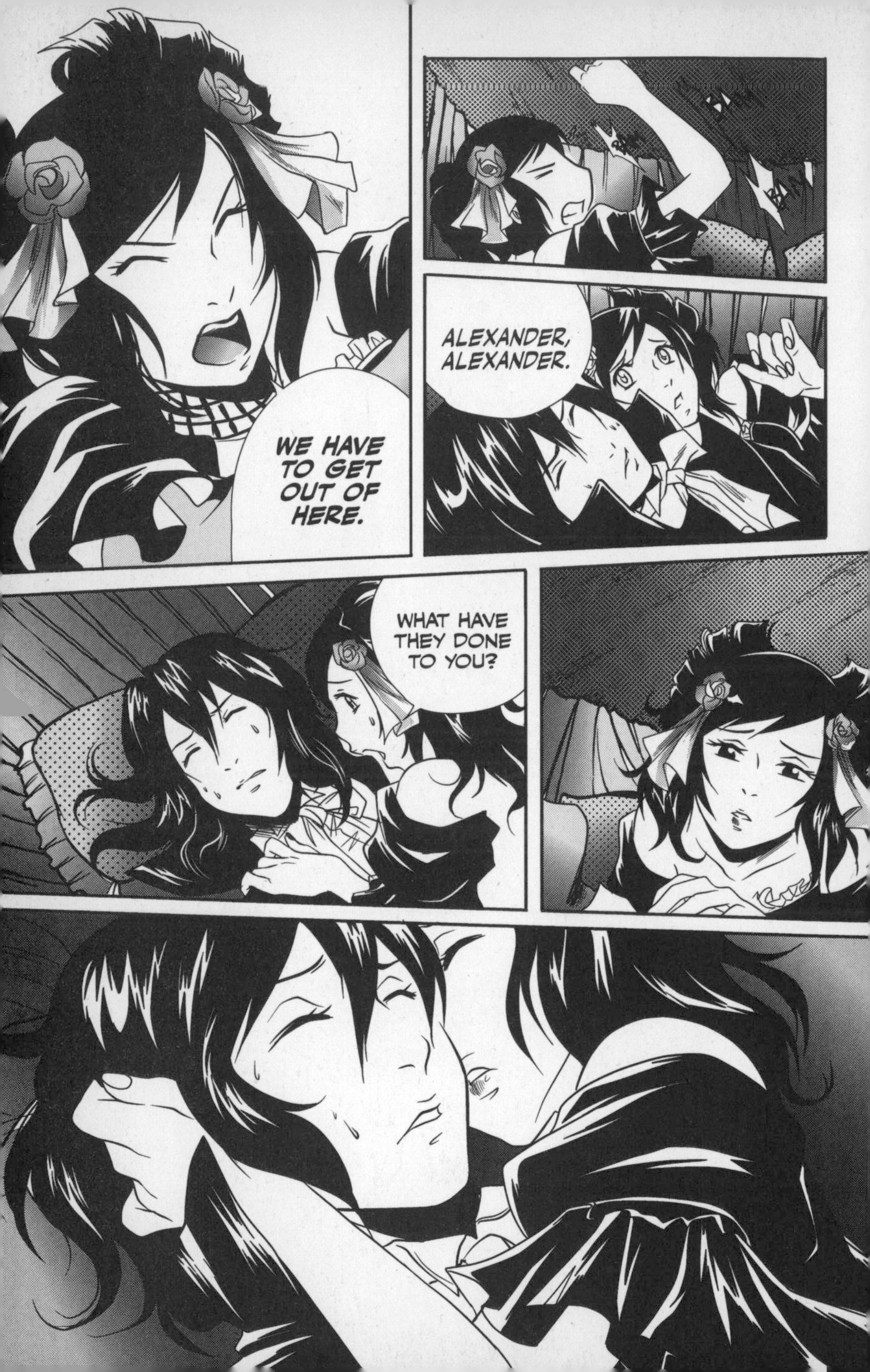
WE HAVE TO GET OUT OF HERE.
ALEXANDER, ALEXANDER.
WHAT HAVE THEY DONE TO YOU?

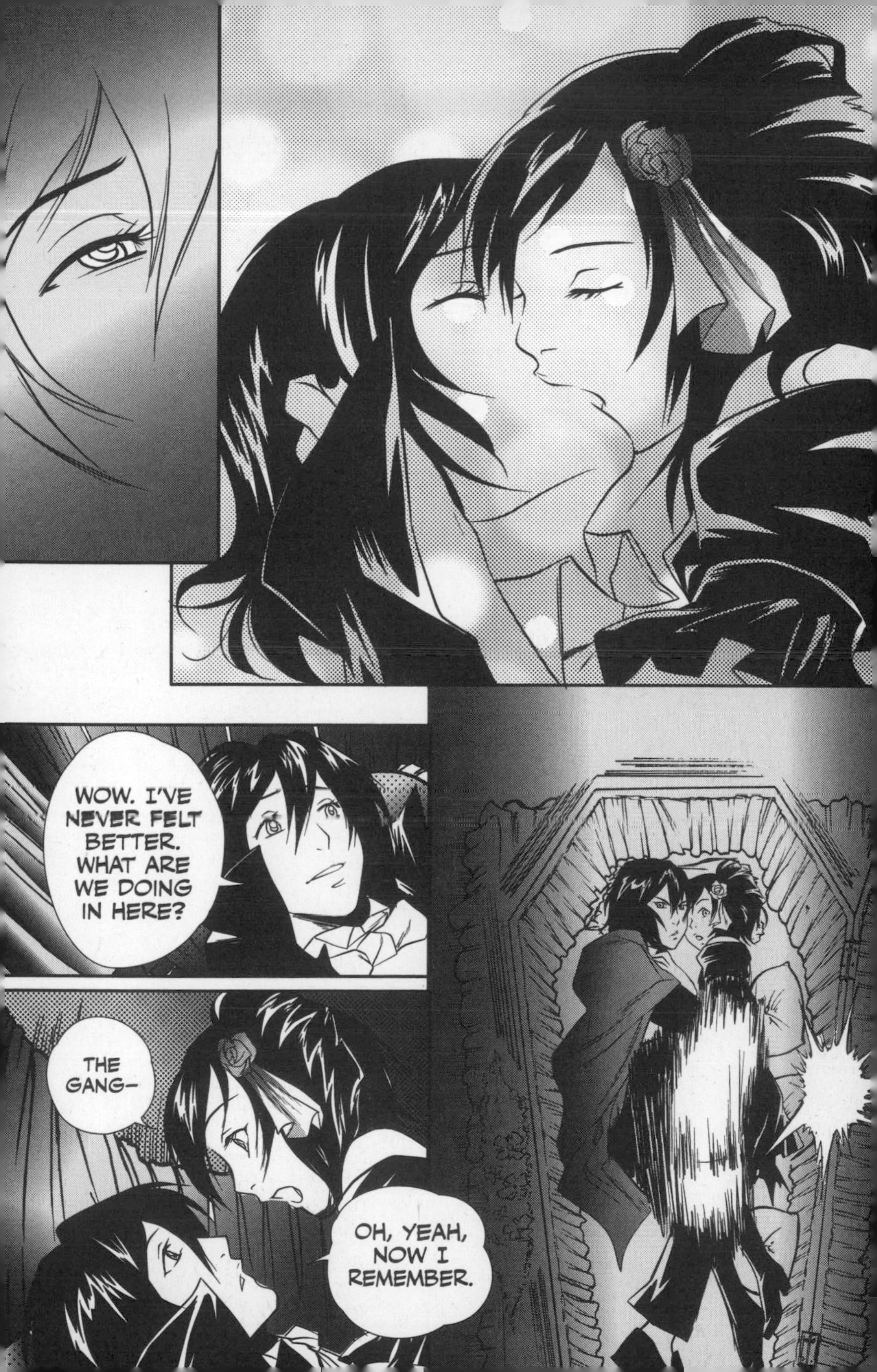
WOW. I'VE NEVER FELT BETTER. WHAT ARE WE DOING IN HERE?
THE GANG—
OH, YEAH, NOW I REMEMBER.

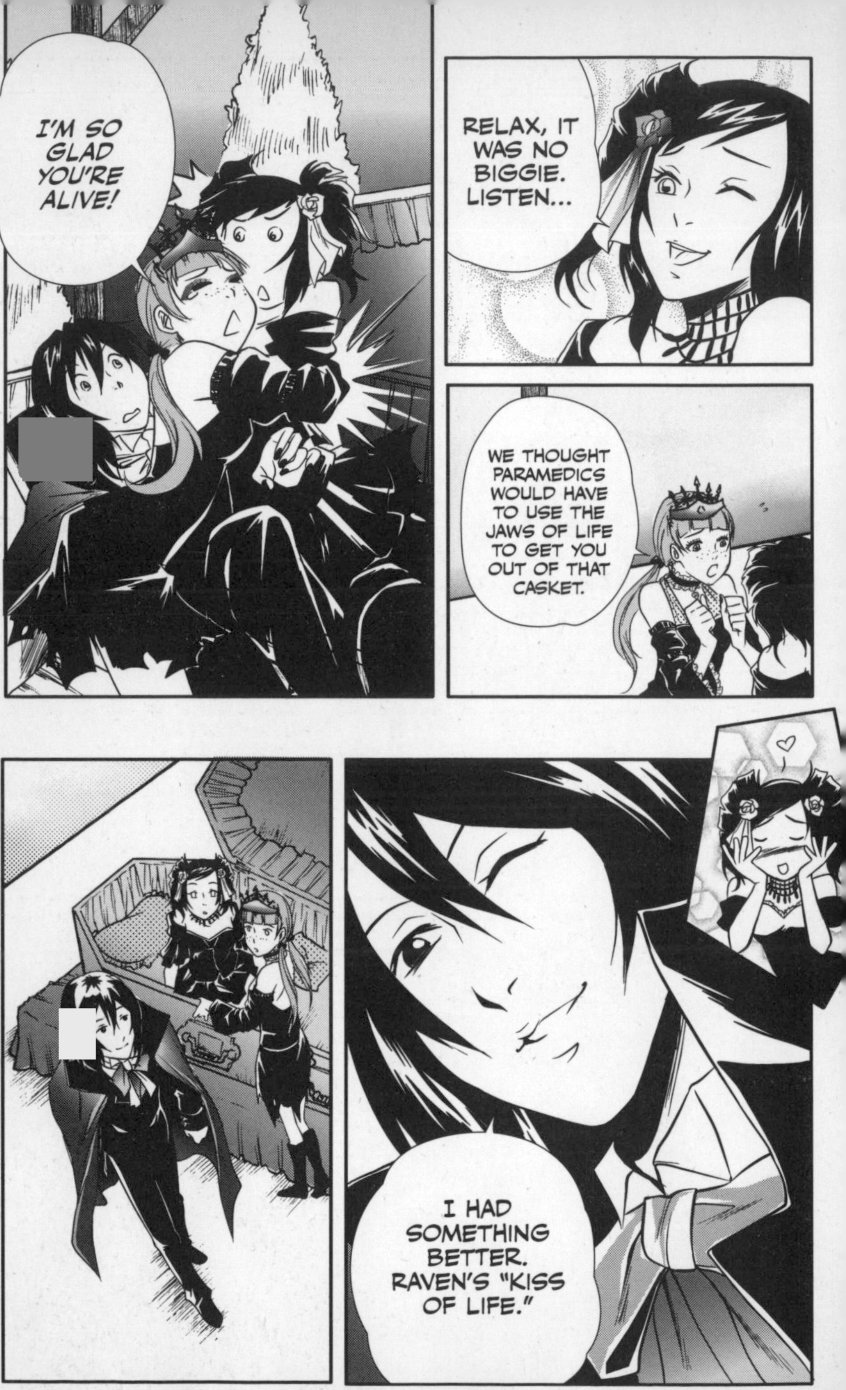
I'M SO GLAD YOU'RE ALIVE!
RELAX, IT WAS NO BIGGIE. LISTEN...
WE THOUGHT PARAMEDICS WOULD HAVE TO USE THE JAWS OF LIFE TO GET YOU OUT OF THAT CASKET.
I HAD SOMETHING BETTER. RAVEN'S "KISS OF LIFE."

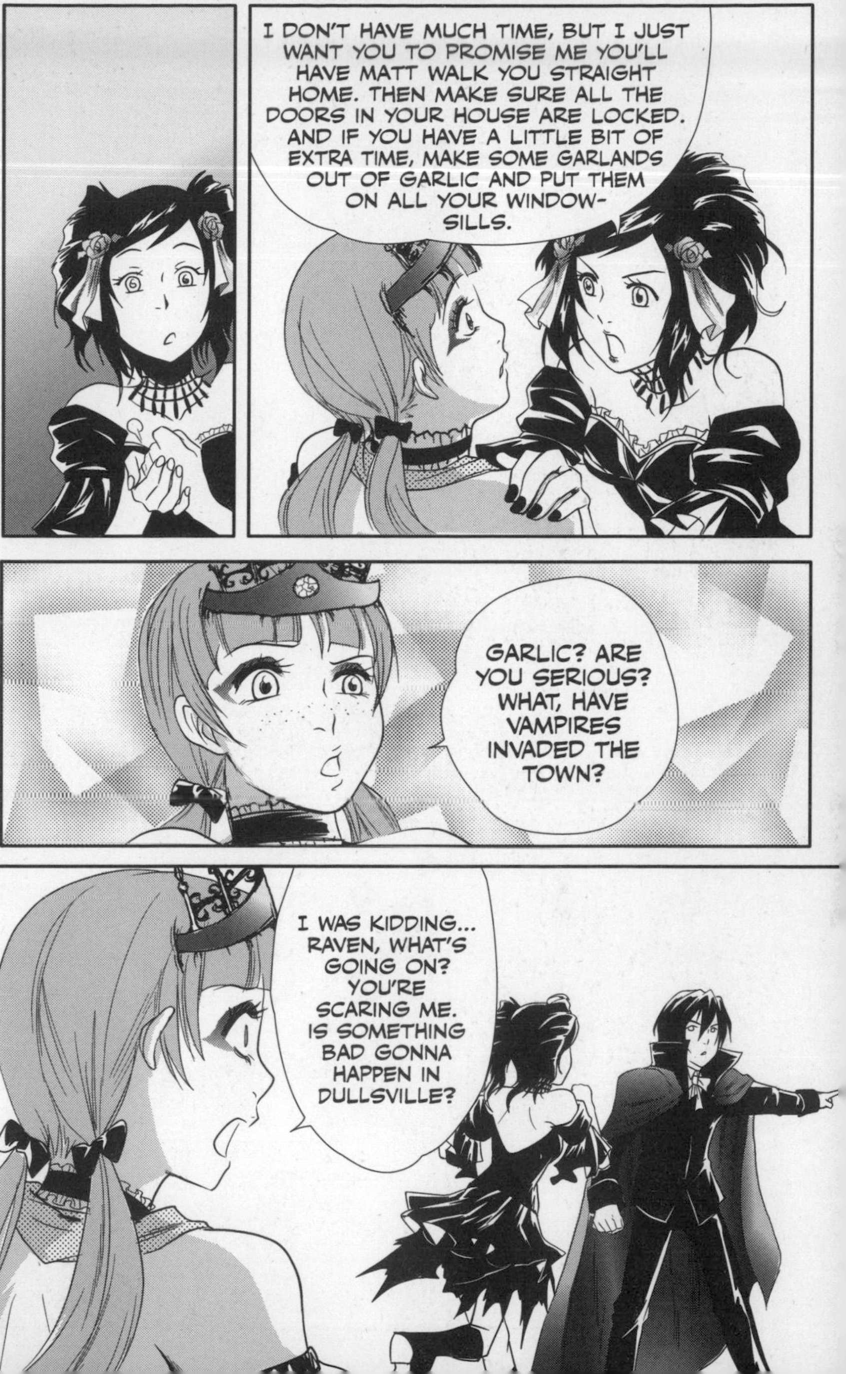
I DON'T HAVE MUCH TIME, BUT I JUST WANT YOU TO PROMISE ME YOU'LL HAVE MATT WALK YOU STRAIGHT HOME. THEN MAKE SURE ALL THE DOORS IN YOUR HOUSE ARE LOCKED. AND IF YOU HAVE A LITTLE BIT OF EXTRA TIME, MAKE SOME GARLANDS OUT OF GARLIC AND PUT THEM ON ALL YOUR WINDOW-SILLS.
GARLIC? ARE YOU SERIOUS? WHAT, HAVE VAMPIRES INVADED THE TOWN?
I WAS KIDDING... RAVEN, WHAT'S GOING ON? YOU'RE SCARING ME. IS SOMETHING BAD GONNA HAPPEN IN DULLSVILLE?

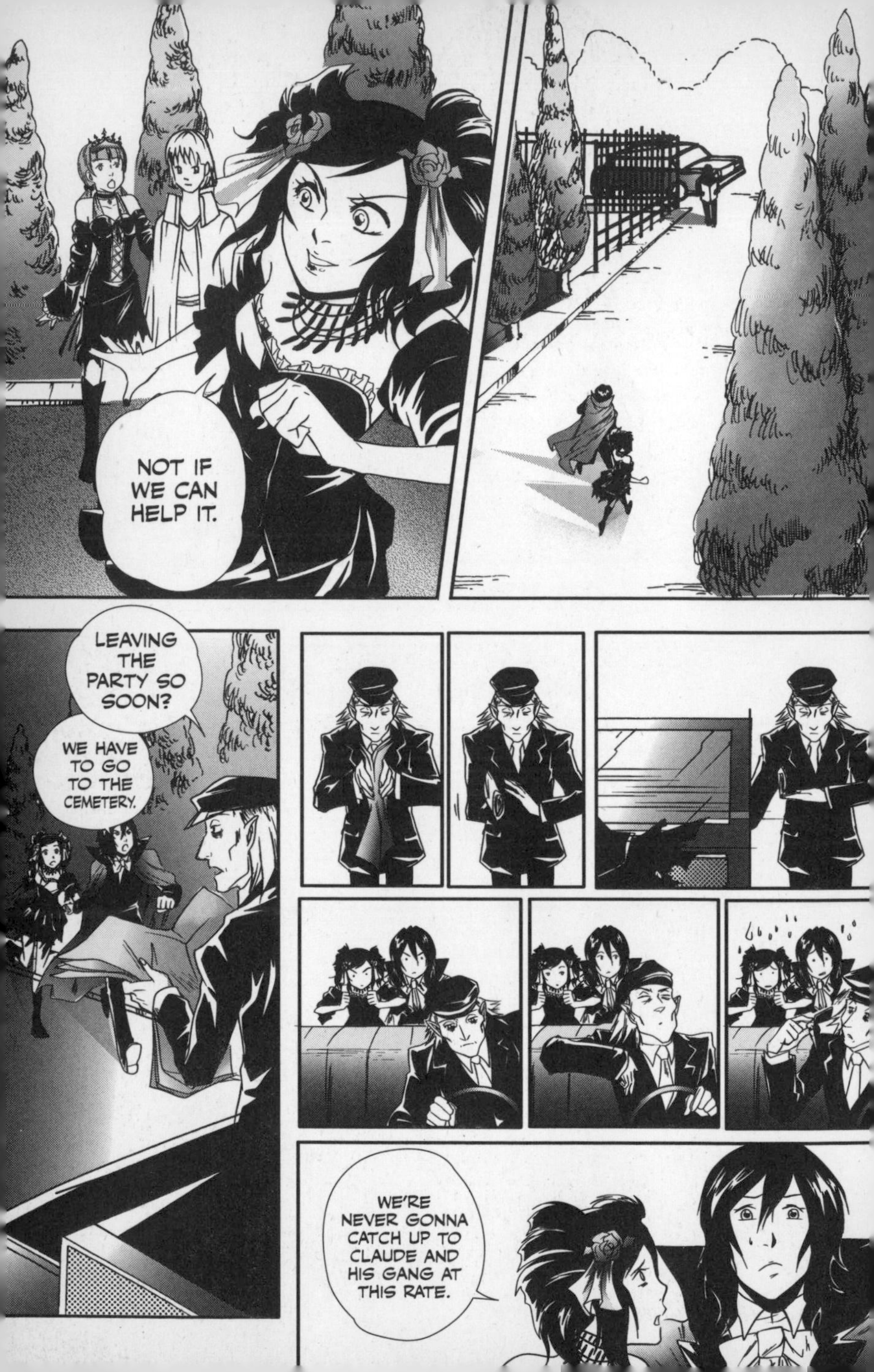
NOT IF WE CAN HELP IT.
LEAVING THE PARTY SO SOON?
WE HAVE TO GO TO THE CEMETERY.
WE'RE NEVER GONNA CATCH UP TO CLAUDE AND HIS GANG AT THIS RATE.

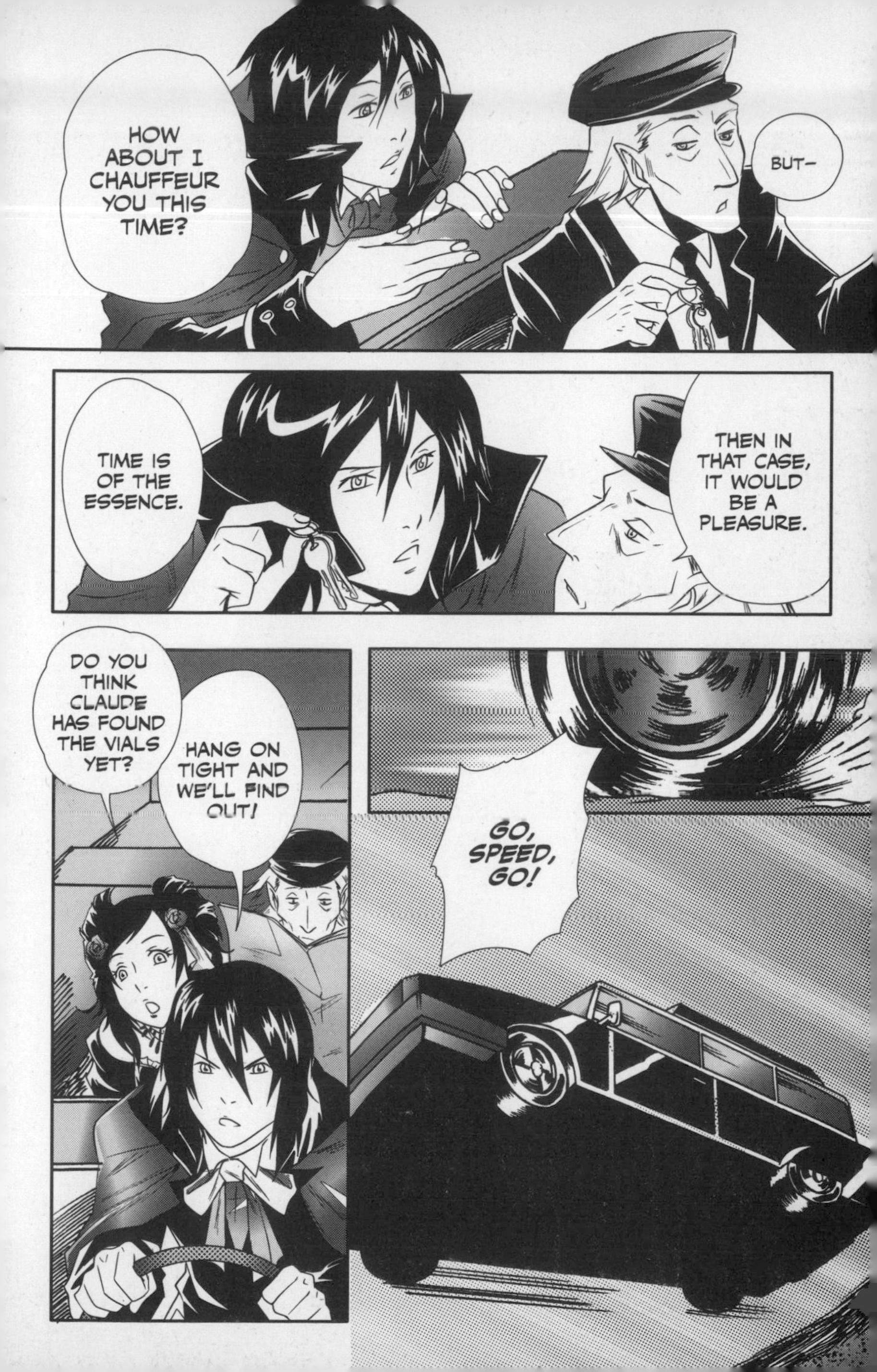
HOW ABOUT I CHAUFFEUR YOU THIS TIME?
BUT–
TIME IS OF THE ESSENCE.
THEN IN THAT CASE, IT WOULD BE A PLEASURE.
DO YOU THINK CLAUDE HAS FOUND THE VIALS YET?
HANG ON TIGHT AND WE'LL FIND OUT!
GO, SPEED, GO!

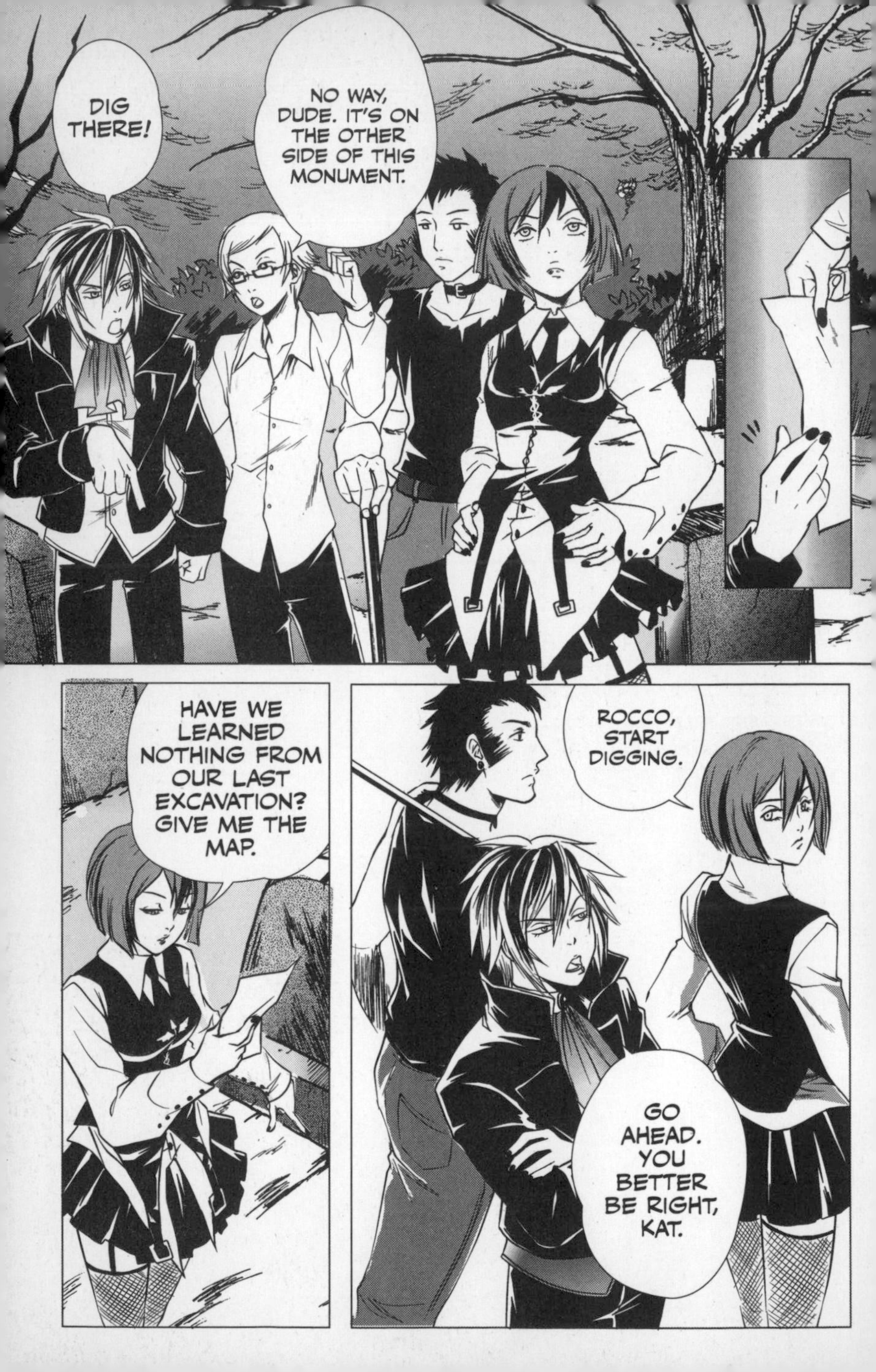
DIG THERE!
NO WAY, DUDE. IT'S ON THE OTHER SIDE OF THIS MONUMENT.
HAVE WE LEARNED NOTHING FROM OUR LAST EXCAVATION? GIVE ME THE MAP.
ROCCO, START DIGGING.
GO AHEAD. YOU BETTER BE RIGHT, KAT.

NEED SOME HELP?

NO, I'M GOOD. LET'S DO IT.

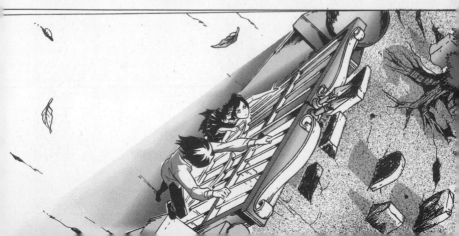

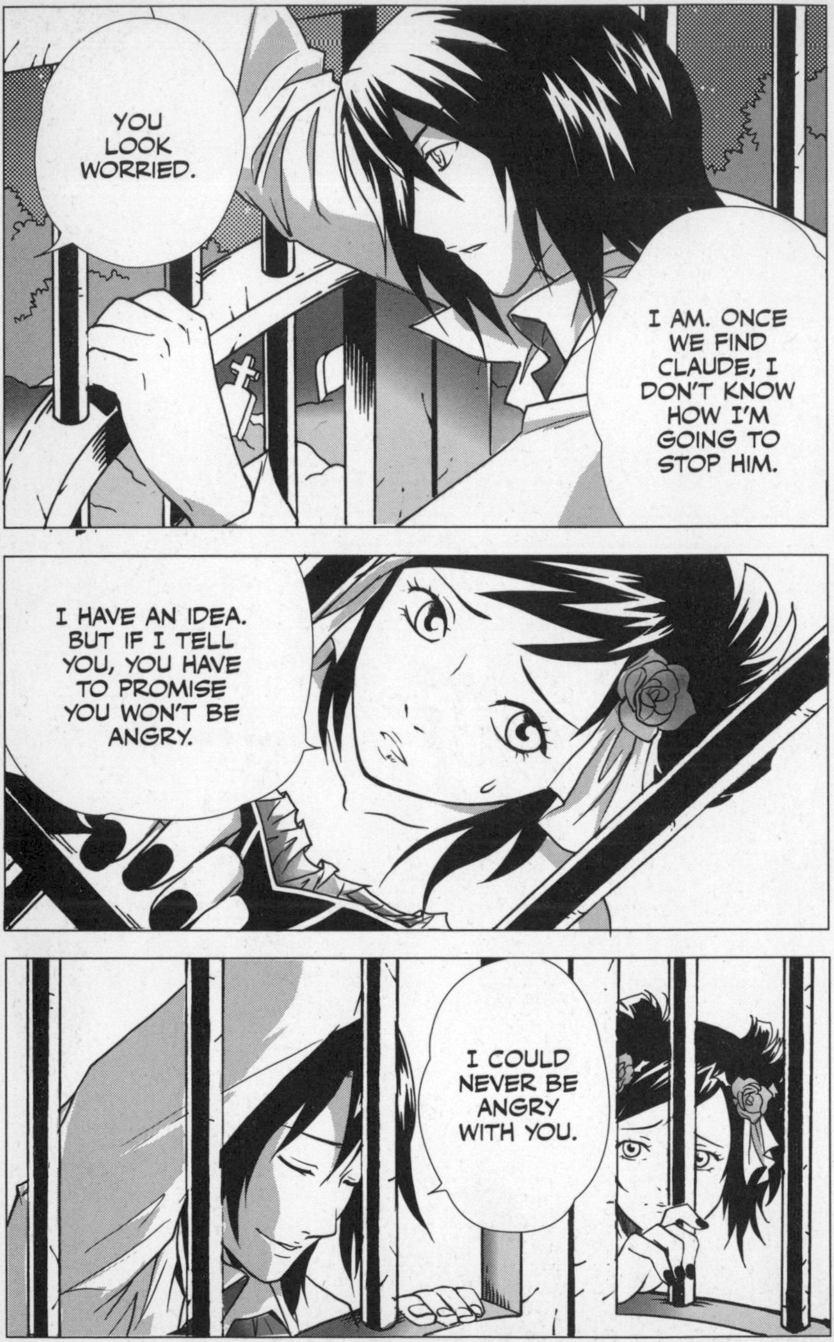
YOU LOOK WORRIED.
I AM. ONCE WE FIND CLAUDE, I DON'T KNOW HOW I'M GOING TO STOP HIM.
I HAVE AN IDEA. BUT IF I TELL YOU, YOU HAVE TO PROMISE YOU WON'T BE ANGRY.
I COULD NEVER BE ANGRY WITH YOU.

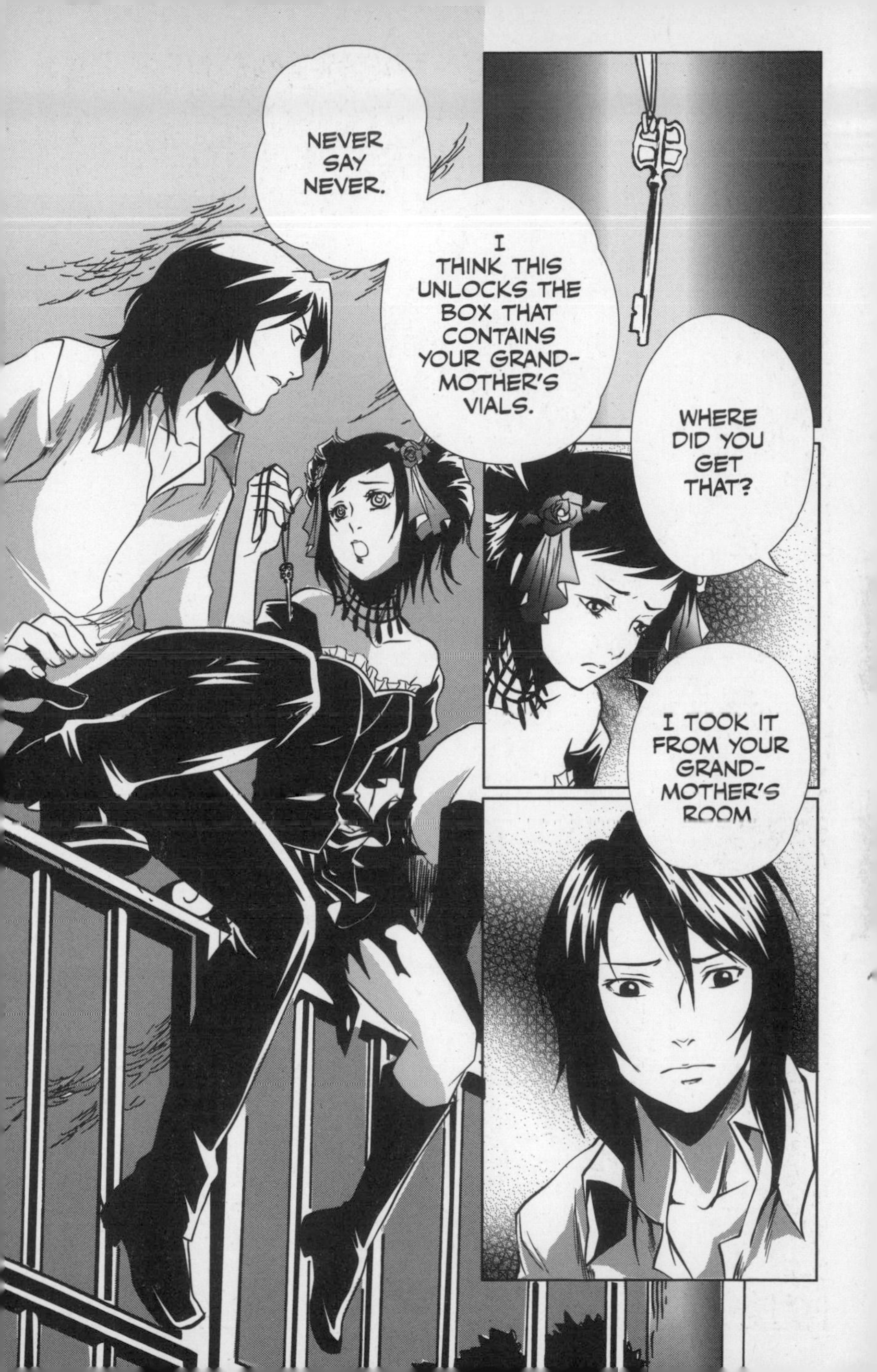
NEVER SAY NEVER.
I THINK THIS UNLOCKS THE BOX THAT CONTAINS YOUR GRAND-MOTHER'S VIALS.
WHERE DID YOU GET THAT?
I TOOK IT FROM YOUR GRAND-MOTHER'S ROOM.

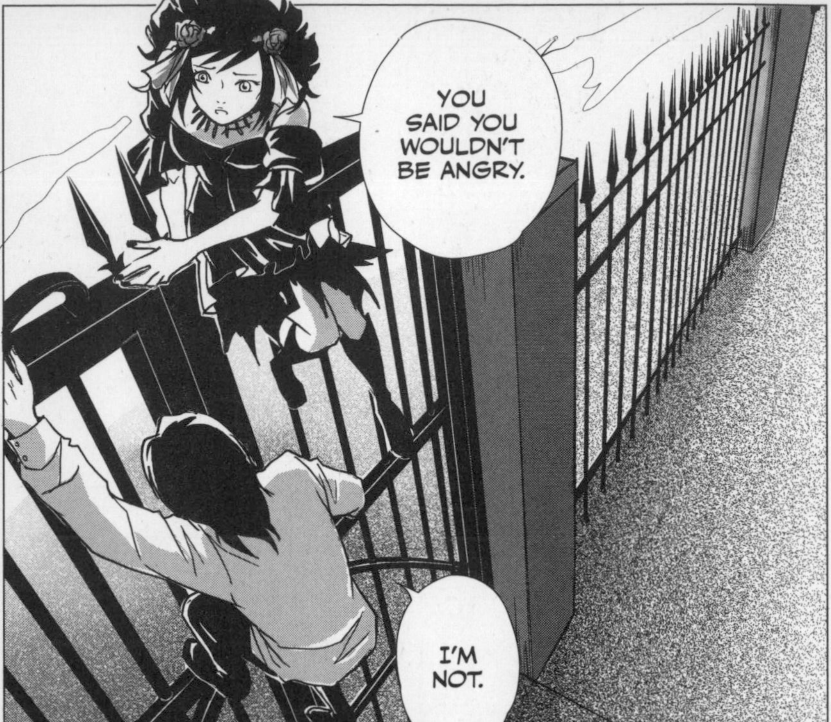
YOU SAID YOU WOULDN'T BE ANGRY.
I'M NOT.
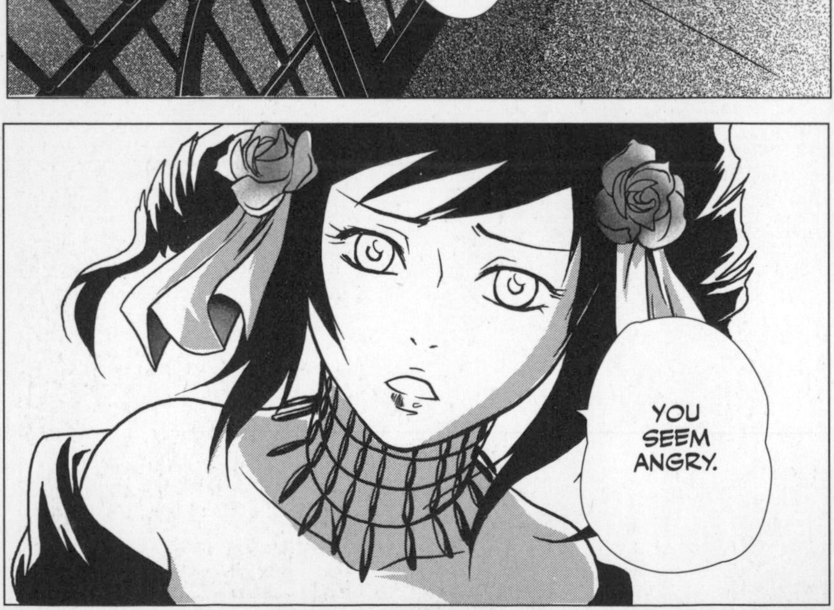
YOU SEEM ANGRY.

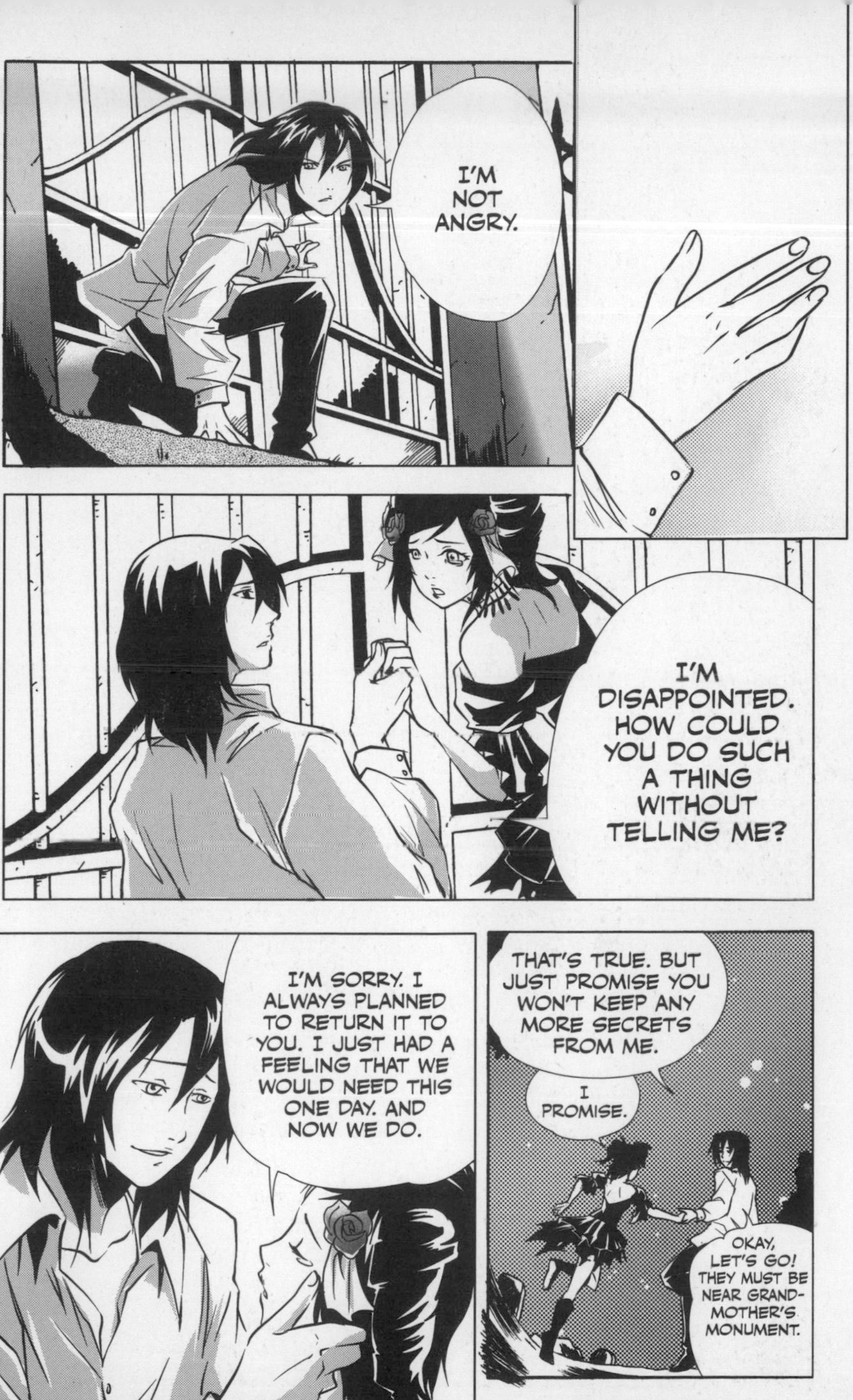
I'M NOT ANGRY.
I'M DISAPPOINTED. HOW COULD YOU DO SUCH A THING WITHOUT TELLING ME?
I'M SORRY. I ALWAYS PLANNED TO RETURN IT TO YOU. I JUST HAD A FEELING THAT WE WOULD NEED THIS ONE DAY. AND NOW WE DO.
THAT'S TRUE. BUT JUST PROMISE YOU WON'T KEEP ANY MORE SECRETS FROM ME.
I PROMISE.
OKAY, LET'S GO! THEY MUST BE NEAR GRAND-MOTHER'S MONUMENT.

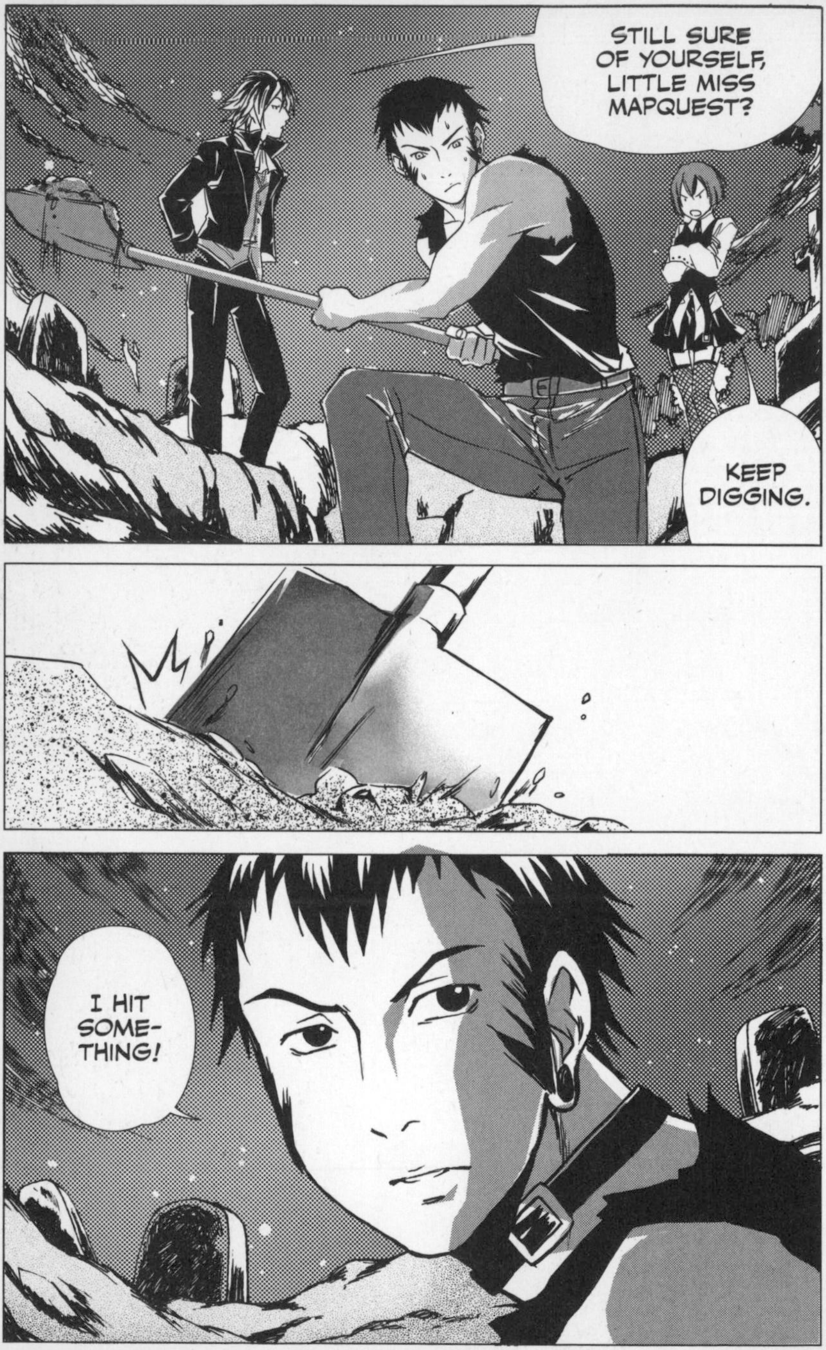
STILL SURE OF YOURSELF, LITTLE MISS MAPQUEST?
KEEP DIGGING.
I HIT SOME-THING!

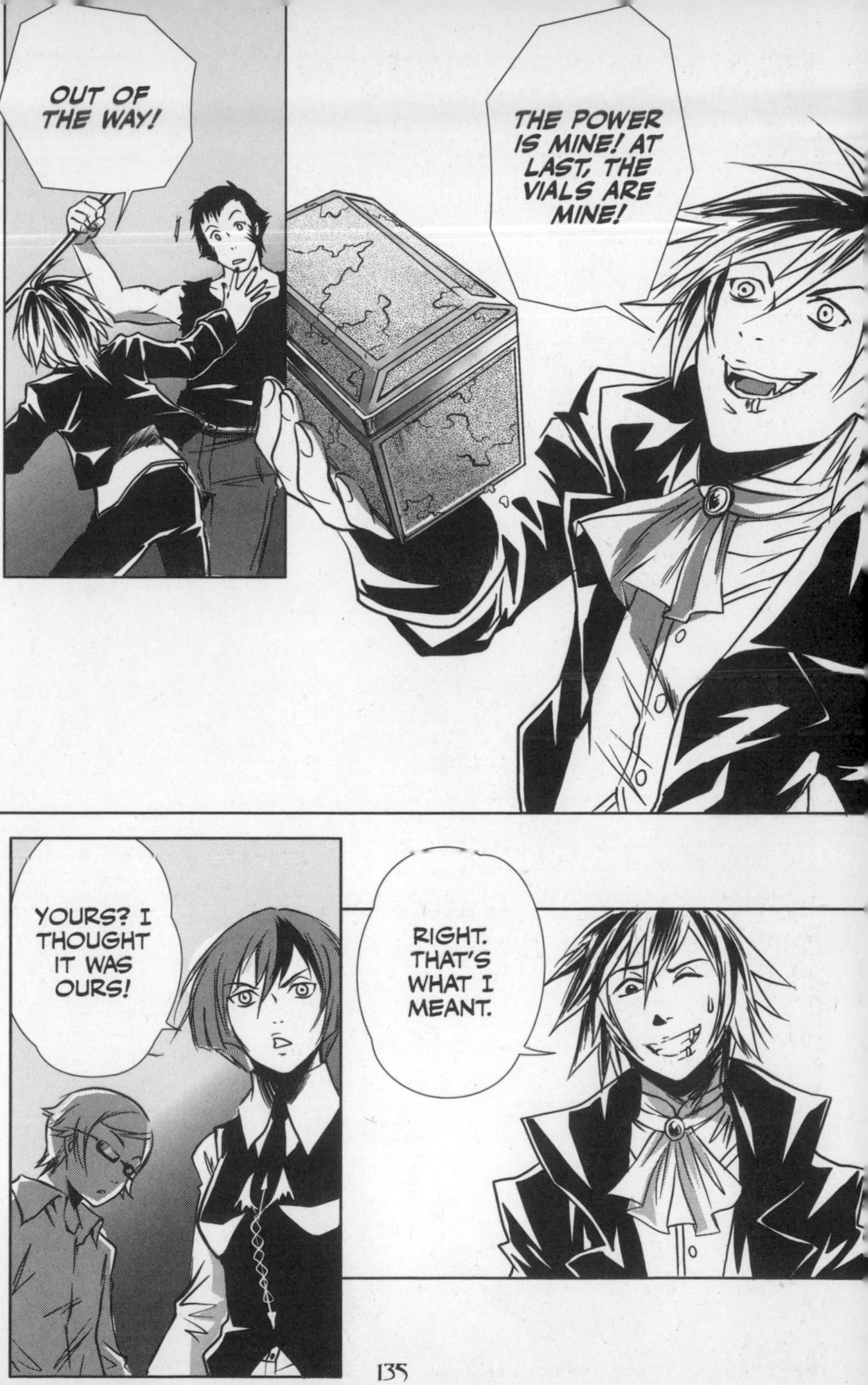
OUT OF THE WAY!
THE POWER IS MINE! AT LAST, THE VIALS ARE MINE!
YOURS? I THOUGHT IT WAS OURS!
RIGHT. THAT'S WHAT I MEANT.

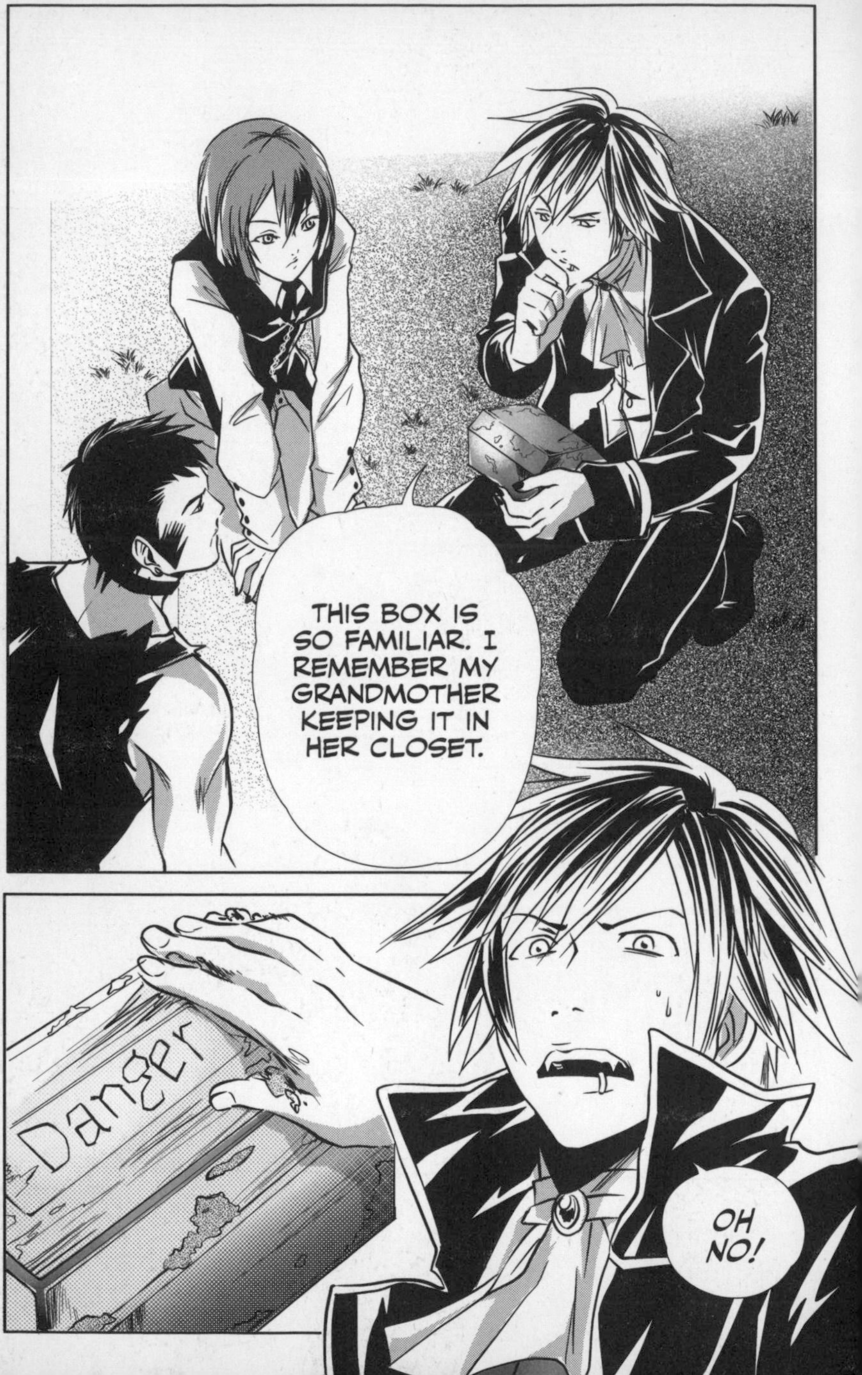
THIS BOX IS SO FAMILIAR. I REMEMBER MY GRANDMOTHER KEEPING IT IN HER CLOSET.
Danger
OH NO!

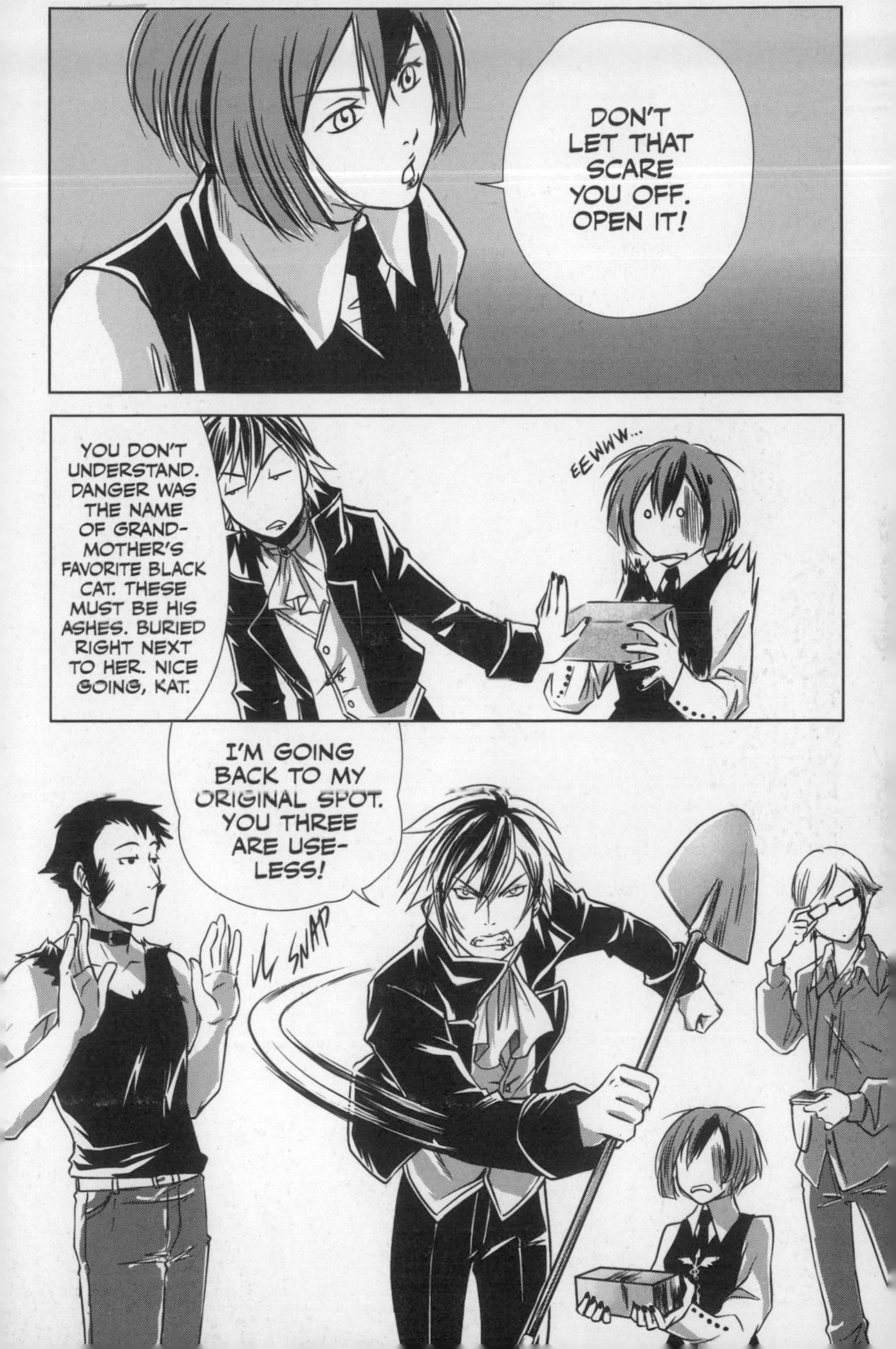
DON'T LET THAT SCARE YOU OFF. OPEN IT!
YOU DON'T UNDERSTAND. DANGER WAS THE NAME OF GRAND-MOTHER'S FAVORITE BLACK CAT. THESE MUST BE HIS ASHES. BURIED RIGHT NEXT TO HER. NICE GOING, KAT.
EEWWW...
I'M GOING BACK TO MY ORIGINAL SPOT. YOU THREE ARE USE-LESS!
SNAP

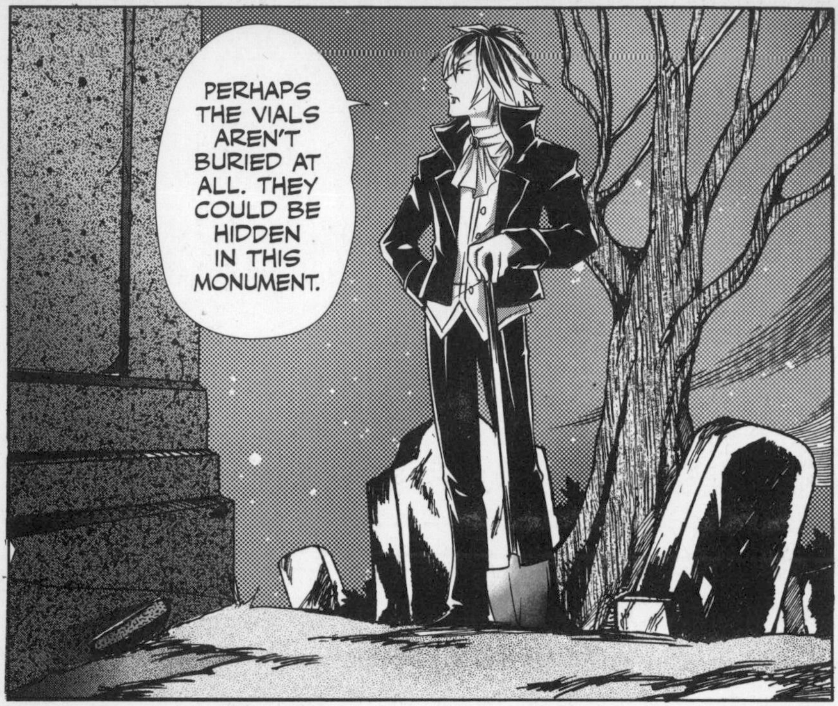
PERHAPS THE VIALS AREN'T BURIED AT ALL. THEY COULD BE HIDDEN IN THIS MONUMENT.
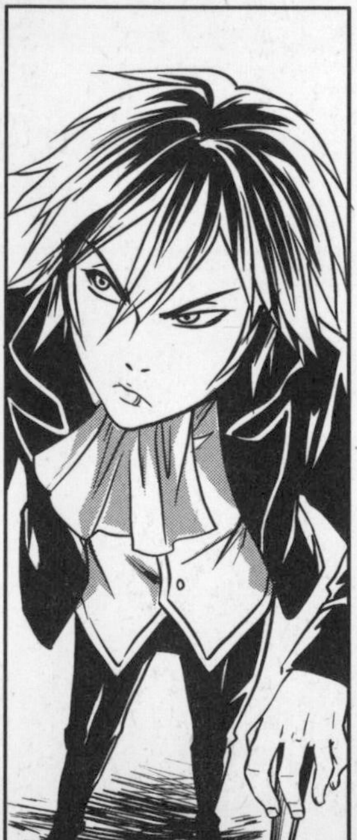
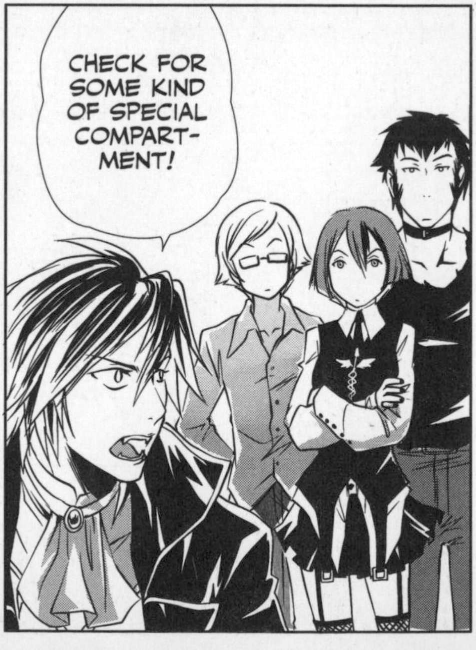
CHECK FOR SOME KIND OF SPECIAL COMPART-MENT!

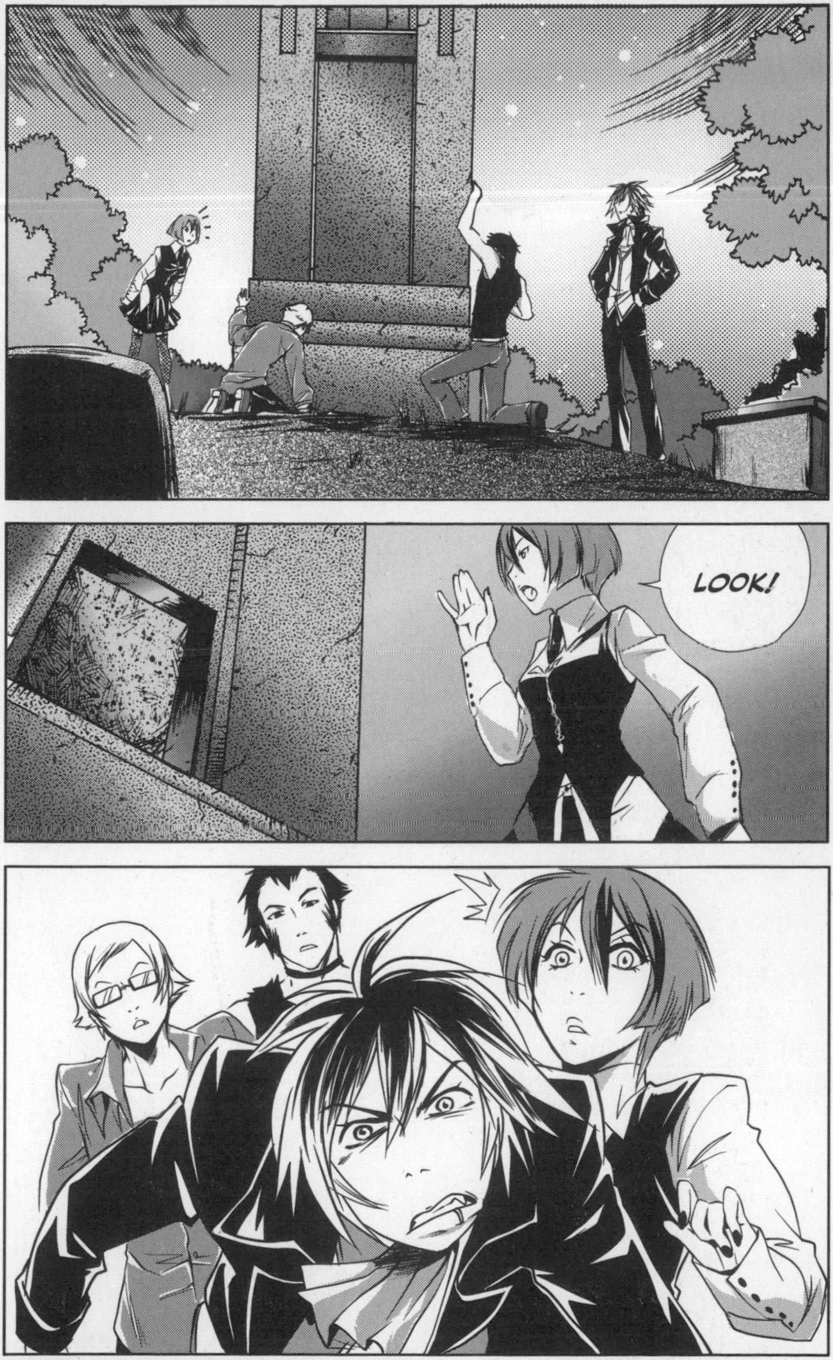
LOOK!

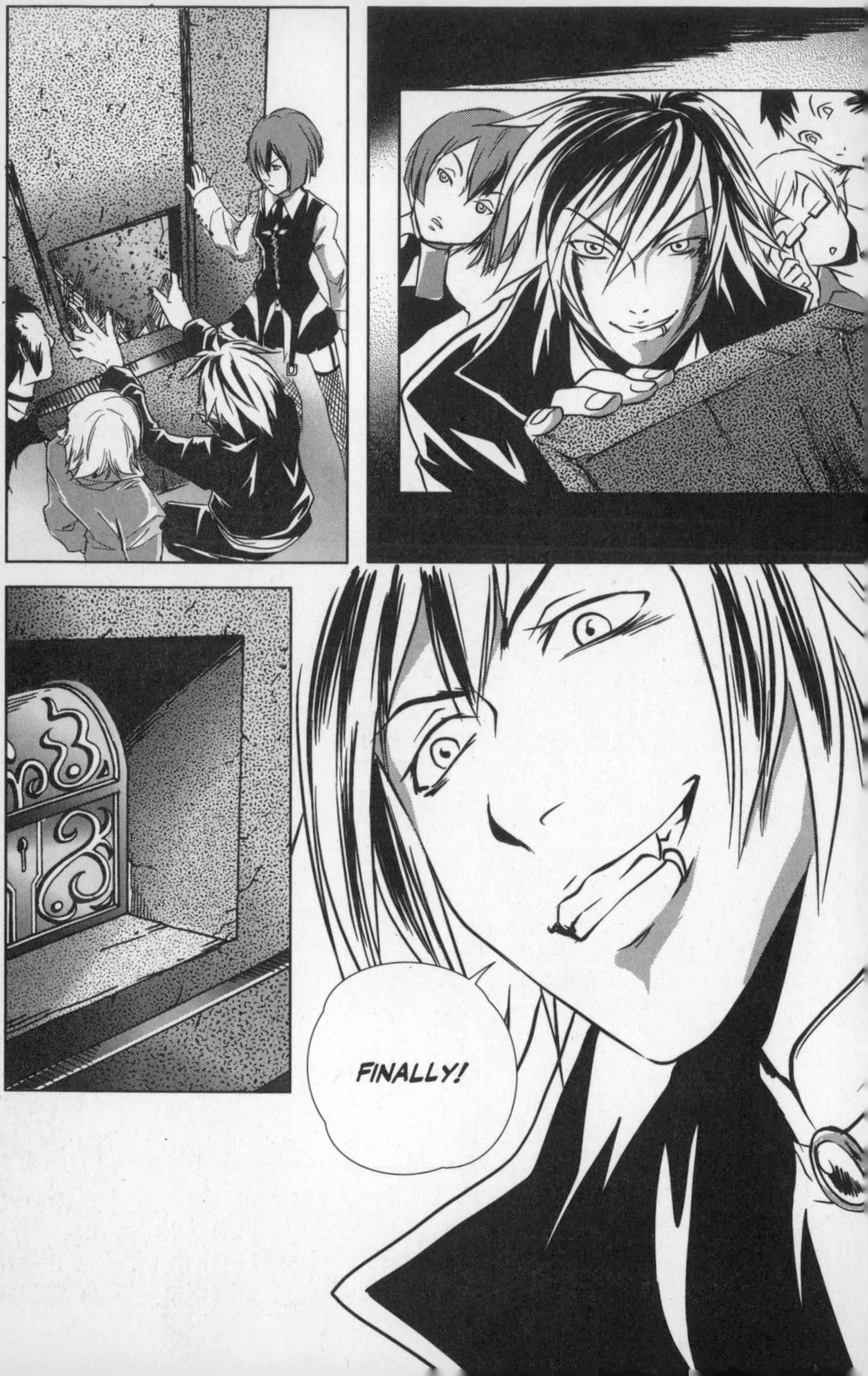
FINALLY!

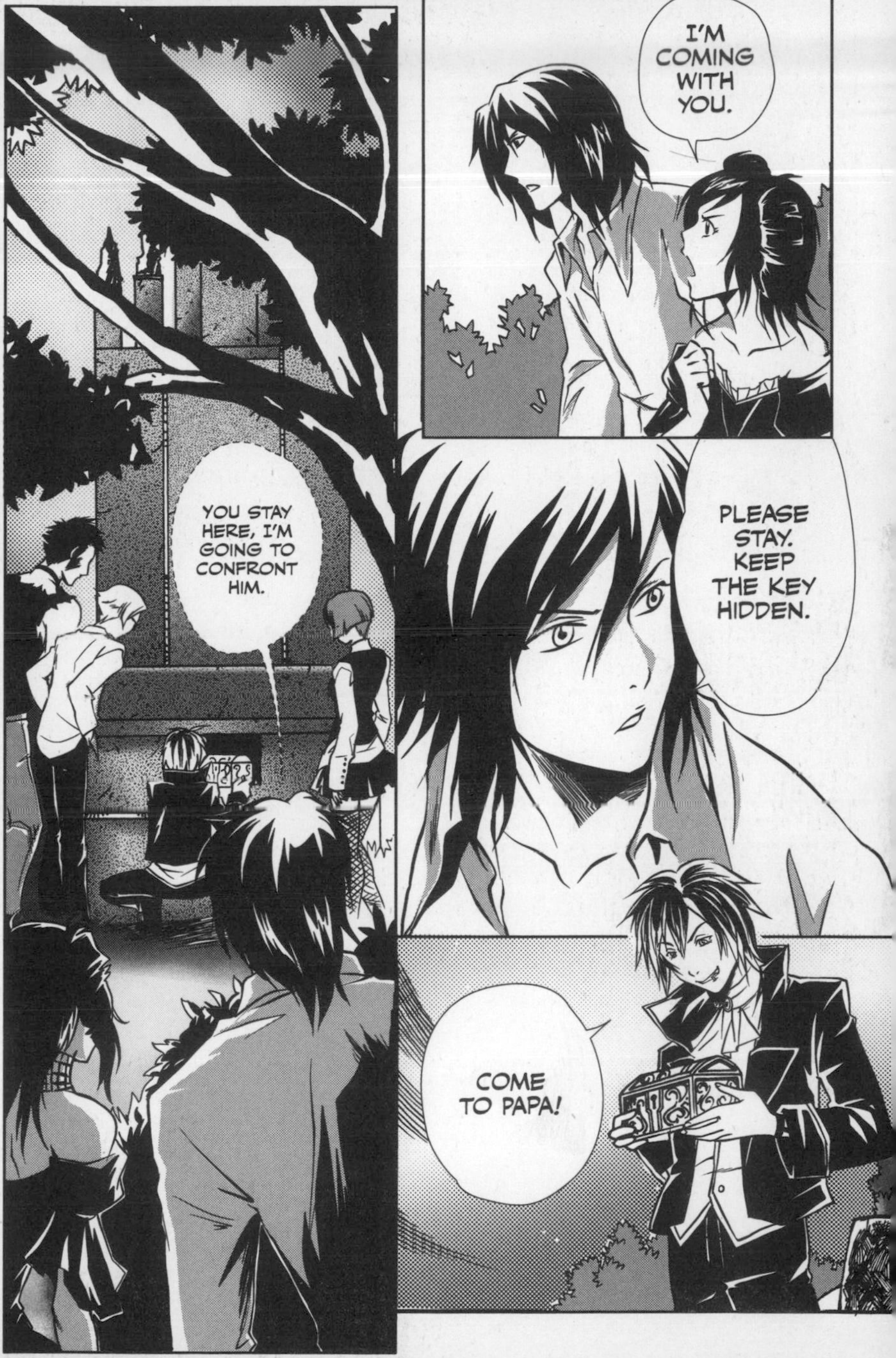
YOU STAY HERE, I'M GOING TO CONFRONT HIM.
I'M COMING WITH YOU.
PLEASE STAY. KEEP THE KEY HIDDEN.
COME TO PAPA!

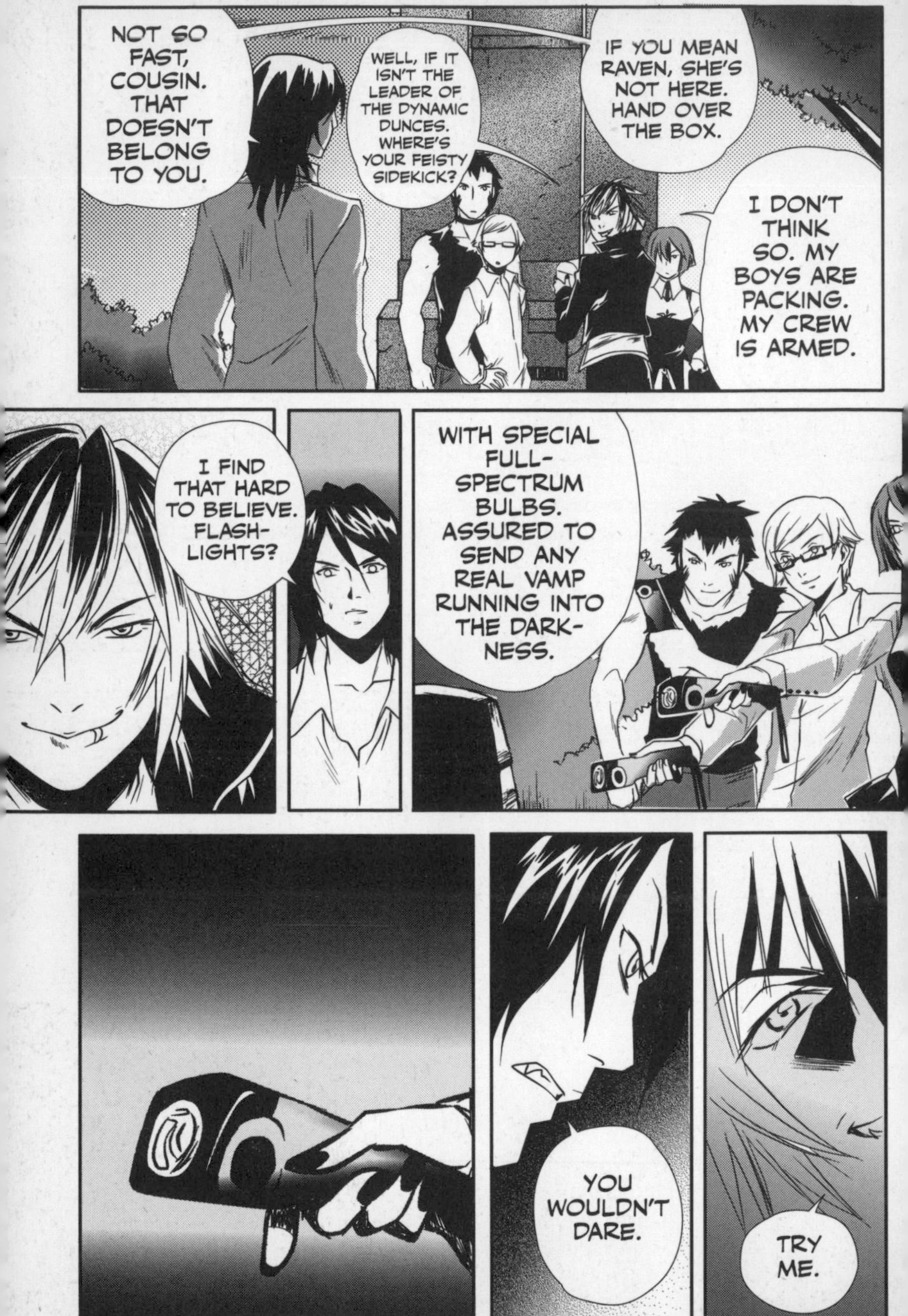
NOT SO FAST, COUSIN. THAT DOESN'T BELONG TO YOU.
WELL, IF IT ISN'T THE LEADER OF THE DYNAMIC DUNCES. WHERE'S YOUR FEISTY SIDEKICK?
IF YOU MEAN RAVEN, SHE'S NOT HERE. HAND OVER THE BOX.
I DON'T THINK SO. MY BOYS ARE PACKING. MY CREW IS ARMED.
I FIND THAT HARD TO BELIEVE. FLASH-LIGHTS?
WITH SPECIAL FULL-SPECTRUM BULBS. ASSURED TO SEND ANY REAL VAMP RUNNING INTO THE DARK-NESS.
YOU WOULDN'T DARE.
TRY ME.

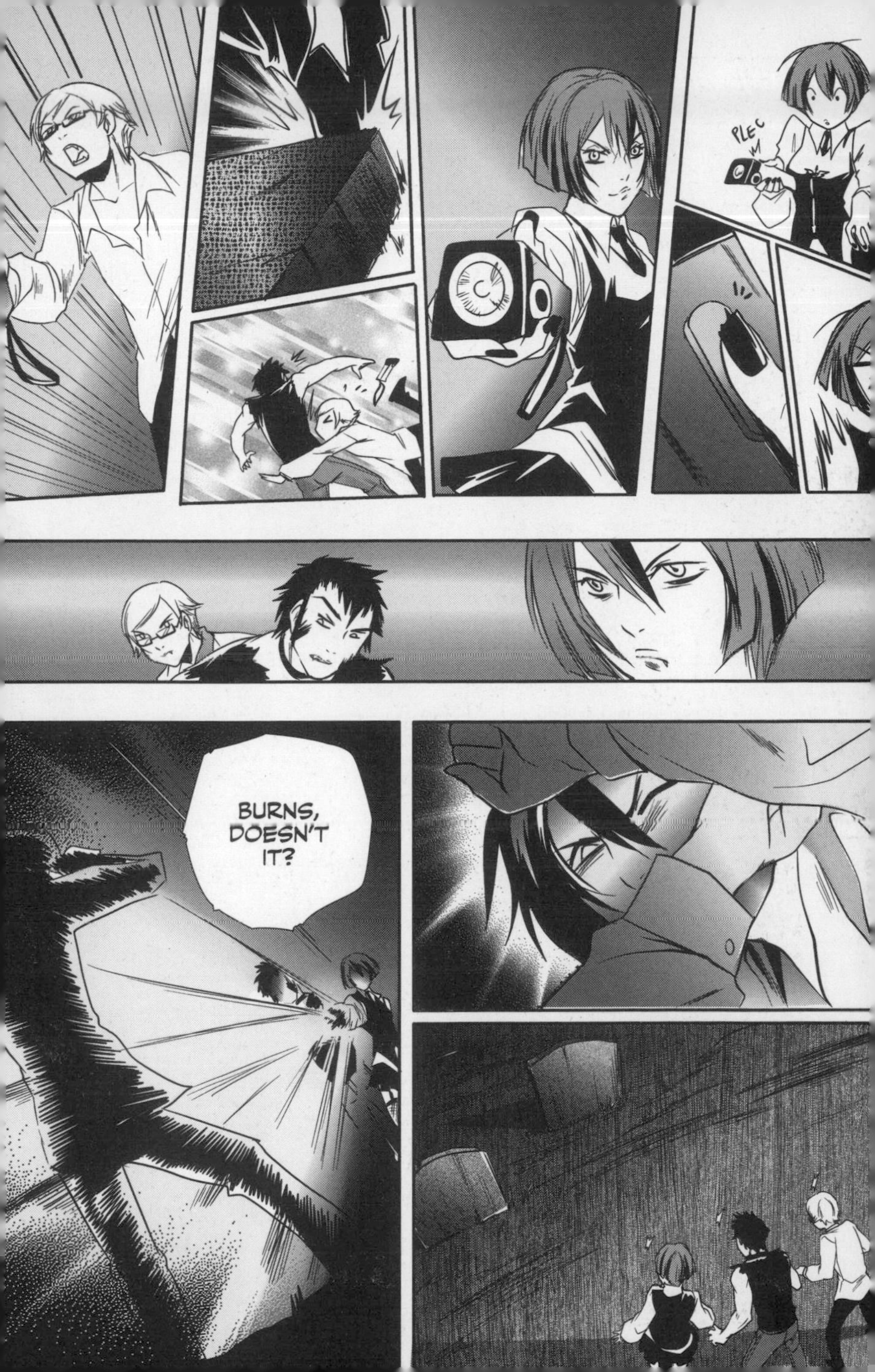
PLEC
BURNS, DOESN'T IT?

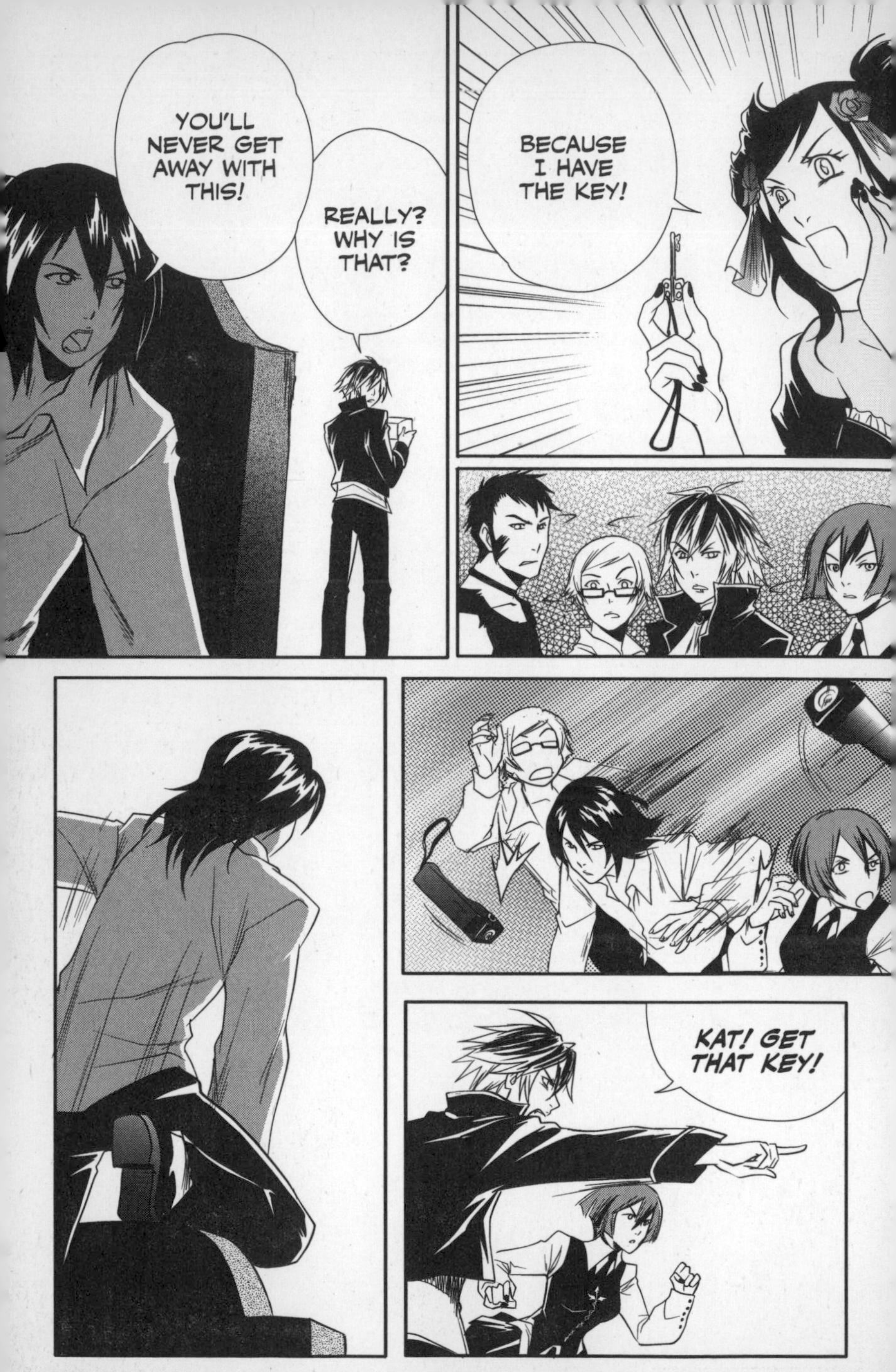
YOU'LL NEVER GET AWAY WITH THIS!
REALLY? WHY IS THAT?
BECAUSE I HAVE THE KEY!
KAT! GET THAT KEY!

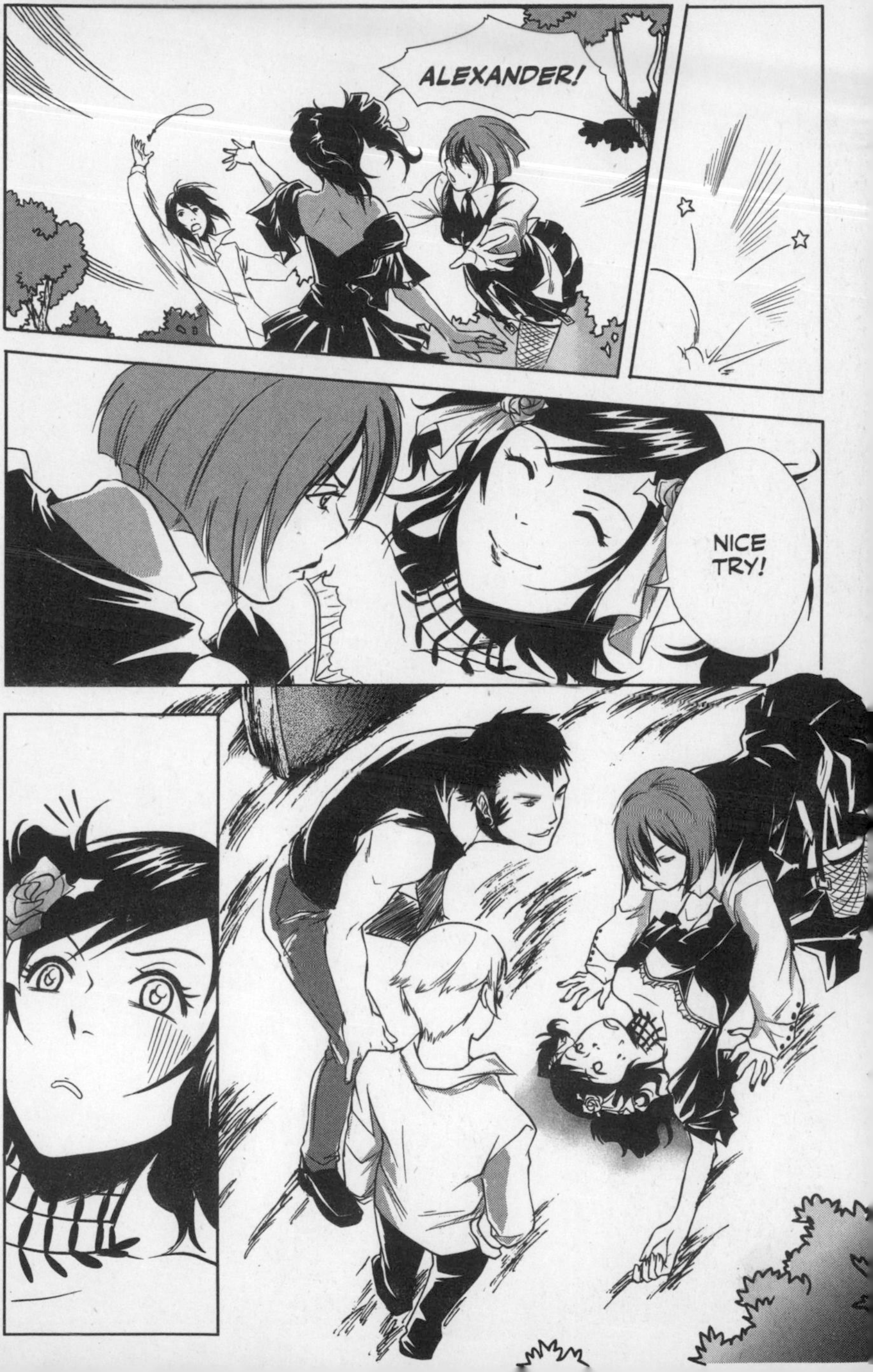
ALEXANDER!
NICE TRY!

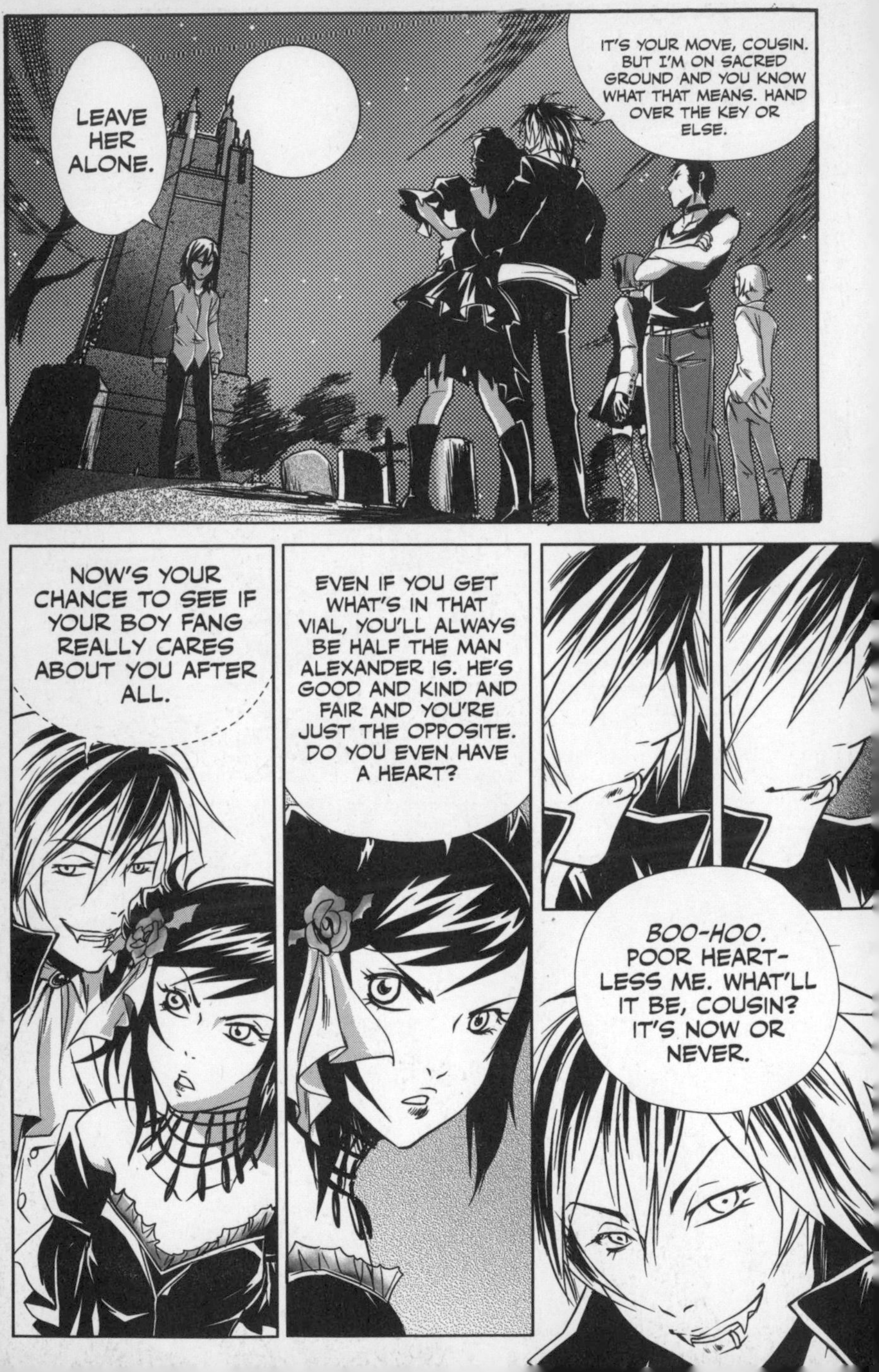
LEAVE HER ALONE.
IT'S YOUR MOVE, COUSIN. BUT I'M ON SACRED GROUND AND YOU KNOW WHAT THAT MEANS. HAND OVER THE KEY OR ELSE.
NOW'S YOUR CHANCE TO SEE IF YOUR BOY FANG REALLY CARES ABOUT YOU AFTER ALL.
EVEN IF YOU GET WHAT'S IN THAT VIAL, YOU'LL ALWAYS BE HALF THE MAN ALEXANDER IS. HE'S GOOD AND KIND AND FAIR AND YOU'RE JUST THE OPPOSITE. DO YOU EVEN HAVE A HEART?
BOO-HOO. POOR HEART-LESS ME. WHAT'LL IT BE, COUSIN? IT'S NOW OR NEVER.

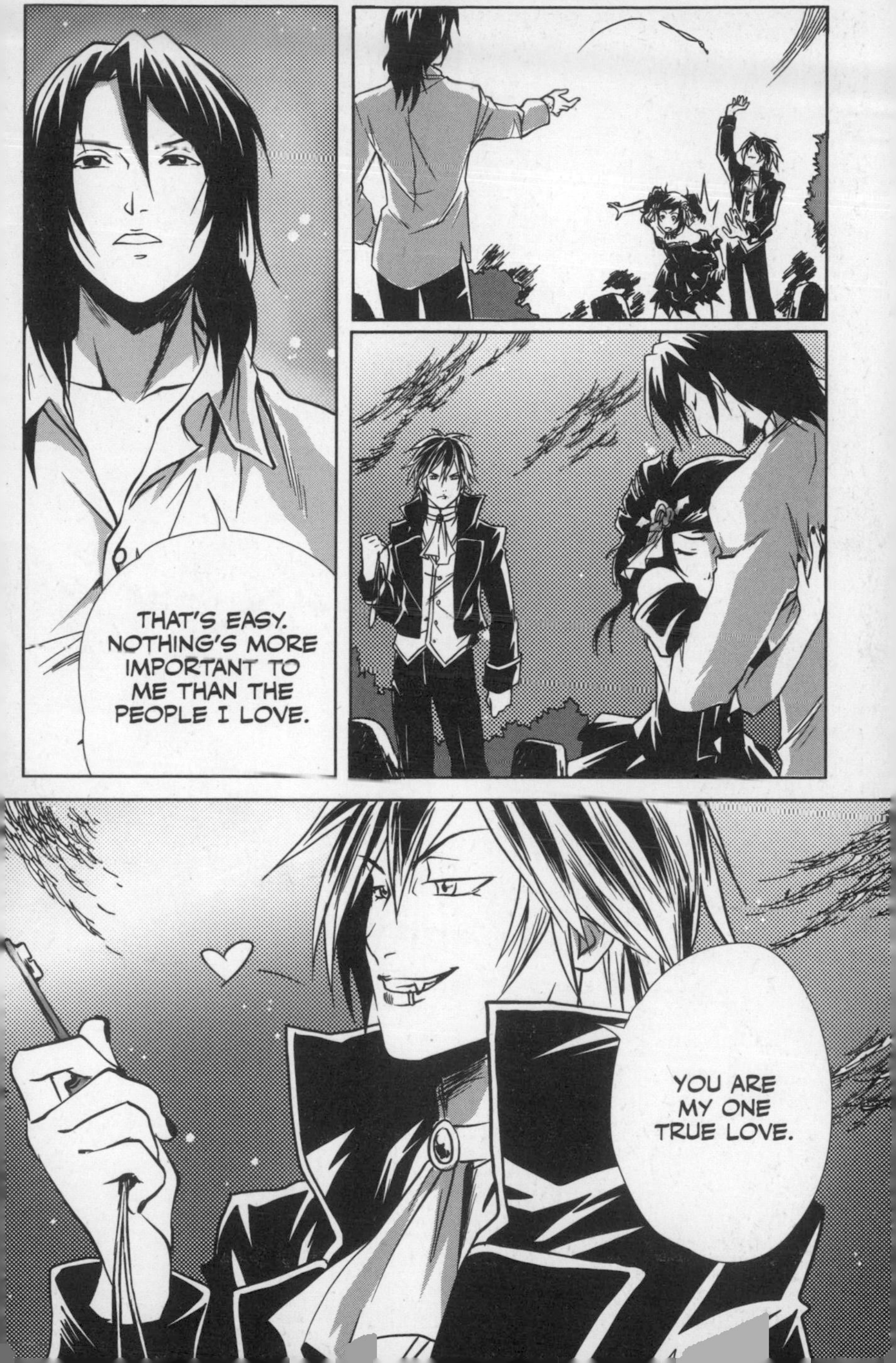
THAT'S EASY. NOTHING'S MORE IMPORTANT TO ME THAN THE PEOPLE I LOVE.
YOU ARE MY ONE TRUE LOVE.

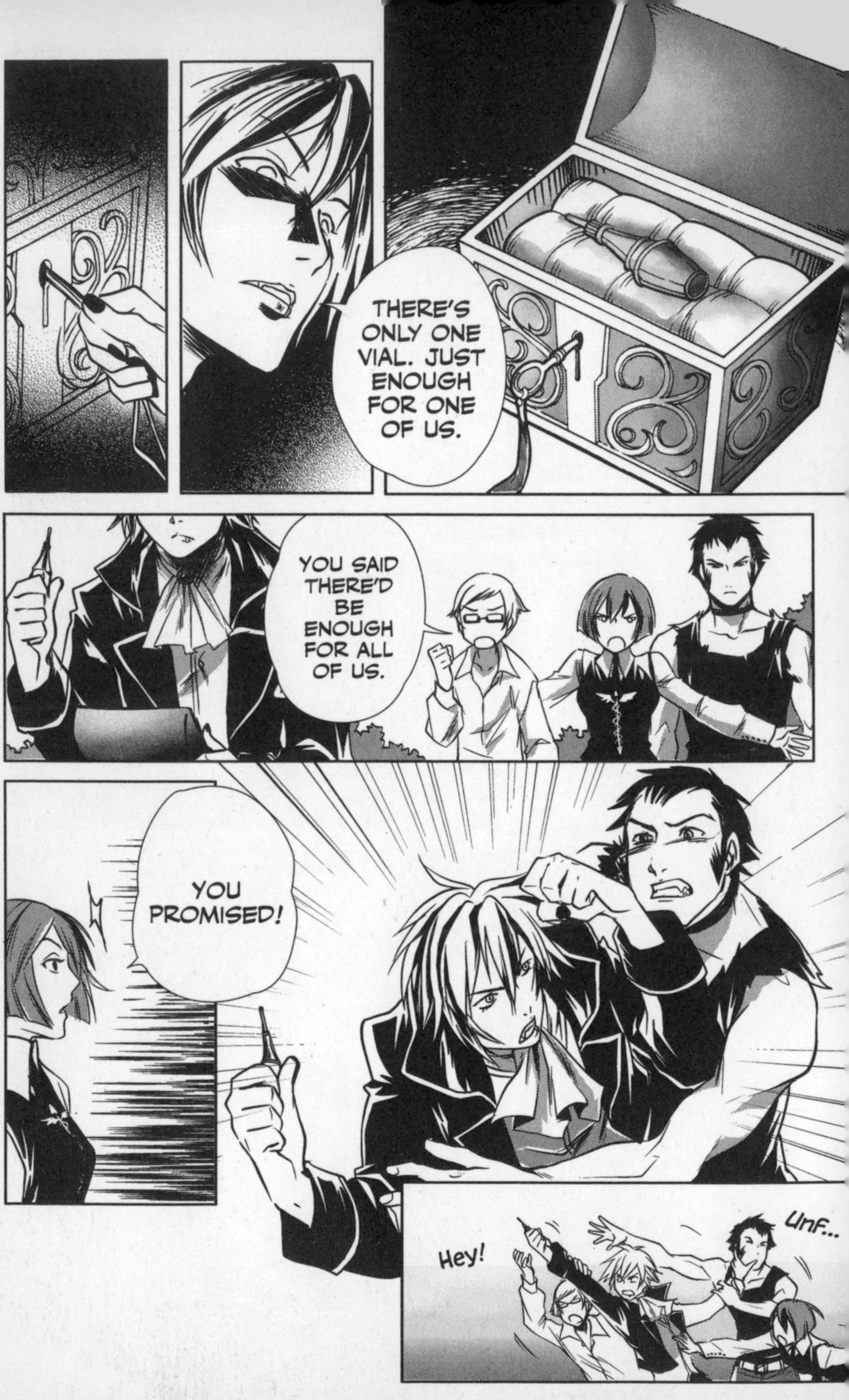
THERE'S ONLY ONE VIAL. JUST ENOUGH FOR ONE OF US.
YOU SAID THERE'D BE ENOUGH FOR ALL OF US.
YOU PROMISED!
Hey!
Unf...

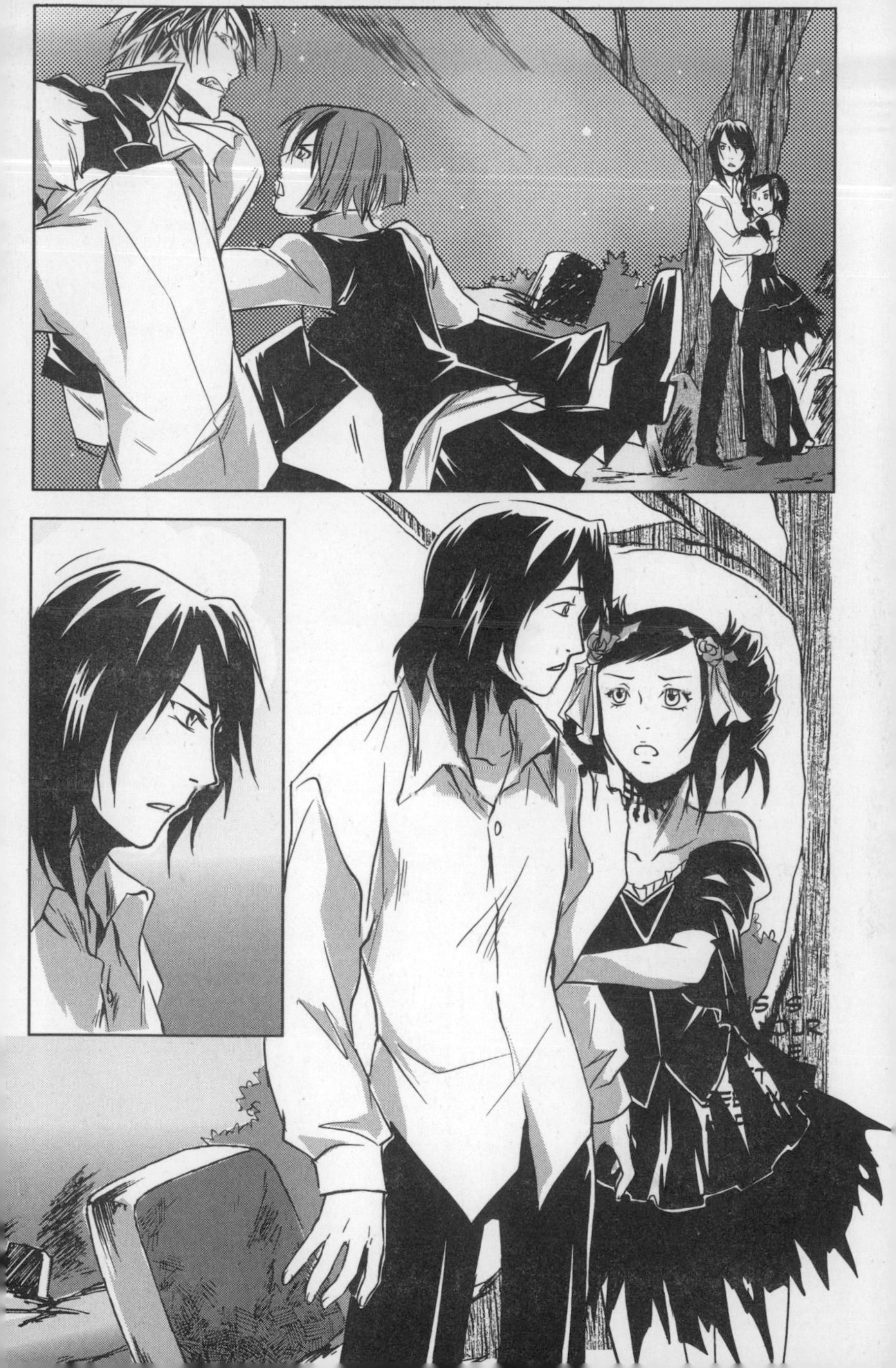

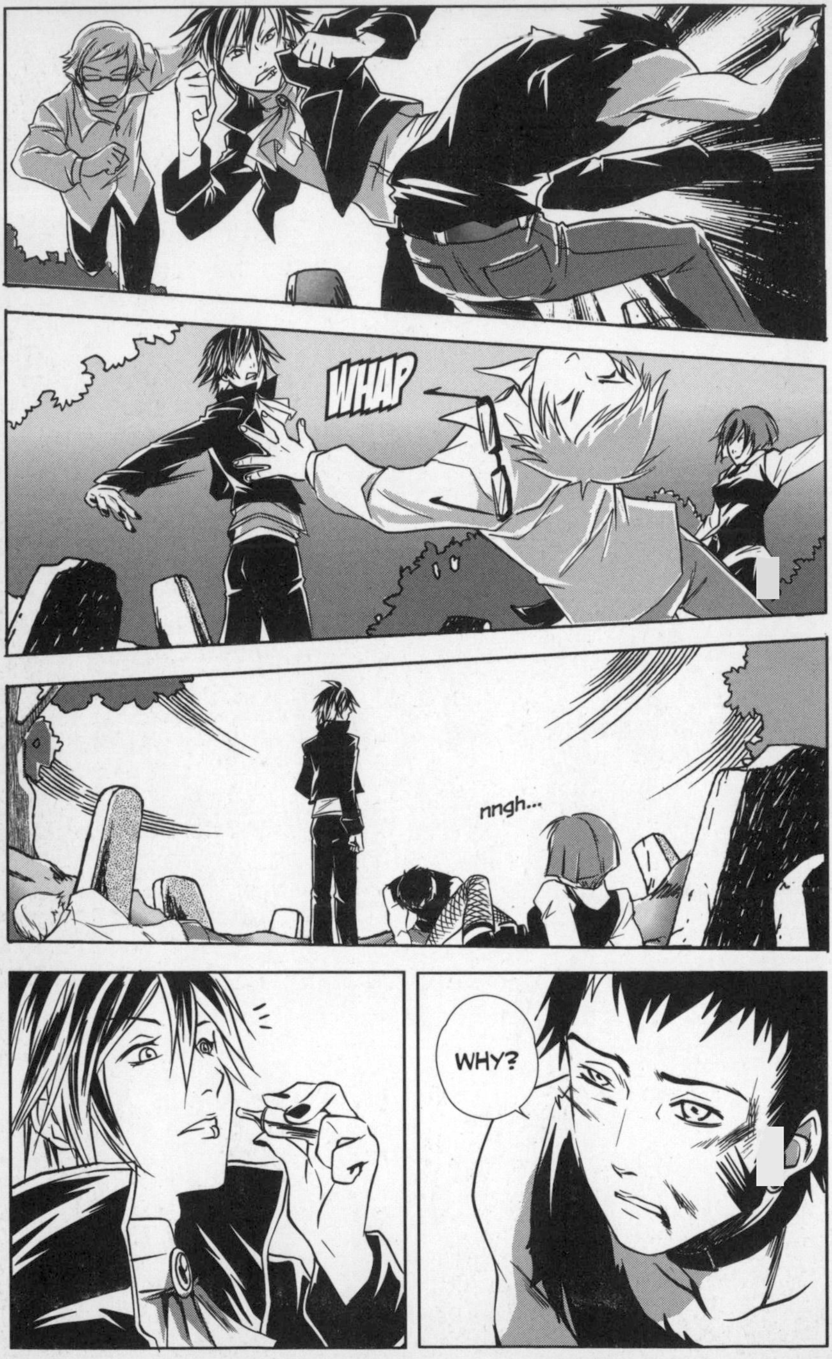
WHAP
nngh...
WHY?

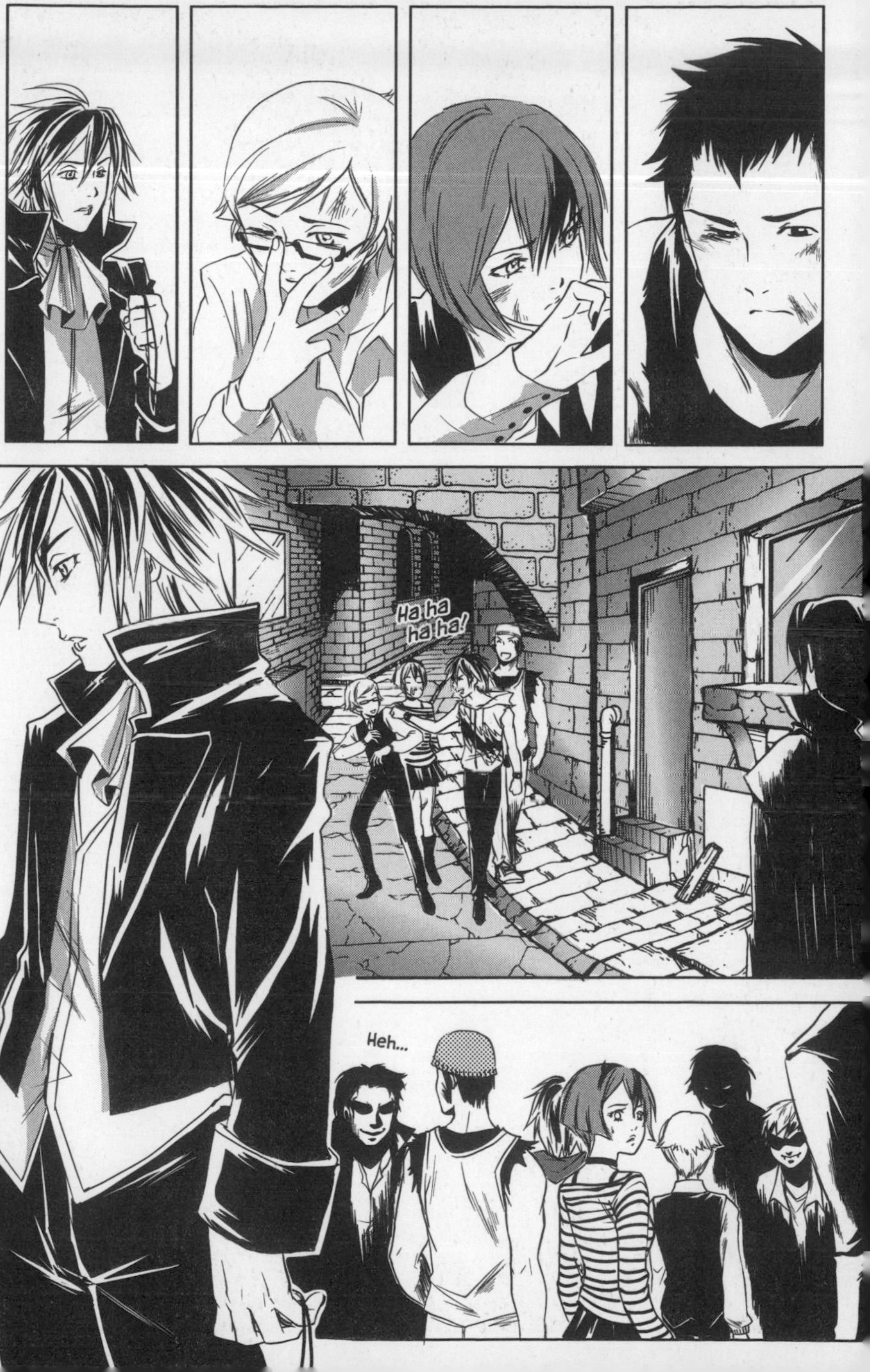
Ha ha ha ha!
Heh...

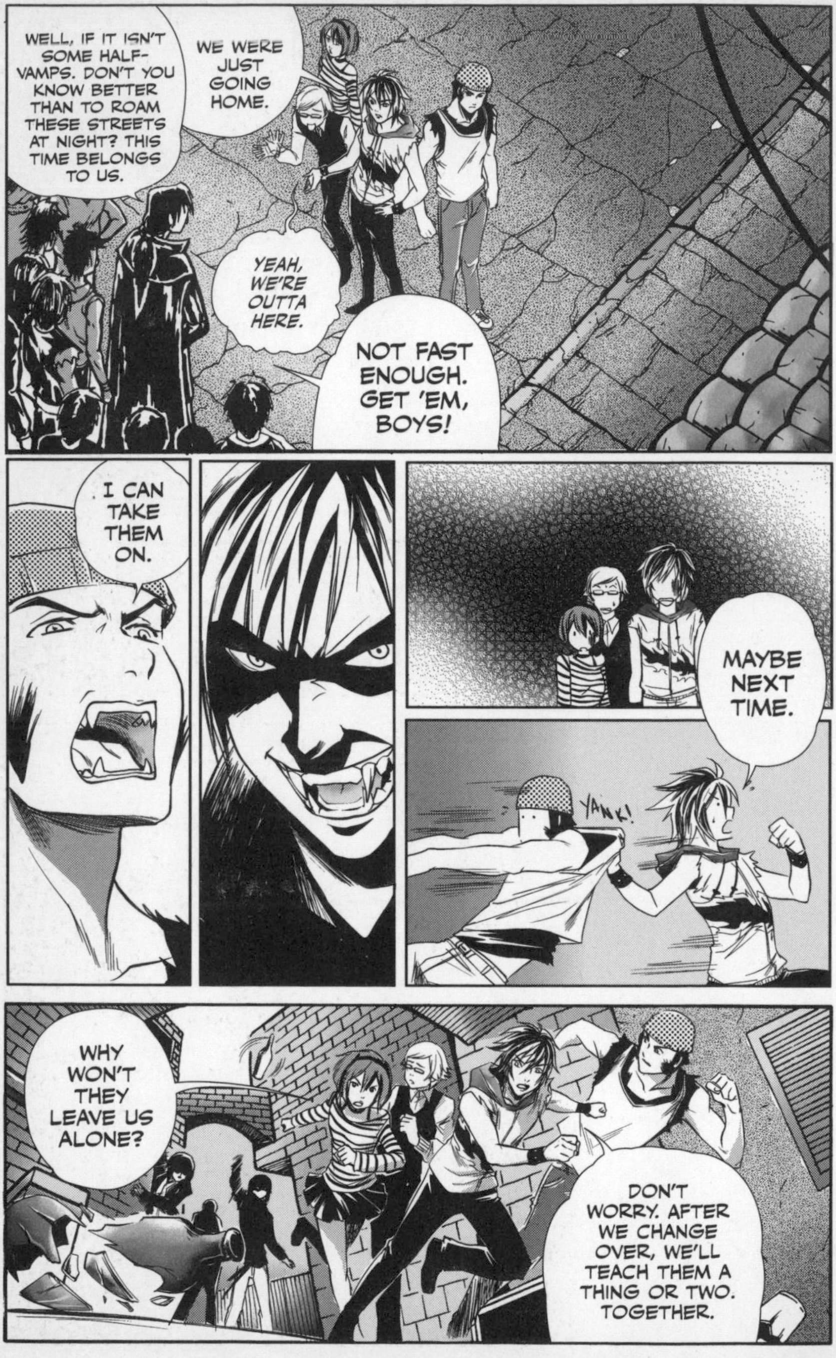
WELL, IF IT ISN'T SOME HALF-VAMPS. DON'T YOU KNOW BETTER THAN TO ROAM THESE STREETS AT NIGHT? THIS TIME BELONGS TO US.
WE WERE JUST GOING HOME.
YEAH, WE'RE OUTTA HERE.
NOT FAST ENOUGH. GET 'EM, BOYS!
I CAN TAKE THEM ON.
MAYBE NEXT TIME.
YANK!
WHY WON'T THEY LEAVE US ALONE?
DON'T WORRY. AFTER WE CHANGE OVER, WE'LL TEACH THEM A THING OR TWO. TOGETHER.

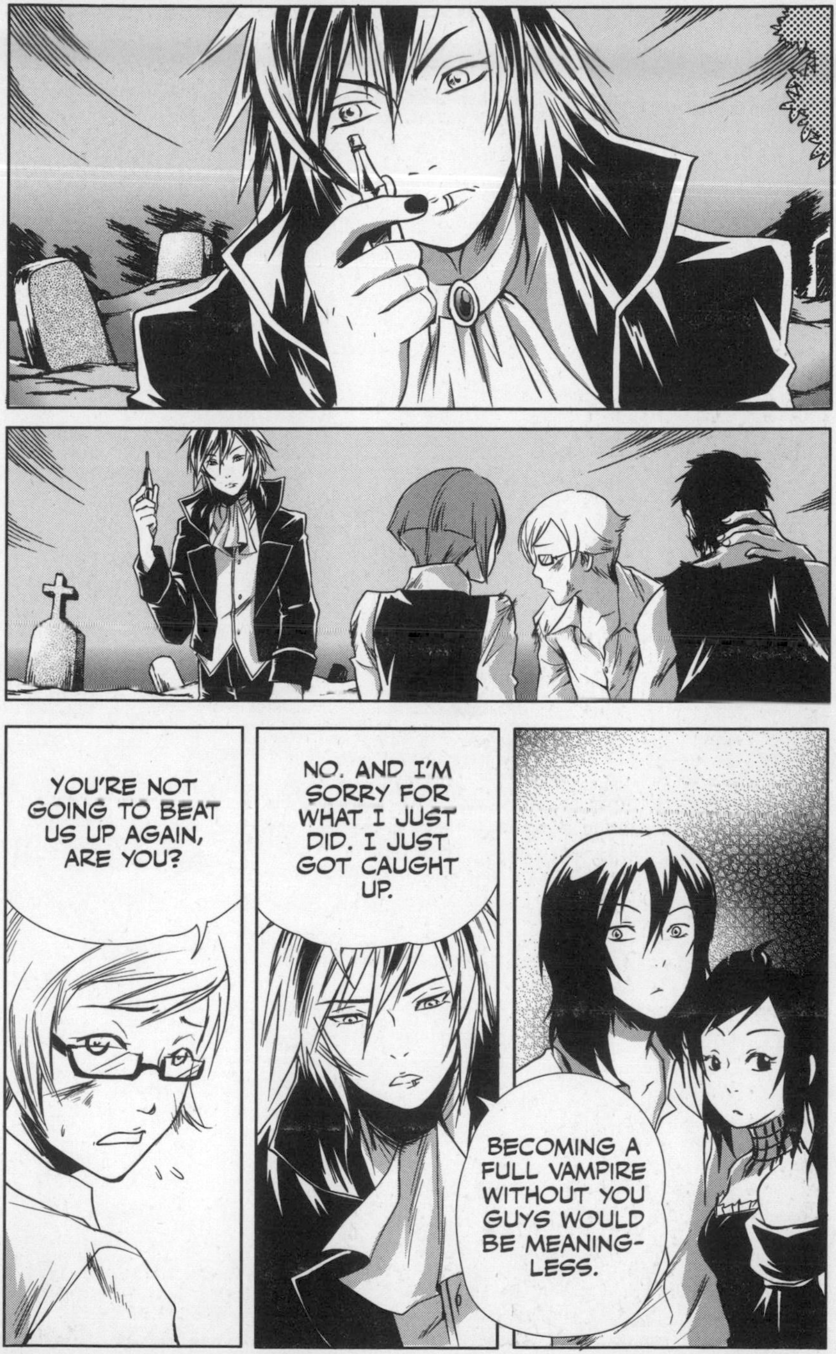
YOU'RE NOT GOING TO BEAT US UP AGAIN, ARE YOU?
NO. AND I'M SORRY FOR WHAT I JUST DID. I JUST GOT CAUGHT UP.
BECOMING A FULL VAMPIRE WITHOUT YOU GUYS WOULD BE MEANING-LESS.

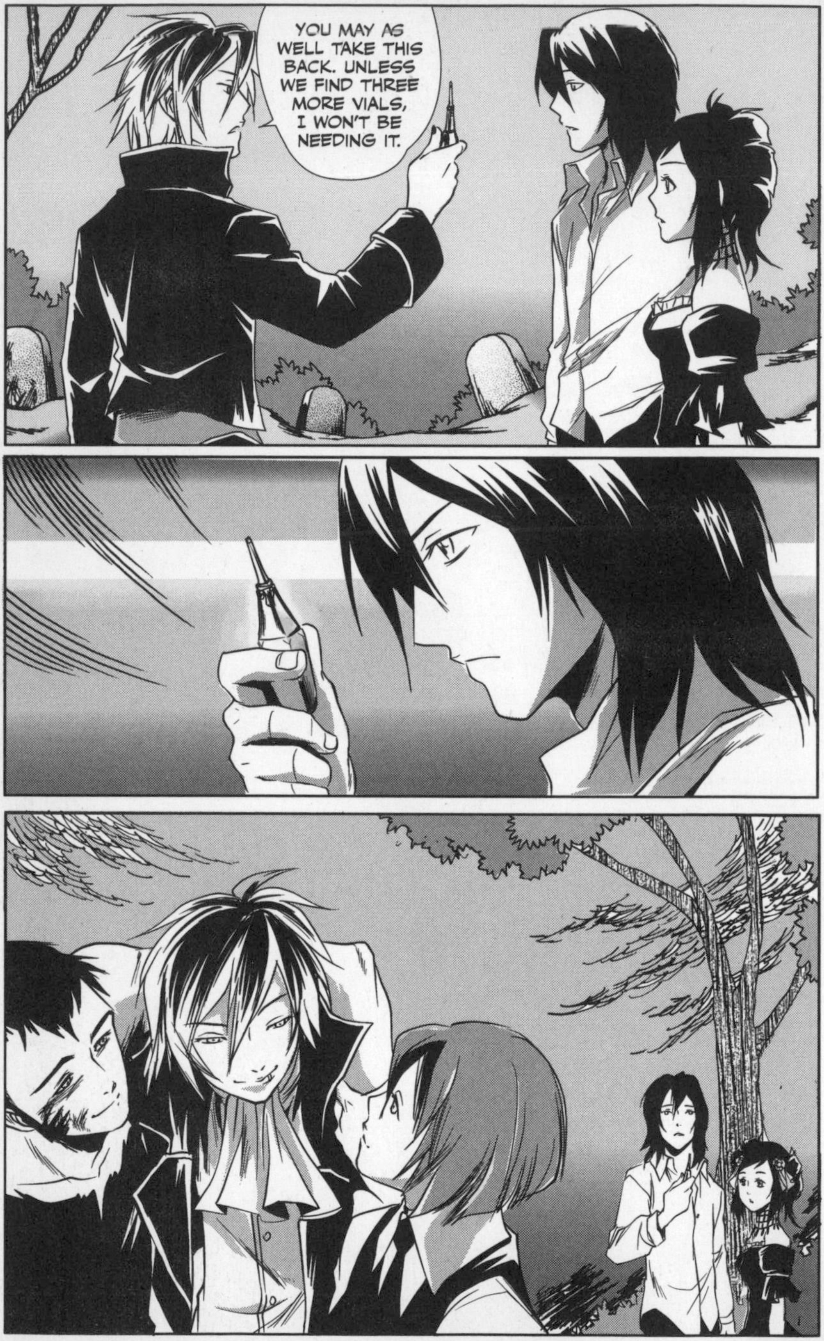
YOU MAY AS WELL TAKE THIS BACK. UNLESS WE FIND THREE MORE VIALS, I WON'T BE NEEDING IT.

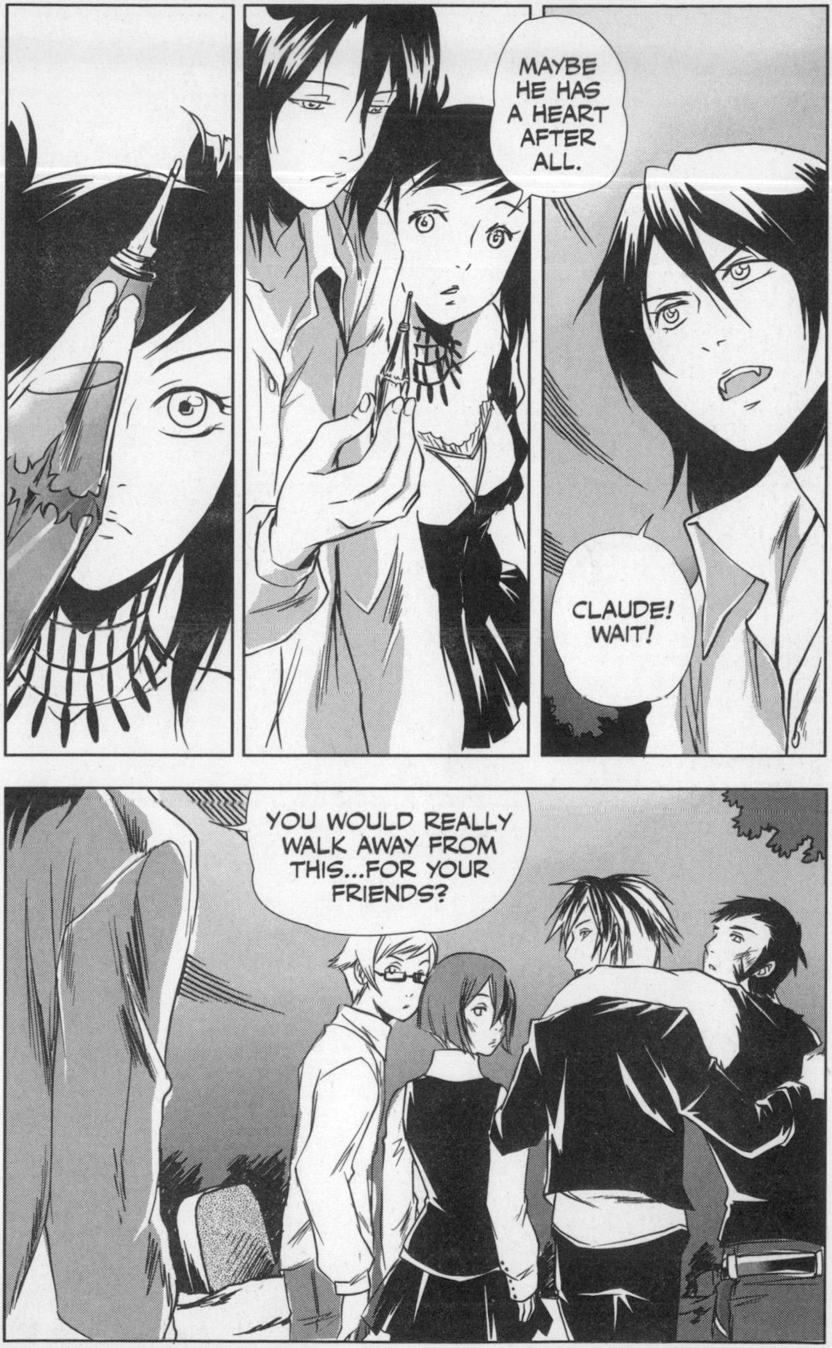
MAYBE HE HAS A HEART AFTER ALL.
CLAUDE! WAIT!
YOU WOULD REALLY WALK AWAY FROM THIS...FOR YOUR FRIENDS?

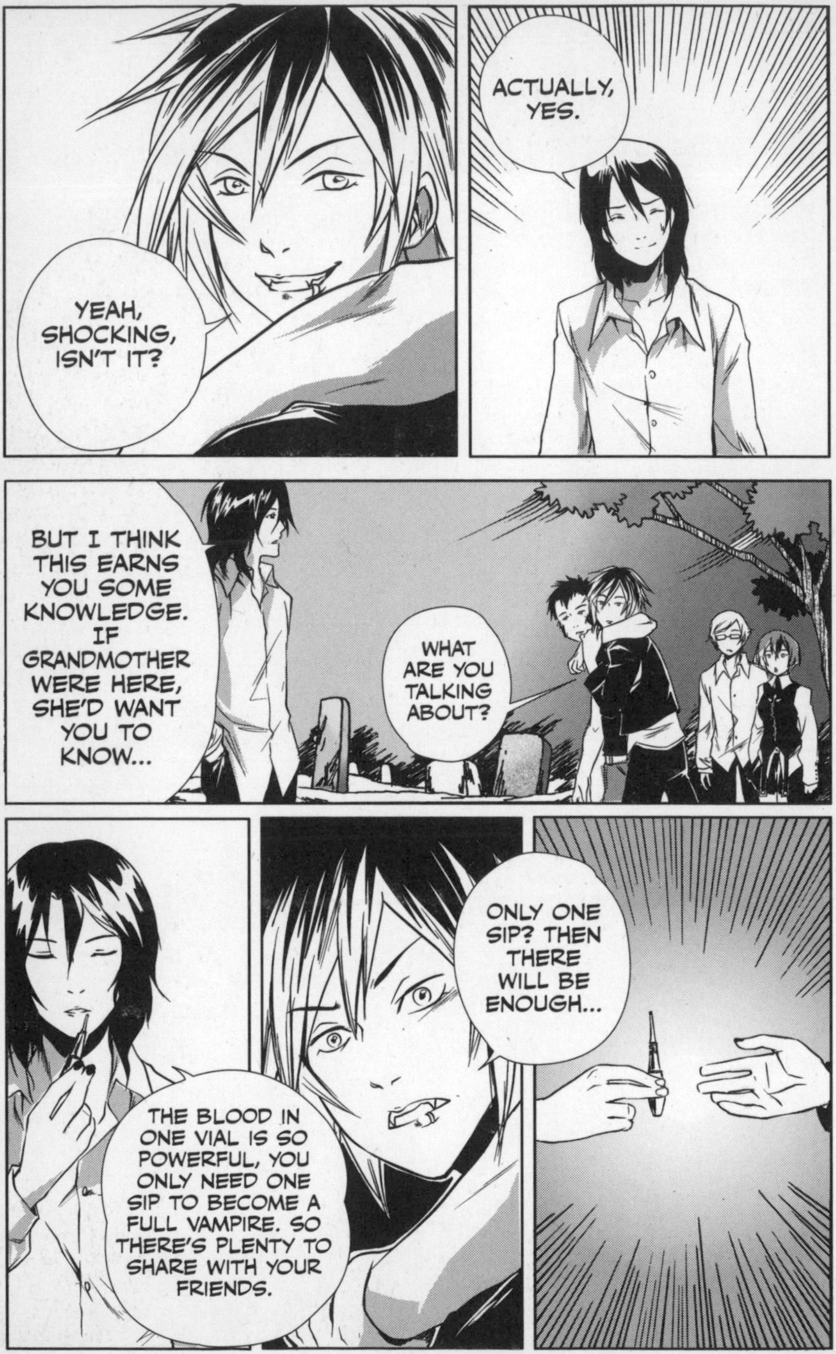
YEAH, SHOCKING, ISN'T IT?
ACTUALLY, YES.
BUT I THINK THIS EARNS YOU SOME KNOWLEDGE. IF GRANDMOTHER WERE HERE, SHE'D WANT YOU TO KNOW...
WHAT ARE YOU TALKING ABOUT?
THE BLOOD IN ONE VIAL IS SO POWERFUL, YOU ONLY NEED ONE SIP TO BECOME A FULL VAMPIRE. SO THERE'S PLENTY TO SHARE WITH YOUR FRIENDS.
ONLY ONE SIP? THEN THERE WILL BE ENOUGH...

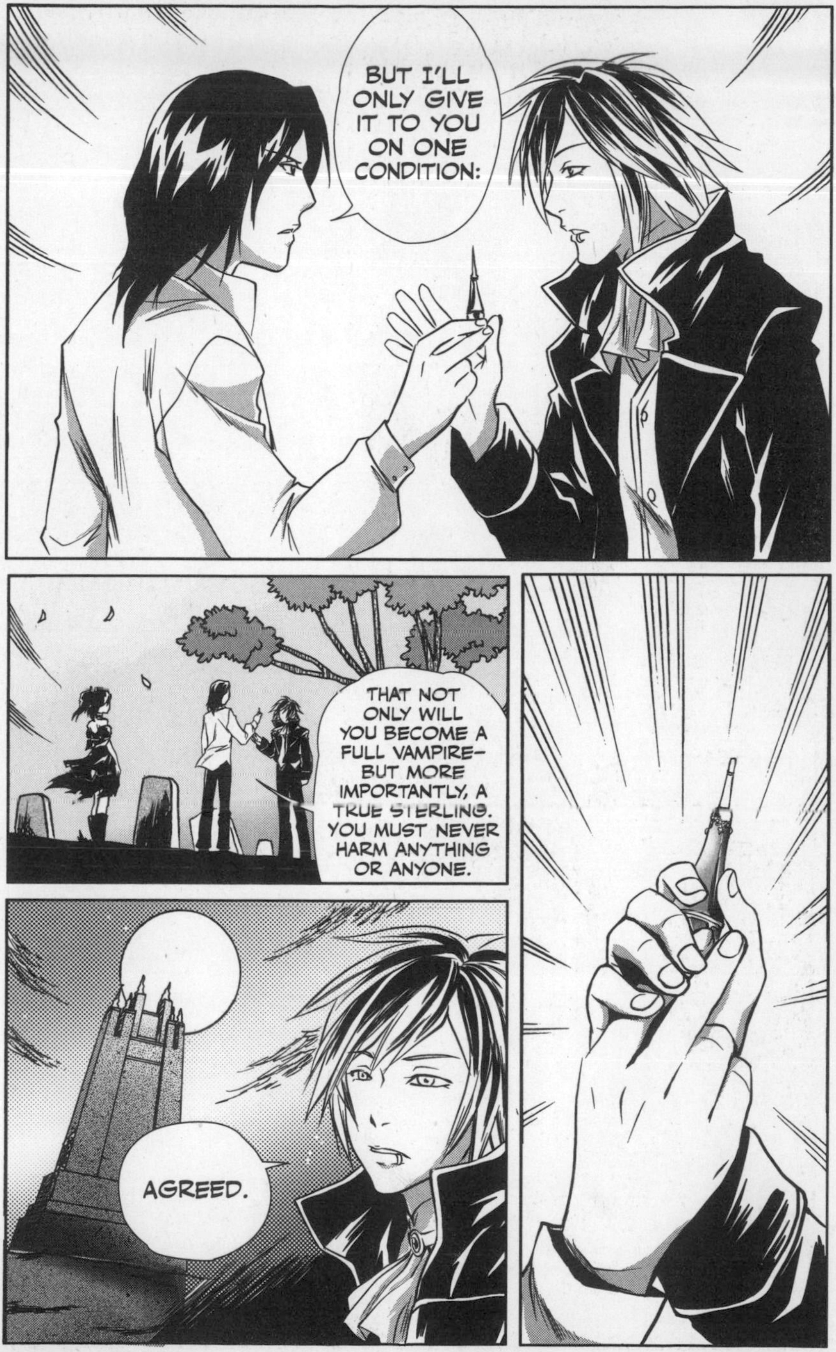
BUT I'LL ONLY GIVE IT TO YOU ON ONE CONDITION:
THAT NOT ONLY WILL YOU BECOME A FULL VAMPIRE—BUT MORE IMPORTANTLY, A TRUE STERLING. YOU MUST NEVER HARM ANYTHING OR ANYONE.
AGREED.

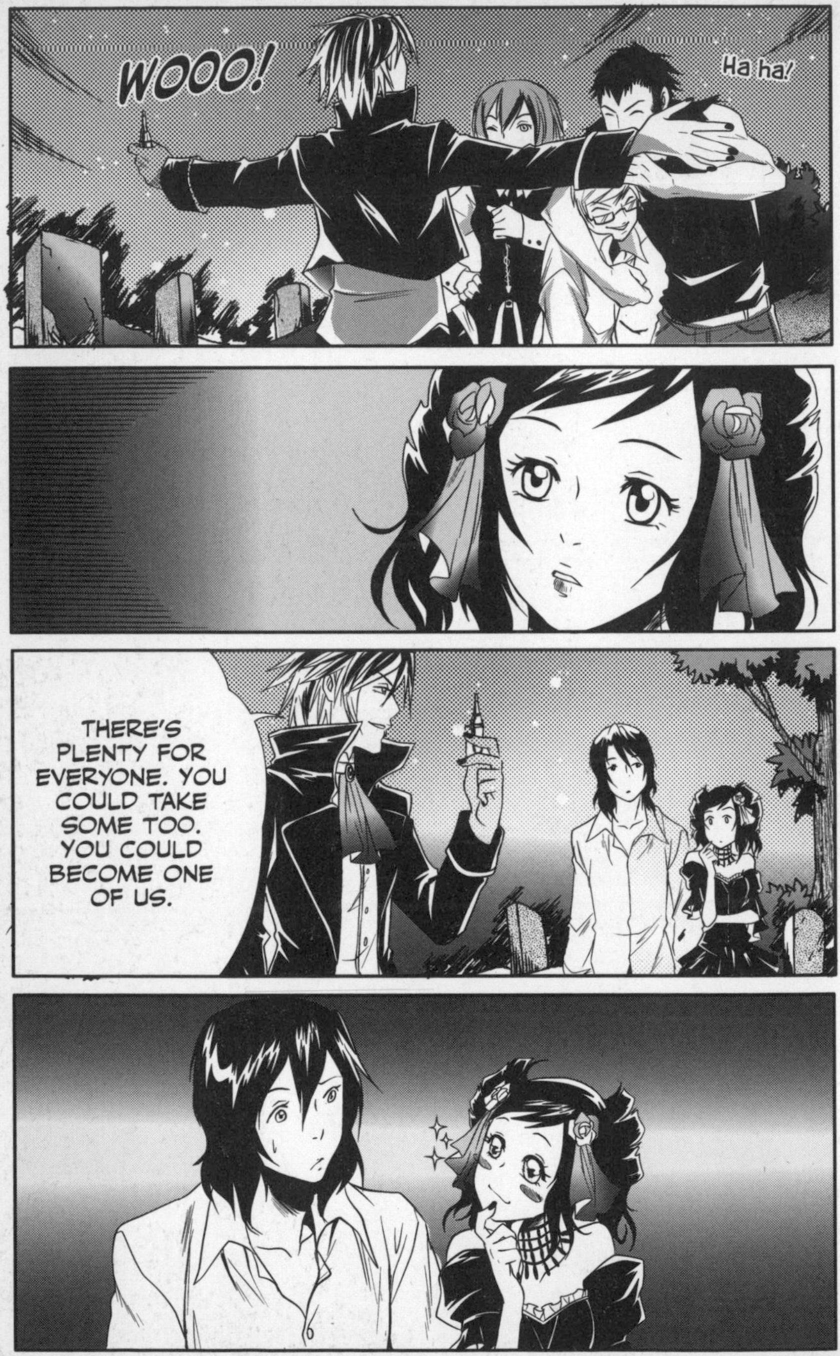
WOOO!
Ha ha!
THERE'S PLENTY FOR EVERYONE. YOU COULD TAKE SOME TOO. YOU COULD BECOME ONE OF US.

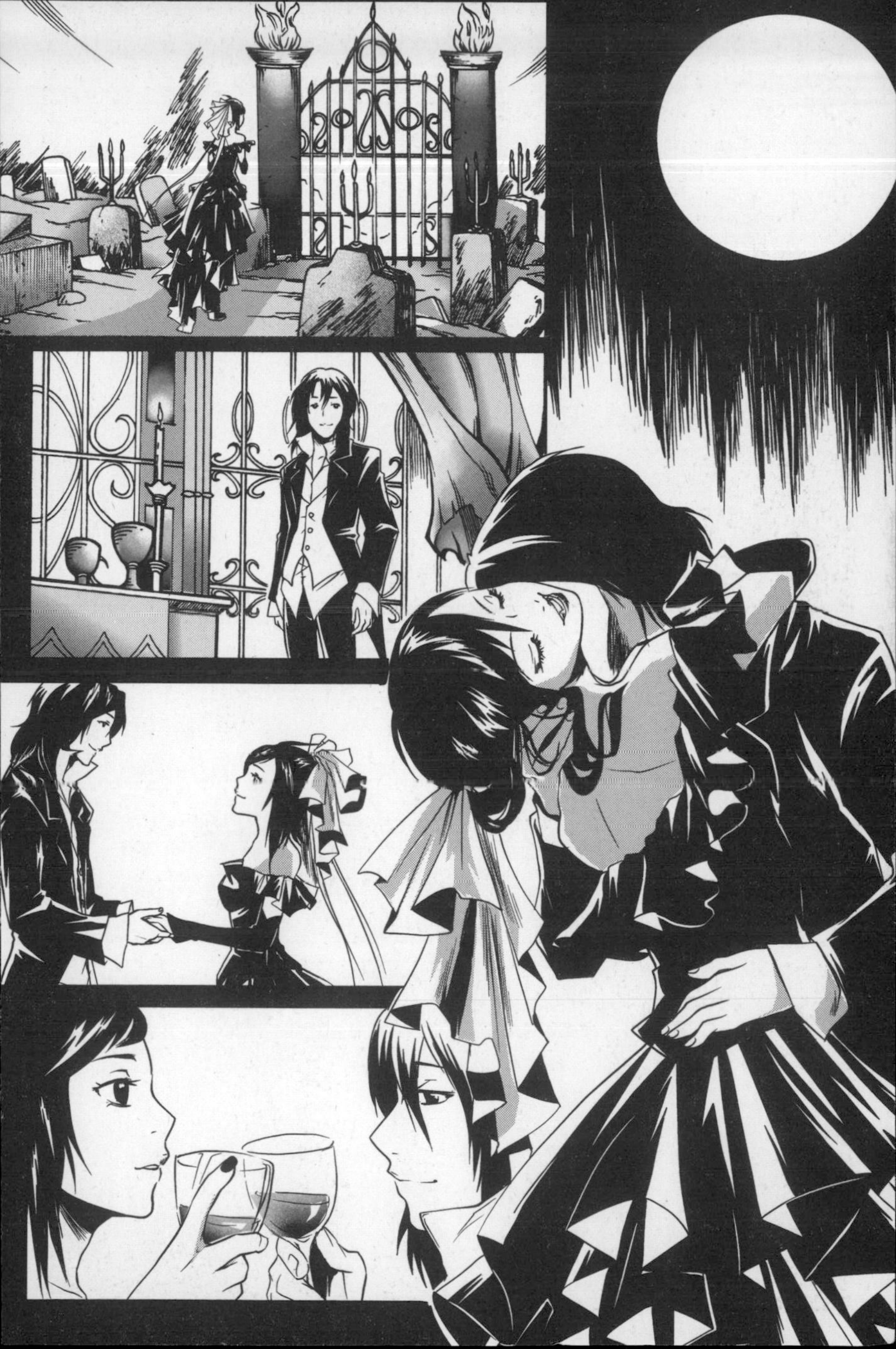

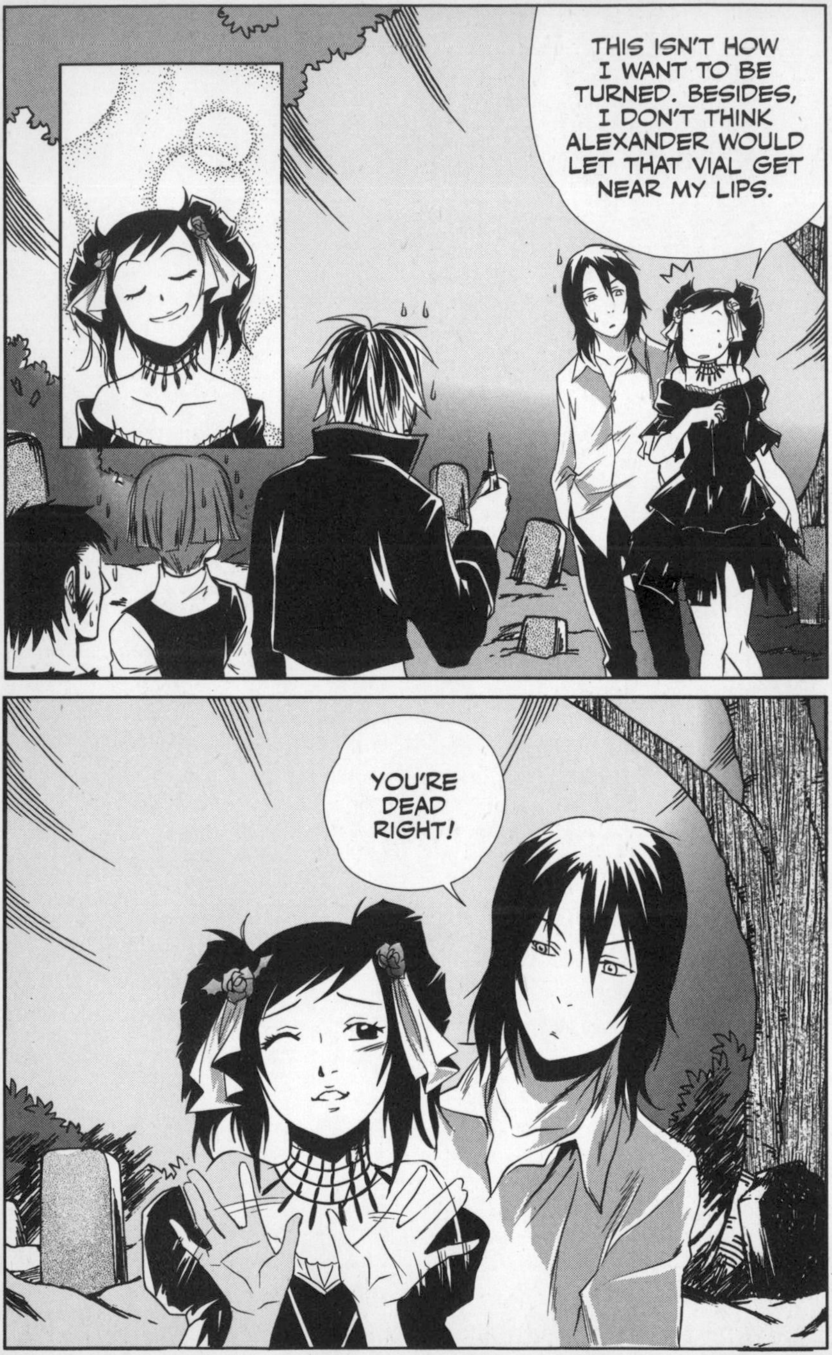
THIS ISN'T HOW I WANT TO BE TURNED. BESIDES, I DON'T THINK ALEXANDER WOULD LET THAT VIAL GET NEAR MY LIPS.
YOU'RE DEAD RIGHT!

THANK YOU, COUSIN. I AM INDEBTED TO YOU. YOU'VE SET US ON A COURSE FROM WHICH WE CAN'T RETURN.

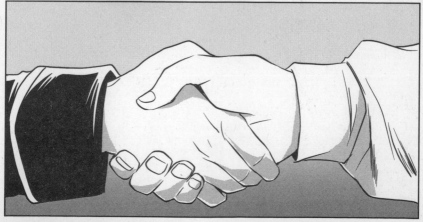

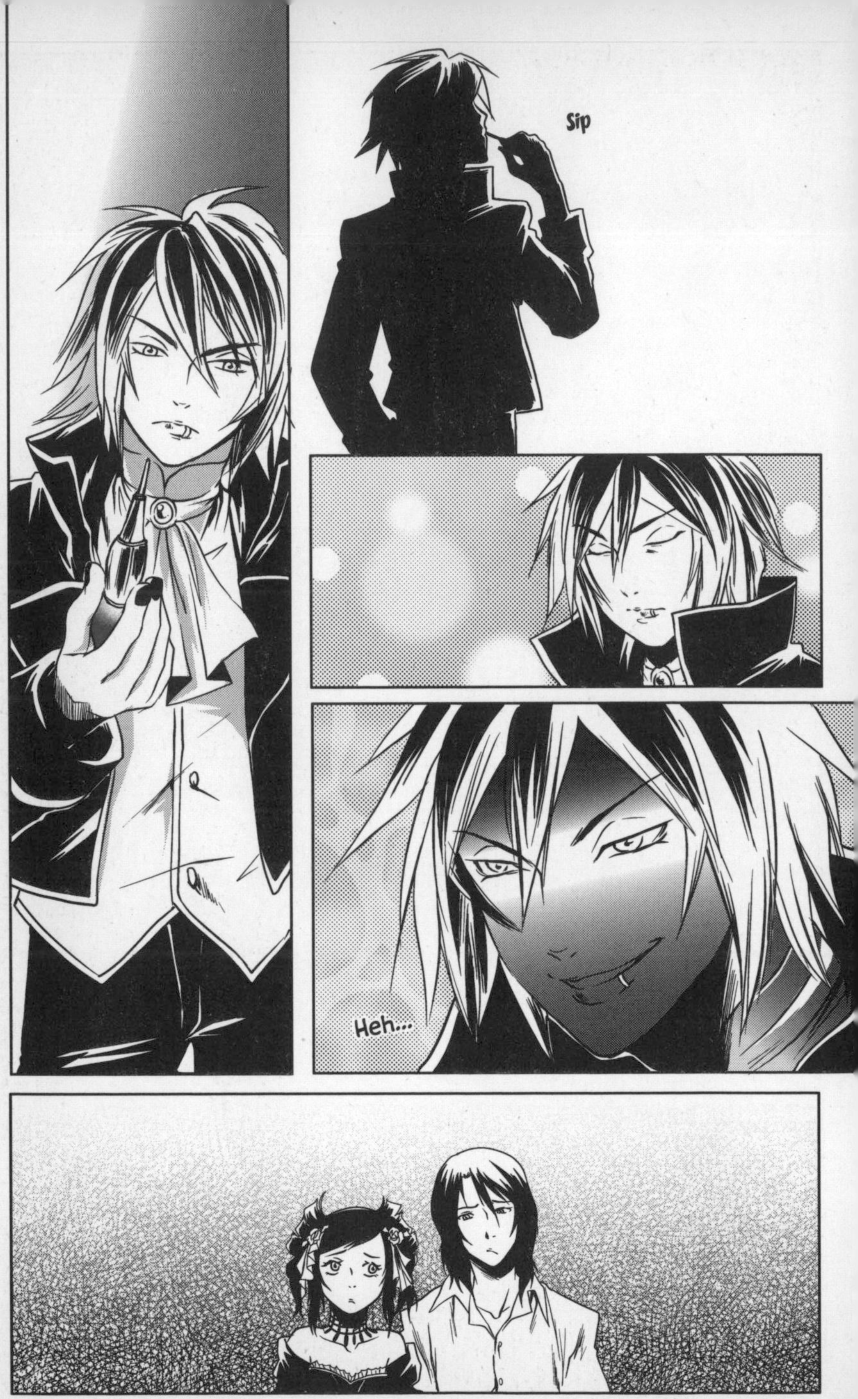
Sip
Heh...

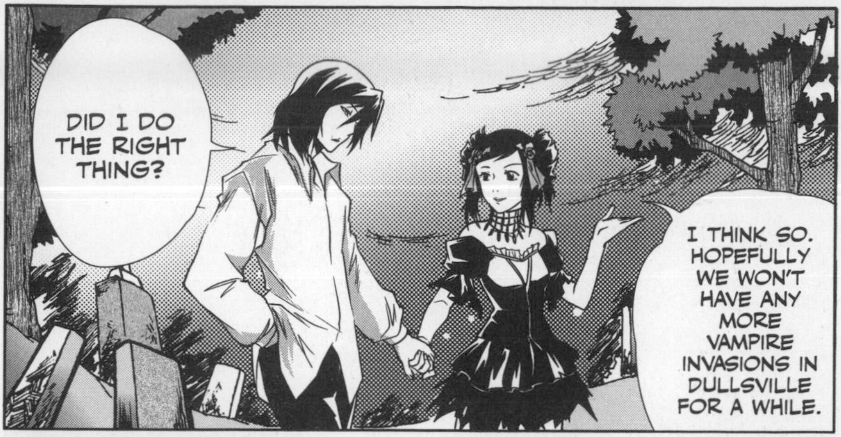
DID I DO THE RIGHT THING?
I THINK SO. HOPEFULLY WE WON'T HAVE ANY MORE VAMPIRE INVASIONS IN DULLSVILLE FOR A WHILE.

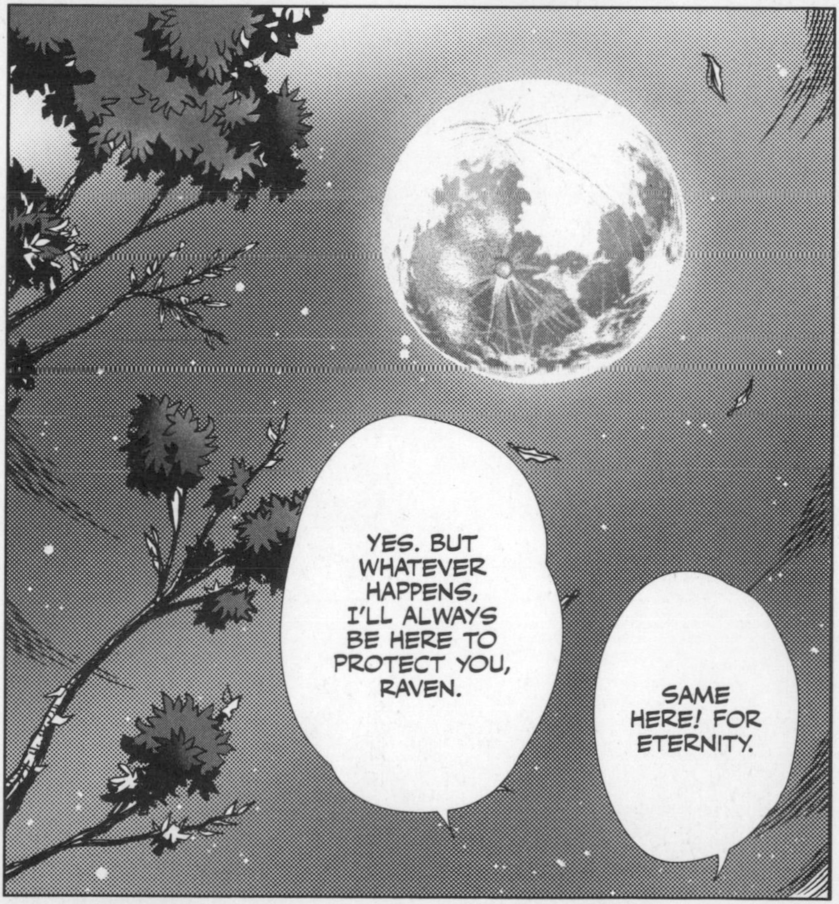
YES. BUT WHATEVER HAPPENS, I'LL ALWAYS BE HERE TO PROTECT YOU, RAVEN.
SAME HERE! FOR ETERNITY.

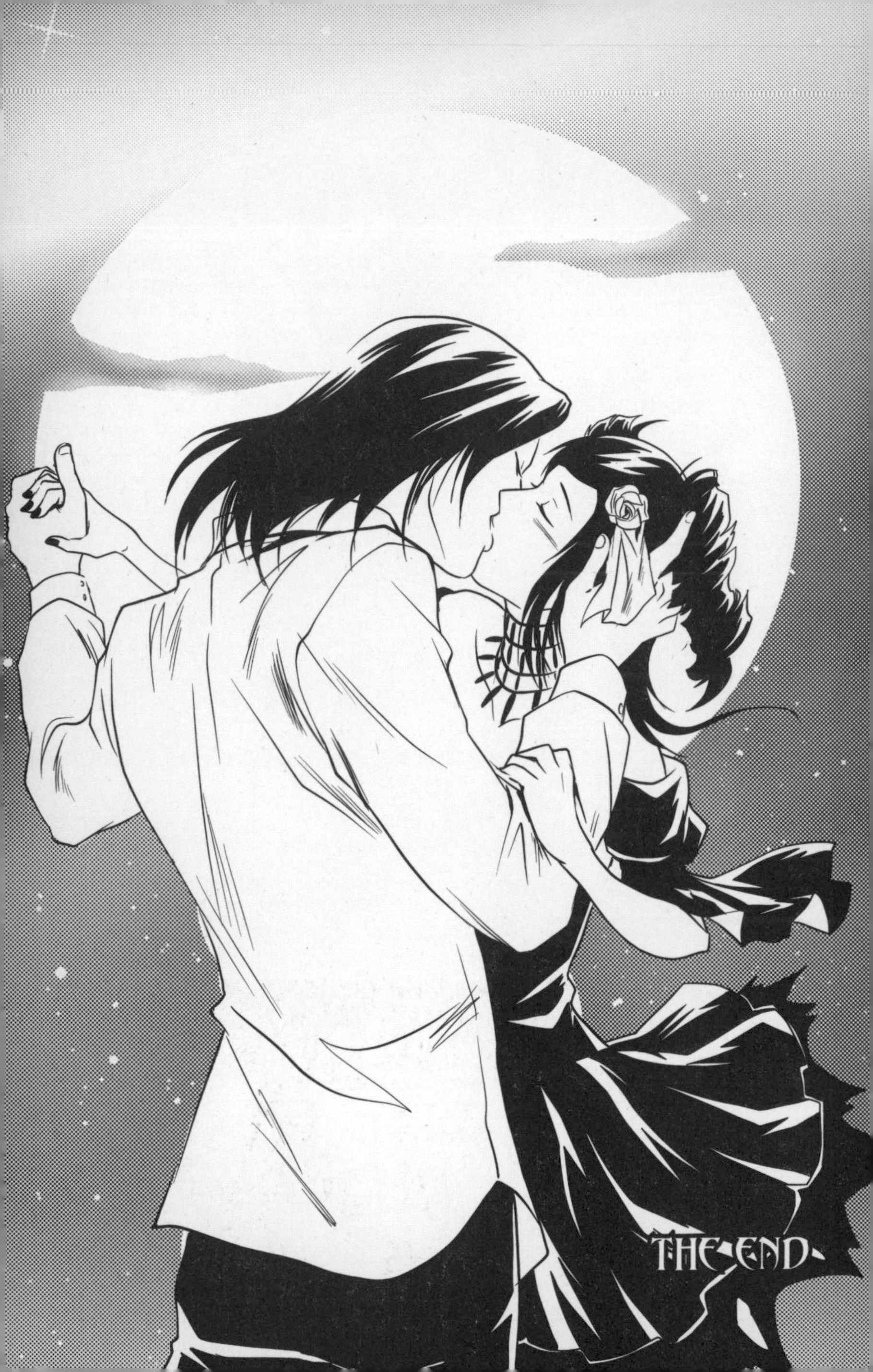
THE END

Hey, Guys and Ghouls,

It's been a blast publishing the manga series Vampire Kisses: Blood Relatives.

I'm so thankful to all of you fangtastic readers who've been following the stories of Raven and Alexander in both the manga and novels.

It's been very exciting to see Raven, Alexander, Becky, and Trevor come to life in art. Even Nerd Boy (Raven's little brother, Billy). He's so adorable!

And to top it off, creating the new half-vampire gang has been so much fun. Claude is one hot trouble-maker and Kat, Tripp, and Rocco are matchless sidekicks. Making the manga has been an incredible process—from dreaming up new character concepts to seeing the artists' spectacular designs.

Many of you continue to send me amazing fan art. I've posted some pieces on my website (www.ellenschreiber.com) and also keep them for my own collection. There is so much talent out there and I'm inspired by your creativity!

Enjoy the sampling of fan art on the following pages.
And check out my Vampire Kisses novels too!

Thanks so much for reading!

Many fangs,
Ellen :)

Fan Art

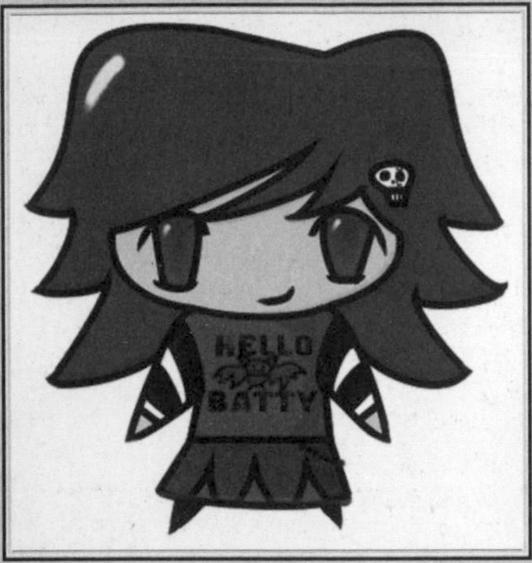
HELLO
BATTY

By DQ

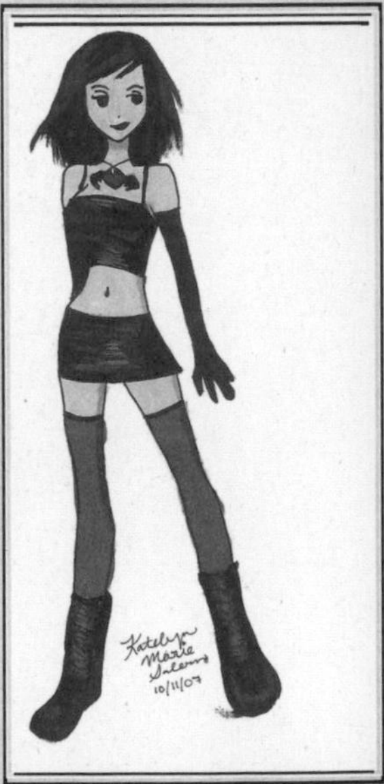
Katelyn
Marie
Salerno
10/11/07

By Katelyn Salerno

Fan Art

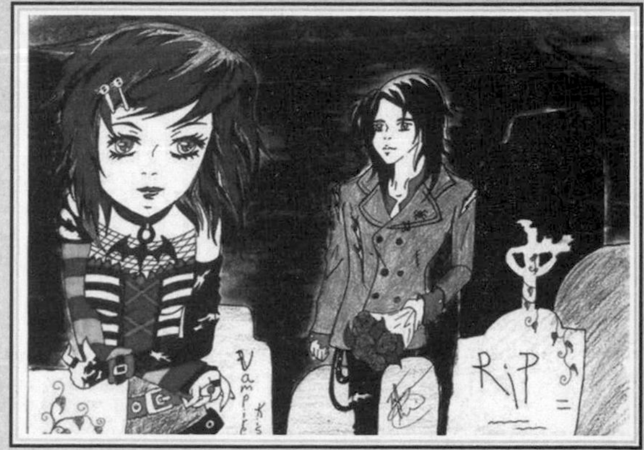
RIP

By Tiffany M.

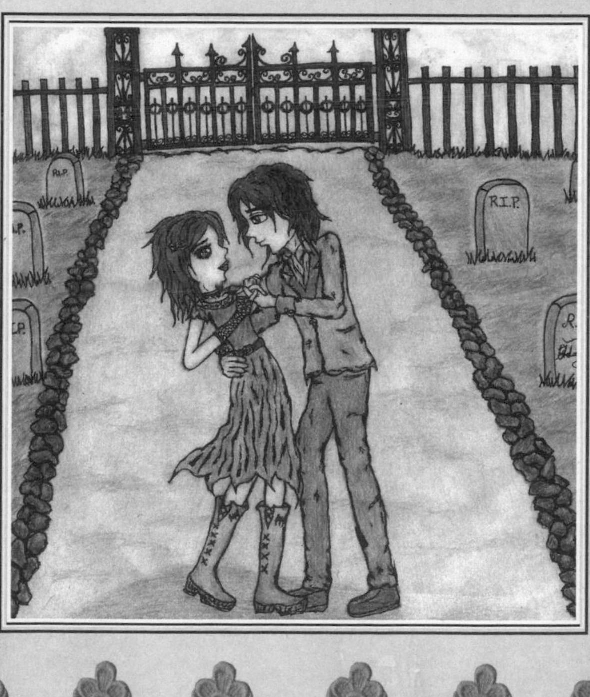
R.I.P.
R.I.P.

By Chelsea Chang

Fan Art

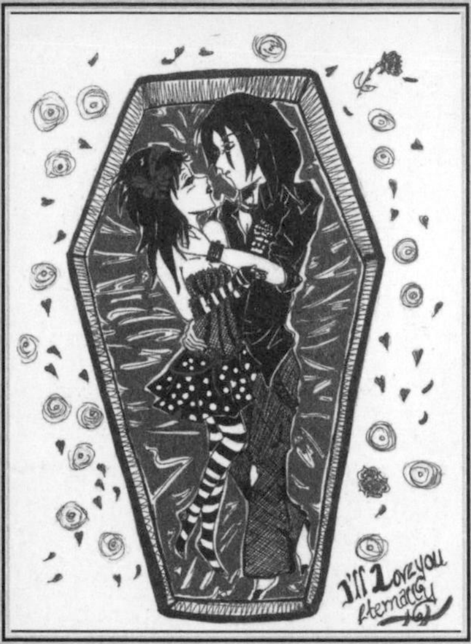
I'll Love you Eternally

By Kassandra Hamel Monahan

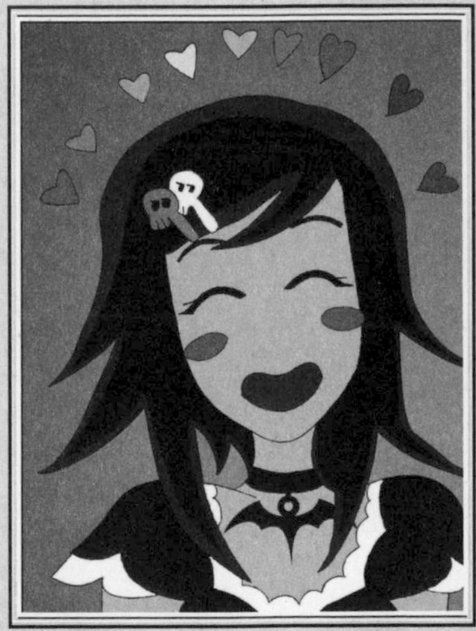

By Alexandra Nightmare

Fan Art

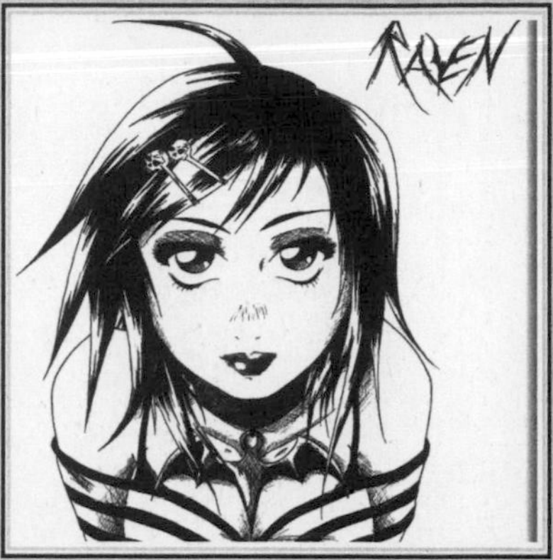
RAVEN

By Casey "Ryoko" Mullins

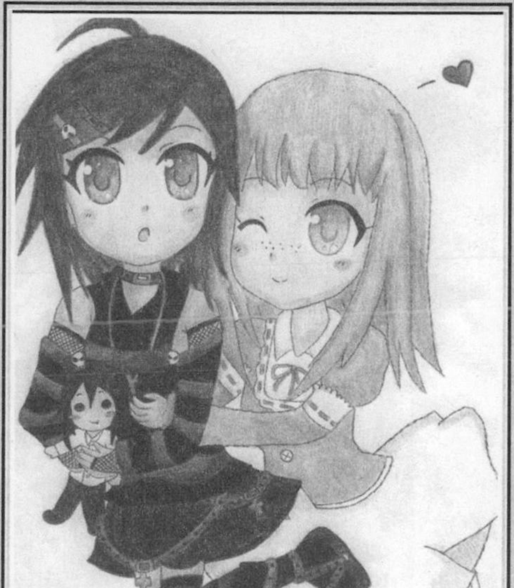

By Teshana Miles

Fan Art

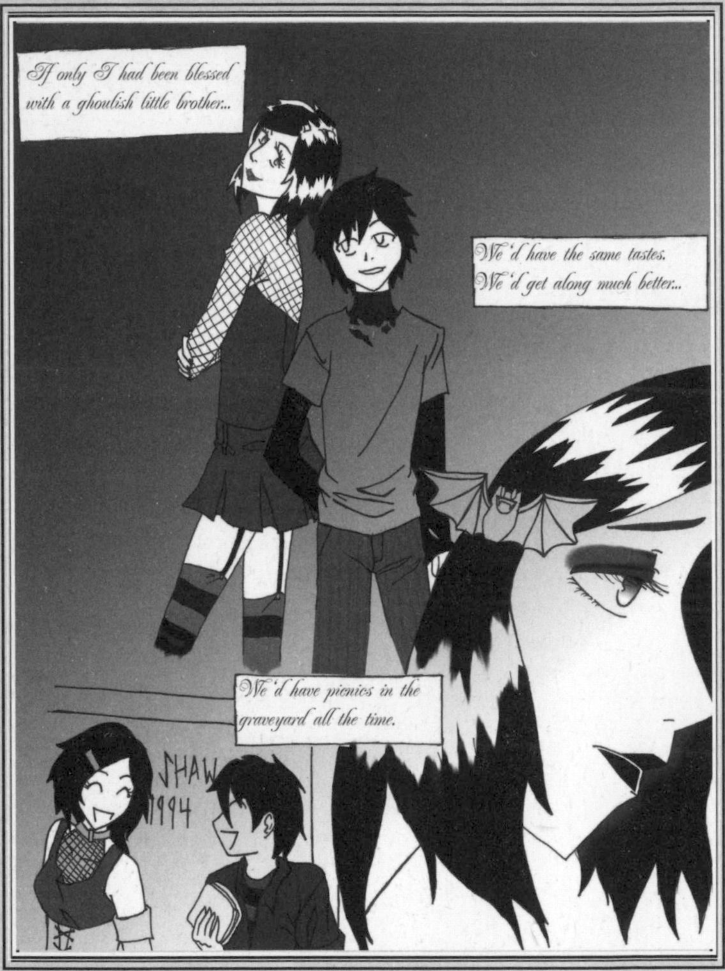
If only I had been blessed with a ghoulish little brother...
We'd have the same tastes. We'd get along much better...
We'd have picnics in the graveyard all the time.
SHAW 1994

By Savannah Sheets

Fan Art

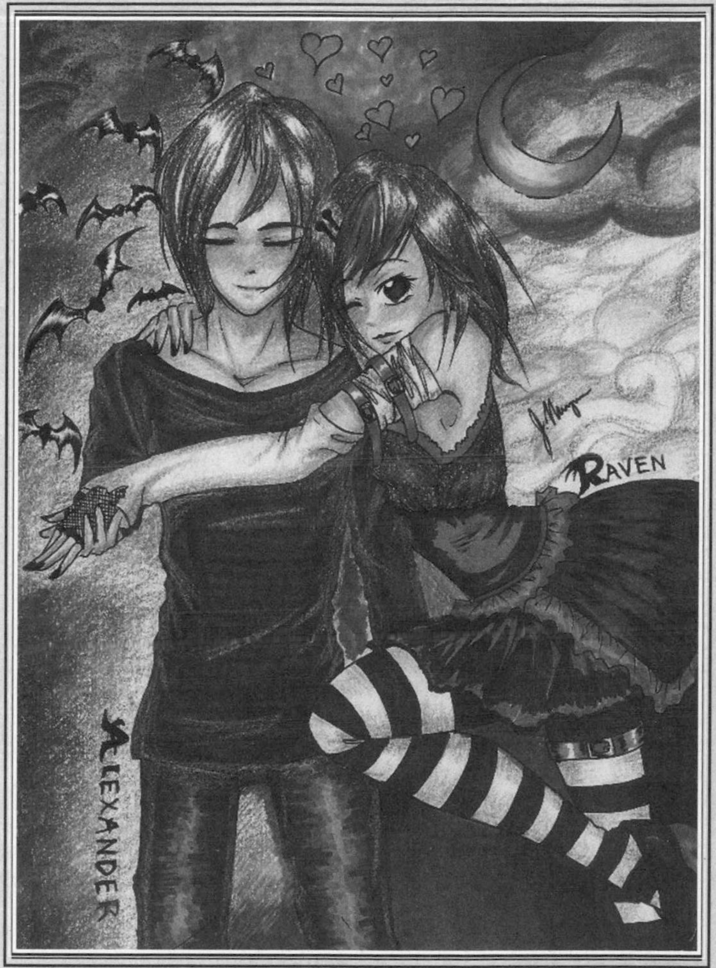
RAVEN
ALEXANDER

By Jessica Morgan

Fan Art

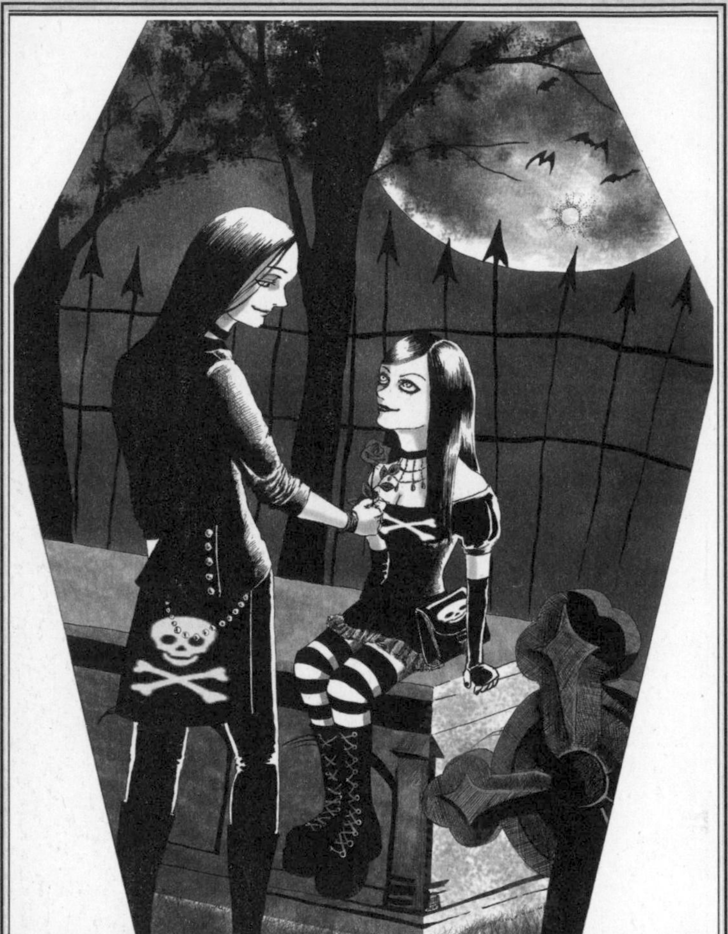

By Mai Aimheart

Fan Art

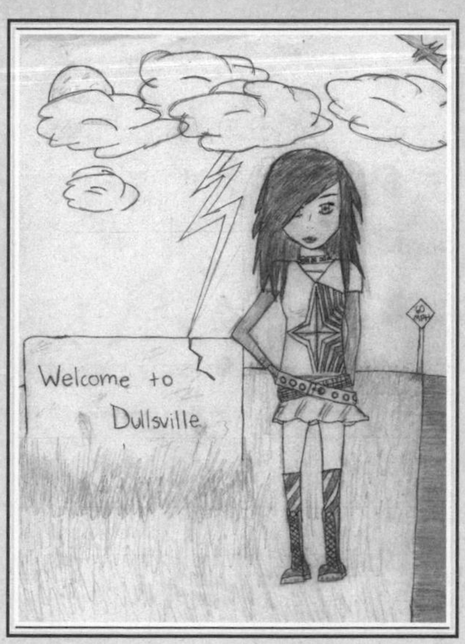

Welcome to
Dullsville

By Natalie Renee Tran

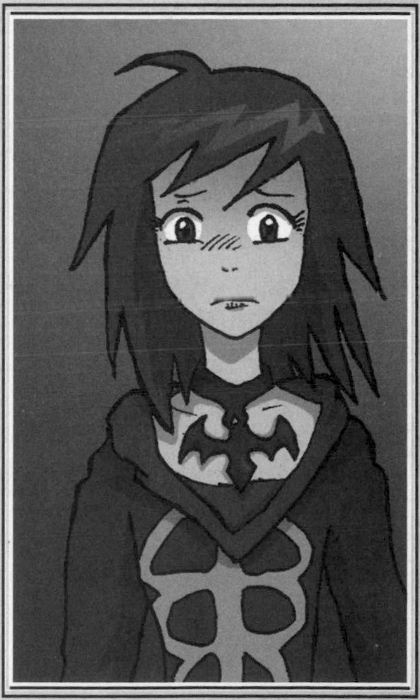

By Ethan Williams

Fan Art

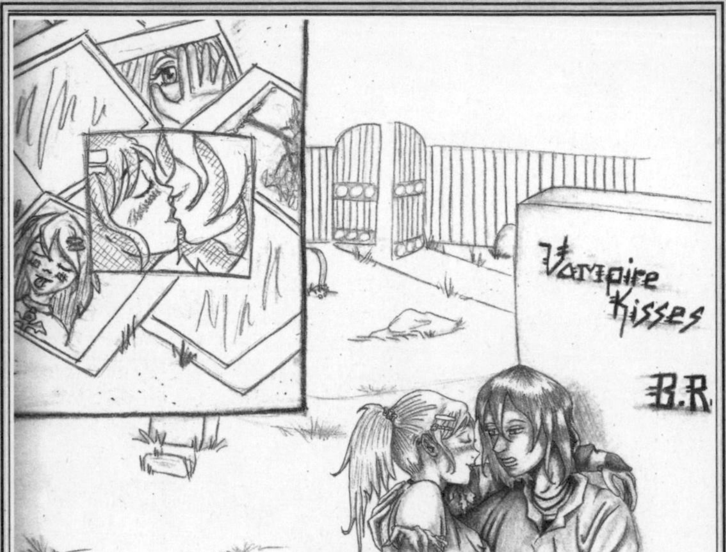
Vampire Kisses
B.R.

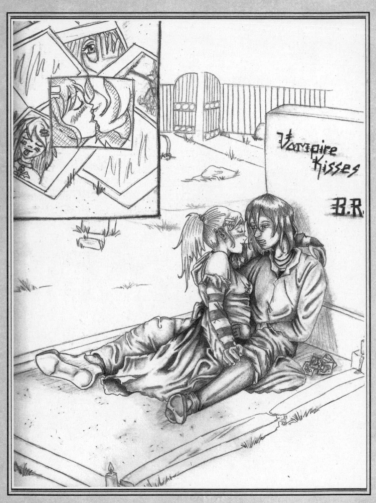

By Brittany Harris

Fan Art

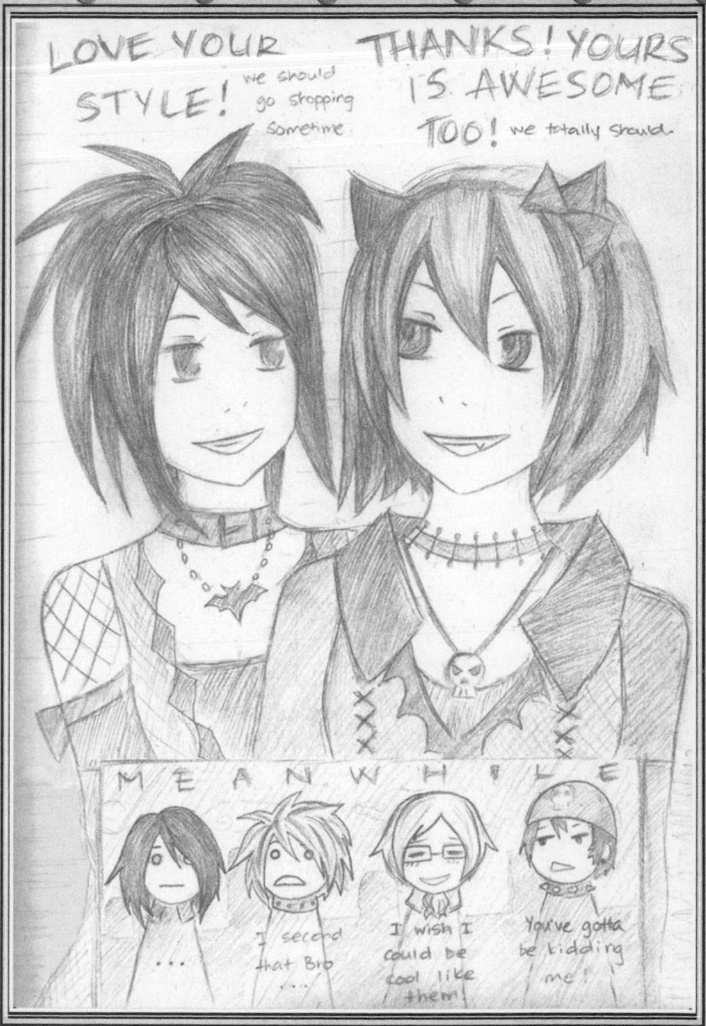
LOVE YOUR STYLE!
we should go shopping sometime
THANKS! YOURS IS AWESOME TOO!
we totally should.
MEANWHILE
...
I second that Bro ...
I wish I could be cool like them!
You've gotta be kidding me!

By GM

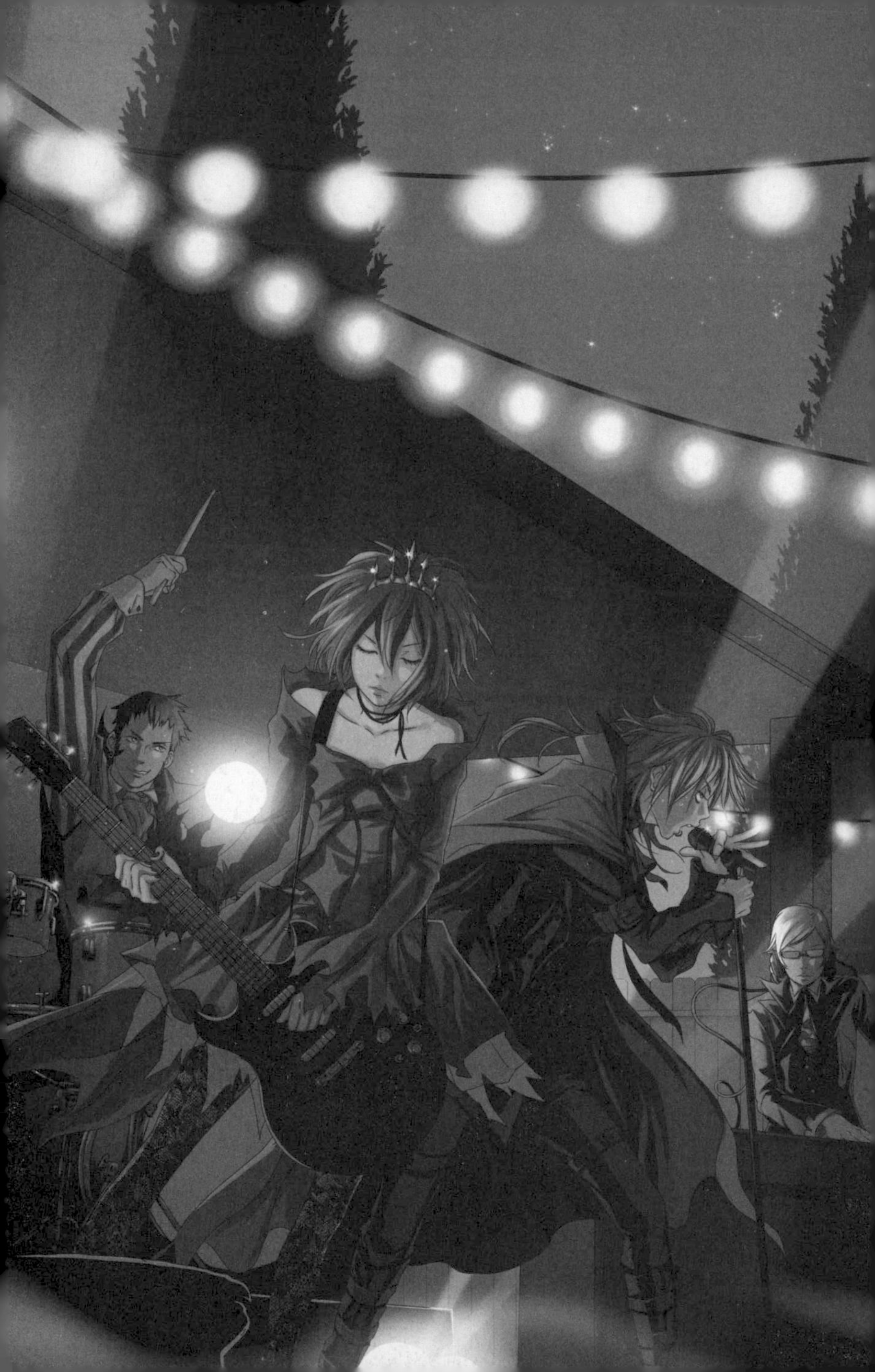

Keep reading for more of Raven and
Alexander's unusual romance in:

Vampire Kisses 6
Royal Blood

1

Special Delivery

The letter arrived mysteriously.

I imagined the deliverer was an enigmatic figure masked in a centuries-old black hooded cloak, slipping undetected through the darkness past the Mansion's wrought-iron gate. He may have approached the Sterlings' haunted-looking house in a hearse. Or perhaps he'd flown over the menacing fence in the form of a bat.

By nightfall, the Mansion's mailbox was usually as hollow as an empty coffin, sitting lonely at the bottom of Benson Hill, at the end of a long and windy driveway. So the letter would go unnoticed for several hours as I was stolen away in Alexander's attic room, pressed against my

1

vampire boyfriend's deathly pale, but full of life, lips.

Several weeks had passed since Alexander and I had returned from our adventure in Hipsterville, and though Alexander hadn't bitten, he did make this mortal feel a part of the Underworld. During that time, we began to experience the vampire life without distractions. There was no school to interrupt my daytime sleep, no Trevor Mitchell to be a thorn in my side, and no Dullsville High students to ridicule my dark attire. There were no teen vampires lurking in the cemetery, disrupting Alexander's and my stardust dates. No threat of a preteen Nosferatu attempting to turn my younger brother and his nerd-mate immortal. Free of the feuding Maxwells, Alexander and I were now able to unite our mortal and immortal worlds as one.

I was also beginning to do something I'd never had the opportunity to do before—make the Mansion my home. And why shouldn't I? On a dare, in my youth, I'd snuck into it by squeezing through the abandoned estate's broken basement window. Now, invited, I could confidently walk right up its splintered stone path and through its creaky unlocked front door.

I had never been so happy in my life.

I transformed the Mansion into Alexander's and my private vampire castle. I felt like a medieval queen and

Alexander was my handsome king. Instead of spending the rest of summer break in my tiny bedroom, I suddenly had full reign over a palatial estate. I replaced Alexander's torn and aged bedroom curtain with a brand-new black lace one. I added some candelabras I'd found at a rummage sale to the ones his grandmother had brought from Romania. I placed black roses in pewter vases and lavender-scented votives and rose petals on all the empty hall and antique end tables.

Jameson, Alexander's butler, didn't seem to mind. In fact, he even appeared to delight in a woman's (or, in my case, teen girl's) touch around the barren estate.

It even seemed like the Mansion itself was amused by my presence. The floors appeared to give an extra squeak when I ran over them, as if the uneven boards were greeting my stay. The wind sounded louder than I'd remembered as it whistled through the cracked windowpanes. The creaking in the foundation warmly echoed off the hollow walls at a higher volume than it had before.

The massive house glistened with candles and cobwebs.

During the day I nestled in Alexander's corpse-cold arms, cuddling in his coffin. At night we cranked Rob Zombie and had midnight showings of *Fright Night*.

Alexander gave me the next best thing to a sparkling

diamond ring—a dresser drawer. His dresser was as ancient as Dracula himself. A family-owned chipped oak bureau with glass knobs held his clothes in five three-foot-long drawers. Alexander emptied the middle one for me, to be filled with anything I liked. One of the glass handles had broken and he replaced it with a wooden raven. There was even a lock on the dresser. At first I thought it was a facade, but on closer inspection it was revealed to be real. Whereas everything in my bedroom—clothes, magazines, hair products—was cast about in an unorganized mess, my drawer at the Mansion was in perfect order. Alexander brought out the best in me. It held a pair of socks, my Emily the Strange hoodie, a few T-shirts, and a bat-shaped sachet. I often felt jealous of the accessories I left there, which got to call the Mansion their home, while I returned to my house on Dullsville Drive.

I even managed to bake at the Mansion. I prepared ghost-shaped cookies, cupcakes with witch hats, and chocolate Rice Krispie treats. With my new independence I found a side of me that I didn't know existed.

My parents were pleased too, as long as I returned home for dinner and didn't stay out after midnight. My spirits were high and they were content that I wasn't hiding under the covers all summer long.

Alexander seemed happier, too—and inspired. When

we weren't roaming the cemetery at night, he painted landscapes and portraits of me. He began to churn out one beauty after another. Many of them were upbeat pictures of places around town we'd visited. The golf course, Dullsville High, Oakley Park, Hatsy's Diner, the swings at Evans Park, and the historic library. These paintings were bright and vivid and sweet and reflected his fondness for the town. I knew he had truly found his home here.

But unbeknownst to Alexander and me, all that was about to be changed by the letter that awaited him under the glow of the Mansion's lights.

Alexander took my hand in his as we left the Mansion and strolled down its drive. When we reached the gate, he drew me close.

"These last few weeks have been great. This is how it should always be. Just you and me."

"For eternity?" I asked, and stared up at him.

His hair hung sexily over his soulful eyes. There was a contentment I hadn't seen in Alexander. He gave me a long, breathtaking, weak-knee-making kiss. When we finally broke apart, something alongside the mailbox caught a reflection from the streetlight. The mailbox flag was sticking up.

"Funny. Does the mailman deliver your post at night? I thought only I knew your true identity."

Alexander appeared puzzled, too.

"Jameson is diligent about bringing the mail in as soon as it arrives."

"Well, that couldn't have been later than noon," I said. "Maybe they made a special delivery."

"I'll get it later," Alexander resolved with a shrug and put his arm around my shoulder. "I'll walk you home first."

"Forget that," I said before he could lead me away. "Maybe it's an invite to a party. Or notification that you won a trip to London."

"Or it could be a batch of coupons for pizza."

I glared up at him.

"Well, we'll never know unless you open it," I said coyly.

Alexander paused. Then he reluctantly leaned against the rickety box. He reached his pale fingers out to open the lid when we were struck with a few drops of rain.

"That's funny. It's not supposed to rain until tomorrow," I said.

Alexander drew back the metal door. "Be my guest."

I stared into the rusty mailbox, which was as dark as any tomb.

I half expected to see a detached hand holding out a letter. This was, after all, a vampire's mailbox. But I saw nothing.

"Are you afraid? It won't bite. But I might," he said, tickling me in the side.

"You promise?" I giggled as a few more drops of rain tapped me on the head. I imagined I could get snapped by a bird protecting its young or a field mouse hoping for a snack. I took a deep breath and reached my black chipped fingernailed hand into the dark box but felt only a spiderweb. I reached in farther, allowing my ashen palm to disappear until I couldn't even see my Eve L wristband. Then I felt something pointy.

"It's not a package," I said, yanking it out. I had grasped a single standard-size black envelope.

I held it toward the streetlight. The letter looked odd. First of all, there wasn't a stamp, or even a postmark. Perhaps I had been right about a fang-toothed flying mailman. In perfect beautiful silver calligraphy it read: MR. ALEXANDER STERLING.

As I handed the envelope to my boyfriend, a few sprinkles of rain hit the letter A and the ink began to run.

"Looks like I'll have to drive you home," he said resignedly.

Alexander tucked the letter into his jacket and took my hand and we raced up the mile-long driveway, escaping into the Mansion.

I stood in the foyer of the magnificent Mansion. Lavender wafted through the estate. A new portrait of me stared back, a substitute for one of the original portraits that once lined the hallway.

"There's no return address," I remarked, smoothing out my hair.

"I recognize the handwriting."

"Really? Then who is it from? A long-lost girlfriend?"

"No."

"Are you sure?"

"I'm sure."

"I bet you get millions of love letters from old girlfriends."

Alexander placed the envelope on a hallway table. "Wait here while I ask Jameson for his car keys."

"Aren't you going to open the letter?"

"Eventually."

Alexander was patient and disinterested. I was neither.

"You must tell me who it's from," I said, snatching his mail. "Or *I'll* open it," I teased.

Alexander paused. "It's from my parents."

"Really?" I asked, surprised.

It had been ages since Alexander's parents had been to Dullsville, and Alexander rarely spoke of them. Most of the time, I forgot they existed.

"Well, open it up," I pushed, handing it back to him. "Maybe they sent you a check."

Alexander took a white gold **S**-shaped letter opener lying on the hall table. Unlike me, who ripped open mail like a wild animal, Alexander carefully severed the envelope.

He opened the black letter, which had a blood-red border. A check didn't fall out. Not even a Romanian leu.

Alexander began to read the letter to himself.

"What does it say?" I asked, bouncing around him and desperately trying to take a peek. But all I could make out was regal-looking letterhead with an inscription I couldn't decipher.

Alexander playfully held the letter out of my sight. But when he finished reading, he turned serious.

"What does it say?" I asked again.

Without answering, he put the letter in the envelope and returned it to the table. "I'll take you home now."

"What does it say?" I repeated.

"Nothing really."

"Your parents wrote to tell you nothing?"

"Uh-huh."

"Is everyone okay?"

"Yes."

"So why aren't you smiling?"

Then I thought maybe reading a handwritten note from them made him homesick. A creepy but kind butler wasn't a substitute for parents in a lonely old estate.

"I'm sure you miss them. I bet you wish you could see them soon."

"I will," he said. "They're arriving tomorrow."

"Tomorrow?" I asked, shocked.

"Yes," Alexander said, almost melancholy. "That means things are about to change."

I glanced around the Mansion. We felt like two teens who'd trashed the house with a party only to find their parents were returning from their vacation early.

"Our 'coffin clutches' will have to end," I said.

Alexander nodded reluctantly.

"And my decorations will have to be removed."

"It looks that way."

"What about my drawer?"

"I found the dresser key," he said with a smile.

As Alexander closed the door behind us, I managed to catch a last glimpse of the black rose petals lying on the hallway table. The painting of me would have to be shelved and the original ones returned. The votives would have to be stored away.

One thing was for sure: This time Alexander, not Jameson, would have to clean up the Mansion.

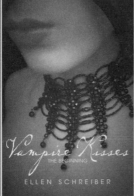
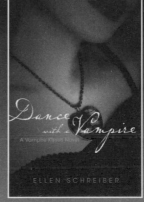